# White
# Ghost
# Ridge

ALSO BY CAROL COFFEY

*The Butterfly State*

*The Penance Room*

*Winter Flowers*

*The Incredible Life of Jonathan Doe*

*The Pact*

*Published by Poolbeg*

A DETECTIVE LOCKLEAR MYSTERY

# White Ghost Ridge

## Carol Coffey

POOLBEG
CRIMSON

Published 2019 by Crimson
an imprint of Poolbeg Press Ltd
123 Grange Hill, Baldoyle,
Dublin 13, Ireland
Email: poolbeg@poolbeg.com

A catalogue record for this book is available from the British Library.


ISBN 978178199-7765

Printed and bound by CPI Group (UK) Ltd, Croydon, CR0 4YY


www.poolbeg.com

# ABOUT THE AUTHOR

Carol Coffey was born in Dublin but now lives in West Wicklow. A teacher by profession, she has worked in the area of special education for over thirty years.

Carol has used her extensive background in special education throughout her writing. Her first book, *The Butterfly State*, centres around a young girl, Tess Byrne, whose communication difficulties caused by autism result in her incarceration in a psychiatric institution for so-called disturbed children.

Since then she has written four more critically acclaimed novels. *The Penance Room* is set in Australia where she lived for over ten years. It is multifaceted but provides an insight into the impact of deafness and its resultant isolation on the emotional well-being of a child. *Winter Flowers* explores the impact of generational dysfunction on the development of children. *The Incredible Life of Jonathan Doe*, set in America, delves into our perception of identity, about finding out who we are and where we truly belong.

Carol's fifth novel, *The Pact*, introduced her readers to a new character, Detective Sergeant Locklear, a Native American cop whose battle with his own demons is matched by the strange and complex cases he faces working for the Richmond PD.

*White Ghost Ridge* sees the return of the maladjusted and socially awkward Locklear and his trooper, Josefina Mendoza, as they battle to save their friend Lee Carter from a murder conviction.

# ACKNOWLEDGEMENTS

A sincere thank you to all the staff of Poolbeg Press for their support. In particular, I'd like to thank Paula Campbell for her encouragement over the years. Thank you also to David Prendergast and Caroline Maloney of Poolbeg Press. As always, a special thank you to Gaye Shortland for her keen observations and humour during the editing process. Finally, thanks to my husband David for his endless patience.

*For my late aunt, Maura Coffey,*
*for kindnesses never forgotten*

# Chapter 1

It was the suspect's hands that Locklear first noticed as he entered the interrogation room where the man sat on a hard plastic chair, his fingers splayed out, tense and claw-like on the table in front of him. A narrow bandage was wound around his left hand and his head was bowed so low it appeared that he was sleeping.

Locklear placed his coffee cup gently on the table and quietly acknowledged the young cop who stood on guard with his back to the wall of the windowless room. A fluorescent light above the table flickered periodically and, at that early morning hour, the only sound to be heard was the distant hum of the station's air-conditioning system. Locklear took his notebook and small pen from his back pocket and pulled a seat out from the table, lowering his tired body into its ill-fitting frame.

The suspect looked up. His bright-blue eyes were wide open but Locklear had already known that the man had not been sleeping but was praying.

Lee Carter had changed since the last time Locklear had seen him. His thick blond hair was cut tight to his scalp. He was thinner and his face had lost that boyish look which had irritated Locklear when they had first met in Dayton on a case. The ex-trooper had later taken up a research post at Virginia Commonwealth University. He had tried to keep in contact with Locklear since he moved his family to Richmond two years previously but, aside from spending some time together on one or two outings their mutual friend Josefina Mendoza had begged Locklear to attend, they had not seen each other much.

Right at this moment, Locklear was glad he had rebuffed Carter's more recent invitations to join him and his close-knit family for gatherings in his cosy backyard. The sheer domesticity of those get-togethers, the ordinariness of them, was too much for him. Kowalski, the station's boss, was on vacation overseas and would know that Locklear had what could be described as a personal relationship with the suspect which would preclude his involvement in the case. But Benson, Kowalski's loud-mouthed stand-in who was trying to make a name for himself in the force, did not.

Looking over the evidence, Locklear knew Carter didn't stand a chance of being found innocent. Not with what the cops had on him. Only Locklear and Mendoza knew that there was no way their gentle friend was involved in a serious crime, that there was no way he was guilty of murder. Sooner or later though, Benson would figure out the link and Locklear would be moved off the case. Locklear already knew that so he wanted to waste no time before he was replaced with some second-rate detective like Diaz or Hill who wouldn't recognise an important lead if it walked up and slapped them.

Locklear thought over the murder scene he had just come from and where his trooper Mendoza was still bagging up the evidence.

Richmond University professor, Alec Holton, had been found dead at his desk in his upmarket apartment on Creek Avenue with a four-inch hunting knife in his neck. Neighbours had said that the single man lived alone with only the old grey cat who had hissed at Locklear from a nearby armchair. According to one neighbour, visits from occasional male partners whose relationship with Holton rarely lasted more than a few months had become rare in recent weeks with the man spending much of his downtime alone.

Holton was roughly sixty years of age and had a shock of white, wiry hair. His complexion was as pale as his hair and he had the physique of a man who spent many years sitting behind a desk. His stomach bulged over his grey polyester pants and his legs and arms were the thin and wasted extremities of a man who was unaccustomed to physical exercise.

Locklear had focused on the victim's facial expression as the crescendo of Pagliacci boomed through the opulent office. Alec Holton's open green eyes looked shocked. A half-empty bottle of brandy sat on his desk beside an empty glass. There was no sign of forced entry so Holton had most likely known the murderer well enough to allow him or her entry to his home, or else the person had keys and had let themselves in and taken the man, whose desk faced away from the office door, by surprise.

More startling than the neck wound was the neat

3

horizontal cut along the British-born man's hairline, as though someone had tried to scalp him. The old rusted knife did not have a handle and the exposed section of the blade was covered in blood. The coroner at the scene said, based on the high volume of blood on the victim's face, the hairline cut was made while Holton was still alive but most likely after the knife had been plunged into his carotid artery.

"Looks like the Indians are on the warpath," one cop quipped.

Locklear glanced at Jo Mendoza who stood on the periphery, surveying the scene. He watched her tense at the cop's comment but she had no need to be worried. He was not easily offended and the cop, like most people he encountered, hadn't registered his Native American features.

He noticed that his trooper looked tired. He observed that she had gained a few much-needed pounds but her large bosom remained at odds with her lean body and gained her the unsolicited attention of male cops who then took offence when his sharp-tongued trooper rightfully put them in their place. Mendoza's sexual orientation heightened the interest from some of the dumber cops who had been heard on more than one occasion making inappropriate comments to the tough trooper. Kowalski's intervention had not put an end to the jibes completely. Locklear's offer to knock some heads together was met with scorn from Mendoza who insisted she was well able to stand up for herself. Some men, Locklear reasoned, were pigs. He noticed Mendoza's normally shiny hair looked dull and was tied in a tight bun on top of her head. She wore no make-up save for the thick line of black eyeliner which accentuated her deep brown eyes and brown skin.

Locklear shifted his focus to his surroundings. Alec Holton's apartment was expensively decorated. Modern art covered the stark white walls, and antiques, placed on expensive oak furniture, seemed to adorn every corner of the apartment. Even the tall steel columns that supported the high ceilings were decorated with artwork. Two seemingly identical, lavish Persian rugs covered either end of the dark-oak office floor.

Locklear moved to an even larger reception room directly across the hall which was decorated in much the same way. The bathroom next door was, on the other hand, functional and was dismally decorated with the tiny black and white tiles seen in thousands of apartments across the country. A towel hung halfway outside the laundry basket and the air in the windowless room was damp and musty.

The small kitchen to the rear of the apartment was similarly tiled and held only a couple of worn dusty cupboards, a small dining table which was covered with a long, old-fashioned oil tablecloth and two chairs. Locklear opened the fridge but there was nothing inside except a half loaf of stale bread and a container of sour milk.

The bedroom adjoined the kitchen and faced the side of the building. Nothing had been disturbed in the clinical white room whose only contents were a neatly made bed, a bedside locker and an ornate antique wardrobe which was too large for the room. There were no paintings or other ornaments which was in stark contrast to the other areas of the large apartment.

Mendoza lifted a photo of Holton and an old lady from the top of the locker.

"Must be his mother," she said, more to herself than Locklear. "How sweet."

Her boss made no response.

Locklear opened the bedroom window which led onto the apartment's fire escape. Heavy rain had continued to fall from early the previous evening and the pavement surrounding the exclusive building glistened in the early-summer downpour. The floor inside the bedroom was completely dry and the window had been locked so the perp had not gained access to the apartment through the fire escape.

"I take it there's no other way into this apartment?" Mendoza asked the janitor who had been roused from his bed to answer any questions they might have.

Mateo Moretti looked like he should be long retired. The man was around seventy and had hobbled into the apartment on two bad hips and a knee that clicked as he walked.

"No."

Locklear dismissed the janitor back to his bed and sighed. He opened the wardrobe which contained a row of equally dull but expensive tweed jackets and an array of polyester pants in varying shades of grey. Locklear lifted a shoebox down from the top shelf and lifted its loose lid with gloved hands.

He showed the contents to Mendoza who placed her gloved hands into the box and rummaged through the loose one-hundred-dollar bills.

"There must be thousands of dollars here. Well, at least we can rule out robbery."

Locklear returned to the victim's office and stared at the

body from the doorway. He was known to spend longer at crime scenes than any other detective at the station. He moved slowly across the room and circumnavigated the body six times slowly – three times clockwise and three times in the opposite direction – much to the bemusement of the other cops in the room. All except Mendoza. His trooper knew his ways and knew he would see something no-one else would.

Locklear knelt and examined the phone which lay on its side at Holton's feet. He pressed the redial button to check the last number phoned from the line. It was the emergency services. Someone had tried to call for help. He phoned 911 and asked for the tape to be replayed to him. He listened as a man's voice asked weakly for the police. The next few words were muffled followed by the word *Carter*. Locklear thought he recognised the voice or, if not the voice, the intonation. It was an American accent and therefore not the voice of the British-born professor who lay dead in front of him and who, in any event, would more likely have asked for an ambulance than an apartment full of cops.

The victim's computer, which sat in the centre of the desk, pulsated with white light. An open box used to store USB sticks lay empty on the desk. The sticks scattered on the ground around the victim's comfortably shoed feet were broken. One, which was smeared with a bloodied thumbprint, was sitting in a port in the computer. Locklear gently pushed the stick in further and beckoned for Mendoza to assist him. He knew nothing about computers and had refused Kowalski's requests for him to attend training. He had only two years left in the force and didn't see any point in an old dog learning new tricks, not when

7

there were young pups to do it for him and not when his particular skills could be put to better use.

He stood back as Mendoza ran her long, gold-varnished fingernails across the keyboard.

Six files appeared on the list. All were named INTENT and were numbered from 1 to 6.

"Do you know what INTENT means?" Locklear asked.

"Apart from the generic meaning of the word? No. Must be a company or an organisation he was dealing with."

Locklear stood back and thought while the three cops at the other end of the room shifted from foot to foot, obviously bored and wanting to get back to the station and their paperwork before their shift ended.

"Don't you think it's a little too convenient that this one stick was left unbroken and happens to be sitting in the computer?" Locklear said.

Mendoza nodded.

Locklear lifted the man's right hand and inspected his thumb which was bloodstained.

"Someone wants us to think Holton took the time to put this key into the computer while he was trying not to bleed to death," he said. "Bag it and take the computer too. Tell O'Brien to check it."

"OK."

"And tell him I said it's a priority!" Locklear barked.

He couldn't deal with the precinct's computer nerd who had recently joined the station. His staring brown eyes and monosyllabic responses to open-ended questions frustrated Locklear who was also not known for his conversation skills. The large dark-pigmented indentation on O'Brien's left cheek also unnerved Locklear, the result, he assumed, of the removal of a birthmark or mole. Its darkness in comparison to the man's pale, washy skin coupled with his short jet-black hair only served to make O'Brien look weak and sickly and, to Locklear's mind, odd.

From his seat in the interrogation room, Locklear shifted his focus from memories of the murder scene to the suspect in front of him. He lifted his cup and grimaced as the cold, bitter taste of the station's cheap coffee hit his palate. He tried to read Carter's expression. It was fear. Locklear studied the bloodied pattern on Carter's shirt and the discernible handprint smeared across the right side of his chest. His pale face was splattered with small dots of blood.

Locklear reached forward and turned the ex-trooper's left hand over. He lifted the bandage to reveal a long, deep wound to his palm.

Locklear sighed. Carter rested his eyes on the tabletop and said nothing.

"You're lefthanded, right?"

Carter nodded and moved his injured hand onto his lap.

"You going to tell me what happened tonight?"

Carter looked at the guard who stared impassively at the wall on the opposite side of the room.

"You can go, trooper," Locklear said quietly.

The young cop hesitated.

"Don't worry," Locklear reassured him. "I think Mr Carter knows he's safe with me."

Carter nodded nervously.

The cop left the room and closed the door quietly behind him.

Locklear reached to turn on the tape recorder but paused as Carter gestured towards it.

"Doesn't the station have a more up-to-date recording system than that old thing?" Carter asked.

"That's what you want to ask about, Lee? Seriously?"

Carter shrugged.

"We do," said Locklear, "but the one in this interview room isn't working."

Carter leaned forward. "I need a lawyer," he said urgently.

Locklear nodded and exhaled. "Yes. You do. Is that Holton's blood on your shirt?"

Carter nodded. Locklear could see tiny tears rise in the mild-mannered researcher's eyes. He looked down and focused on his unopened notebook.

"Then I guess it will be your prints on the knife stuck in Alec Holton's neck?"

Carter nodded again.

"Did you do it, Lee? Did you kill Holton?"

Carter shook his head, loosening the tears that had grown even bigger in his bright-blue, innocent-looking eyes.

"Of course not."

"Well, then you better tell me what happened."

# Chapter 2

Locklear flicked to a blank page in his notebook and picked up his pen. He looked at his watch and jotted down the time.

Carter cleared his throat and moved forward on his seat, slanting his body awkwardly towards the tape recorder.

"Relax," Locklear said, raising his hands in a calming manner towards Carter who was now visibly shaking.

"Shouldn't I wait for my lawyer?"

Locklear stared hard at the ex-trooper.

"You can, if you want to waste my time. As soon as Benson realises I know you, he'll take me off the case and he'll probably decide this interview isn't worth a damn. So, the sooner you tell me what happened the sooner I figure out who's framing you for this murder and why."

Carter nodded.

Locklear switched the tape on and checked his watch again.

"Interview with suspect Lee Carter – murder of Professor Alec Holton. June 10th, 2018. Time 12.46am."

Carter cleared his throat. "I worked with Alec," he said.

"At least I did until about a month ago. He was researching Native American artefacts in South Dakota."

Locklear looked up from his notebook. He felt his heart skip a beat but he didn't know why.

"We had a falling-out. Alec had –" Carter stopped abruptly, as though he just realised that what he had said might amount to motive.

"About?"

"Alec got funding from the university to bring an anthropologist onto his project. My own research project was coming to an end, so I applied and got the job. We got on well, at first anyway."

"What happened?"

"What's going to happen to me?" Carter asked.

Locklear, unsure if his ex-colleague was stalling for time or was only beginning to realise how much trouble he was in, put down his pen and stopped the tape.

"It depends, Lee."

"On?"

"First and foremost, on whether you are guilty or not."

"I already told you I didn't do it!"

"And, secondly, on how much time you are going to continue wasting here. Wasted time is putting distance between me and the person who did this. Right now, the station's money is on you being the killer."

"I want to call Virginia. She doesn't know. She doesn't know about any of this." Carter was referring to his wife.

"You can do that later, after you tell me what happened."

Carter looked deflated and lowered his head towards the table, assuming much the same position as when Locklear had first entered the interrogation room.

"You can also pray later!" Locklear barked.

Carter shot a hard look at his ex-boss.

"Lee – I'm trying to help you. Now, *talk*. From the beginning."

"OK."

Locklear pressed record, re-announced the interview, and Lee once more cleared his throat.

"I was working with Alec Holton until about a month ago. He was researching Native American artefacts in South Dakota. He got funding from the university to study artefacts that had been uncovered during a routine building project out west. He also had access to artefacts on loan from USD –"

"USD?"

"University of South Dakota. He had teamed up with a research project there."

"Go on."

"He'd been working on a number of similar projects since then. I'd been involved in one or two of them in a small way. For this one, he needed me to build up a picture around the artefacts, about the people who used them, how they lived, etc. We did a further dig about four miles from the site with the USD team. It was interesting work … while it lasted."

"Why did it end?"

"There was a falling-out between the research teams on the dig."

"Because?"

"Some of the artefacts were unaccounted for."

Locklear tapped his notebook with the end of his pen. "Stolen?"

13

Carter shrugged. "I don't really know what happened. I was on leave for a week but that Saturday Virginia went to Harrisonburg with the kids to visit her folks …"

The mention of the small Virginian town where he had first met Carter brought Locklear back to his strange and complex investigation in the Mennonite community there. He wondered briefly how they were doing and hoped they had put their unfortunate past behind them.

"I was at a loose end so I decided to go to the lab and catch up on some work. When I got there nothing seemed out of place but when I went to the safe to retrieve some of the artefacts I noticed that some were missing."

"Who else had access to the lab?"

"Just me and Alec. He had one or two grad students doing some PhD research for him, but they didn't have access to the lab unless either Alec or I were there."

"What did you do then?"

"Well, Alec was on vacation so I did what I thought I should do and rang the Dean but he didn't seem worried at all. It was odd. He kept saying Alec must have misplaced them – but I knew something was wrong. When I got back to the lab I did what I thought Alec would have wanted me to do and called the police. But when he got back, Alec was really angry with me. I had never heard him yell like that before. After that, he didn't speak to me for days. As far as I know, the police are still investigating the matter."

"What specifically did he say to you?"

"He wanted to know why I had been there and what the hell I thought I was doing going to the cops. That I shouldn't have gone in, what the hell had I gone in for, something like that."

"Why do you suppose he reacted that way?"

Carter shrugged. "I really don't know. You'd have thought he'd have been as anxious as I was about the artefacts. Especially with what happened on the dig."

Locklear raised his eyebrows. He knew Carter was going to tell him something that was pertinent to the case, something he should have told him as soon as he had sat down. He silently thanked a God he didn't believe in that Carter had given up police work. Carter lacked the street smarts that Mendoza had in spades.

"What happened?"

"Alec usually had four on a dig team but at the last minute he told me that it was just me and him."

"So, that was unusual?"

"Well, yes. There was a lot of physical work to be done. A lot of hours to put in. Alec wasn't exactly the digging kind. He usually sat under an umbrella out of the sun while his team did the physical work. He hated the heat. I wondered how he'd think I could do all that work myself, but he assured me that colleagues from USD would be helping. He also changed the plans at the last minute and arranged for us to go a day early."

"Did he say why?"

"No. He could be precious at times. He was a bit miffed one time about our names appearing side by side on a research paper. He felt he should have been named as lead researcher. He sulked about it for weeks. But overall, he is – was, a good guy."

"So, when you got there?"

Carter focused his eyes on the table. "It was about ten miles outside of a reservation called Pine Ridge."

Locklear moved his gaze from his notebook and looked at Carter. His first station as a young police officer was in Rapid City which he figured was about one hundred miles from the Native American reservation. He remembered driving through it once and recalled the miserable conditions the people were living in and how ill at ease he had been as he drove through its streets. Pine Ridge was then, and probably still was, one of the poorest places in North America.

"It was almost dark by the time we arrived. Alec insisted on us setting up camp which didn't make sense. We had no provisions. We didn't even have water. It would have been better to book into a motel and start afresh in the morning."

"So, he was acting out of character even back then?"

"Yes, he kept checking his phone but the signal was weak. He was really agitated."

"And you didn't ask him what was wrong?"

"I asked him if he was OK but he didn't answer. He hardly said a word all evening. I knew his mother was ill in London. He'd had a call about a day or two before we left saying the old lady had pneumonia and had been moved from her care home to hospital. She's very old. They were very close. I think he was an only child. I assumed he was waiting on news about her."

"So, what happened then?"

"We settled down for the night. There was something wrong with Alec's tent so he had to share mine. That seemed to make him even more agitated. I knew he was awake practically the whole night. I could hear him tossing and turning. The plan for the next day was that Alec would go to town to get provisions and I was going to start the dig while we waited on the rest of the team. The following morning the sun hadn't fully risen when this guy arrives with breakfast."

"Who was he?"

"Alec obviously knew him but he didn't introduce me. He seemed shocked that he was there. Nervous. I ate the breakfast but Alec said he wasn't hungry."

"Describe the man."

"He was white and I *do mean* white. His skin was so pale you could kinda see his veins. He was tall, around six four. Broad build. He had blond hair, slightly greying around the temples and really pale eyes. They were almost colourless."

"Age?"

Carter frowned. He looked over Locklear's features. "About your age."

"What happened then?"

"The guy suggested he and Alec go for a walk. It was clear I wasn't invited so I stayed but I could hear what they were saying until they got a good bit down the track. I heard him ask about me – and then Alec asking him what he was doing there at that time, that they had arranged to meet the previous night. They sort of argued but that was as much as I could hear."

"Do you think this man was a lover or an ex-lover?"

Carter blushed. "Didn't seem that way to me."

"What did Alec do then?"

"I reckon he was gone for about an hour. Then he came back alone. He sat with his head in his hands and he looked so … so lost. I asked him was everything alright and he said there was nothing wrong. That evening the team from

USD arrived. Three in all. A Professor Rosenberg and two grad students. We stayed two more nights. That's when we found the artefacts."

"The ones that went missing?"

Carter nodded.

"And you never discussed the visitor with Alec after that?"

"No. Alec was an unusual guy. He was friendly but, at the same time, he had that reserved British way about him. Even though I looked after his cat when he was away, he was distant. I can't say I ever really got to know him."

"Was he seeing anyone recently?"

Carter shrugged. "Not that I know of. He'd certainly never mention anything to me if he was."

"Who would he mention it to?"

Carter thought for a moment. "There's an old Polish lady in the apartment across from him who he was friendly with. Meara Henschel is her name. She had been a well-known pianist in her day and Alec loved music. They got along very well. If he confided in anyone, it would be her."

"Why didn't he ask the old lady to feed his cat?"

"Alec told me that she's terrified of cats. She mightn't have been able to manage anyway. She's pretty housebound. Uses a wheelchair when she goes out ."

"So he didn't have many friends?"

"No."

Locklear thought about the well-furnished apartment on the better side of town. Despite its lavishness, there had been a feeling of loneliness inside, a feeling he knew others would feel if they visited his own, less salubrious apartment.

"Do professors get paid well?"

Carter shook his head. "I don't think so."

"How could he afford the expensive art in his apartment?"

Carter seemed to need time to think about this. Then, as if he decided he had no answer, he shrugged.

Locklear persevered. "You never thought about how well his apartment was furnished? About all the artwork?"

Carter swallowed. He knew now where Locklear was going and the possibility that his colleague had been involved in something illegal unnerved him.

"He mentioned one time that his father had been in banking, so I guess they were well off. He hinted once that his mother had been disappointed that he had not gone into the family business."

Locklear pondered this. "I guess he would have been due to inherit a lot of money on his mother's death?"

"I guess." Carter shrugged.

"Carter, do you think Alec took the artefacts and, if so, why?"

Carter looked up. Locklear saw something in the man's eyes. An emotion he couldn't quite name. Carter didn't answer.

Locklear ran over the story he'd heard so far.

"You said something happened on the dig. Did you mean apart from this guy arriving?"

Carter swallowed. "Yes."

"And?" Locklear asked impatiently.

"Alec didn't know I saw this or at least I don't think he did. I didn't even tell the Dean or the police because it didn't make sense. I thought there must be an explanation for it. I tried to put it out of my head. On the dig, I found pieces of what I thought was a Native American pipe bowl.

Even though it was covered in dirt you could see this magnificent bright-orange paint on it. I stopped digging and called Alec, but he moved me immediately to work with one of the students about fifty yards away and started digging himself. He saw me glancing over at him while he dug. I was only interested in what the rest of it looked like, but he moved me even further down the dig site to work with Professor Rosenberg who I didn't really like. The professor made out he was a regular friendly guy but there was something about him ... I don't know. I just didn't like him. Neither did Alec – I could tell. But the thing is, later that night I'm sure I saw a larger segment of the bowl in Alec's travel bag." He paused. "We also found a ..." He looked down at his lap while he thought about his next words.

"A *what*, Carter?" Locklear snapped as he rushed some more thoughts down on his notebook. The night was pushing on and he knew how precious these first few hours after a murder were. The trail was still warm but it wouldn't be that way for long. Locklear's cell phone lit up. He glanced at the screen. Mendoza, obviously finished at the crime scene and looking to see where he was. He rejected the call and tried to send his trooper a quick text as Carter continued.

"A Native American fertility figure. That and the bowl, well, they're priceless. They would have been a big find for the university. That is until they had to be returned to whatever tribe they belonged to."

Locklear looked up from his mobile screen. "Returned?"

"Yes, it's the law."

"Was that one of the items that went missing from the safe?"

"No, that's what I'm trying to tell you. I found the fertility figure. Alec and Professor Rosenberg were near me when I unearthed it and they were almost fighting over it. It was weird. I catalogued it but before we left the dig it was missing."

"*You* found it?"

"Yes, well, myself and one of two grad students were digging in the same area."

"Which of the grad students?"

"The white one. I just knew his first name – Tommy. He was a rude kind of kid."

Locklear raised his eyebrows. "The white one? The other was black?"

"No – he was Native. They were an odd pair. They didn't hardly speak to each other or to us even. Tommy was pale with red hair, freckles, glasses. He didn't have sunscreen with him or even a hat. I remember that his skin burnt badly during the dig and Professor Rosenberg had to take him to a doctor in town. The other was real shy. I heard Tommy refer to him 'The Chief' and the kid didn't even seem annoyed. He was slim, pretty tall. Long hair and he wore Grateful Dead T-shirts the whole time we were there. Didn't look to me like either of them had much experience of digs."

"What happened when you all realised it was missing?"

"Rosenberg was incensed. He and Alec argued. Each accused the other of taking it. The two grads and I just stood to one side. We didn't know what else to do."

"Did either of the students look guilty?"

Carter thought for a moment. "No, but the Native one looked to me like he was smiling a little. A weird sort of smile, like he was amused or something." He shook his head. "It was the strangest dig I've been on. Usually there's a bit of camaraderie. We get to know each other well. There was an atmosphere, mostly I think between the two professors, and we hardly spoke. It was uncomfortable."

Locklear sighed. "You didn't answer me when I asked if you suspected that Holton might have stolen those items?"

Carter ran his hands over his scalp. He cried out as his wound brushed off his almost shorn head.

"No! He wouldn't. I don't know why he hid the bowl. Like I said, it makes no sense. Why would he do that? His position, his reputation, his –"

"What would something like the bowl or the fertility figure be worth on the black market?" Locklear interjected.

Carter shook his head. "He wouldn't do that, sir. Not theft. Not Alec."

"I asked you a question, Carter."

Carter looked over Locklear's left shoulder as though there were someone else in the room who had suddenly captured his interest.

"Thousands of dollars," he said then.

"Could someone have been blackmailing him?"

"About what? He was harmless, sir."

"What happened when the police interviewed you and Holton about the missing artefacts from the lab?"

Carter looked down at the table once more.

"Alec told the police that I was the last person to be in the lab and he told the Dean that I had been acting strangely for weeks. The Dean believed Alec over me and I was suspended pending the outcome of the police investigation. Virginia doesn't know. I've been sitting in cafés and parks all day. I couldn't tell her."

"Holton tried to pin this on you. That is until someone got to him. What we need to find out is why. To go over the facts, Alec was the one acting strangely for weeks, meeting people in the desert and not telling you who they were. He was there when an artefact went missing during the dig and conveniently absent when more artefacts went missing from the lab safe. Then he tells the police you were the last person to have been seen with them? Do you still think Alec was harmless?"

Carter met Locklear's eyes and shook his head. "I guess not, sir."

Locklear looked down at his notes. So far, he still didn't have a lot to go on, but one question was burning in his mind. If Alec did all that to Lee, how come Lee went to Holton's apartment the night before?

Then Carter answered without him having to ask. "But he apologised. I got an email from him saying he was sorry for bringing trouble on me. He asked me to come to his apartment around eleven last night and he'd explain everything and that he'd speak with the Dean and clear my name."

Locklear snorted. It was involuntary. Carter was the most naïve person he had ever known.

"And you bought that? You didn't think it was a set-up? That's something he could have done by going to the university himself or meeting you in a public place in broad daylight. Jesus, Carter!"

Carter's lip trembled. "I know," he whimpered. "I trusted him."

23

"I doubt the email came from Holton anyway. My bet is that someone else sent it to you to make sure you were in the wrong place at the wrong time. Seems like Holton isn't the only one trying to set you up. So what happened when you got to the apartment?"

"I pressed the buzzer in the lobby. Alec didn't answer. I had keys …"

Locklear stopped writing on his notepad. "Why'd you have the keys on you? You expected him to be there, didn't you?"

"I told you – I used to feed his cat while he was in England. I parked outside the building and when he didn't buzz me up I took the keys from my glove box and let myself in."

Locklear shook his head wearily. Carter's tale was becoming long and farfetched. No-one would believe him. Locklear himself was beginning to wonder if his innocent-looking friend was telling the truth or if he was being fed a long and very well-rehearsed tale. Although why Carter might lie to him, he didn't know. There was no way he killed Holton.

"Go on."

"When I got to Alec's apartment door I knocked hard but he didn't answer. I let myself in … and … I found him."

"Was he alive?"

"Yes."

"Did you see anyone leave the building as you came in?"

"No. When I got into the office, I could see Alec sitting at his desk with his back to me. He was playing music really loud so I called out but he didn't turn around. It was

24

only when I walked around to the front of his desk that I saw the knife in his neck. He was still alive. I pulled his chair out and tried to stop the bleeding. He looked terrified. He tried to pull the knife out of his neck. I put my hand on the knife to try to stop him. I knew he'd bleed out. The knife had no handle and I cut my hand. I ... I recognised it. It was one of the Native American artefacts that went missing from the lab. Alec grabbed my shirt to pull me closer to him."

Locklear glanced at Carter's shirt which was stained with Holton's bloodied handprint. "So did he say anything?"

"It sounded like '*not intend*'. I think he was trying to say he didn't mean to get me into trouble.

"It wasn't 'not *intent*'?"

Carter ran his hands over his head again. "I don't know. It was barely a whisper."

"Does the word '*intent*' mean anything to you, apart from its general meaning?"

Carter shook his head. "No."

"Go on."

"While I was trying to stop the bleeding, I heard loud banging in the hallway – the cops breaking the door in. Next thing they're in the apartment pointing guns at me and shouting for me to lie on the ground. As they handcuffed me I heard Alec gasp and I knew ... I knew he was dead."

Locklear waited a moment to see if the ex-trooper had anything more to add but Carter had fallen silent. He could see the despair in his eyes.

"Anything else, Lee?"

"No."

Locklear stopped the tape.

"Sir?"

"What?"

"Can I go home now?"

"Carter, you used to be a police officer."

"And?"

"And you were found at the scene with your hand on the knife sticking into the victim's neck. Your shirt is covered in blood and you have a wound on your palm which I dare say forensics will match to the shape of the knife. You know very well that you won't get bail until I can prove that you didn't do this."

Locklear could see the man deflate before his eyes.

Carter sat silently for what seemed like an eternity.

"What are you going to do?" he then asked weakly.

Locklear looked at his watch. It was 2.10am.

"At first light I'll be visiting the home of Meara Henschel. I'm going to review the security tapes from Holton's apartment block and then I'm going to see the Dean."

"What will I do in the meantime?"

Locklear got up and swung open the door. He found the cop half asleep on his feet outside.

"Phone your wife and more importantly ... get yourself a good lawyer."

# Chapter 3

Meara Henschel's apartment sat directly across the hall from Alec Holton's. The apartment was a mirror image of Holton's – like Holton's, its generous front room faced towards the front of the small apartment block. Unlike Holton's however, the room was not lavishly decorated and despite an odd arrangement of antique furniture and paintings, the room was musty and had clearly not been decorated in years.

Henschel's carer placed a pot of coffee on the table in front of her employer and poured cups for Locklear and Mendoza. The young Latina then placed a blanket around the elderly Pole's narrow shoulders and stood erect behind her employer whose small, brown eyes were moist and red.

"Miss Henschel is very upset," she said as she placed her hand on the old lady's shoulder.

Meara moved her hand up and patted the carer's hand, giving Locklear a fleeting glimpse of the five-digit identification number tattooed onto her left forearm. She followed his eyes and quickly dropped her hand to her lap, pulling her worn cardigan sleeve down roughly until it came halfway down her long bony fingers.

"I'm fine now, Rosa, thank you," she said. "You can get on with your work."

Rosa left the room quickly but glanced briefly at the visitors as she went. Mendoza smiled at the young Latina but she avoided her eyes and left the cops to their business.

"You were in a concentration camp?" Locklear asked.

The old lady's lips parted slightly but she did not speak. Locklear watched her tense. Her chin quivered. He looked away, unable to watch the obvious discomfort his comment had caused her.

"Yes. Auschwitz. When I was a small child," she finally replied.

"We can see how upset you are," Mendoza said. "We don't want to take up any more of your time than necessary."

Locklear glanced around the room as the old lady poured cream into her coffee and offered the jug to her visitors. Several black-and-white photographs hung on the wall over an antique bureau. Locklear noticed that none of them seemed to be of the sole resident. He looked down at the carpeted floor which was crowded with an array of large, overgrown plants and made the room appear smaller than Holton's.

"How would describe your relationship with Mr Holton?" Mendoza asked.

"We were very good friends."

"When did you last see him?"

"Thursday evening. He came to borrow some milk. He rarely had anything in to eat. Not since David left."

Locklear noticed the fleeting smile on the old woman's lined face. She spoke, he noticed, in the typical vernacular of Richmondites.

28

"How old were you when you came to the US?" he asked abruptly.

Mendoza turned her head to eye him quizzically.

"I was nine when we were liberated," she replied.

"And your family?" he asked.

"What has that to do with what happened to Alec?" the old woman snapped.

"I'm sorry. I'm just trying to get a picture of how you two became friends. On the face of it, it appears that you had very little in common."

"You could simply ask me," she said.

Locklear could hear the sharpness in the woman's tone.

"Who was David?" Mendoza asked, trying to change the subject and ease the icy stare the old woman had now fixed on her boss who shifted uncomfortably in his seat.

"He was Alec's partner. David Horowitz. They were together for a quite a few years. The relationship didn't work out. He left about a year ago."

"What happened?"

"Alec was completely focused on his work. It was everything to him. I understood that. They met at an art exhibition. It was probably the only thing they had in common – a love of the arts. Otherwise, they were very different. David was a journalist but he wasn't devoted to his work in the same way that Alec was. He was a quietly spoken, unassuming man. David didn't drink. He hated alcohol whereas Alec drank too much. David was devoted to Alec but I think he got tired sitting alone in the apartment while Alec worked late or was away on archaeology digs."

"How did Alec take him leaving?"

"He was upset. I begged him to make it work, to go after him. I warned him not to end up alone like me."

"He obviously didn't listen," Mendoza said.

"Well, not in time. By the time he realised what he'd lost, David had moved back to DC and had taken up a job with the *Post*. He'd also met someone else. Alec rarely dated after that and, if he did, they were usually unsuitable."

"How so?" Locklear asked.

Meara inhaled and swallowed. "They were usually very young and not from good backgrounds."

Mendoza raised her thick dark eyebrows.

"They just used Alec for his money."

"He was well off?" Mendoza asked.

"He didn't earn much but his mother was very kind to him. He had a small yearly income from the family business. He certainly wasn't rich. Anytime he needed money, his mother gave it to him. She loved him so much. It will break her heart when she hears he is gone."

"You've met her?"

"Not in person but we've spoken on the phone a few times over the years."

"Could you tell us more about the younger partners?" Locklear asked.

Meara Henschel shook her head sadly. "Alec was a very lonely man. He went to those awful places, you know. You understand."

Mendoza nodded.

"He spent a lot of money trying to buy company. He had no real friends that I knew of. Just me. I told him that you cannot buy love but he would just smile at me. He would take them to the opera, for expensive meals, on trips, but it always ended the same. They just used him. The last one was the worst."

"Why?" Mendoza asked.

"He was a stage actor, or at least he pretended to Alec that he was. I never heard of anything he claimed to have been in, but Alec was smitten. I hoped it would fizzle out. Alec brought him here once and a pair of my earrings went missing. They were heart-shaped with tiny pearls and they had belonged to my grandmother who had passed them to my cousin Anna – then she left them to me because my mother had worn them on her wedding day so you can imagine how important they were to me. I told Alec but he said I had misplaced them. He was angry with me afterwards because of the implication and didn't come in to see me for weeks. Not until after the night I had to phone the police."

Locklear waited for the old woman to elaborate. She didn't.

He sighed. "Why – and when – did you have to phone the police?"

"I'm sure this is hard for you, Miss Henschel," Mendoza offered.

Meara Henschel nodded. "Alec was like a son to me. I don't think I'll be able to get over it ... after all that's happened. I've been thinking now ... if only I'd told the police everything back then, if only I'd said something." Her eyes filled with tears.

Mendoza stood and took a tissue from a box on the bureau and handed it to the old lady. On her way back to her seat she glared at Locklear in a way that none of his other troopers would ever have gotten away with.

"Simon Caird was his name. He started demanding money from Alec. Alec started wiring his mother for money and she kept sending it. If she'd known what was going on! I should have told her. I should have phoned her."

"Can you tell us exactly what happened that night, please, Miss Henschel?" Mendoza interjected before her boss became annoyed.

"It was a couple of months ago. Alec and Simon had returned from a restaurant. I heard them coming back – Simon always banged the apartment door. He was –uncouth and he drank too much. I could hear him shouting so I got up as quickly as I can manage these days. I couldn't make it across the hall on my own so I phoned Alec to see if he was alright but he didn't answer. Then I heard him shouting out, as though he was in pain. I phoned the police. When they arrived, Alec had a small cut in his neck where that – that awful man had held a knife to his throat."

Locklear and Mendoza glanced quickly at each other.

"What happened then?"

"The police arrested Simon but Alec wouldn't file charges. He begged me not to tell the police about my missing earrings, so I didn't – for his sake. I just couldn't understand the hold Simon had over Alec. I had known Alec a long time and I never saw anyone treat him as badly as Simon did."

"What did Simon look like?" Locklear asked.

"He was tall with dark hair. Handsome, I suppose. About thirty or so. He was always expensively dressed and neat. He reminded me of David when Alec first met him which I guess was partly the reason Alec fell for him. I could see right through him but Alec couldn't."

Locklear pondered this. "Was he Native American?" he asked.

Meara Henschel looked away from Locklear and focused her eyes on the window. He watched her swallow nervously.

"Why would you ask if he was Native American?"

"Just following up on one line of enquiry, that's all."

"No, Simon was white. I think Alec mentioned once that he was of Scottish ancestry."

"Does the name INTENT mean anything to you, Miss Henschel?" Locklear asked. "Did Alec ever mention it?"

"I'm sorry, no."

Locklear sat back in the worn armchair and thought for a moment.

"Do you think Simon was blackmailing Alec?"

Meara Henschel's lower lip dropped down and fresh tears swam in her eyes.

"After the incident, Alec told me he was finished with Simon but he still called to the apartment from time to time. He'd keep ringing the buzzer at all hours of the night until Alec let him in or he'd shout from the pavement knowing Alec would be embarrassed by the attention. Sometimes he managed to get into the building and would bang on Alec's apartment door. Alec would let him in and then he'd leave within minutes. He never told me why Simon was calling but I suspected something was very wrong."

Locklear thought about whether or not he'd reveal his suspicions that Holton was stealing artefacts to fund Simon's lifestyle or else that Simon had found out about Holton stealing and had been blackmailing him to keep quiet – or if he would just leave the old lady with her fond memories of a man who had been like a son to her. He decided on the latter.

"When did you see Caird last?"

"About three weeks ago. Alec wasn't in so he banged on the door for a while and then left."

"So you didn't hear anything last night?"

"Not until the police arrived. I saw them leaving with that nice man Lee from the university who found Alec. I hadn't seen him here for a while. I suspected he and Alec had had a falling-out. Alec fell out with people easily. I loved him but he found it hard to make friends and lost them very easily."

"How well do you know Lee Carter?"

"Not well. He'd come and feed that awful cat Alec has. I'd see him sometimes drop Alec off if they'd worked late. He was polite and seemed like a nice, well-raised young man."

Locklear didn't tell her that the nice polite man was a suspect in the murder of her friend and was still locked up downtown after most probably a sleepless night. Locklear stood and offered her his hand.

She took it from her seated position and blinked. Two heavy tears fell down her lined face. Locklear found himself looking at her concentration camp tattoo, etched on her forearm decades ago but a daily reminder of what she had endured. This time she did not try to hide it.

"I'm truly sorry for your loss," Locklear said.

Henschel nodded. "You'll tell me, won't you, if you find Alec's killer?"

"Yes, of course, but I'll be back soon to ask you some

more questions when you've had time to think about what else might be important for the investigation." He was hoping she would understand that he knew she was withholding information. She was possibly trying to save the reputation of her deceased friend, which Locklear couldn't really understand. Alec Holton was dead and, if there was an afterlife, no doubt Holton didn't much care what the living thought of him anymore. Locklear studied the old lady's face but, apart from a slight swallow, her expression did not alter.

Mendoza touched Henschel's arm before the pair let themselves out into the hallway. Both stood looking at the police tape across Alec Holton's front door.

"Well, are we any nearer to finding out what's going on here, Mendoza?"

Mendoza sighed. "No, sir. If anything, the case has got more complicated. I doubt this Simon guy killed his meal ticket. Still think we should talk to him though. He knows something. That's clear. And we still don't know what INTENT means and I'll wager that it's important."

"Agreed."

"What now?"

"You go ask the janitor for the security tapes. Take them back to the station and study them. I want to know who came in, how long they stayed, what time they left. I'll track down this Simon guy, see what he knows. Stay out of Benson's way. As soon as he realises our connection to Carter you'll be writing parking fines and I'll probably be suspended until Kowalski gets back and deals with me."

When they reached the lobby, Mendoza turned to Locklear.

"Do you think we'll prove Carter is innocent, sarge? I can't stand the thought of him locked up. He won't survive prison – Carter's just not made of that stuff."

Locklear dug his hands into the pockets of his worn jeans. "Then we better get busy."

# Chapter 4

It wasn't hard for Locklear to find Simon Caird. The man had a record consisting of one prior for prostitution and one for possession. He was also wanted for questioning for robbery of a rich old widow in his hometown of Tucson, Arizona. She had been paying Caird for his company. Caird had skipped town before the case progressed any further. Locklear had found out by calling in a favour from a station secretary he used to know before she moved from New York to Tucson with her Arizonan husband. An outstanding arrest warrant was still in operation on the man in his home state. Caird was facing his third strike which explained the pressure he presumably put on Holton not to press charges for assault.

Locklear parked across the street from the rundown house Caird rented and watched the house for a while. He needed to determine if Caird was alone. He didn't think the petty criminal was particularly dangerous but he wasn't sure about his associates and whether any of them might enjoy putting a bullet into a cop's head for fun. When he saw no sign of activity, he locked the car and walked slowly across the road. He crept up the three stones steps and listened at the door but heard nothing.

Locklear unhooked his gun, pulled back the screen door and knocked loudly.

The cheap wooden door, which had a large indentation at foot level, opened halfway. A thick security chain thwarted Locklear's plan to rush into the house before Caird had time to refuse a visit but he knew instantly that the man in front of him was Alec's ex-lover. Meara's description of the man was good but gone were the fancy clothes and neat attire. Caird was dressed in dirty jeans and a torn T-shirt. He was barefoot and unshaven and smelt of beer and cigarettes. In seconds, Locklear read the shocked expression on Caird's face and knew the man was about to close the door. He forced his foot inside but Caird kept pushing the door until, with no other option, Locklear pulled back his limb. The door slammed and Locklear listened while the back screen door screeched. He ran around to the side of the unfenced and unmowed yard and raised his piece just as Caird reached the top of the seven-foot wall of wire which ran at the back of the property.

"*Get down!*"

Caird kept his hands on the top railing while he considered his options: try to get over the fence and get shot doing so or drop to the ground. He decided to drop.

He raised his arms and waited for Locklear to speak.

"Lie on the ground – put your hands behind your back," Locklear ordered.

"Who are you?" Caird asked.

"Detective Sergeant Locklear – Richmond PD. I'm here to talk to you about your friend, Alec Holton."

Caird studied the man's appearance – his worn jeans, his unpolished boots, his surprisingly neatly pressed shirt. He studied the man's face for even longer than he studied his clothes. In particular he focused on his hair, thick black hair which was too long for a cop and his dark brown eyes which gave little of his intention away.

"You're not a fucking cop."

"Why would you say that?"

"You're one of them Indians that's after Alec."

"Didn't anyone ever tell you that most Native Americans find the name 'Indian' offensive?" Locklear said, despite sometimes using the term himself.

Caird didn't reply.

"Lie on the ground. Face down."

"Don't kill me, please. I don't know anything. I swear. All I saw was a few emails. Honest."

Locklear reached towards his back pocket, pulled out a pair of handcuffs and cuffed the writhing man. The screen door opened and a heavily pregnant woman came out onto the back porch. Locklear focused in on her hands. They were empty save for a lighted cigarette.

"Who's that?" Locklear asked.

"My fucking sister."

The woman laughed.

Locklear pulled Caird to his feet and dragged him towards the house.

"Anyone else in there?" he asked.

"Just my two-year-old kid," the woman replied, grinning.

Locklear pulled Caird closer to where the woman stood until he was close enough to see the small lines around her eyes and the circle of white powder caked to her nostrils.

Despite her advanced pregnancy, the woman was painfully thin. She pulled on her cigarette and blew smoke into Locklear's face. Locklear stared at the heart-shaped pearl earrings in the woman's ears which were at odds with her cheap clothes and bleached-blonde hair.

"Our kid," she added, glancing at Caird as he continued to writhe against Locklear's firm grip.

"You sure made a fool of Alec Holton," Locklear said to Caird as he pushed him into the house. A half-snorted line of coke lay on a glass coffee table beside a rolled-up $20 bill. "And I don't only mean the fact that you were spending the money he gave you on coke. I mean because he thought you and he were a couple. I'd say he had no idea you were straight and that you had a family."

"He can't complain. I also used some of that money for expensive acting lessons. Looks like his investment paid off," Caird sneered.

The woman laughed out loud. It was the throaty, deep laugh of a heavy smoker. A child began to cry in an adjoining room but she didn't move.

"See to the fucking kid!" Caird barked.

The woman stared a cold hard stare at Caird before she turned to leave the room.

"Wait," Locklear said. "Before you go, you'd better give me those earrings or I'll be taking you as well as your boyfriend downtown."

"What for?"

"Receipt of stolen property."

Despite her swollen belly and without, Locklear noticed, as much as even a slight change of expression, the pregnant woman walked swiftly over to Caird.

"You bastard! You said you bought these for me!" She slapped Caird's face and then tore the earrings from her ears and dropped them into Locklear's waiting hand.

The woman dropped her thin body into a worn armchair and seemed to forget the crying infant in the next room. She lit another cigarette and inhaled deeply. Locklear watched as her hands began to shake. He could see the woman come down from the line she had obviously snorted earlier – her elation slowly being replaced with feelings of agitation and anger.

"What did he do?" she asked Locklear.

"He's wanted for questioning about the murder of his, and your, meal ticket."

Caird pulled away from Locklear and turned to face him. The look on his face told Locklear that the con artist had no idea Holton was dead.

"*What? He's dead? Murdered?*"

"You know he is."

"I swear I didn't know – I didn't kill him."

"I'd say he did it OK," the woman said. "When'd it happen?"

Locklear didn't answer. He could see the disappointed woman was trying to draw him into a domestic and he didn't have time for games. Her steady supply of money had just dried up and clearly she had little other use for Caird.

"In fact, today is the first time he's been here for about a week," she added.

"What the fuck are you doing, Nat?"

She stood and smiled at Caird and then walked towards the door of the room where the infant had continued to cry.

"Don't rush back with him," she said to Locklear. "I don't care if I never see that loser again."

Locklear waited until she returned with the infant on her hip. He focused on the thin black-haired child and the dirty clothes he was dressed in.

"Looks like it's just you and me, boy," she said as she swayed.

That one line brought Locklear back more than half a century. He stood and stared at the woman as though he had woken from a dream. He took in her emaciated frame, her shoeless feet, her worn face that might once have been beautiful and her dilated expressionless black pupils, before shaking himself free of a memory he had tried hard to forget.

"Well, get on, Geronimo, get him out of my face," she jeered.

Locklear lifted his phone and asked for two cars. One to take Caird downtown and one from Child Protection Services. He hoped that CPS would take the kid somewhere he would be safe. The unborn kid he could do nothing for. He closed the phone and stared at the woman but all he saw was his mother's dark, doleful eyes staring back at him.

Less than twenty-four hours after Locklear interviewed Lee Carter in the interrogation room, Simon Caird was seated in the same chair in the same room with the same cop staring idly at the wall. That was where the similarities ended though as, while Caird wore the expression of a man who knew he was in trouble, he was no stranger to interrogation.

Locklear stared hard at the man, trying to decide which

tactic would get him furthest, especially as he knew he was running out of time. He had looked in on Carter when he got back to the station and the man looked like death. He was refusing all food and drink and, according to the night sergeant's records, had been heard sobbing in his cell, begging to see his wife. The rostered sergeant had taken almost all of the quiet man's clothes and had put Carter on suicide watch, moving him to a cell which was checked every fifteen minutes to ensure the anxious man did not attempt to take his own life. The thought of that upset Locklear deeply. He knew Carter was innocent and he was never wrong.

"Where were you last night?"

Caird smiled and rocked back on his chair until its front legs left the floor.

"I want a lawyer."

"You'll get one," Locklear retorted. "When I'm ready."

"Guess we'll be sitting here all day then cos I'm not saying shit to you until I speak to a lawyer."

Locklear stared at this man who had made a fool of the victim. He wondered how someone could do that, prey on the vulnerabilities of a lonely man and not show as much as an ounce of remorse now that he was dead.

"I saw your record, Caird. Even if you don't go down for this, you're wanted on charges of robbery in Arizona which will be your third strike. I'll make sure you're escorted on the next flight back to Tucson where you'll face prison. It'll be a long time before you see your family again. Your kid will be born while you're behind bars."

The smug smile slowly faded on Caird's face but he regained his composure quickly.

"You saw that bitch. She ain't no prize. Wouldn't mind a break from her."

"And your kid? Looks like she doesn't give a damn about him."

The earlier image of Caird's girlfriend swaying back and forth came back to him but, instead of Nat, it was his mother standing in the kitchen of their rented home, swaying on her feet in front of him. It was just after another boyfriend had decided to leave them. He had liked the man but he could no longer remember his name. There had been a lot of names to remember. Some he remembered more, for all the wrong reasons. "It's just you and me, boy," she had said as the man's car spun away from their trailer-trash home and her words had filled him with dread and fear. Alcohol had been his beautiful mother's poison as it was to become his. He shook his head and managed to block his mother from his thoughts.

"He ain't my kid. She says he is but I'm not stupid. Look, I was at home last night and every night this week. Just me and the kid. Nat started taking off in the evenings. So I stayed in. She'd probably leave the kid alone if I didn't, so that's where I was. Bitch was probably meeting up with some old boyfriend or something."

"So you care about him and there's another baby on the way."

Caird did not answer.

"I know you didn't kill Holton, Caird. You don't have the guts for that sort of thing and he was giving you enough money to feed your coke habit and hers too. What I want to know is why he was paying you off. If you cooperate, I'll speak to my boss. See what I can do to ensure you don't do time."

Caird shifted in his seat. "And if I don't?"

"I'll make sure you go down for blackmail, possession and theft of property from Holton's neighbour. And that's before we turn you over to the Arizona PD to face charges there."

Caird seemed to need a moment to consider his options. He blinked and nodded his head slightly.

"OK. I'll tell you what I know but if it ain't important I still walk, right?"

Locklear pulled his chair closer to the small metal table.

"You better make sure it's important, Caird."

"Can I have a cigarette?" he asked.

Locklear shook his head. "I don't smoke."

He pressed record on the tape recorder and announced the interview.

"OK. So you were extorting money from Holton?"

"I was playing him. So what? He was lonely and he was stinking rich."

"He wasn't rich, Caird. He was calling his elderly mother in England for the money to keep you quiet."

Caird shrugged. "So what?"

"Where'd you meet him?"

"At a downturn club."

"Holton didn't seem the type to go to clubs," Locklear said.

"Not that sort of club. High class. Discreet. Men only. Big joining fee. Likes of me was polished up and made to walk around like candy or sit at the bar looking mysterious. Good earner though."

"Go on."

"A friend put me on to it. I didn't think I could do it at

first. I mostly dealt with old ladies looking for a bit of fun but, then, a hooker's a hooker right? I coked up and got on with it. I was only there a few weeks when Alec walked in. Could tell he was an easy mark from the moment I laid eyes on him. He had 'desperate' written all over him."

"So, what? He walked up to you and asked for sex?"

"Doesn't work like that. I told you. Well, not usually anyway. It was high class. I had to dress up like a dog's dinner, speak right, have a whole story about how I was a starving actor. Owner made sure all us young guys looked like Christmas to the customers. Alec asked me to dinner. Took me to a show. Few weeks in he told me he was in love with me and that he didn't care if I was an escort, that I could start over." Caird laughed at the memory and licked his dry lips. "Anyway, I put a hook in his mouth and reeled him in. I bided my time before I told him about my elderly mother and her medical bills. He gave me a check to cover her costs. I came back for more. Alec paid." He began to laugh again as another memory surfaced. "One time I told him if I couldn't pay her medical bills I was going to have to take her out of the facility and go back to Arizona to look after her. Alec nearly died of shock. Said he couldn't bear it if we were separated."

"Do you have a sick mother?" Locklear asked even though he already knew the answer.

"Never met my mother. Except for the first few minutes of my life, I guess. My older brother told me she walked out of the hospital three hours after I was born, leaving him sitting on a seat in the lobby and me in the nursery without even a name. We grew up in state care. A few foster homes, orphanages."

"And how was that for you?"

"Happy times," he said sarcastically.

"I take it you don't want that for your kid? For either of them?"

"No," Caird replied quietly.

"So, when and how did you start blackmailing Holton?"

"We were at his apartment one night. I heard him arguing with his cousin on the phone. Some snob in London. She wanted to know why Alec was asking his mother for so much money. He got mad and hung up on her. Drank himself into a near coma on brandy and fell into bed with his clothes on. I start snooping around."

Locklear shot Caird a look. "And?"

"He had a filing cabinet so I looked through to see if he had any bank statements. I was hoping to find out just how much cash I was playing with."

"But you didn't find anything?"

"No. Then I tried his computer. I looked through his emails. Mostly work stuff. Then I found an email thread from some Indian outfit ..." He started to laugh loudly and pointed at Locklear. "I thought you were one of them. I mean, I seriously never met an Indian cop before."

Locklear didn't react. "What was in the emails?"

"The oldest email accused Alec of 'sleeping with the white ghost'. That's all. I thought it was funny."

"And the others?"

"There were three more. All a few weeks apart. Demanding that Alec return sacred property to its rightful owners. Next two threatened to inform the police that he was stealing artefacts. Last email said they were coming for him. There were no replies from Alec."

Locklear pondered the information. The reference to the white ghost made him think about the description of the man who had turned up at Alec's dig site. Carter said the man was very pale with blondish-greyish hair. It was a long shot but it was something. O'Brien was still working on Holton's computer but there was no way of knowing if it had been wiped clean and the only 'evidence' left would be what the real killer wanted him to find.

"So, you start putting the squeeze on him?"

"Not at first. He was still splashing the cash he had on me. Then it started to run out. That cousin of his went to court in England to stop him getting any more of his mother's money. She won too. Old lady had some sort of dementia. Alec started to refuse when I asked him for money. One night, we came back to his apartment. Nat and I were desperate for a fix. I did what I had to do to try softening him up a little and then asked him for money. He refused. He said he didn't have any. So I said I'd cut him, right? I wouldn't have. That's not my scene. I'm small-time stuff. But he wouldn't back down. I put a knife to his neck and just about nicked him. He screamed like a baby. Old lady across the hall rang the cops. Alec didn't press charges because I told him I knew what he'd done and I'd have had no problem telling what I knew if I had to."

Locklear thought about this for a moment. Something didn't quite add up. The timeframe of the emails meant that Holton had been stealing Native American artefacts *before* Caird started blackmailing him.

"Who were the emails from? A name?"

Caird smiled again. "They all ended with '*Toh-way cheen*' so I guess that was his name.

Locklear sighed and hoped that O'Brien could figure out where in the US the emails had come from.

"There's more," Caird said. "But if I tell you, I definitely walk?"

Locklear thought about what Benson would have to say about that but decided he'd risk it.

"OK. If it's good – you'll walk."

"I came to the apartment one day with Alec. An Indian had arrived at the building earlier. Knocked on the old woman's door across the hall by accident and threatened her. Alec and me got out of the elevator and Alec and the Indian started arguing."

"Date?"

"I dunno. Maybe a Saturday? Alec wasn't working so it must have been the weekend. I went into Alec's apartment while this was going on. It was none of my business. But I could hear everything. I watched the whole thing through the peephole. The Native guy had a big tattoo of a feather on his cheek. He left and Alec went into his office in the apartment to make a call. I heard him telling whoever he called what happened and telling them to sort it out. Then Alec got really drunk. He was terrified. Didn't wake up the next day until after two. He went over to the old lady to check on her. Two days later I see a photo of the Indian on the news – saying he'd been pushed off a bridge in Richmond."

"You didn't go to the police?"

"You fucking kidding me? This was gold dust. I had Alec where I wanted him. I only had to show up at the apartment and I got cash. No more favours for it neither."

"Any idea where he was getting it from?"

"Wasn't my problem."

Locklear sighed again and tapped his pen off the metal table.

"We done here?" Caird asked.

"Yes. For now."

"Bad news, sarge," Mendoza said out in the busy station.

"Shoot."

"No-one except Carter came anywhere near Holton's apartment door on the night he was killed."

"No-one? You sure."

"Yes. I spent two hours going over the footage."

Locklear glanced over to where O'Brien was sitting staring into his computer screen.

He walked up to him.

"Check Holton's phone records and see who he phoned each Saturday for the last number of weeks. I want that information yesterday, O'Brien."

O'Brien pulled a face and did not look up from his screen.

"O'Brien?"

"Yes?"

"When I speak to you, you look at me and you say 'Yes, sir'. Got it?"

"Yes, sir," O'Brien replied as he narrowed his dark pools at Locklear.

"Come on, Mendoza," Locklear said, stalking towards the entrance.

"Where to now?" she asked.

"Back to the innocent-looking Meara Henschel. Seems the old lady knows even more than I thought she did."

# Chapter 5

Locklear could see the light flicker behind Meara Henschel's peephole as the old lady stood behind her door and tried to decide whether or not to let him and his trooper inside. He took her missing earrings out of his pocket and dangled them in front of the peephole until she pulled back the chain and unclasped the lock on her door.

Meara put her hand out and waited for Locklear to drop her treasured earrings into her hand. Then she stood to one side and motioned for the pair to come in.

"Where did you find them?"

"Does it matter?"

"Thank you," she replied with glistening eyes.

The old lady was not surprised to see the sergeant and his trooper again only a day after their first visit. She had known the sergeant had realised she had not told him all that she knew about her long-term friend. She had loved Alec and even now her overriding emotion was to protect the man she looked on as a son. Even when she knew it was too late. Even now that she knew it no longer really mattered to Alec.

When her visitors were seated she sat in silence and waited to see how much Locklear had figured out and how much she might still be able to keep to herself. If not for Alec's sake, then for his family.

Locklear matched her silence with a brooding stare but the woman remained silent.

It was Mendoza who broke the quiet of the room.

"We know you didn't tell us everything about Alec," she said. "We also think we know why. You loved him. You wanted to protect him. But what you're actually doing is protecting his killer. We don't want to cause you any more upset than you've already been through and we don't want to take you downtown for questioning – but if we have to, if it means we can find out what happened to Alec Holton, then we will. So, we'd advise you to tell us what you know and don't waste any more of our time."

Locklear squirmed a little at his trooper's forthrightness towards the old lady but Mendoza's tactics appeared to throw Meara off guard. She glanced quickly at Locklear before focusing her tired swollen eyes on Mendoza.

"I admit that I didn't tell you everything and you're right – it was to protect Alec's reputation. It's his family I'm thinking of. I didn't want to upset his mother."

"Holton's mother is in the early stages of dementia," Locklear said. "She's a ward of court in the UK. She may not even understand that he is dead."

"He has a cousin. She's a British diplomat. It could ruin her career."

Locklear took out his pen and notepad. "Her name?"

"Amelia Hirsch."

Locklear jotted down the name and inhaled. "Now, tell

us everything about the day a Native American mistakenly knocked on your door."

Meara rubbed her lined hands together as though she was cold while Locklear sweated in the heat of the apartment. A radiator clicked beside him. The temperature outside was around 32°C yet the old woman had the heating on.

"Do you mind if I turn that down?" he asked.

"Yes, I mind," Meara snapped. "I doubt you'll be here long enough to melt," she added curtly. "I gather you've spoken with Simon Caird."

Locklear nodded.

"Did he kill Alec?" she asked.

Locklear did not answer.

"The Native American," Mendoza interjected swiftly.

Meara cut her a sharp glance.

"Alec wasn't here when the man arrived. I don't know if he knocked at his apartment. I don't even know how he got into the building, but the carpet-cleaning company were here so perhaps they'd left the front door open while they were working. I'd asked the janitor if the men would clean two of my rugs while they were here so when I heard the knock at my door, I thought it was them. My carer wasn't here so it took me a while to get to the door and by the time I reached it he was yelling and pounding on it."

"What was he yelling?" Locklear asked.

"He was just calling out Alec's name and some foreign words, repeating the same thing over and over."

"Foreign? Have you any idea what language it was?" Mendoza asked.

"I'm sorry, no. I didn't recognise it and I've a good knowledge of languages. I speak five."

"Really?" Mendoza replied.

Locklear could hear the admiration in his trooper's voice. He wasn't sure if Mendoza was genuinely impressed or if she was putting on the charm to get as much out of the old lady as they could.

"Yes. My native Polish, of course. I speak some Russian, German and English. I learnt Italian while studying music."

"I speak Spanish," Mendoza offered for no apparent reason.

"I should imagine that you do. You *are* Hispanic," Meara replied curtly.

"Gee, you're tough but, sweetie, so are we," Mendoza said. "Now that we've become friends, you need to get to the point. If you'd prefer your rich neighbours to see you being brought downtown in a marked car, Sergeant Locklear would be happy to arrange it. So, get to the point."

Meara pursed her thin lips.

"As he repeated those words over and over, do you remember them?" Locklear asked.

"Yes, It was '*lakotayate*' or something close to that."

"Do you mean *Lakota Oyate*?"

"Possibly. He said it very fast."

"Do you know what it means?" Mendoza asked Locklear.

"Well, Miss Henschel, that's not foreign," he sniped. "*Lakota Oyate* means 'Lakota People' or 'Lakota Nation'. It's one of the languages of America's first people."

"So what happened when he knocked?" Mendoza asked to distract from Locklear's sarcasm.

"I opened the door and he seemed surprised to see me. He looked past me into my apartment and insisted on speaking with Professor Holton. I said Alec didn't live here. Just then the elevator door opened and Alec and Simon got out. Alec and the man argued. Simon fled like a scared little rabbit into Alec's apartment. The Indian had a small box which he thrust into Alec's hand. He called him a traitor."

"Traitor? So, he and Alec knew each other?"

"Yes, it seemed that way," Meara replied weakly.

"Then what?"

"He said Alec would pay for the betrayal. That they'd be coming for him unless he put things right."

"Did he say anything else?"

"No. But Alec was terrified. He tried to explain that it wasn't his fault. He tried to hold onto the man, to reason with him and the man pushed him and began to say those words again over and over. Alec grabbed onto him. He was trying to make him stay. They struggled a bit. The box fell and burst open. The Indian picked up the contents from the floor and took off down the stairwell."

"What was in it?" Mendoza asked.

Meara began to cry and both Locklear and Mendoza could see the sharp old woman's tears were heartfelt.

"Something I saw too much of already in my life. Something I tried hard to forget. It was a human skull."

"Did you ask Alec later what it was all about?"

"Not until the next day. He stayed in the apartment all evening with that Simon. It showed me how caught up he was with that man. I'd have expected him to call after something like that happened. He knew how upset I was. When he called the next afternoon, he was dreadfully hung over and in need of a shower. It looked like he'd slept in the clothes he was wearing."

"Did you ask him outright or did he just tell you?"

"I asked him."

"And?" Locklear said.

"He said that some time back he'd been trying to help a local tribe block further digging on a sacred site. He'd come up against the Dean of his university and some other university he'd been working with about it. Alec said the tribe had turned on him and were blaming him for missing items that were to be returned to them. Alec said he feared for his life."

"What did you do then?" Mendoza asked.

"I was horrified. I'd never seen Alec so ... so vulnerable. Someone was threatening to kill him and even if they weren't really going to do it, even if it was an idle threat, he should go to the police – but he wouldn't. I had to do something so I phoned the number I had for his cousin. Alec had given it to me in case of an emergency."

"Was she alarmed? Had she had any idea that he was in trouble before that?"

"She sounded worried but, no, she seemed to have no idea that Alec had such problems."

Locklear watched as the woman's face clouded over. Her lips moved as though she was trying to make sense of something.

"What?" Mendoza asked.

Meara shook her head. "She seemed so refined when I spoke with her that day. I asked her if I should call the police but she said there was no need. She thanked me for telling her. She said she'd talk to him, that she'd help him sort it out. When I got off the phone I was relieved."

"But you were wrong?"

"Yes."

"How so?" Locklear asked.

"I tried to reach her on her landline to tell her Alec was dead. It rang out so I phoned her on the second number Alec had given me. It was a cell-phone number. Amelia travelled a lot with the diplomatic services."

"Did she answer?" Locklear asked.

"Yes. I was shaking when I heard her voice. I dreaded telling her that Alec was gone. I assumed she'd be devastated."

"Assumed? Why, what did she say?" Mendoza asked.

"I decided to just come right out and say it. I prefer that myself. There is no other way to give such terrible news. I remember the day a prisoner in the adult section of the camp told me my parents were dead, that in fact they had been dead for weeks. He sought me out when he had reason to work in the area I was placed in. He walked up to me and he just said it and I remembered how I appreciated his honesty although I was just a child. So I did the same. I said: 'Amelia – Alec is dead'."

Meara stopped speaking and looked down at her lined hands. She shook her head and heavy tears fell down her worn face.

"She said ... she said 'Don't ever call this number again' and hung up. I haven't heard from her since."

Locklear eyed Mendoza. Amelia Hirsch had two reasons to be glad her cousin was dead as far as he could see. First, once Holton's mother died, Hirsch would be the sole heir to what was possibly a substantial banking fortune and, second, the public figure could no longer be embarrassed by whatever her troubled cousin had got himself involved in.

"I'm sorry," Mendoza offered.

"Alec was a weak man but a good man. You need to know that. Whatever trouble he was in you can be sure it was something that had got out of hand. Something that was beyond his control."

Locklear nodded and sat silently for a while, thinking. Then he rose to his feet.

"Thank you," he said.

He and Mendoza let themselves out while Meara remained seated in the soaring temperature of her overheated apartment.

Locklear's phone rang. "O'Brien," he muttered to Mendoza and answered.

He listened as the curt man told him that there had been only one Saturday night in the past number of weeks that any calls had been made from Holton's home phone. He nodded as he absorbed the information.

"Sartre's office, huh?" he said. "The only call."

Mendoza eyed him quizzically.

"Right, Mendoza," he said as he ended the call. "You need to go back to the janitor. See if he still has the security tapes from the day the Native American called. We might see something that neither Caird nor Henschel remembered. Then, go back to the station and pull the record on this native guy's murder. Find out as much as you can about him, who he was, anything that will explain what he had against Holton."

"What are you going to do?"

Locklear looked at his watch. "I'm going to Richmond University. I think it's time I had a chat with the Dean."

58

# Chapter 6

Gerard Sartre was younger than Locklear had expected him to be. The Dean of the prestigious university sat in a leather chesterfield armchair and beckoned for Locklear to take the chair facing his in the large office which felt chilly despite the searing summer heat. He reached across the desk and shook Locklear's hand warmly but did not stand.

He was dressed in similar clothing to those hanging in Holton's stuffy wardrobe – a crisp white shirt over tan corduroy trousers. Locklear glanced down at the man's small feet which were clad in comfortable brown shoes under which Locklear could see socks of an almost identical shade. Sartre was not wearing a tie which Locklear noted did not fit in with his pristine, albeit boring appearance. He had light-brown hair, tan skin and small brown eyes. From the level of his head on the chair, Locklear could tell that he was not a tall man and was probably barely five foot eight. Locklear placed him at being around forty-five years old and wondered how the man had achieved the most prestigious position at the university at such a young age.

"Can I offer you something to drink?" Sartre asked.

Locklear zoned in on the man's accent, the crisp consonants and over-accentuated vowels typical of the cut-glass accents of the British upper class.

"No, thank you. You're British?"

"French-born, actually. My parents moved to London when I was a child. I came here to do my PhD. I met my wife here at the university. She's from London and was also doing her PhD. In politics, of all things! How utterly boring. Unfortunately, we were just getting settled here when she got a post back in London. So, we have to travel a lot just to see each other. But, well, *c'est la vie*!" He smiled.

"I'm here about Alec Holton," Locklear began.

Sartre nodded and waited.

"Can you think of any reason why anyone would want to kill him?"

"No," Sartre replied.

"Do you think that Holton was involved in anything illegal? Anything that could bring unscrupulous people into his life?"

Sartre hardly raised his thin, brown eyebrows. "No."

Locklear weighed up the man and knew it was going to be one of those interviews where he had to drag information from the person. He could never understand how those who resorted to this tactic didn't realise that it made them look guilty, that talking was more likely to make them look innocent than staring stone-faced while waiting for a cop to ask the next question.

He needed to knock the man off his smug perch.

"I know about the investigation into the theft of Native American artefacts at the university."

Sartre stared back at Locklear. "What's that got to do with Professor Holton?"

"The items were stolen from his lab, weren't they? And the police have made no arrests yet. Whoever stole those items is still out there. Maybe Holton knew who they were? Maybe they were blackmailing him? Maybe he was going to tell the police everything he knew and the thieves killed him?"

"That's a lot of maybes, Sergeant Locklear. And you're wrong. One of our employees stole those items. The police are working on the investigation. I've even heard that Mr Carter is locked up downtown as a suspect in Professor Holton's murder. So, it's a closed case, as the police would say. A fait-accompli, sergeant."

Locklear leant forward. He could feel the anger rising in his throat.

"It's *Detective Sergeant*, Mr Sartre –"

"Professor," Sartre corrected him.

"Professor Sartre. I worked with Lee Carter and consider myself to know the man well. There's no way he stole those items and there's definitely no way he killed Holton or anyone else for that matter. Somebody is setting him up and I intend to find out who that person is."

A sly sneer washed over Sartre's face. "Well, your colleagues Detectives Hill and Diaz believe they have enough to convict your, em, friend … of the theft of priceless Native American artefacts."

"There's no evidence of that," Locklear retorted.

"No? The security footage shows that the only one who entered the lab that morning was Carter. I interviewed Professor Holton myself and everything was accounted for before he went on leave. It was Carter who seemed wary of giving information. He hardly spoke when I questioned him. He just kept insisting that he didn't take anything. The man was shaking like a leaf. You're telling me that he had nothing to hide?"

"He was covering for Holton. He saw Holton take things from the dig site. He didn't say anything out of respect for Holton."

"Well, I guess there's no way he can prove that now, is there? Not with Professor Holton being dead."

"How convenient. Can I ask why you don't suspect Holton of any wrongdoing?"

"Professor Holton worked at this university for thirty years. He had an exemplary record. Carter did his undergraduate and graduate work here but he's only been employed here for a couple of years. Do the math," Sartre replied smugly.

Locklear leant far back into his chair until the leather buttons dug into his head. He shifted again.

"I know about the other missing artefacts – the ones that went missing in South Dakota. I also know that the day a Native American arrived at Holton's apartment, Holton called someone looking for help and that that someone was you."

The smile slowly faded from Sartre's face.

"I also know that neither you nor the USD Dean reported those particular items missing. I checked. So don't bother lying. You didn't think I wouldn't look into things before I sat down here, did you?"

"Holton called me because there had been some difficulties with local tribes, I'll admit. Seems they've been threatening our teams on dig sites. We have our permits and we stick to the law. Perhaps those people stole the items themselves? Did you consider that?"

"Those people? You can't steal things you already own," Locklear retorted.

Sartre scanned Locklear's features and laughed openly.

"Now, now, sergeant. Don't make this personal. If you can't be ... objective, then perhaps you shouldn't be on this case? Your ... em ... ethnicity ... and the fact that you're a friend of the suspect ... well, I think they're grounds for you to be taken off the case. Don't you think? I might even call Captain Benson myself. As a concerned citizen only, you understand."

Locklear stood and backed off a few steps.

"I see right through you, Sartre, and you're hiding something dirty. I don't know what it is but, believe me, I will find out and when I do I'll be back."

Sartre grinned.

Locklear flung open the wood-panelled door until it slammed into the expensively decorated wall of Sartre's office.

As he walked to his car, he phoned Mendoza.

"Sarge?" she answered.

"Where are you?"

"At the station. I've been to Holton's apartment block and got the tapes you wanted. The janitor, Matteo Moretti, was only too happy to help me. Seems Miss Henschel has been looking down her nose at him since he started working there and he had an axe to grind. I'm going to look through the tapes now and then I'll look for the record on the Native American's murder."

"Leave the tapes for now. Our time's up. Go to O'Brien and take whatever he's got off Holton's computer. Then look for the sheet on the Native American's murder. Hide what you can on your person."

"What's going on, sarge?"

"Just do it," Locklear growled.

He snapped the phone shut and drove at speed to the station, hoping all the way that Benson would not see him until he had a chance to see Carter again. He parked roughly at the back of the station and rapped on the metal back door where he hoped Al Gervaso would be on duty. The long-serving officer would let Locklear into the cells through the back corridor and wouldn't ask any questions about him using an entry into the building which was reserved for taking prisoners securely to court or to prison.

He knocked loudly on the door again and Gervaso pulled the hatch back.

"Sergeant?" Gervaso asked.

"Let me in, Gervaso."

Gervaso scanned the area to the right and left of the detective sergeant to make sure no-one was forcing him to gain entry through the secure door to try to break out any of the five prisoners he now had in his charge. He knew he didn't need to be worried. Locklear was the type of cop that criminals would have to kill first, but he still had to be careful.

Assured that Locklear was alone, he entered the code and the door sprang open.

"Jesus, sarge, you'll get me fired for this. You know no-one's allowed in this way."

Locklear pushed past Gervaso and walked down to the

cell that Carter was being held in. He found his friend lying on a bed in his underwear. The heat in his cell was turned up to ensure he didn't freeze. If it were possible, Carter seemed to have lost even more weight than when he'd seen him less than twenty-four hours earlier. His face looked like it was sinking in around his cheekbones and his eyelids were dark and swollen. He stood shakily and approached the bars.

"I'm going to get you out of here, Lee. You need to believe that."

Carter nodded.

"But it's going to take some time and, until then, you need to keep your head. You need to eat. You need to do it for Virginia and the kids. If you do all that, they'll move you to a cell with another person. You'll be safer that way."

"Safer from what, sarge?"

"I think your Dean is somehow involved and now he knows I know you." Locklear shook his head, reflecting on his stupidity in telling Sartre about their former relationship. "That puts you in danger, Lee, so … I'm going to try to get you bailed or at the very least moved out of this station. I'll call in a favour. But if I fail, if you're kept here, then for God sake get yourself off suicide watch and into a shared cell."

Carter nodded. "I told Virginia everything. She's upset. I don't know if she completely believes me. She can't understand how I can be arrested for something I didn't do."

"She'll come around."

Carter looked as though he was about to cry.

Locklear fixed his eyes on the filthy cell wall and tapped his foot on the cold tiled floor.

"You'll be fine," he finally said.

Carter did not respond.

"Do you trust me, Lee?"

"Yes," he replied weakly.

"Then hang in there. I'll prove you didn't do this. You have my word."

Locklear heard a small whimper rise up from Carter's dry throat.

He glanced down the corridor. "Gervaso?"

"Yes, sarge."

"This man's feeling better now. Give him his clothes, get him some food and drink. Then move him to a shared cell."

"Sarge, the captain said –"

"That's an order, Gervaso. He's just playing games, that's all. We've got a silver-spoon guy here. Seems he's used to getting his own way. Doesn't like sharing."

"Anyone in particular you want me to put him in with?"

"Someone who won't look for trouble but can handle themselves."

Gervaso looked over the long, thin, weak-looking man and nodded.

"OK, sarge, you're the boss."

Locklear walked to the end of the corridor and waited while Gervaso buzzed him into the main station building.

He walked towards Mendoza's desk and immediately sensed that Benson was around.

She nodded at him, a nod which said she had done as he asked.

He walked past her and glanced sideways at Diaz and Hill who were both seated at their desks. Diaz had his feet up on his and was slurping a store-bought coffee while Hill played solitaire on his computer. Both men grinned as he pulled out his chair to sit at his desk on the far side of the room from where he could see Benson's serious head bob furiously on the phone in his glass-panelled office.

"Someone's in trouble, Locklear – can you guess who it is?" Diaz sneered. "And hey, if you think that your friend will get bail on account of his lilywhite face and clean sheet, think again. We've enough on him to make sure he doesn't see daylight for years."

"Fuck you," Mendoza spat from her desk.

Locklear did not bite. He didn't have time right now to joke with Ernie and Bert, as Mendoza had nicknamed them. He two-finger-typed Sartre's name into the record system but no matches came up. He glanced briefly towards Benson and Benson's eyes locked onto him. He tried to enter Sartre's name into the general search which Mendoza referred to as 'Google' but there were too many hits for him to focus on anything useful before Benson's door opened abruptly.

"Locklear. In here – now!"

Locklear cleared his search and took anything he needed from his desk drawer. He knew what was coming. He had known it since he sat down with Carter on the night his friend was arrested.

He walked into the glass-panelled office and did not bother to sit. Suspensions didn't take long. He had witnessed many of them. Granted, it had never happened to him. Kowalski had come close to it a few times but had always found ways of getting Locklear out of his sight for a week or two until things blew over as they usually did.

But Benson was different. Benson was a climber, a crowd-pleaser and a would-be politician, who had obviously reacted to a call from Sartre.

The whole station came to a dead stop while all eyes focused on the two men behind the glass screen. The desk sergeant's phone went unanswered as cops waited with bated breath to see what Locklear would do.

Benson seemed suddenly nervous of the attention that was on him. He was aware that there wasn't a person in the station who wasn't missing Kowalski and that the good impression he had thought he'd make by running the station with an iron fist had backfired on him and that, if asked, there wasn't a person in the room who liked him. Nobody except Diaz and Hill that is, who he had already figured out were two bootlickers and were the two laziest cops he had ever had the misfortune to know.

"Badge, keys, gun," he said quietly.

Locklear threw all three items onto the desk and waited.

"You're suspended," Benson said as quietly as he could.

"I know," Locklear replied loudly.

Benson's shoulders rose upwards, as though he was expecting a row.

Locklear remained quiet.

"You aren't going to ask why?" Benson asked.

"Does it matter?"

"Guess not," Benson replied as he gathered up Locklear's things and placed them in Kowalski's safe behind the desk.

"How long?" Locklear asked.

"Until Kowalski gets back and decides what to do with you. I spoke to him. He's mad as hell."

Locklear looked at the year-in-view calendar on

68

Kowalski's wall where his captain had marked his return. June 21st, 2018.

"So, about ten days?"

Benson nodded.

"That should be all I need," Locklear replied.

"Need for what?" Benson barked, his voice now rising.

Locklear ignored the question. He swung open the glass door in much the same way as he had done leaving Sartre's office and walked out.

He made his way to the parking lot and waited for Mendoza to come out as he knew she would.

It took longer than he expected. Benson must be in full flow.

Twenty minutes later, she opened the passenger door of his car and slid onto the worn, dirty seat.

She held up a computer stick and grinned.

"O'Brien gave me this. I'll tell you what else he said later."

"Well, what's your punishment?" he asked her.

"Desk duty," she said. "Two weeks."

"You got off lightly. After all, you knew Carter as well as I did."

"Ah, but you're my boss. I told Benson I was only following orders."

Locklear grinned as he looked at the row of cars parked in front of the building and noticed two royal-blue Ford trucks parked side by side.

"I see Ernie and Bert have identical new wheels. Wonder how they can afford those cars on their salary?" he mused as he leaned his head out of the window and made a note of their plates.

"What I wonder about is what's with the 'parking side by side' thing. It's like a pissing contest between those two weirdos."

"You got any vacation due? I could use your help on this case," Locklear asked.

Mendoza laughed. "Lots. Think I'll take them from today. At least I don't need to arrange for someone to look after Santiago."

Her seven-year-old son was in Mexico with her mother. Mendoza's grandmother was very ill so they would be at least a few weeks there. Her grandmother had moved from her village to live in Mexico City with Mendoza's aunt some years back but her aunt died and her grandmother lived alone there now. She'd had to take Santiago out of school a few weeks early as she didn't have anyone else to look after him. Her mother would make sure he kept up with his schoolwork there.

Locklear watched as the cop's eyes clouded over.

"You missing him?"

"Yeah, but it's not that. He's having a great time. It's just that ..."

Locklear waited.

"Manuel is living in Mexico now. He left the force about a year ago. I only heard that recently from a buddy working in my last precinct. Seems he's joined some church-run charity helping victims of domestic violence in Mexico City – mostly women and their kids." She grimaced. "Seems he's found God there."

"That's good, isn't it? After what he did to you, maybe he's trying to make amends?" Locklear offered.

Mendoza shook her head. "Santiago put a post on

Facebook saying that he's in Mexico for the summer and Manuel made contact with him. I was against it but it seemed like Santy was happy to hear from him. My mom said maybe he has changed, that maybe it would be good for Santy to have a father figure but ..." Mendoza trailed off.

"But you don't believe he's changed?"

"I don't think people can change. Not like that. I don't want him being in contact with Santy."

"Then refuse it. He hasn't seen the kid in years. He has no right to ask to be part of his life now."

"I thought about that, but Santy seems to really want to see him so I've said yes. He's so aware that other kids dads live with them and he doesn't have that. My brother lives in New York. I rarely see him so it's not like Santy has a male role model. I have to do what's right by him. I'll allow it once and see how it goes."

"He has me," Locklear replied.

Mendoza smiled. It had taken her sullen boss almost two years to learn how to speak to her son and their interaction mostly involved Locklear throwing a baseball back and forth to Santy in her backyard while the boy nattered on about a range of topics Locklear had no understanding of or interest in.

"So," Mendoza began, "where do we begin?"

"Ever been to South Dakota?"

# Chapter 7

It took until the following afternoon for Locklear and Mendoza to get a flight to Rapid City which was as close as Locklear could get to the place he felt held the key to what happened to Holton in Richmond. The pair had spent the morning together in Locklear's dusty apartment, discussing what they knew so far and, more importantly, what they didn't.

Mendoza had listened in as Locklear phoned Kowalski and asked as a favour to get Carter bailed. The captain berated Locklear for his handling of the case so far – namely for neglecting to inform his replacement that Carter was in fact a friend of his. Mendoza could tell that Locklear was losing the argument and it was only when he became emotional and resorted to yelling at his boss to get Carter out of jail that Kowalski relented.

Kowalski was the only person, she knew, apart from herself, who showed any kindness or understanding towards their mutual friend and colleague. She knew Kowalski and Locklear went back a long way and wondered how much their captain knew about Locklear's past and if this caused him to give way to Locklear more than he did to any of his other staff.

O'Brien had told a disappointed Mendoza that he hadn't found any more emails of interest on Holton's computer – only the four Caird had reported seeing. He had found nothing on an organisation named INTENT and reported that the files entitled INTENT were empty. Neither had he found any evidence of the email Carter insisted Holton had sent to him inviting him to call to his apartment, an email which had also miraculously disappeared from Carter's inbox.

"Someone very clever is messing with their computers," O'Brien had said, without looking at Mendoza as he typed.

"There's someone smarter than you?" she'd quipped.

O'Brien did not react to the compliment but continued to do various searches on his computer while Mendoza stood over him.

He had, thankfully, figured out what the words *Toh-way-cheen* which appeared at the end of the emails meant. It was not a person's name as Caird had thought but was in fact a Sioux term for '*to revenge*'.

Locklear only expressed mild interest when Mendoza informed him that O'Brien's maternal grandmother had been a Lakota Sioux and that the IT nerd had spent many of his summers with her in South Dakota. O'Brien had also figured out that Holton's relationship with the man who had shown up at his apartment – Albert Whitefeather, a Native American army veteran from Rapid City – had been in existence for a couple of years and it was only the more recent emails that showed any signs of aggression towards Holton.

73

O'Brien had also managed to find a record of an assault on a museum curator in New York who reported that a Native American had tied him up at his home and had cut along his hairline in an hour-long attack. This matched the MO's of two Native Americans, one of whom was Whitefeather – but Whitefeather's alibi was watertight and the second suspect was in prison at the time of the attack.

After an hour-long stop, the American Airlines flight took off on the last leg of the six-hour flight to Rapid City. Mendoza sat in the window seat and stared out at the clear blue sky as the plane made its way westwards to a state she had never been to. When she tired of gazing at the horizon, she focused on her sleeping boss who had placed himself in the aisle seat as his long legs would not fit into the cramped economy seat beside her. As they had settled into their seats, she'd noticed the relief on his face when he realised that there was no-one else allocated to the three-seat row and that he would not have to come into close proximity to her during the flight. She knew her boss did not like to be touched and especially did not like it when *she* touched him. Mendoza often wondered what had happened to Locklear to make him so averse to human contact. He was a good man, a kind man, who tried hard to cover up his compassion for people with his gruff personality and sharp retorts. But she knew that deep down he was like a hurt child who had built a protective wall around himself and that she, and possibly Kowalski, were the only two people who had become as close to Locklear as he was ever likely to permit another human being to be. Mendoza mused that she and Locklear were alike in a way. She had been both physically and emotionally hurt by the husband who was trying to push his way back into her life. She had closed the wounds he had inflicted on her, both physical and psychological, had licked both scars through her love for her child and her commitment to her work and she had succeeded. She did not need Manuel in her life, not when she had tried so hard to give their son the security he had lacked in the early years of his life. Her ex-husband was remarried now. She had found his new family's Facebook page and had stared into the face of the pretty Mexican widow and her two young sons sitting proudly beside her new American husband. One boy looked to be around the same age or slightly younger than Santy while the other was no more than two or three years old. The young Latina's physical similarities to Mendoza did not go unnoticed by her. Both women had the same long, unruly black hair and deep brown eyes. The woman also shared Mendoza's high cheekbones and small nose. It was almost like Manuel had sought out a woman who looked like her and the idea of this made her shiver. She did not believe for one moment that her husband had turned over a new leaf. But for now she would watch and wait in the hope that her ex-husband had changed and would not hurt her child. She suspected Locklear had endured a different form of abuse which made him separate from all those around him, made him avoid connections, attachments and emotions. Whatever happened to her boss in his early life had had a lasting impact on him and she did not want this happening to her only child. She hoped that Locklear might someday feel close enough to her to tell her what he had endured but doubted that this would ever happen. She knew other cops that had worked alongside him for decades yet knew nothing about his life outside of the station.

Mendoza leant across the empty seat between them, a representation she felt of their relationship, near enough to touch but yet so very far. Despite her sexual orientation, there was something about her boss that attracted her. She looked into his face and reasoned that he was a handsome man. His hair was thick and black and his face had that high-cheek-boned chiselled look that she found attractive. She raised her hand and was about to touch his unshaven face when he half-opened his eyes. She pulled back and pretended to fuss with the thin airline blanket that had fallen to his lap, pulling it roughly upwards to cover his arms. He closed his eyes but she knew that he was awake.

She lifted her phone and checked for messages from Santiago but there were none. She grinned at the expletives and threats in Benson's response to her email that she had decided to take urgent leave. She responded with a simple "OK" to her temporary boss, knowing this would annoy him further and knowing that she, like Locklear, would have to face the music when Kowalski returned.

As they approached landing, the plane began to rock back and forth. The sky lit up and loud thuds erupted through the cabin. Mendoza gripped Locklear's hand. She was not afraid of flying but she hated turbulence. She felt him tense in his seat but he did not pull away as she would have expected. He kept his eyes closed tight and did not look at her. The thunder became louder and she began to mutter some words of comfort to herself.

"Stop praying. It's just a storm. They happen here all the time," he said without opening his eyes.

"I wasn't praying," she retorted, releasing his hand.

"You were. Might as well have Carter with us."

Mendoza laughed. "I hope he's OK."

"Me too," he replied softly.

The plane came down with a loud thump and rocked back and forth on the runway until it finally came to an abrupt stop. When the passengers began to applaud, Mendoza saw no reason to join in. It was expected that the pilot would deliver them onto terra firma as he or she was paid to do, and Mendoza saw no reason why she should congratulate them for doing so.

When they entered the terminal, Locklear made his way purposefully to the shopping area and bought a light-brown Stetson. He placed it firmly on his head.

"Looks good on you," Mendoza said with a grin.

Locklear's phone beeped. He listened to a message from Carter. He was free on strict bail conditions and had taken Locklear's advice and gone somewhere no-one would expect to find him but which would not break the terms of his bail.

Locklear pressed redial and clenched his hand in fury when the naive ex-trooper answered his phone.

"That was a test, Carter. Don't answer your phone. I don't trust this guy Sartre and he has your number. I told you I think he's involved. Somehow."

"Sir, I doubt it, he hardly even knows me. Why would he try pin something like this on me?"

"Because you're an easy mark and so was Holton so don't end up like him. Tell your wife and kids to go stay with relatives. *Don't* text me to tell me where you are. *Don't* contact me or Mendoza at all. Get yourself a burner phone and give the number to the guy whose jaw you think I broke. When we met, remember? If I need you, I'll contact him."

"My fa–"

"*God damn it, Carter. Don't say one more goddamn word.*"

"You think my phone is bugged?"

"Goodbye, Carter. I'll let you know when this is all over."

Locklear snapped his phone shut and looked for the terminal exit.

They made their way outside.

Mendoza stood gazing out at the mountain range which surrounded the small regional airport. Dark storm-clouds, peppered with purple and red hues, hung over the top of the range. A flash of lightning lit up the sky, turning the mountains into a blanket of scarlet silk.

"It's beautiful," she said, more to herself than to her boss who showed little interest in their surroundings.

Locklear pulled his bag onto his shoulder and walked fast, leaving Mendoza trailing after him pulling a large suitcase behind her.

"You travel light," she gasped as she caught up with him at the cab terminal.

"You don't," he replied curtly.

Locklear hailed the first cab and eased himself into the front seat. He looked over at the driver who weighed about a hundred pounds and was drinking coffee from a steaming cup. Locklear sniffed and caught a familiar aroma. Whiskey.

"Nope," he said as he got out and pulled their luggage from the car.

He raised his hand and gestured to the next cab driver who was parked second on the line.

"Didn't like the look of him?" Mendoza asked.

Locklear ignored the question as he threw his bag into the waiting cab. He checked the driver over. A woman. She had an easy smile and a photo of her three teenage kids on the dash. He returned her smile and tipped his hat.

"Motel 6, East Latrobe Street, please, ma'am," he said as he fastened his seatbelt.

Mendoza noticed how relaxed her boss had suddenly become.

"Is this home to you?" she asked from the back seat of the cab.

Locklear did not answer but thought about the question posed to him. No one place was home, he reasoned, when you've moved around as much as he had. Everywhere and anywhere was home.

Locklear looked out of the window as they turned onto Highway 44 and thought about the time he had spent in the small town. He stared silently as they passed green fields and farmhouses and as the sun set he felt his mood darken. He had come back here in his youth because it was the place his mother had wanted to spend the last months of her life. She had given birth to him here, he knew, with no family around her. No husband. No boyfriend. Not one person to care for her. In nine days, on June 21st, it would be exactly fifty-eight years to the day that he had been born in a small free clinic in the poorer part of town. The name she had given at reception had not been her real name, or if it had he could find no birth record for Wachiwi Locklear matching his mother's age. He did not know for sure if she had been born in South Dakota or if she had come from another state to Rapid City to give birth to him, and so his efforts to find whatever kin she had resulted in failure because he had nothing to go on. Not even her unusual first name led to any firm leads. In time, he gave up looking because he reasoned that if anyone was still looking, if anyone still wanted Wachiwi after all of these years, they would have found her. Only once did he remember someone coming for them, or rather, for his mother because the Indian that barged into their trailer showed no interest in Locklear and, if anything, objected to his very presence. Whoever that man had been, his mother did not want to do whatever it was he had asked her to do. Locklear was still just a boy at the time and if he did not understand their words, he understood that this man wanted his mother to do something she would not agree to. He had honoured his mother's dying wishes and had rented a small house in the south-east of the town but the move only added to the agitation and confusion her illness caused. She did not recognise any place or anyone. She had not been back to the state since his birth and he spent those last months wondering what she had hoped for, who exactly she had been looking for. In time, she stopped speaking English and wandered around the house mumbling in her native tongue. During those sad and lonely weeks he wished more than anything that he had learnt to speak his mother's language. Instead, he understood only when she was hungry or scared. The time came when he could no longer care for her and he could still remember what she was wearing when he drove her to a care facility only a couple of hundred yards from the place she had given birth to him. A nurse held her hand as he walked away from her in her faded purple floral dress, her long hair spread around her narrow shoulders, still dark despite her middle age with only a few stray white hairs framing her brown, smiling face. She had waved to him as he left, not knowing or understanding that he was leaving her in someone else's care. Not knowing who he was. It occurred to him then, despite his youth, that he had never known her and that now he never would. The secrets Wachiwi kept from him during his troubled youth died with his mother and sentenced him to a rootless life without any family or place to call his own. With the passing years, he understood that she had come looking for something in Rapid City but by the time they returned to the place that had bound them together, her condition deteriorated so quickly that her memories were washed away, drowned under the rising tide of dementia. His mother had come back to South Dakota to find herself but it was too late. She had roamed around the country for too long for her to ever find whatever it was that haunted her tormented mind. In the weeks coming up to her death she called out, almost endlessly, some words he could not understand. He had written those words down as best he could in the hope that they would lead him somewhere, to someone. He remembered them still. *Magaskawee. Chaska.* His mother said those two words with a love and longing that almost hurt him to hear. But *akecheta* – a word she did not say often, was said with a venom and hatred that had not come naturally to the woman he had known. Wachiwi had loathed only herself and, by consequence, her son. He checked maps across South Dakota in the hope that these were places she had known, places perhaps where she had once lived, but found nothing. In time, he could no longer bring himself to visit her. He could no longer bear to watch her suffering, to watch her mind search for something that was always beyond her reach. The day he got the call to say she had died, he cried alone in the last home they had shared together. Their journey together was over. He was alone, alone in a different way to the loneliness he felt trying to care for her during her troubled drinking days, during the days she went missing and abandoned him as a teenager, leaving him to fend for himself with whatever money she had left behind. But she always came back to him. His mother always returned and they would carry on wordlessly as though she had never left. He would never know where his mother went during those brief times she drove away or what she was running away from and he would never have any answers to the questions he had about who his mother had been or where she had come from.

Slowly, the green fields gave way to service stations, pizza joints and small casinos. Farmhouses disappeared and were replaced with fragile-looking houses that were easy pickings for the many storms that swept through the city. Locklear moved his eyes to the other side of the highway to avoid looking at a large, rundown trailer park perched at the side of the highway. He had spent too many years cooped up in that kind of cheap accommodation and couldn't bear to look at them, no matter what city he happened to find himself in. He counted three large pawn joints along the road which told him that the city still had that edge to it, that side of poverty that made poor people desperate to pawn whatever valuables they owned, money that would most likely only put food on the table for a week until they had to repeat the whole process over again.

The cab swung right onto Campbell Street and drove three more blocks until it merged onto East North Street. After one block they turned left onto East Anamose Street, a street he was familiar with and where he had worked for a short time as a rookie cop before eventually getting a transfer to New York and then to Richmond. They followed the long road as it wound its way through a sandy expanse on either side. They took Luna Avenue and then Eglin before taking a sharp right onto Pine, eventually turning sharply left onto Latrobe and into the lot of Motel 6.

Locklear took off his seat belt and surveyed the basic motel which he had handpicked because of its narrow, brightly lit car park which would afford him a view of people coming and going from the lot.

"Sarge?" Mendoza asked.

"Huh?" he replied, looking back at his trooper.

"I asked you back there if this was home?"

"It is. For now."

# Chapter 8

Motel 6 was exactly like dozens of motels Locklear had stayed in during his long police career which took him throughout Virginia on cases Kowalski knew no-one else could solve. He turned the key in the door at the end of a long corridor and took in the room. The large neatly made bed and the small wooden bedside locker took up most of the small space. A tiny dining table and one chair sat just inside the door under a long narrow window which faced out into the parking lot. At the other side of the room an old-fashioned TV stood atop a faded dressing table. A wood-panelled door on the other side of the bed led to the bathroom which was small but functional and painted the same shade of bright orange as the bedroom.

Locklear looked at his watch. It was a little after 10.30 pm. Although the room had cooled from what was probably a hot June day. He turned on the air conditioner but found it was broken. He banged twice on the white metal casing but the machine was dead. He noted the lack of a coffee machine or fridge and looked at his watch.

He jumped into the shower, shaved and knocked on Mendoza's door which was next to his.

His trooper opened the door in her bathrobe. Her hair was loose and she had removed all of the heavy make-up she had worn earlier that day. Locklear reasoned that she looked more beautiful without it.

"You up for starting work?"

Mendoza yawned. "Sure."

After a quick meal and two strong coffees in the diner adjacent to their motel, Locklear and Mendoza made their way on foot to the rundown motel which was listed as Albert Whitefeather's last known address. As they approached the single-storey building, Mendoza smirked at the motel's name. *Heaven Motel.*

"If this is heaven, show me hell," she quipped as she took in the row of three intoxicated men sitting on the pavement outside.

There were no cars parked in the motel driveway which looked like it had become a permanent home to homeless people with addiction problems. One of the men, a Native American around fifty years of age, stood and moved towards Mendoza. His two older companions, one white and one Latino, smiled toothless grins as their friend pushed a coffee cup which contained a few nickels and a one-dollar coin into her face.

"Spare a dollar and save your life," he said with a laugh.

Mendoza ignored him.

Locklear opened the screen door and waited until his trooper was safely inside before glaring at the man.

"Relax," Mendoza said.

"Neither of us are armed, remember?" Locklear replied.

"He looks like a strong breeze would blow him over and I can handle myself, OK?"

The pair stood just inside the small reception area which was furnished with a solid pine desk which ran the length of the room and could only be accessed through a small gate which was obviously locked from the inside. A lone woman was sitting on a red plastic chair behind the tall desk. Locklear could just about see the crown of her grey curled hair from where he stood. The tiny area inexplicably smelt of urine. Mendoza looked into the two visible corners, hoping the presence of a dog or cat would explain the nauseating aroma but she saw neither.

"What a dump," she whispered to Locklear.

Together they approached the desk and leant on its stained ridge but the woman, who could probably barely make out the print she was reading through her thick glasses, did not look up from the glossy magazine she appeared to be lost in. Mendoza coughed.

"Yes?" the woman said, without even glancing at the cop.

"This is Detective Sergeant Locklear and I am Trooper Mendoza. We're here to take a look around Albert Whitefeather's room," Mendoza said confidently.

Locklear squirmed in his shoes. Neither he nor Mendoza had any jurisdiction in South Dakota and even though they had agreed earlier that pretending to be local cops would be their only way to find out about Whitefeather, it did not sit well with him.

"You got ID?" the woman asked as she eyed the two plainclothes cops.

Mendoza pulled out her ID and kept her finger over the Virginia PD seal. She thrust it forward.

The woman squinted at the photo and looked at Mendoza. "What happened to the other cops who were here?" she asked. "Thought they'd finished up everything. And why aren't you in uniform?"

"We're detectives, ma'am," Mendoza replied. "We here to do follow-up. See if there's anything they missed."

The woman nodded. She stood and earmarked the article she was reading. Locklear glanced at the heading which read 'How to Change Your Life in Thirty Days'. He smiled to himself. It wouldn't be hard to change your life in even one day if you ended up working in a dump like the motel he was standing in. Any change at all would surely improve the lot of the woman in front of him. Quitting was the first idea which came to his mind. He wondered briefly how she had ended up working alone at night in what was obviously a dangerous working environment.

"I'm Norma Macken. I do the night shift here."

"How long have you worked here?" Locklear asked.

"Oh, about twenty-five, twenty-six years," she replied. Mendoza's mouth opened in disbelief.

"*Raymond!*" Norma suddenly screamed. "I'll have to wait for my son to man the reception." Dropping her voice to a low whisper, she added: "Can't take your eyes off the desk, believe me."

"You live here as well?" Locklear asked.

"Yes. Room and board and a small wage but, well, it suits us."

The three waited in silence for Raymond to appear. They could hear the muffled sounds of a single male voice behind a door which sat to one side of the reception desk. The words suddenly became clearer as the speaker began to shout – arguing about the quality of the shit and price he wanted for it.

"*Raymond!*" Norma called out again nervously.

The side door opened and a heavily bearded, overweight man of around thirty in an Iron Maiden T-shirt and pizza-stained shorts walked through, phone in hand.

"*I'm doing business. What the fuck are you calling me for?*" he screamed.

Mendoza sniffed the air which had suddenly become filled with the aroma of marijuana. It was a welcome change from the smell of urine which was beginning to make her feel sick.

Locklear looked at the pair and immediately understood their history. He pictured a young Norma, abandoned by whatever cretin she'd had the misfortune to hook up with, roaming around with a young child and a desperate need to put an affordable roof over their heads and food on the table. This job offered her both. For some reason she had stayed. The reason, he figured, was Raymond. The man didn't look like he had turned out so good. Norma, it seemed, would be handing out keys in the stinking lobby and feeding pizza to her lazy, dopehead son until she took her last breath.

Norma blushed and nodded urgently towards the visitors.

"These are cops," she warned. "Detectives come about Albert."

Raymond took a few steps back, as though putting two feet between him and the cops might dampen the smell wafting towards them. Mendoza decided to use the opportunity in front of her to the fullest advantage.

"Listen, we're not interested in whatever you're smoking or how much of it you happen to have stashed in your room. We want to see Whitefeather's room, take a look through his stuff. Let us do that and we'll be out of your hair. We won't see any need to tell whoever owns this joint that you're running a little sideline from the property. Will we, Detective Sergeant Locklear?"

Locklear shook his head but did not speak.

Mother and son exchanged looks.

Norma nodded. "Thank you. But Albert's room has been cleaned out. His stuff is here though, in lock-up. No-one came for it. The other cops didn't seem interested in it. I didn't have the heart to throw it out, Albert having fought for our country and all."

Locklear and Mendoza followed the woman through a series of doors behind the reception area while Raymond remained behind on guard. They waited while Norma pulled a large bunch of keys from a chain around her neck and unlocked a cage in a back room.

"I keep these on me all the time. Even sleep with them. Can't trust anyone these days," she said, looking at Locklear as though she knew the man understood her, understood her life, her struggles and above all, her disappointments. A single tear welled up in her eyes. She took off her thick bifocals and wiped them roughly with her sleeve.

"Raymond is a good boy," she said, still looking at Locklear.

"I'm sure he is," Mendoza offered.

Locklear looked away and focused his eyes on the cage which held only a bicycle with two flat tyres, two oil paintings and three cardboard boxes on top of a broken bureau.

"That's all there is," she said as she lifted one of the paintings and admired the rural scenery. "He liked to paint. He was getting real good at it. Rest of the stuff is in those three boxes. Hard to think that's what a life comes down to, isn't it?"

Mendoza opened one of the boxes and began leafing through its contents. "How come no-one has claimed it? Doesn't Whitefeather have any family?"

"He has a younger sister, Cindy. Geddis is her married name. She's a teacher at the school on Columbus. He talked about her a lot."

"How well did you know him?" Locklear asked, breaking his silence which he could see had begun to make Norma nervous. He understood the woman and sensed that she preferred people who talked a lot. It filled the air and probably made her feel less lonely.

"Fairly well. Albert was a nice man. He'd come into the reception at night to talk to me. Sometimes he'd bring me a coffee from the diner even though he could hardly afford to feed himself. Albert was a sweet guy. I miss him."

"How long had he lived here?" Mendoza asked.

"Oh, about five, maybe six years."

"He wasn't married? Kids?"

Norma shook her head.

Mendoza lifted an envelope from the box and read it.

"Why does it say Albert Mills?" she asked.

Locklear took the envelope from Mendoza and read the name and address.

"That's from the army pension people. I phoned them

and told them Albert was dead. Most of them Indians got a regular name and an Indian name which can change a few times during their lives during naming ceremonies.

Mendoza looked at her boss. "Did you know that?" she asked.

Locklear shook his head.

"Was Albert from this town?" he asked.

"Yes. He was born here. I don't know exactly where. Far as I know both parents are passed on now."

"Did he ever have any visitors? His sister, did she ever come here?" Mendoza asked.

"Albert lived with Cindy and her family for a couple of years when he got back from Iraq but it didn't work out. He told me that until the war he had a normal life. He had a good job working for some antique place that restored furniture, paintings, that sort of thing. Had a good future ahead of him. After 9/11, he enlisted because he was a proud American. He wanted to defend his country, least that's what he thought until he got to Iraq and saw what was really going on."

"What was going on?" Mendoza asked.

Norma moved the second box and pulled Albert's dog-tags from it.

"Well, I'll never know if some of it was in his head. He had a drink problem and he took a lot of painkillers. He was wounded in Iraq. Shot. Had two, maybe three operations but he didn't get any better. He was in a lot of pain. Army sent him to lots of doctors but they didn't help. He made complaints about what had gone on during the war. He wrote to Washington and to newspapers, he did everything he could to make the situation public but no-one would listen to him. When the army suggested a psychiatric evaluation, Albert willingly went to prove them wrong. He thought it would help his case. He went two or three times, told the psychiatrist what he'd experienced over there, what he saw. But the shrink said he was mentally ill, diagnosed him with paranoid-schizophrenia. After that, Albert broke off all ties with the army. He just kept going to the free clinic downtown for prescriptions for painkillers and he kept drinking. After a while his sister couldn't have him at her house anymore. She's got three little girls and she didn't want them seeing that. Albert moved in here then. About four or five years ago, he started to come good. He got involved in AA, stopped drinking. He didn't stop the pills though. I'd see him walk through the lot here sometimes and he'd look as though he was in so much pain that he could hardly move. He'd go back to his room, take a bunch of pills. Wouldn't see him until the next day. Guess he couldn't get through the night without them. He joined a Native American group and he got real interested in his heritage. He'd stop here sometimes at night on his way back from a meeting and tell me all about the Lakota history and how he was a proud Sioux. He changed his name to Albert Whitefeather which had been his family's original name. He said the naming ceremony was a real proud day for him."

Mendoza glanced at her boss and noticed how engrossed he was in Albert's story. The two men had a lot in common. A Native American heritage both had grown up knowing nothing about. They had both served in the army, had a history of alcoholism and lived solitary, lonely lives. She lifted a photo of a young Native American woman, a white man and a tall, handsome Native man with three small girls.

"Is that Albert?" she asked, pointing at the Native American man.

Norma nodded. "That was before he got that awful tattoo on his face."

Mendoza replaced the photo neatly on top of something flat inside the box. She glanced down and saw it was a small laptop. She lifted it out.

"Can we take this? For evidence?" she asked.

Norma blushed. "It was missing from his room when the cops searched it. I noticed it as soon as I let them in because it was always on the table in his room. He'd sit in the library most days looking things up. He had a real interest in history. I knew straight away that Raymond took it so I couldn't say anything. You won't tell, will you? He didn't mean anything by it. He just loves computers, that's all. I took it off him but by then the cops had finished up here so I just boxed it up with the rest of his stuff. I phoned his sister and left a message at her work to say come and get Albert's stuff but she never came."

Mendoza put the laptop down and began rifling through the dead man's things to check for anything else that might be useful.

"Do you know the name of the group he joined or how we'd make contact with them?" Locklear asked.

"No. Sorry. Is it important?"

"Maybe."

"I think you'd be best speaking to his sister. Albert did say once that she was dead set against him becoming involved with them so I'm sure she knows where you'd find them. I don't know why she didn't want him joining though. He seemed so happy. Like he finally had a purpose, that he belonged somewhere."

"You know Albert died in Richmond – do you know why he went there or even how he afforded to fly there?" Locklear asked.

Norma shrugged.

"I'm sorry, no. He definitely wouldn't have had money for flights or anything like that, but he did go away a lot. Sometimes he'd be missing for a few days. I never asked him about where he was when he'd get back. I figured it was to do with the group he'd joined. Last few days though before he went missing for good, he wasn't himself. He was keeping to himself more. He seemed nervous. I told him someone had come here one night looking for him while he was away. The man tried to talk Raymond into letting him into Albert's room. Ray refused and the man threatened him. When I described the man to Albert, he was shaking. I never seen him so upset."

"What did the man look like?"

"Raymond said he looked like a 'weird ghost dude'." Norma smiled sadly. "My son has a way with words."

"So, very pale-skinned, blond?"

"Guess so. Ray said he was really tall too."

"The man Carter saw at the dig site," Mendoza said quietly to Locklear.

He nodded and turned back to the woman.

"You didn't tell us what Albert thought was going on in Iraq," he said.

Norma placed Albert's army dog-tags back in the cardboard box and closed it.

"Albert said that some senior members of his unit were

stealing Iraqi stuff and bringing them back to the US on army aircraft to sell illegally here."

"Stuff?" Locklear asked.

"You know, museum stuff – valuable things. He said when he found out about it, his corporal sent him on what Albert called a 'routine walk-through' and he was shot."

"And he thought that was somehow the army's fault?" Locklear asked incredulously.

"Yes," Norma added simply. "He was shot in the back."

Locklear waited for more.

"So?" Mendoza asked.

"By an American bullet."

Locklear endured a sleepless night in his strange bed which he already knew would only be home for a short time. The local newspaper he had pored over before he tried to sleep did not tire his busy mind as reading normally would. Articles recounting the hopeless situation many Native Americans found themselves in when they arrived in Rapid City scratched at his mind and hindered his attempts to sleep. The fruitless search for work and the cycle of poverty and homelessness haunted him as he tossed and turned in the uncomfortable, unfamiliar bed. The newspaper's historical section only served to heighten his agitation until, with little chance of rest, he got up and stared out the long narrow window at traffic passing by the quiet motel.

He thought about the investigation which he hoped would soon take them out of the city of his birth. He had not thought about how he might feel or if indeed he'd feel anything on his return to Rapid City, but he had not anticipated the unease he had felt during the short cab ride through the streets of the city. He had not thought about the anxiety that would rise up through him as he walked with Mendoza through some of the familiar streets, streets he had followed his confused mother around as she searched for something he could not see and she could not name.

He went back to bed and tried to sleep again.

At dawn, he got up, stretched out his sore back, dressed and went to Mendoza's door. He heard some movement inside so he knocked lightly.

The door opened immediately to a smiling Mendoza, again in her bathrobe.

"Come on in."

Locklear stepped inside.

On her bed sat Whitefeather's old laptop.

Locklear looked at its blank screen. "Find anything?"

"No. Tried three times to get into it but couldn't guess his password. It's locked now. Only hope is O'Brien might be able to figure it out, but I doubt he could do it remotely."

"Can't see O'Brien helping us, Mendoza. He doesn't seem the helpful type."

Mendoza grinned. "Hang on, sarge. I've got something to tell you. I guess he cottoned on to the fact that I was up to something when I asked him to rush things through for me and he was listening in when Benson very publicly put me on desk duty. He's a good deal more on our side than you think. As I was leaving to follow you out of the building, he called me and handed me a stick key and said, 'Here's the files you wanted'. I thought he'd forgotten that he'd already given me what little there was on Holton's laptop on a key earlier. I thought nothing of it. You know as well as I do how weird he can be, so I just took the stick and put it into my pocket.

I remembered it last night and decided I'd better put the info onto my own laptop. It wasn't another copy of the emails from Whitefeather to Holton. There was only one file on it named '*I never gave this to you*'."

"What was in it?"

Mendoza placed her laptop on the small dining table inside the door and opened the file.

Locklear took the lone seat at the table. Mendoza stood behind him.

"Holton's bank statements?" he said as he scanned the page in front of him.

"O'Brien obviously downloaded them from Holton's laptop. Until a few months ago, nothing was amiss. There were a few international transfers from the UK – most likely from his mother. No large amounts. Usually around $2000-$3000 each time."

"And then?"

"Then everything changes. The UK transfers keep coming but there are more of them and the amount being sent keeps increasing, up to $20,000 one time. Within a couple of days in each case, the money is gone from Holton's account."

"Do we know where it went?"

"No – cash withdrawal each time."

"That explains the cash in Holton's closet." He swung around to look at her. "Why do you think O'Brien is helping us, Mendoza? If he's found out, he'll probably lose his job."

"You're suspicious of him?"

"I'm suspicious of almost everyone. I need to know why he's doing this."

Mendoza looked down at her clasped hands and reflected on her boss's words.

"I guess Kowalski, me and probably Carter are the only three people in the world that you trust."

Locklear made no reply.

"Sarge, you've only known me and Carter a couple of years though I suppose you've known Kowalski best part of your life but what happened to everyone else? There must have been other people in your life? People you trusted, loved?"

Locklear coughed nervously as he did each time anyone got too personal with him. He looked into Mendoza's eyes and saw only sincerity in the huge brown pools.

"I guess everyone else let me down. Or I let them down. Either way, it doesn't matter anymore, Mendoza. Now, can we get on with the job?"

Mendoza sighed. "Well, maybe O'Brien is helping because the missing artefacts are Native American? He's part Native so I guess it bothered him."

Locklear thought about this for a moment and wondered if the Native American aspect to the case bothered him. He decided it didn't. A case was a case. Someone was doing something wrong and it didn't matter to him who they were or to whom they were doing it. He would find them and bring them to justice.

"OK. We need to keep in contact with O'Brien. We're on the outside now. He's the only one who can get information for us."

"There's more, sarge." Mendoza leaned over Locklear's shoulder to open another document on the laptop. He pulled back a little from the contact. "Look – O'Brien also included more information on Whitefeather's death than I'd been able to grab before Benson called me into his office."

Locklear scanned the document which was lengthy and detailed. "Sum it up, Mendoza."

She went and sat on the bed and he turned around to face her.

"Seems the cops haven't ruled out suicide because Albert supposedly had mental-health problems. There was a witness at the scene, a Ms Mai Nguyen who was driving home from working late when she saw a man on the US1 Bridge, fighting with Whitefeather. They struggled and Nguyen said as she passed she saw the man lift Whitefeather up and throw him off the bridge."

"Throw him? The rail on that bridge must be five feet tall, maybe higher. How big was Albert?"

"Autopsy report says he was 5ft 10, weighed about 160 pounds."

"Took a big man to do that. Any description?"

Mendoza grinned. "Nguyen told cops who arrived at the scene that the man was very tall and that he was wearing a long dark coat with a hood. She said when she drove past him the man looked into her car but then took off. It was dusk but Nguyen said she could still see enough to say he was definitely white. She said he was extraordinarily pale and that he looked ..."

"Like a ghost," Locklear said, finishing her sentence.

"Right. And there's more. When cops came to Nguyen's workplace to interview her the next day she suddenly couldn't remember having given that description. She said she couldn't remember what he looked like. She also said that it was possible that the man was trying to stop Whitefeather from jumping off the bridge. Two cops interviewed her and put on the sheet that the witness was shaking."

"So you think someone got to her?"

"Yes. Someone you've already met. Nguyen works at the University of Richmond. She's the Dean's private secretary. Gerard Sartre sat beside her throughout the interview, holding her hand."

"Was it our friends Diaz and Hill who interviewed her?"" Locklear asked.

Mendoza nodded.

"OK. I'd better give O'Brien a call," Locklear said.

"No, he doesn't like you. I'll do it."

"Not that I care, Mendoza, but *why* exactly does O'Brien not like me?"

Mendoza laughed, picking up a hairbrush and pulling it through her unruly hair. "Maybe because of the way you speak to him?"

"I speak to everyone that way."

"Doesn't mean it doesn't piss him off, sarge. I think you and O'Brien are more alike than you think. One-worded answers to open-ended questions. The things that annoy you about him are exactly the reasons I think he doesn't like you. Two peas in a pod."

Locklear frowned and stood.

"Well, sarge, what's next?"

"We're going to pay a visit to Whitefeather's sister, Cindy. See if she knows any ghosts."

# Chapter 9

The car Locklear and Mendoza hired was inconspicuous enough to blend into the neighbourhood where Cindy Geddis worked as a pre-school teacher on the other side of Rapid City. The eight-year-old tan-coloured Chevrolet Impala looked like the local car of choice and Locklear noticed several similar albeit slightly older models pass as they made their way to their destination. They drove in silence along Joseph Street past a long line of cheap houses, thrift food stores and so many small Indian casinos that Locklear lost count. Small churches stood side by side with gambling houses, liquor stores and homeless shelters. They pulled into a gas station beside the *Save a Lot* store and watched two intoxicated men fight on the pavement. Locklear, unable to watch the men fight over a cheap bottle of wine, fixed his eyes to the ground as he put the gas-tank cap on.

"You OK?" Mendoza asked as she returned from the store with two fresh coffees.

"Yeah."

Locklear drove back onto Joseph Street and followed

straight for three miles until he reached the turn for East Patrick Street. He took a right over the railway line and drove past a huge billboard advertising Mount Rushmore with the slogan *Do Big Things*.

"Oh, if we have time, I've got to see that. Might never be back this way again," Mendoza said.

Locklear snorted.

"What?"

"You want to go to see the place white people carved their faces into a granite mountain to show their dominance over the aboriginal population who held those hills sacred?"

Mendoza thought for a moment. "I guess not. Jeez, sarge, I had no idea you felt that way ... that you ... well ... cared."

Locklear tightened his grip on the wheel as he passed almost identical stores to those on Joseph Street except Patrick Street had even more casinos and fewer churches than those he had counted on Joseph.

"I don't," he said. "It's just ... wrong."

"Take the next left," Mendoza said as she turned off the route planner on her phone.

Locklear pulled into the huge parking lot which was thronged with cars as parents dropped their children off to the large, two-storey school.

"There must be a hundred kids here and even more parents," Mendoza said. "How are we going to find her in this crowd? We can't go inside and ask, can we?"

"No. Best we can hope for is to get her attention in the parking lot. See if she'll talk to us."

They sat in silence as they looked out for the Native American woman they'd seen in the photo in Whitefeather's sad cardboard box. Three Native American women passed right by the car but were older and looked like they were dropping their grandchildren off for the day. One woman matching Cindy Geddis's age and appearance could be seen parking a blue Toyota on the far side of the lot but when she got out of the car she ushered two boys and not three girls inside. When the children were safely inside, she drove off at speed, obviously late for whatever job awaited her.

It took another eleven minutes for the crowd to fade until only four adults remained in the parking lot. Three women and one man. Two of the women were white and were attempting to herd the remaining smaller children into a line-up in front of the main door. The man had his back to Locklear's car and was carrying a little girl. In front of him and obscured from view was a woman who was much smaller than him. The only view Locklear could get of her was the faint outline of a green skirt blowing in the early-morning breeze. From the distant view Locklear had, the man appeared to be white but the child in his arms whose face was partially obscured by the man's shoulder, looked Native. Locklear waited a while longer but the pair seemed to be lost in conversation.

"*Move*," Locklear said aloud as he waited for the man to step aside and give him a view of the woman.

Another moment passed and a shrill bell rang out across the lot. The man leant forward and kissed the woman. He stepped back, giving Locklear a good enough view to confirm that the woman was Whitefeather's sister. The man handed the child to her and got into his car. As he drove away, Cindy Geddis was still standing in the lot, smiling and waving with the child in her arms.

103

"I think I should talk to her on my own, sarge."

"Why?"

"I just have a feeling she'll be more comfortable talking to me."

Locklear shrugged and leaned his sore back into the seat.

"OK."

Mendoza opened the door and moved swiftly across the lot. She took out her badge and was flashing it before Locklear had a chance to remind her to take a gentle approach. He watched as the smile faded from Geddis's face. Whitefeather's sister stared at the badge and then glared at its owner. Mendoza started to deliver whatever speech she had rehearsed and Locklear wished he was close enough to hear but already knew the interview was not going to go well. He watched as the woman asked one of the two remaining teachers to take her child into the school. Once alone, Geddis placed her hands firmly on her hips and glowered at Mendoza.

Mendoza apparently kept to her script, no doubt trying to explain why she was there and how the murder of Alec Holton in Richmond more than seventeen hundred miles away had led to her brother and subsequently to her. He watched as the woman spoke. Geddis's anger was obvious as she waved her arms about. Mendoza, unperturbed, persisted. She interrupted Geddis and continued to talk. Geddis seemed to soften but only a little. She spoke some more and Locklear wondered at what point Mendoza would feel it was OK for him to join in. He waited for her signal and continued to watch as Mendoza moved a little toward the woman and put her hand on her shoulder. The woman began to weep. Mendoza comforted her and kept talking. Geddis softened some more and start talking again. She seemed to be giving Mendoza information that might be useful, judging by the fact that Mendoza took a notebook out of the back pocket of her mannish trousers and wrote some notes as she nodded sympathetically. He waited some more but the two women seemed to have a lot to discuss so he tapped on the dashboard but did not take his eyes off the pair.

When Mendoza finally turned in his direction, he watched as she pointed towards the car and, obviously, to him. Geddis raised her hand to her eyes to block out the sun and get a good look at the man Mendoza had obviously introduced as her sergeant. Locklear got out of the car but, as he stepped forward to join them, something in the woman's face made him freeze. Cindy Geddis's mouth turned into an O. Her eyes opened wide and she turned her head from side to side so slightly that Locklear might have missed it had he not been so fixated on her expression. Cindy Geddis was scared. Scared of him. Geddis turned her face to Mendoza and said something. A short sentence. No more than three or four words. Then she disappeared into the building.

Mendoza turned again and stared at Locklear with an expression of confusion on her face. She looked down at her notebook, flipped its cover over and shoved it roughly into the back pocket of her pants. She walked to the car and got into the passenger seat.

Locklear climbed back in. "What the hell happened?" he barked.

Mendoza looked at her boss and tried to formulate her sentence.

105

"Well?" Locklear growled. Geddis was their only lead. Without her, they might as well pack up and fly back to Richmond and accept that Carter was going to prison for a very long time. "Mendoza, speak, what did she say, just there, just before she took off? The rest you can tell me later."

"She said '*It's not possible*'."

"What did she mean? W*hat's* not possible?"

"You, sarge. What she meant was *you're* not possible. Earlier you said let's go and see if Cindy Geddis knows any ghosts? Well, looks like it's you, sarge. You're the ghost."

Locklear and Mendoza sat in the diner across from their motel and ordered a late breakfast. Locklear moved his pancakes around the plate, trying to make sense of Geddis's reaction towards him. He came up with nothing and waited for Mendoza to finish her huge bacon sandwich. He gulped down the last of his strong bitter coffee and waited.

"So, you have absolutely no idea why Cindy looked at you that way?" Mendoza asked through a mouthful of bread and bacon.

"None."

"Looked to me like she recognised you."

Locklear snorted. "How could she? She would have been a small child when I last lived in this town, if she was even born at all. And I think we can take it I've changed a bit in the last thirty-plus years?"

"I guess, sarge," Mendoza said with a smile.

Locklear ordered more coffee and listened as Mendoza recounted Cindy Geddis's story of Albert Whitefeather's descent into an obsession that was to cost him his life. He

106

learnt that Albert and Cindy's parents had come from the Pine Ridge reservation to settle in Rapid City in the hope of a more prosperous life. Cindy said that her parents had not been political and had wanted only two things for their children – education and stability which the Native American couple found in the then bustling town of Rapid City. Both worked hard to buy their own home: Albert Mills Senior had been employed as a wood-turner and his wife, Catherine, worked as a cook in a local diner. Neither of Whitefeather's parents had experienced a Native American upbringing, being forcibly taken from their parents to be educated in Christian-run boarding schools in much the same way as their parents had been before them. Mills Senior did not drink alcohol as he had seen the destruction it had visited on his community and the young couple wanted to distance themselves from their past and, by default, from their community. When the pair married they left Pine Ridge for good, visiting only on occasional holidays or to attend the funerals of relatives. Both of their children were born in Rapid City and Cindy said she had received a conventional upbringing in which their Native American heritage was rarely discussed. Both she and her brother were raised as Catholics and attended local state schools. When their parents died, Albert was already working in Sioux City and Cindy had married. Albert, she said, returned from Iraq a broken and damaged man, both physically and emotionally. She believed his story of stolen Iraqi artefacts and also believed that when he reported this a member of his own unit shot him.

Locklear, immersed in the story, had a question. "If that's true, why didn't they finish him off? Why let him live to tell the tale?"

"Cindy said when Albert was shot, he remembered lying on the ground, face down. He heard feet approaching him and prepared himself for death. Next thing he heard shouting. Then two of his buddies were pulling him by the arms towards safety. He heard his commander shouting for them to desist and leave the private where he lay. They ignored him and dragged Whitefeather to safety. He was taken to their makeshift hospital and I guess, once he was there, there were too many people around him. Army couldn't risk killing him then. The bullet was removed from his spine and he was flown back to the US as soon as he was strong enough."

"Did you happen to get the names of his buddies?"

"Sure did. Private Patrick Lewis and Private Sandra Torres. Both now civilians. Lewis runs a bait-and-tackle store in Sioux City. As far as Cindy knows, Torres moves around a lot but she's also originally from Sioux City. Lewis might know where we can find her."

"What else?"

"When Albert returned to the US he needed two more surgeries on his back. Neither were successful and he became dependant on painkillers. He couldn't get back to his old job which he had loved. With nothing else to do all day, he began writing to Washington about the stolen artefacts. His letters were ignored. Then he started writing to newspapers. He got some exposure but mostly local rags looking for seedy stories. Army began to put the squeeze on him. Cindy said twice they stopped paying his disability pension, only reinstating it when a shrink said Albert was mentally ill. She reckons that's what they wanted. If they couldn't kill him, they had to discredit him. Make people think he was crazy. Albert started to drink and his behaviour resulted in tensions in Cindy's marriage. Her husband wanted him out. She kept trying to keep the peace. She said he became obsessed with stolen artefacts from around the world, spent all day on his computer. By the way, I have his password. Thankfully I got it off her before she locked onto your scary face! He began joining anti-war protests. Actually, he joined any protest group he could find. But, and this is key, the only Native American group he joined was the Pine Ridge Native American rights group and they're legit, sarge. I told Cindy that the motel manager said Cindy hadn't wanted Albert joining these groups but she said she had no problem with Albert joining PRNA. It's a small group which is part of a chain of sister-groups all over America and Albert mostly attended meetings in Rapid City. Their aim is to gain equal rights for Native Americans. They lobby the government to honour treaties by returning land and Native American artefacts to their respective tribes. But she went on to tell me that, after joining the group, Albert became acquainted with more radicalised Native Americans although she never knew who they were or anything really about them. Two things happened to send Cindy over the edge. Firstly, Albert was arrested for throwing a stone through the Dean's window in the University of South Dakota."

"Was that Rosenberg? I think Lee mentioned him."

"She didn't say."

"And the second thing?"

"A man came to Cindy's door twice looking for Albert. The first time Cindy's eldest daughter was home alone. Cindy had only been gone for ten minutes to drop her two younger daughters to a dance lesson, so she was scared that the man was actually staking out the house. Second time he came back the man scared her. It was the final straw. She had to ask Albert to go. Said it broke her heart."

"What did he look like?"

"I planned on asking her for a description after I told her that there had been a witness to her brother's murder. I had hoped to make the point that now that the witness wouldn't talk, our investigation into who killed Holton and possibly her brother had stalled. I pointed over to you and, when she saw you, she took off."

Locklear finished his coffee and stood painfully.

"Let's check out and head to Sioux City. It's a long drive. About 400 miles."

Mendoza stood and lifted a doughnut from a plate on their table. She shoved half of it in her mouth and rubbed the cinnamon from her fingers onto her pants.

Locklear grimaced. "How ladylike!"

"How sexist!" she retorted.

They walked across the road to their motel. Inside Raymond was working the day shift and was waiting to deliver something Locklear had ordered from him.

The drug-dealer was wearing the same pizza-stained shorts and torn T-shirt. Norma was nowhere to be seen.

"First time I ever sold burners to a cop," he said with a grin.

Locklear lifted the two cell phones and switched them on.

"They're both working?"

"Yes, and definitely untraceable."

Locklear placed a fold of money onto the counter. He threw one of the phones to Mendoza.

"Here, disable your GPS, turn your cell off and take the battery out. Then, give the number on that cell case to your mom. Make sure she knows not to share it with anyone else."

He turned to walk away but then turned back quickly and suddenly grabbed Raymond by the neck and pushed him into the wall.

"Jesus, man, take them ... for free!"

"I pay my own way in this world, Raymond. What I want from you is your word to stop disrespecting your mother. What I mean by that is no yelling, no leaving your mother to do work that she shouldn't be doing alone while you peddle drugs in the only home she could manage to give you. And no living off her. You pay your way. You make her life as easy as you can. I've asked some cop friends to check in here. Plainclothes cops. I may even be back this way and I'll check in on her myself and you don't want to disappoint me. So, you be nice."

Locklear loosened his grip from the startled man and backed away.

Mendoza smirked.

Back in his room, Locklear phoned Carter's father. He said his name, told Seth Carter to get the number to his son and hung up.

When the two arrived back at reception with their keys, Raymond was scrubbing urine from the floor tiles with a brush.

Locklear threw his luggage into the trunk and grappled with Mendoza's case to lift it in too.

"I got it, sarge," she said.

They got into the car.

"That was nice, what you did for Norma there," Mendoza said. "You're a good man, Locklear – but don't worry – I won't tell anyone at the station. Your dirty little secret is safe with me."

Locklear turned on the ignition and signalled out of the lot.

"Thought you were crap at technology? How'd you know so much about burner phones?"

"I learn what I have to, Mendoza."

"Why can't we fly?"

Locklear looked at his watch. It was only a little after 11am.

"Next flight to Sioux City is probably not until tomorrow morning. That's a day wasted when we could have already been where we want to go. Time is running out for Lee, Mendoza. I can feel it."

# Chapter 10

Mendoza remained silent until Locklear drove out of Rapid City and swung right onto Highway 14 heading eastwards. She could feel her boss visibly relax as he nestled into the driver's seat and stared silently at the grey expanse of road ahead of him. Soon the road became empty save for a few truckers heading east or pulling into large diners scattered along the isolated roadway. They passed a road sign which said 'Sioux City 340 miles'. The silence in the car was beginning to grate on the young cop's nerves.

"Jeez, sarge. We better think of something to talk about or at least put the radio on."

"I can't think if the radio is on," Locklear snapped back.

Mendoza sighed and looked out of the window as they passed the turn-off for Box Elder and wondered what kind of place the small town was. She tapped her long nails onto the dash and tried to occupy her mind by reading the dozens of billboards that littered the highway. She knew better than to ask her boss if it had been hard for him being back in the town where he had been born and where she knew his mother had died, although the details of the woman's death and what passed between mother and son in those last few months remained unknown to her. Locklear's past was a closed book and the only information she learnt about him and what he had been through was gleaned from how he interacted with the world, how he hated bullies like Raymond and how protective he was of her. All she knew about her boss's mother was her first name: Wachiwi. She could easily imagine how he had been with his mother when she was alive, that he had been a good son. She wondered if Wachiwi had been a good mother to him in return but something told her that this had not been the case.

"Did your mother have an Indian name as well as the name Locklear? You know, like Albert did?"

"Huh?"

"I know her first name was Wachiwi and that's native, right? But Locklear, that doesn't sound native, does it? I wonder if she also had an Indian last name?"

"Mendoza!" Locklear warned.

"OK, OK!" she replied, putting her hands up in mock surrender. "I just wondered."

The emptiness of the road did not alter with the exception of large trailer parks dotted along the highway.

"Can I ask one more question, sarge?"

Locklear shook his head but his subordinate persevered.

"Was Locklear your father's name?"

Locklear waited a while before answering. Mendoza watched him as his mouth moved silently, obviously formulating an answer that he was comfortable with. He came up with nothing.

"I don't know. I never found a birth cert or a marriage cert for my mother. Things were different then. Records weren't kept like they are now, especially in her ... community."

"One more question?"

"You said *that* was your last one, Mendoza."

"I know but ... do you think your father ... well, do you think he was white?"

"What do *you* think?" Locklear barked.

Mendoza tensed at the tone of Locklear's voice. She had obviously hit a nerve. She looked at her boss and took in his deep brown eyes, his thick, black straight hair which always looked like it needed to be cut and his light-brown skin which was no darker than the skin of any white man who spent time in the summer sunshine.

"I think he was white," she whispered.

Locklear made no response.

"Would it bother you if he was?"

Silence.

Mendoza knew that would be all she'd get out of him and that pushing any further could possibly anger her boss.

They passed the turn-off for 173$^{rd}$ Avenue which amused Mendoza. "Not sure why they name these 'turn-offs'. There's damn all here to turn off for."

"Do you have to use bad language, Mendoza?"

"You say *damn* all the time."

"Well, that's different."

"Why? Because I'm a woman? Didn't your mother ever cuss?"

"No. She didn't."

The terrain changed a little, revealing small hills on either side of the motorway and the incline of bigger hills

115

in the distance. The land looked drier and the heat rose up from the asphalt in silvery waves.

"Can we stop for some water?"

Locklear nodded. "There's a small place called Wasta a few miles up. I'll pull in there."

"You travel this road a lot, sarge?"

"Few times," he replied.

He signalled and turned off the road, pulling roughly up in front of a convenience store in the tiny dot that was Wasta.

Mendoza bought a coffee and some water while Locklear filled the car with gas. She wandered around and looked out into the rising heat.

"I could never live anywhere like this, sarge. It'd kill me. I mean, what do people *do* all day?"

Locklear scanned the small outpost which consisted of a service station, gift store and a small convenience store. A tiny post office which looked like an afterthought was in an old house at the end of the row. To Locklear, the place looked like peace.

They drove back onto the road and crossed the Cheyenne River. A sign told Mendoza that Sioux City was now only 303 miles away and a town called Badlands 11 miles. They passed the town of Wall which was slightly larger but no less unimpressive than Wasta was.

Badlands was nothing more than a trading post and a camping area which no-one appeared to be using.

"Why is it called Badlands?" Mendoza asked

"It was translated from the Lakota language meaning the land was poor. It's dry here. There's little water, hence the name."

"Did your mother teach you that?"

"No."

"Then how do you know it?"

"I told you before, I was a cop in Rapid City for a while. Sometimes we'd be handling a case that originated in the city but trailed back to one of the reservations. We'd have to come out and speak to the tribal cops. I got to know some of them well."

"Did they ever ask about you being part native?"

"Does every Hispanic person you meet ask you about being Mexican?"

"Well no, but this is different."

"How?"

"It just is. I mean, you might have found out something about your mother."

Locklear made no reply.

"Didn't *you* ever bring it up?"

"No. Look, my mother could have been from anywhere. Look at this land. There are dozens of reservations here, if she was even from SD. I don't know. It's a big country."

"So the tribal cops, they didn't notice?"

"Mendoza, will you goddamn well drop it?"

Mendoza got the message and sulked for a moment in the passenger seat until she spotted the turn-off for a town called Kadoka.

"I'm starving," she said.

"Mendoza, seriously, how are you so skinny? We just ate breakfast."

"Two hours ago," she pleaded.

Locklear signalled and took the off-ramp.

They settled into a red faux-leather seat in the nearest

diner and ate wordlessly. Mendoza paid despite Locklear's protests at the cashier's desk.

"You don't always have to pay, you know," she said as they settled back into the car to drive the last leg of the journey.

Mendoza tensed up and held onto the roof as they drove over the huge, clear water of the Missouri River.

"What's the matter?" Locklear asked.

"Nothing. I can't swim so I always get nervous driving over water."

As they passed Chamberlain airport followed by Kimball municipal airport, Mendoza turned to Locklear.

"That's three airports in all that I've seen on this journey. I'm sure we could have flown here."

"I don't want to use our cards any more than we have to. We'll use cash as much as possible from here on. We don't know who's involved in this case or how big it is. Someone might be keeping an eye on our travel plans. The road is safer and it's easier to get away fast if we need to."

"You're really expecting trouble on this one, aren't you?"

Locklear did not answer.

Mendoza fell quiet as they travelled silently through the towns of Pierre, Huron and Iroquois. The names were so exotic to her yet she could see the poverty in the towns, the deprivation. She glanced at Locklear several times but he was looking straight ahead.

They drove by the town of De Smet. She grinned at the billboard advertising tours of the homeplace of Laura Ingalls Wilder.

"Guess you don't want to stop and take in a tour of our

country's history of white settlement?" she said with a laugh.

"Doubt it," Locklear replied and smiled.

It was the first time she had seen her boss smile all day.

"You know, one of my aunts was convinced that our family had very little Spanish blood and that, apart from one or two more recent intermarriages, we were Aztecs and part of the indigenous people known as Tlaxcaltecs. A few years back she did a DNA test. When the results came back she discovered that we were 91% Spanish with very little actual native blood. I remember that she was upset for weeks."

Mendoza laughed. Locklear didn't.

"Your point?" he asked.

"Well, I guess my point is that my ancestors were colonialists. God knows what shit they did when they arrived in South America. My point is that it was so long ago, really, so does it matter now? Doesn't change who we are now, does it?"

Locklear looked out at the rundown clapboards and empty streets of Iroquois. Outside of the wooden convenience store, two Native men stood on the porch, side by side, passing the time by looking at the farmland across the road that their ancestors had probably once owned.

"It only wouldn't matter if we were all equal now, Mendoza."

Together they drove on through Arlington and came to the end of the E14 in the town of Brookings where they took a right onto 29, crossing the Big Sioux River. When they finally arrived at the outskirts of Sioux City, Mendoza looked at the clock on the dash which read 5.45pm.

"Took longer than you thought," she said.

"I didn't factor in stopping for lunch. Or coffee."

"Jeez, sorry for being human and needing food. Speaking of which ..."

"I want to catch Lewis before he closes up his store for the day. Then, we can eat."

"Couple of beers wouldn't go astray."

"Do what you want then, Mendoza. I'll just eat."

Locklear drove more slowly as he searched for the exit for 77. They exited and then drove on to Western Parkway. He crossed Hamilton Boulevard and turned onto Myrtle Street which was a long winding road full of retail outlets and small speciality stores.

The fishing store was located at the very end of the street beside a closed cell-phone store. Locklear parked on the opposite side of the road and watched a tall, lean black man in his mid-thirties carry fishing supplies into the store as he prepared to close for the day.

Ex-Private Patrick Lewis walked with a slight limp and still wore an army buzz cut. His body looked toned and fit under his expensive Stone Island T-shirt and Cavelli jeans. Lewis looked like a man who looked after himself but there was something about his movements that told Locklear the man had not been born into money and that he wore his wealth with the disdain of someone from humble beginnings. Locklear scanned the parking lot which was empty except for a red Ford F-150 Lariat which was parked right outside Lewis's store.

"Well, shall we do this one together?" Locklear asked.

Mendoza looked Lewis up and down and tried to form her opinion of what kind of interviewee he would be. She decided that interviewing Lewis warranted a team approach.

"Together," she replied.

Locklear got out of the car and waited for Mendoza to join him. He knew by the look on Lewis's face that he knew they weren't looking for fish bait.

Lewis glanced nervously around him, lifted the last of the equipment from the pavement and walked inside.

He stood to one side to let them in and pulled the metal shutter down.

"Looks like you were expecting us. Did Cindy Geddis phone you?"

Lewis nodded.

"So, you know we're looking into her brother's murder?"

"I saw it in the newspaper. I heard it was suicide."

"Is that what you believe?" Mendoza asked.

Lewis looked around his store and set his eyes on the rows of fishing rods lined up against the wall of his small business.

"Doesn't matter what I think. It's what I know that matters and what I know is that you have no jurisdiction here."

"Albert was your friend. Thought you might like to help put his killer behind bars."

Lewis glared at the cop and pulled his lips into a fine line.

Locklear walked to the wall and looked at a photo of Lewis fishing on a boat with an older black man. A photo beside it showed the same man looking younger and wearing a military uniform.

121

"This your dad?"

Lewis nodded. "He lives for fishing. We spend almost every moment we get on the Missouri River.

"What do you fish for?" Locklear replied, feigning interest in an activity he had never done and had no inclination to ever try.

"Mostly wall eye."

"I see your dad served in the army."

"Yes, he did."

Locklear nodded. "I did my own time too," he said.

Mendoza listened to Locklear's attempts to soften Lewis up.

"Your dad must be proud that you followed in his footsteps," she said.

"Some, I guess. I only did it for him," Lewis responded, quieter now.

"I was saying, Albert was your friend?" Mendoza said.

"I only saw Albert twice since I got back from Iraq, both times to visit him in the hospital. I phoned him at his sister's house once or twice after that but that was years ago. Heard nothing from him since."

Lewis turned the key in his cash register and flipped the main light switch leaving the room in a gloomy, washy security light.

"There was a witness said he was thrown over that bridge in Richmond," Mendoza said.

Lewis looked Mendoza up and down and then focused his eyes on Locklear.

"I don't know anything about that."

"We know," Locklear said. "We want to know what happened in Iraq."

Lewis thought for a moment. "I don't want any trouble."

"We're not here to cause you any," Locklear replied.

"I told the army police all of this years ago."

"Well, now *we'd* like to hear it."

Lewis sighed and moved roughly past them, locking the shutter from the inside.

"Come into the back."

Mendoza, unsure if it was safe, looked at Locklear who remained rooted to the spot.

"We can talk here," Locklear said.

"Ain't going to do nothing to you. Just want to sit down."

Lewis pulled his trouser leg up to reveal a prosthetic leg from just above the knee.

"This time of day it gets sore."

"That happen in Iraq?" Locklear asked.

Lewis nodded. "Blew straight off in a land mine. I never felt any pain at the time. Only reason I knew I'd been hit bad was the look on my buddy's face."

"Was that Torres?" Mendoza asked.

Lewis nodded. "Torres lost an eye in that blast and some of her hearing but still she helped me, leaned on my leg for close to a half hour trying to stop the blood until help arrived. We'd both passed out by then. Woke up in the hospital."

"We want to talk to Torres. We heard she's originally from this town. Is she around?"

"Yes, but I wouldn't recommend that. In fact, I'm asking you not to. Torres has been through a lot. She never recovered from Iraq. Torres lived for the army. It's all she ever wanted to do. Her family has a long military history.

Discharge cut her up pretty bad. She still goes around in fatigues. Last I heard, she was homeless and was sleeping on her friends' couches. She used to sleep in there sometimes." He gestured, pointing to the back room.

Mendoza leaned past him and looked inside while Locklear remained where he was. The room was furnished with a filing cabinet, small desk and chair and a worn couch that looked like it had been purchased in a charity store. An old-fashioned TV, covered in a film of fine white dust, sat on top of the filing cabinet and was switched off. The small room had only one window, set high on the western wall through which the evening sun threw strands of golden rays across the otherwise dismal room. A narrow door located at the back of the room was closed.

"What's in there?" Mendoza asked, pointing.

"Just a toilet, small kitchen and my storeroom. That's all."

Locklear stepped forward and gestured to the man to go inside first.

They followed him in.

Lewis lowered himself heavily into the low-set couch and sighed while Mendoza sat at its other end. Locklear took the chair at the desk and waited.

"I was really sorry to hear about Mills," Lewis said. "He was a good buddy."

"Tell us what happened in Iraq? About when he was shot."

"What's the point in dragging all of this up? We told the army police then and nothing happened. Mills is dead. What will talking about this shit achieve?"

"It might prove why he was murdered."

124

"I don't think one thing had anything to do with the other. From what his sister said, Albert got mixed up with some Indian movement and met people who got him to do all sorts of crazy shit. Almost landed him in jail. Seems like he pissed off the wrong people."

"He found out that Iraqi artefacts were being stolen during the war. Seems like the man had a conscience and wanted to expose the same thing happening to artefacts belonging to his own people," Mendoza said.

"Albert never even spoke about being Native when I knew him. I mean, I could see he was, but he never mentioned it. America has moved on. This shit shouldn't matter anymore. I never spoke to him about my people being brought to the US as slaves – and Torres, I guess her people were Spanish or something. We were just all Americans together. Just buddies. Ain't that what the United States is supposed to be about?"

"Doesn't always work like that," Locklear replied.

Lewis shifted on the couch and rubbed his thigh. "Yeah, well, it should."

"Torres is single?" Mendoza asked. She wanted to know if Lewis and Torres had ever been in a relationship.

"Widowed."

"How old is she?" Mendoza asked.

Lewis shrugged. "We were in high school together. I left early. I hated school. She was in the same year. Guess she's about thirty-four, thirty-five."

"Pretty young to be widowed," Mendoza said.

Lewis looked from Locklear to Mendoza and bit down on his lower lip. "Her husband was with us in Iraq. He went missing."

He fell silent. He closed his eyes for a moment as though he was reliving some terror. Mendoza watched as he swallowed. His opened his eyes again but fixed them on the wall.

"Look, I got nothing else to say. Please, just leave me alone. I don't like remembering this stuff."

Locklear lifted an invoice from the desk and scanned it. "This fishing stuff is expensive – must have cost a lot to set this store up."

Lewis continued to stare at the wall.

Locklear looked down at Lewis's leg and back to his face.

"How much did the army pay you for your leg?"

Lewis did not reply.

"Come on. I can see you didn't come from a rich family who set you up here and you said yourself that you didn't even finish high school. So the money the army paid out in compensation for your leg helped you set up this store. Gave you a way of making a living. Why not? You deserve it. But my guess is they paid more than the odds for a leg. I saw your car out there. Pretty classy. Not every fishing-tackle store-owner owns a brand-new pick-up. You probably don't even need to come here. I'd say you could even afford to have someone run this place for you."

Lewis dropped his gaze and fixed his eyes on the ground.

"Could it be the settlement required a certain ... silence on your part?"

"Could be," Lewis said without looking up.

"Things didn't go so well for Albert, Lewis," Locklear said. "He didn't get any big settlement. The army found all sorts of ways to tie him up in knots until he got so mad they had him diagnosed with a mental illness. Maybe what he saw in Iraq did make him crazy. We'll never know. But maybe you'd do him the honour of speaking up and telling us what you know. Maybe you'd do that for him?"

Mendoza stood, walked to where Locklear sat and leaned against the desk.

Both she and her boss stared at Lewis in his low seat.

"OK. But I never talked to you? To either of you?"

Locklear and Mendoza nodded in unison.

"It started with Torres' husband, Nick Hughes. He was a good guy but he was highly strung. Always on edge. Didn't trust anyone – big into conspiracy theories. Pretty much no-one wanted to be put on patrol with him cos he'd bring you down. Make you regret being in the army, make you not too proud to be an American. He started telling a few of the company that he heard that stuff from a bombed museum was being sent to the US on army aircraft in munition crates. We all laughed. At first anyway. It wasn't us who blew up the museum and he wanted us to believe the army went in then under fire to take a few fucking vases and paintings?"

Lewis laughed. It was the short, hysterical laugh of a man who had seen things he wished he hadn't. Things that altered the course of his life for ever.

"Few days after that, another museum was hit. It was in a busy area, in the centre of the city. Lots of casualties. We did what we could. It was ... hard to forget. Women, children, dead, just lying in the street. We were trying to look for survivors, our own and civilians. Going through the streets, checking bodies, moving on if there was nothing we could do and always looking up into the buildings for

127

snipers. It was hell. I was near the back door of the museum trying to help a little boy whose chest was full of shrapnel. Kid dies in my arms. I can still remember his mother's screams. I put him in her arms and I walked off. Nothing I could do. Next thing I see is my commander bringing a few men into the back entrance with crates. I followed them in. I actually thought, Jesus, they're going to blow up this beautiful building. That's how dumb I was. That's what a fucking naive idiot I was."

He fell silent.

"Then you saw it for yourself?" Mendoza urged him.

"It took me a few minutes to get across the rubble but when I got inside there was nobody there. I could hear voices underneath me like there was a basement or something. Someone called out, asked who was there. I knew something wrong was happening and it'd be smart to get myself out of there. I got back across the street and waited in a building that wasn't much more than rubble. I could still hear my unit shouting around the street so I knew I'd be safe for a few minutes anyway. After a while everything went quiet and I figured I'd left it too late to get out. I couldn't hear my unit. Then I saw Torres. She'd come looking for me. She came under fire so I shot back, trying to cover her till she got to me. We hid in the building till the firing stopped. Next thing a truck pulled up behind the museum. We were looking right into the fucking door from across the street and we saw a few privates carry three crates out under heavy guard. Torres and I kept out of sight. The crates looked a lot heavier being carried out than they were going in. We didn't see where they went but three days later Albert, Hughes and I were among a small group asked to drive to the airstrip and help load a transport flying back to the States. There were five crates in all and lots of the usual stuff going back. When we were carrying them on, Hughes asked the staff sergeant – Bissett was his name – what's in the crates? I mean, they're for storing ammunition and they were heavy. Why would we fly munition back in the middle of a war?"

"So what happened?" Locklear asked.

"Staff sergeant tells Hughes not to ask questions and just follow orders. We load the plane and another truck arrives with more shit for loading. We start loading that too and then the sergeant gets a call, walks away. We're inside the transport at the time and Hughes has the bright idea to open one of the crates. Albert says it's a good idea. Hughes picks up a crowbar and starts at it. Albert helps him but I just stand there pleading with them to leave it alone. I say I want nothing to do with it but they won't stop, so I walk off but before I jump down I hear Hughes cussing like he's seen something big. I turn and in his hand he has some weird stone tablet thing. Looks ancient. I go back. Like a fool. I should have walked away."

Lewis's chin quivered and Mendoza and Locklear gave the man a moment to compose himself.

"Crate was full of those artefacts. Stolen goods. All heading for the US." Lewis shook his head and inhaled deeply. "Hughes put the thing back in the crate and pushed down the lid again. Couple minutes later we jumped down off the transport together and saw the sergeant there looking at us. Probably the guilty looks on our faces told him we knew what was going on. There were four, maybe five privates guarding the airstrip so I think he knew he couldn't do anything to us there and then.'

"And after that Whitefeather got shot?" Mendoza asked.

"When we got back to base, Albert and Hughes went directly to our corporal and told him what they saw. I told them not to, but they wouldn't listen. Corporal was a guy named Drabek. Real ambitious guy. Drabek came to me and asked what I had seen."

Lewis hung his head and thought for a moment. He looked up again and locked his eyes into Mendoza's deep brown pools.

"I told him I didn't see nothing."

He swallowed. Guilt washed over his face. His chin quivered again.

"So you sold them out?" Locklear said.

"I did the smart thing. I did the only thing I could to get out of that godforsaken country in one piece."

"But you didn't," Mendoza said.

Lewis eyed Mendoza questioningly.

"You didn't get out in one piece, did you?" she clarified as she glanced at Lewis's metal leg.

"What happened?" Locklear asked.

"Day after we looked into those crates, Nick Hughes came to Torres and told her he was being sent to another base on an errand – with just a driver. Torres never heard from him again. Army records said they had no record of Hughes being asked to leave the base and recorded his status as AWOL. Neither he nor the driver ever made it to the other base. Same day, about twenty of us were sent on a mission. Albert was in the frontline, Torres and I were second. It was a routine walk. Next thing we hear firing. I looked up, searching buildings in front of us. Nothing behind us except sand. No buildings. Nowhere for anyone to hide. Then I see Albert lying on the ground, bullet in his back. I shouted for Torres and we start dragging him backwards. We start coming under fire from buildings to the front. Whole time corporal's shouting at us to leave him, shouting that Mills is dead but we could hear him groaning so we kept pulling him back with us. Two more privates ran to us and we carried Albert to safety. All this time Drabek is screaming at us. He tells me and Torres to go back towards the buildings but we're under heavy fire. Rest of the troop all looking at each other, wondering what the fuck is going on with Drabek and he backs down. Mills is taken to hospital and they take the bullet out. After he recovers he starts to tell anyone who would listen that someone in his own unit shot him in the back. When the bullet came back as one of our own, Drabek said what happened to Albert was an accident. Army believed him. Soon as Albert was strong enough, he got flown out to where Drabek couldn't get to him."

"So Drabek already got Hughes out of the way and he obviously thought Albert would be killed," Mendoza said. "Seems like his plan was to get rid of all three of you on that walk-out. You must have known he'd find another way to get you. What did you do next?"

"Torres had a big idea to go to a sergeant by the name of Walsh. Torres had served under her before. She trusted Walsh.

"Susan Walsh? From New Jersey?" Locklear asked quickly.
"Yeah. That's her."

Mendoza watched Locklear's reaction to the name. She couldn't decide if he seemed pleased or upset.

"You know her?" she asked.

Locklear nodded. "We had a mutual acquaintance. Long time ago. What happened then?"

"Walsh heard us out. Took statements. She interviewed Drabek and Bissett but both denied the accusations. That night, another staff sergeant, this nerdy guy by the name of Braff, orders me and Torres to go on a night walk out past the perimeter of the base. He was a real piece of work. Not one of the guys. Well educated, thought he was better than the rest of us."

"A night walk? That makes no sense," Locklear said.

"Yes, that's what I said too."

"So, you went?"

"Had no fucking choice. Orders. Torres and I gunned up. Went walking."

"Until you stepped on a landmine."

Lewis nodded. "It was an AP mine. Buried about twenty feet outside the camp. Right where we swept the area each and every day before we went out on walks. There was no landmine there that morning. Someone buried it on the exact path they knew Torres and I would have to take."

"'Someone' meaning the US Army?" Mendoza asked.

"There's no way insurgents could get that close to the camp without being noticed. 24-hour guard, lights, everything. Army planted that mine there itself. Couldn't shoot us, right? Not with what happened to Mills. Drabek didn't need any more heat than what was already on him. He had to think of another way to get rid of us."

"How did he explain what happened to you?"

"When Torres and I woke up in hospital, we found ourselves under military guard – not that I was in a position to run anywhere." Lewis glanced down at his prosthetic leg. "Seems we were found with priceless Iraqi artefacts in backpacks and enough clothes and supplies to escape with. Someone worked hard to make it look like we'd meant to go AWOL."

"But to where?" Locklear asked.

"Exactly. The story Drabek made up made us look like thieves and it also made us look stupid. Drabek also said there was no order for us to go on a night walk. Braff said he never spoke to either Torres or me. We both knew we were beat."

"What about Walsh's investigation?'

"Now that Torres and I were caught with the artefacts, looked to Walsh like we were trying to cover our tracks. Drabek told her he had suspected us of stealing and was watching us, added in that we must have figured this out and tried to blame it on him. Walsh dropped the whole thing. Heard later that Drabek and Braff were promoted. Bissett was sent home and was later decorated."

"So that left only one thing for the army to do?"

Lewis nodded. "Both Torres and I were dishonourably discharged. Flown home first chance army got to get rid of us."

Locklear looked around the room and then at Lewis's expensive clothes.

"Something must have changed their minds," Locklear said.

Lewis blew out. "I was home a few months. Had to move back in with my folks. Army had me on minimal pension. I was depressed. I couldn't afford the rehab I needed. Medical bills were piling up. Spent all my time fighting them for what I was due. Life was hell."

"And then you decided to go and see Mills," Locklear said as he pieced the sequence of events together.

"Albert was locked in a psych ward. They were treating him for paranoia. I went to see him. Felt sorry for him. His spine was fucked. He was in awful pain. Army were doing their best to make life a misery for him because he just wouldn't shut up. Same happened to Torres. She was drinking very heavily by then. Lost her house cos she couldn't make the repayments. Nick Hughes' body was never recovered in Iraq. Fine print in his life insurance policy said no body, no payment. Albert and I talked about what we saw in those crates and what happened to the stuff. I didn't know nothing about antiques but Albert did. I didn't get an education but I had street smarts. Albert was smart in a different way. He knew everything there was to know about antiques, what they were worth, what kind of people bought them. Thing was he was locked in a loony bin and no-one would listen to him. He was sure those items were being sold here for big money to private collectors. It got me thinking. I start searching the internet, looking for artefacts for sale – and guess what?"

Mendoza nodded and sighed.

"There were fucking hundreds of priceless things for sale and not just from Iraq. You could pretty much find anything you wanted from anywhere in the world. I made contact with one of the sellers and used a false name. Pretended I was looking for something bigger. He put me in contact with a Mr Braff – no less. I knew straight away that it was the same Braff I served with. I turned up at the meeting I arranged but sat in my car across the street until I was sure it was him. I took photos of him sitting in his car with the go-between who I found out was a convicted criminal. There was another guy in the back. Then I drove off. Had a think about what I'd do that wouldn't get me killed. I did a search for Walsh. I knew she was straight, knew she had nothing to do with what happened. She was easy to find. Got herself a good job in Washington. She didn't need anyone knowing how she fucked up, how priceless Iraqi artefacts were being stolen right under her nose. Told her to put things right with me and the army or I'd start yelling."

Lewis trailed off and sat with a look of defiance on his face.

"So Walsh put pressure on the army to compensate you?" Locklear said.

"You're smarter than you look," Lewis replied.

"And Torres?"

Lewis rubbed his thigh again and the defiance slowly faded from his face.

"Torres wouldn't play ball. All she wanted was for the army to admit what had been going on. Like that would happen. I told her, get what the fuck you can because if you think the army cares about the truth, you're crazy. Albert was intent on exposing what was happening to artefacts from his own community but he knew this thing was way bigger than that. He said he'd written to Walsh, told her all about it. Walsh never replied. You have no idea how big this is. It goes all the way to the top. Not just America. There are lots of people involved, high-profile people in Europe and Asia. People who wouldn't want what they're up to getting out."

"You could have offered Torres money. At the very least you could have helped get a roof over her head."

"I tried but Torres didn't want my help. She kept fighting the army till there was no fight left in her. Eventually she gave up trying. Hit the bottle."

"But at least Torres kept her dignity," Mendoza said.

Lewis's eyes darkened. "Dignity? You think Torres has dignity? Torres is a drunk who turns tricks just for food!"

Mendoza stood. Locklear took her lead and together they made their way to the front door.

Lewis followed and unlocked the metal shutter. He pulled it partially up and stood to one side. Mendoza ducked under the shutter.

Locklear held his card out. "If you think of anything we need to know, phone my station. Ask for a cop called O'Brien. He'll know how to get a message through to myself or Mendoza."

Lewis nodded and placed the card on a small table inside the door.

Locklear hunched down to get under the shutter. Looking back at Lewis, he asked, "Where will we find Torres?"

Patrick Lewis didn't react at first, then raised the shutter further and stuck his head out. He looked up the street and motioned his head towards a blurred green light in the distance.

"Happy Hour in O'Sullivan's," he said.

# Chapter 11

Locklear took a seat in the far corner of the bar and ordered two steaks while Mendoza walked around the watering-hole looking for Torres. Locklear chose the seat due to its strategic location from where he could watch everyone entering and leaving the busy bar.

Mendoza returned and sat heavily in the seat beside him and stared out into the crowd. She had just got off the phone from her son and her mother and was still upset by the conversation. He had listened in as they drove the short distance to the bar and gleaned that the kid's father had been late taking him back to his grandmother and that, according to her, his trooper's reformed Catholic ex-husband had been asking the kid about Mendoza's drinking.

Locklear had wanted for some time to talk to Mendoza about her drinking, about how she couldn't seem to go more than a couple of nights without alcohol. It was a road he recognised and one he did not want her travelling. For some there was no turning back. He was one of the lucky ones but his sobriety was still a daily struggle to maintain.

"Any sign of her?" he asked.

"Not yet but this place is packed. Hard to see through the crowd. But I see you didn't order me a beer," Mendoza said as she lifted a soda from the dirty tabletop.

"You're on duty," Locklear replied quietly.

Mendoza shrugged. "I'm officially on vacation," she retorted.

"I've been thinking about the word INTENT and the fact that even O'Brien can't seem to find anything on this. I wonder if it's some underground organisation which is working to expose the theft of artefacts?"

The waitress arrived and placed two huge steaks on the table in front of them.

Mendoza lifted a French fry from her plate and nodded. "You could be right. But if it is a secret organisation, how the hell are we going to find who's running it and from where?"

"When we check into the motel, search Whitefeather's laptop and see if you can come up with anything."

Mendoza mock-saluted her boss and pulled her chair closer to the table to eat. Locklear was still munching his way through the well-done steak after she had cleared her plate.

Mendoza nudged him with her foot under the table and nodded towards the bar where a woman dressed in a khaki vest and army fatigues was climbing onto a high bar stool.

"Looks like we found Torres," she said.

Locklear looked the thin woman over and nodded. The ex-army private looked just as Lewis had described her. Sandra Torres' black hair was shorn tight into her head. Locklear could see the faint outline of a tattoo of an American flag on her right arm.

Mendoza finished her soda in one gulp.

"I got this," she said as she stood. She made her way over to the bar.

Locklear watched from his corner as Mendoza signalled the barman for a beer. She glanced back at him, grinning, and he frowned and shook his head.

"Hi," Mendoza said as she lifted herself onto the bar stool beside Torres which had just been vacated by a man who had obviously tried and failed to chat her up.

Mendoza tried not to look at the vertical scar that ran above and below Torres' left eye or the poor-quality glass eye which was smaller and a lighter colour than Torres' remaining dark-brown iris.

Torres studied Mendoza in return. She looked over Mendoza's unflattering suit pants and loose-fitting shirt and then focused on her eager face.

"I'm not gay," Torres said.

Mendoza, unperturbed, persisted. "That's not why I sat here."

"Good," Torres replied.

"I'm a cop," Mendoza added.

Torres put down her beer and swung around to face Mendoza. She did not speak.

"I'm investigating the death of Albert Whitefeather. You would have known him in Iraq as Albert Mills."

"Who asked you to speak to me?" Torres asked nervously as her eyes darted around the packed room. If she noticed Locklear sitting in the corner staring, she did not say anything. Mendoza could feel her boss's eyes bore into her as he watched her interview a person in a less than professional setting.

"A friend of yours – Patrick Lewis," Mendoza replied.

"He's no fucking friend of mine," Torres replied.

"You were in Iraq with Lewis. And with Mills. Lewis said you sometimes used to sleep at his place."

Torres laughed. "Once. When I was wasted. I don't even remember getting there. Seems Lewis was in a bar I was drinking in and took me home when I made a fool of myself. That was a few years back so he if told you we're friends, he's a fucking liar. Lewis is a sell-out. A phony."

Mendoza suddenly realised that Torres was slightly inebriated and must have been drinking in another area of the bar or someplace else before she arrived in O'Sullivan's.

"Can I get you a beer?" Mendoza asked.

Torres took her cigarettes off the bar and lit one. "Whiskey," she replied.

Mendoza ordered a whiskey and another beer for herself. They sat in silence until the drinks came.

Mendoza picked up the bottle and drank the beer down in three long gulps.

Torres smiled. "I was on my last five dollars. Good job you showed up," she said and she downed the amber liquid in one. She shivered from the rush as Mendoza raised a hand and signalled for another round.

She shoved the second drink in front of Torres.

"Tell me all you know about Whitefeather," she said.

"I'll need to be a bit more drunk than this," Torres replied, downing the second whiskey. "And make them doubles."

Mendoza raised her hand again and the barman approached, this time with the whiskey bottle.

From his seat Locklear could see him eye Mendoza carefully. He saw him glare meaningfully at Torres as he filled her glass, as if in warning. By the dismissive wave of the woman's hand, Locklear knew that he had figured Mendoza was a cop and was protecting a regular from being questioned under the influence.

The barman shrugged, added a glass for Mendoza and poured. Locklear cringed from his seat and, unable to watch, looked away into the crowd and instead watched a band setting up for the night.

He couldn't help but glance back occasionally at the bar. Torres was talking. A lot. He hoped Mendoza was getting something useful out of her while simultaneously feeling guilty that Mendoza was interviewing someone under these conditions.

Time passed and the women kept on drinking. At last Locklear could not sit by any longer. He stood and walked to the bar.

As Mendoza raised her hand to order another round of drinks Locklear pulled it down roughly and held onto it.

"You've had enough to drink," he said.

"Who's this? Your dad?" Torres sneered.

Mendoza belched and laughed. "He thinks he is – he's my boss," she slurred. "Sarge, this is Sandra. Sandra, this is Detective Sergeant O. Locklear. No-one knows what the O stands for. It's a secret."

"*You're drunk*," Locklear hissed.

Mendoza, surprised by the venom with which he uttered those words, seemed to suddenly sober up.

"*Sarge!*" she replied.

Locklear thought he could see a faint downturn of her lips. His trooper's eyes welled up. He took her by both hands and pulled her to her feet.

Drawing her aside, he leant in close to her and lowered his voice.

"This is wrong, Mendoza. You're taking advantage of a vulnerable woman."

Mendoza nodded slightly and turned to look at Torres. Then she walked back to her.

"I'm sorry. If you think of anything else, call this number and ask for O'Brien," she whispered as she wrote down his name and the number for the station on a napkin. "Mention Detective Locklear." She added his name to the napkin and handed it to Torres.

Torres shrugged, stuck the napkin in her trouser pocket and turned her back on Mendoza. She nudged a grey-haired sporty-looking man standing at the bar beside her. When he turned to her, she wrapped her arms around him.

"Johnny, get me a drink," she pleaded.

Johnny quickly ordered Torres' next whiskey.

Locklear drove to the nearest motel he could find. He paid for two rooms with cash and struggled to get Mendoza into hers. He lay her down on the bed and found she was snoring before he took her shoes off. He moved her hair from her face and stood there for a moment, then sighed and pulled the covers over her.

He left a note on the bedside locker telling her where they were and his room number.

He closed the door gently and went to his own room where he sat for an hour before lying down fully clothed on yet another uncomfortable bed. He watched the stars glimmer in the dark night sky through the blinds which he had only half closed. An hour passed, then two, as the details of the case floated in his troubled mind. When he finally slept all he could hear was Mendoza's voice laughing about his undisclosed first name and her question the day before about whether or not his mother had had a name other than the Indian name she used. The realisation that there might be a record of his mother somewhere, a record under a name he had no way of discovering, marred his dreams as he tossed and turned in the unfamiliar bed.

He woke to the sound of banging on his door. He jumped up in the darkened room and, unsure where he was, waited a moment while the sound of knocking continued. He turned on a table lamp and opened the door.

Mendoza stood there, pale, shaken and barefoot.

"I'm sorry," she said. "I shouldn't have done that. It was unprofessional. I'm sorry. It was just ... that call from my mom. It upset me. I wasn't thinking straight. Santy and this job are all I have. I think Manuel is trying to take him from me. Then, that look you gave me in the bar. It hurt. I don't want to lose your respect." She started to cry.

He put his arm around her and led her into the room.

"Can I stay here? I don't want to be on my own tonight."

Locklear sat her on the bed. He pulled the covers back and beckoned for her to lie down.

She lay back and watched as he moved to the table under the window and sat on the hard plastic chair.

"I don't mind if you sleep in the bed too," she said.

Locklear remained where he was and stared out at what remained of the night. He listened to her faint snores as the sky brightened and then fell into a deep sleep, his chin sunk down on his chest.

When Locklear woke the sun was high in the summer sky and Mendoza was gone. His neck and back ached and, when he stood, he found that so did the rest of his muscles. He rotated his head and stretched in an attempt to loosen up.

He was relieved to see a coffee machine in the corner of the room that hadn't been there when they'd checked in the night before. He made coffee and drank it quickly while he thought about what their next steps might be.

He quickly showered and gathered his belongings and knocked lightly on Mendoza's motel-room door. When she opened it Locklear could see the signs of a heavy hangover on her face. She was showered and dressed but there were deep lines underneath her eyes and he could still get the faint aroma of whiskey from her breath.

She looked guiltily at the ground and stood aside for him to come in.

"Sarge, I ..."

Locklear raised his hand to stop her.

"Forget it, Mendoza. I made a lot of mistakes when I was drinking. Did a lot of stupid things. But I do want to say, as your friend, that you need to look at your drinking."

Mendoza nodded but kept her eyes on the linoleum floor.

"Thank you," she whispered.

"You hungry?" he asked.

"Always," she said and smiled.

Locklear waited while Mendoza packed up her things. When she had finished, she zipped up her case and opened the door.

"Where to?" she asked.

"Vermillion," he replied.

Mendoza eyed her boss quizzically.

"University of South Dakota. Think it's time we talked to its dean."

# Chapter 12

The large breakfast Mendoza and Locklear ate in yet another forgettable diner did little to make Mendoza feel any better. Her head ached mercilessly and her stomach churned from the effects of the copious amounts of whiskey she had drunk the night before. Locklear, knowing her blood-alcohol level would be still above the driving limit, insisted on driving despite his fatigue.

"Sorry for keeping you up half the night," Mendoza said to her silent companion.

Locklear smiled a half smile and shrugged. "I guess I've had better reasons for a woman to keep me up all night."

"Yeah, and I guess *that* was more fun!" she said, smiling through the pain.

She glanced at her boss.

"Can I explain my behaviour, sarge? I feel like we need to clear the air."

"It's not necessary."

"I need to."

Locklear sighed. "OK."

"I was upset about the call from my mom and I have a

feeling Manuel's trying to take Santy from me."

"You already told me that last night when you came to my room – and said you were sorry."

"Did I? Can't remember."

"But, Mendoza, how could Manuel take Santy? He hasn't seen the kid in years and he was violent when he was married to you. Goddamn it, he even hit your son. No court in this country is going to give him custody of Santy."

"I hope you're right, sarge. He's trying to paint himself as a reformed man but I know he's not. I feel that something is up with all of this Christian-movement stuff. Mom thinks he's changed. She says he's even living in some commune that offers homes to single women and their children."

"And not to homeless men? Families? I don't like the sound of that."

"Me neither."

"Maybe you should tell your mom to come back with Santy to Richmond now so you'll know he's safe."

"My grandma is still real sick. Mom is her only surviving daughter. She's needed there. I can't ask her to do that. It's bad enough that I rely on her to look after Santy for me."

"Look, Mendoza, if you want to call it a day on this case, fly to Mexico and take Santy home. I can manage from here. Your son is more important than any case."

"Thanks, sarge, but I told Mom last night – no more visits from Manuel. He can't force this unless he takes me back to court and you're right about the history of abuse – last time it didn't go well for him because of that. So, it's OK – I'm not going anywhere until we see this case through."

Mendoza reached across the car and touched her boss's hand tenderly.

"I can't understand why some woman didn't snap you up, sarge. I mean, I'd say you're hard to live with, a perfectionist for sure and not a talker, but you're a good man and ... kind of cute."

"What makes you think no woman ever tried?"

"Like Susan Walsh? I saw how you reacted when Lewis mentioned her name. Was she an old girlfriend?"

Locklear snorted. "No. Nothing like that. We know ... well, we both knew someone a long time ago. And not that it's any of your business but I was a lousy boyfriend. I was always working and, when I wasn't working, I was drinking. I guess I wasn't the settling-down kind. Women got tired waiting for something to happen that I knew was never going to."

"Any regrets?"

Locklear shrugged. "Just that it would have been more honest of me to have told them upfront that I wasn't the marrying kind. Other than that, what would be the point of regrets? I'm the same person now as I was then."

"But you're not drinking. Maybe things would be different? And, don't you get lonely?"

Locklear made no answer as he swung onto the N29 heading westwards.

"OK, well, I guess *that* conversation is over," Mendoza said.

They inched along the Missouri River and then headed in a northerly direction. Within minutes they crossed the Big Sioux River and left the state of Iowa behind, heading once more into South Dakota Territory.

Locklear still remained silent and focused on the featureless highway that stretched out before them.

"OK, well, after I woke up with the hangover from hell," Mendoza said at last, "I logged on to Whitefeather's laptop –"

"First, tell me what Torres told you," Locklear interrupted.

Mendoza closed her eyes and massaged her throbbing temples. She did not want to be reminded so soon of the error of judgement she had made or how she had used a vulnerable woman to further the case.

"Nothing more than what Lewis told us. She's pretty sad."

"She must have said something."

Mendoza sighed. "She sits in that bar most days looking for people to buy her drinks. A sad end to someone who had a long military career planned. She still hopes her husband is alive although I guess she knows deep down that he was murdered as soon as he cleared the base. Seems they were happily married. Her parents have disowned her because of her drinking. They retired to a small ranch about thirty miles out of town. She has a sister who helps her but only just. Sister has two kids and lives in town. She's close to the parents and doesn't pretend that she sees Torres. Brother is an ex-army man and now a local cop. Passes her by in the street. Her dad was pretty high up in the military. Decorated. Feels she embarrassed him making accusations against the army. Only reason she stays in town is she doesn't have anywhere else to go. Army have her tied into a minimal pension. Doesn't even pay enough for her to afford rent."

"Waste of a good army private," Locklear said quietly.

"At the moment she's crashing in a caravan parked on

148

an empty lot her sister is planning on building a new house on, but that's going to change as soon as her sister's army husband comes back from overseas duty in a couple of months. Torres said she doesn't get along with her brother-in-law and that he won't want her around his kids."

Locklear blew out. "Can't she get a job? Start over?"

"Seems she used to work in that bar. She said the owner O'Sullivan had to fire her for drinking on the job. Torres said O'Sullivan gave her more warnings than he ever gave anyone else. Small town. Word gets around. No-one will hire her. She did say though that O'Sullivan is good to her. He's ex-army too. She said he's sweet on her, but she's not interested. She said as far as she's concerned she has a husband. O'Sullivan gives her food for free."

"In return for?" Locklear asked sarcastically.

"She didn't go into the details but I guess she's got to find a way of surviving."

"Seems you got a lot of really personal information out of her," Locklear said quietly.

Mendoza looked out the window.

"I know. I was out of order, sir. It won't happen again," she whispered.

"And what of less personal stuff? The case, remember?"

"She liked Albert a lot. Feels bad about what happened to him."

"Was she in contact with him?"

Mendoza shook her head. "She said she hasn't seen or heard from Whitefeather since he was taken back to the US for treatment. She knows Lewis has seen him though. Lewis told her how bad things were for Albert, but I guess she had her own problems to deal with."

Locklear, clearly uncomfortable about Torres' situation, tried to think of something to say.

Mendoza eased his discomfort. "I asked her – if the army retracted her discharge, would she serve again?"

"And?"

"She said that she'd go back in a heartbeat. Can you believe that? After all they did to her."

Locklear thought for a moment. "I guess she understands that the whole army isn't corrupt. She and her husband, well, they were just unlucky. OK, tell me about what you found on Whitefeather's computer."

"It was mostly newspaper articles that he had saved on his laptop."

"About?"

"Almost all were local newspaper reports on demonstrations he was present at, which were arranged by the Pine Ridge Native American group. Mostly at dig sites where the locals were objecting to the government issuing archaeological passes to universities. The reports said that Natives claimed that the items found were not being returned to their respective tribes and also that sacred burial grounds were being disturbed."

"Hence the arrival of Whitefeather at Holton's apartment with a skull in his hand."

"I must have read twenty or so similar stories but there was one newspaper article that caught my eye because the photo from the article was like a get-together photo of who's who in our investigation."

Locklear turned his head and stared at his trooper. "Well?" he barked.

"Not so loud, sarge! God, seriously, this is the worst

pain I've ever felt," she said as she rubbed her throbbing temples.

"You had a baby, Mendoza. How on earth could a headache be worse than childbirth?"

"Santy was delivered by C-section. He had a big head. I had small hips. So –"

"OK! Way too much information, Mendoza."

Mendoza laughed. "Well, this photo made the front page. It was about a dig site outside of Pine Ridge."

"That's where Carter was."

"Yes, but this one was two years before Carter was there."

"Go on."

"The story was that USD and Richmond University were granted access to a dig site that both universities felt still held archaeological items which were of national interest. The local Sioux tribe said they had agreed to three previous digs at the site in the preceding fifteen years and that there was nothing more of interest there and they objected to the presence of teams on their land. There was a major demonstration at the site. Representatives from most of the sister groups flew or drove in to support the local Sioux. Eventually the government backed down and blocked access to the site for both universities."

"But Carter was there earlier this year."

"Seems he was operating without a permit," Mendoza replied.

"He wouldn't have known that. Holton tricked him."

"Looks like Holton was operating a dig without consent and that Rosenberg from USD was involved. Do you want to see the photo?" Mendoza lifted Whitefeather's laptop from the floor in front of her.

Locklear pulled off the highway at the next exit and drove into a gas station. He put the car into park and took the open laptop from Mendoza.

The photo was of a large gathering of Native American demonstrators. A female journalist stood to the left of the photo in front of three white men. Locklear instantly recognised Holton, who stood next to a man in his mid-sixties. Locklear remembered that Holton had been around six foot. The white-haired man stood several inches shorter than him so this was not the tall man Carter had seen at the dig site, the same man that Raymond had called the "weird ghost dude".

"A journalist was investigating the legitimacy of the digs and both universities sent their senior staff to put their case forward," Mendoza went on. "The journalist arranged to take a photo of the academics at the site, but word got out and a huge number of Native American protestors showed up." She placed her fingernail on a man standing to the right of the photo. "That's Albert Whitefeather. I recognise him from the photo we found with his stuff at his motel."

Locklear scanned the faces of the rest of the people. One other face stood out for him, a side profile of a young man in the background dressed in Native American clothes, standing beside an older Native American couple.

"You see anyone else you recognise?" he asked.

Mendoza took another look at the photo. "No."

"I do."

"Who?"

Locklear ignored her question. "Email it to O'Brien. Tell him it's from me."

Mendoza shrugged.

Locklear pulled the laptop closer and looked at Whitefeather.

He wore the traditional long straight hair and a strange hat, similar to a bowler except squatter with a band of orange and brown beads around it.

He then focused on Holton. He had not seen the man alive but he didn't look much different to the body Locklear had stood over only days before. He was thin, with the exception of a moderately big belly which hung over his grey pants. He was the only one of the three who was smiling. His eyes were not looking directly at the photographer but at another person in the crowd. Locklear followed the direction of his gaze.

"Looks like Holton's smiling at Whitefeather," he said.

"Yes, I noticed that. Looks to me like the men were friends. I stared at the photo for a long time this morning and – that smile – it's saying something. Like they shared a secret."

Locklear nodded and pondered, looking over the photo. He scanned down to the list of names underneath.

"The man in the middle is Rosenberg," he said. "At least we know what he looks like now." He closed the laptop and tapped his fingers on its worn cover.

"How are you going to play the talk with Rosenberg?" Mendoza asked. "Looks like he and Sartre knew each other well. Maybe Sartre has tipped him off, told him not to speak to you. Could even be dangerous, sarge. If these people are involved in what we suspect they are, they'll do what they need to prevent it from becoming public."

Locklear thought for a moment. "He doesn't know what I look like. Maybe I could pose as a Native looking to sell something valuable that I found on my land. Tell him I hear he's in the market?"

Mendoza's eyebrows shot up in surprise. "*You*, sarge? First, you'd never pull it off and, second and more importantly, that's entrapment. Even if he bought it, the information would be inadmissible in court. Also, if we went in fast like that, it'd kill any other leads we might have got. Who knows what we'll uncover if we keep going? I have a feeling about this one, sarge. I think even Lewis didn't fully understand how big this thing is. I think we need to step lightly."

Locklear nodded and turned the key in the ignition.

"OK. You're right. I trained you well," he said with grin.

"Was that a test?"

"Sure, we'll go with that," he said and laughed.

# Chapter 13

Locklear settled into his usual silent mood as the car travelled through the towns of Jefferson and Elk Point, heading north on the N29. He swung a sharp left at Junction City onto route 50 in the direction of Vermillion. When he reached the busy town, he took a right onto North University Street and made his way to the Old Main building where the university administrative services were housed.

He pulled up and stood out onto the curb. He motioned to the coffee house on the corner as Mendoza joined him.

"Think it's best if we split up. Two of us making queries might lead to questions we don't want to answer," he said.

"And what? My job is to get the *coffee*?"

"Yes. And donuts please. I'm going to go into the admin office here to see if I can find out where we'd find Rosenberg. This place is huge. We'll meet back here in five. Decide on our plan from there."

Mendoza sulked as she made her way across the road.

Locklear climbed the five stones steps into the building, stopping only to read the plaque on the wall which dated the building to 1883. He stepped back down to take in the three-storey building whose light brick shone in the early summer sun. It was, he thought, a beautiful building with an impressive Palladian facade. On top, a decorative pillared dome sat on a narrow tower-like structure which on each side housed a round window which reflected the brilliant blue South Dakota sky. Locklear stood for a moment longer and wondered about the people who built the structure, wondering if they had known that their creation would look as good today as it did when it was built in what was a very different America.

He made his way back up the steps and opened the narrow door into an open office area. Two women sat behind large oak desks and were busy typing into computers. One was also talking on the phone, uttering monosyllabic responses to her caller as her fingers deftly raced across the keyboard.

The other, a Native American woman of around fifty, looked up and smiled warmly at him.

Locklear approached her desk and looked at her name badge. *Kayawi Duta*.

"How can I help you?" she asked.

"I'm looking for Professor Rosenberg's office."

"You don't look like an archaeologist," she said with a grin.

Locklear returned her smile. The woman was beautiful. He found himself glancing at her left hand and found himself slightly disappointed to see a narrow gold band on her fourth finger. The woman noticed and smiled shyly.

"My meeting is about something else," he said.

"What time is your appointment?"

"Well, I don't exactly have an appointment," Locklear said and grinned.

Kayawi pursed her lips. "Then, you'll want to knock on the professor's door when his private secretary has gone for lunch. The Prof normally eats his at his desk. Barbara is like a Rottweiler. None shall pass without an appointment."

"And Barbara's lunch is at?"

Kayawi looked at the clock on the wall. It was twenty past twelve.

"In about ten minutes. Lucky for you she's a creature of habit! East Hall building," she said, handing Locklear a map.

Locklear scanned the map and memorised each turn he needed to take to get to the other side of the huge campus.

"Can I ask you one more thing?" he asked quietly.

Kayawi looked towards her colleague and got to her feet. She walked away and beckoned to him.

He followed her.

She turned, leaned in and whispered to him.

"You're a cop, aren't you?"

Locklear glanced at the other woman and, deciding she was too busy typing and giving her caller short, sharp answers to listen in, nodded.

"Is Professor Rosenberg in some kind of trouble?" she whispered.

Locklear thought he could see a glint in the woman's eyes, as though Kayawi Duta was hoping he'd say yes. He didn't answer but hoped his smile would give the woman the satisfaction she needed. Rosenberg was obviously not popular in the university or, at the very least, was not popular with Kayawi.

"What do you need to know?"

"Rosenberg had two grad students on a recent dig with him outside Pine Ridge," he said.

Locklear watched Kayawi's face darken and hastened to make his case.

"I can see that this is a huge campus. There must be thousands of students here but I was hoping, given the area of speciality, that you might know who they are. They were both very young. One had red hair, pale, freckles. He wore glasses. The other was a young Native American. He was tall, had long hair and wears Grateful Dead T-shirts."

"You didn't get this information from me," Kayawi said.

"I didn't."

"Neither of those kids are grad students. They're not even archaeology students."

Locklear thought back to Carter's comment that neither of the young men seemed to have had any experience of digs.

"I'm pretty sure the redheaded kid was Tommy Rosenberg," she said.

"Is he related to Professor Rosenberg?"

"Yes. He's his grandson. He was studying drama here. He dropped out a few weeks back. Word is the apple didn't fall at or even near the tree. Flunked out in all his exams and it's not the most taxing course he chose. I'd say Professor Rosenberg decided to pull Tommy out of here before he embarrassed him."

Locklear absorbed this information.

Kayawi's colleague's call ended. The woman stood and stared at Locklear and Kayawi.

"I'm going to lunch," she barked and went out a door behind the reception area.

"She's pleasant," Locklear remarked.

Kayawi laughed. "And you got her on a good day!"

"And the other kid?" Locklear asked.

"The Grateful Dead T-shirt and the fact that he was with Tommy Rosenberg can only mean one kid. He's a second-year law student here."

"Name?"

"I know his first name is Jim. He's a nice kid. Always willing to help out with anything. Hard to see what they have in common. Let me look up the 2$^{nd}$ year law enrolments."

Locklear followed her back to her desk where she typed on her keyboard and waited.

"I don't think Tommy had any other friends on campus. My son is a student here and he says Rosenberg is really spoiled and obnoxious. The other students didn't really take to him."

The computer beeped.

"Hunter. That's his last name. Jim Hunter. Bright kid. An A student. He won a scholarship to come here."

"Address? Cell-phone number?"

Kayawi typed in some more and looked puzzled as she looked at the screen that opened on her computer.

"Seems like he enrolled using a Vermillion address. It's a street a few blocks from here but it's not current. Could be he just rented there until the semester started in his first year. He dorms here now. I guess any correspondence the university has for him is posted to the dorm."

"Do you have any idea how I can contact him?"

"He wouldn't have left the university for summer break

yet. His class still have one exam to complete which is on later today. Plus he's got a couple of casual jobs on campus to earn some extra money. His dorm is at Coyote Village, North of Campus. You might find him there. But I remember talking to him here last summer. He was helping out moving furniture and that sort of thing and I'm fairly sure he said he came from Pine Ridge – so if you don't find him here, you could try the reservation."

Locklear leaned over the counter and looked at the university ID of the young man who had been on the dig with Carter. Jim Hunter was only twenty years old and already looked like he had the weight of the world on his shoulders. One big question raced in Locklear's mind: why a Native American kid would help Rosenberg on an illegal dig in his own community.

"You said neither of them are archaeology students. Why would they have been on a dig?" Locklear asked.

Kayawi shrugged. "I don't know. Archaeology students are normally queuing up to work with Professor Rosenberg. His work is internationally renowned. He usually has three, maybe four, grad students doing research with him at any given time. So that makes no sense. He had an assistant who used to look after PhD applicants. I'm sure Dr. Walter Braff would have been able to explain that, but he left a while ago."

Locklear's jaw dropped. Braff was the name of the man who had served with Lewis, Torres and Whitefeather in Iraq and was also the man Lewis said was selling stolen Iraqi artefacts. And he had been working here, with Rosenberg, in the archaeology department of a major university with access to national treasures.

160

"Did you say *Braff*?"

Kayawi nodded but the crease in her brow and the tight line of her lips told Locklear she knew she had probably said too much. He watched a deep blush rise up her neck and face.

"I take it you weren't too keen on Braff either?"

Kayawi did not answer immediately but the expression on her face told Locklear everything he needed to know.

"Walter Braff never said much," she said. "He was very aloof. None of us even knew what his qualifications were. Professor Rosenberg hired him. We used to joke here that his PhD was gained from research in how to alienate yourself from your colleagues."

"You doubted that he was qualified?"

"Well, let's just say that when any of the other archaeology lecturers tried to engage him in topics, he never joined in the conversation, even when he was directly asked for his opinion on things. One lecturer asked him where he'd completed his studies but he just walked away. Never answered. No-one, except maybe Professor Rosenberg, liked Braff."

"And Rosenberg?"

"Professor Rosenberg is different. Very genial, pleasant. Good manners and that, but you don't want to be alone with him in his office. Likes young, good-looking female staff. I've worked here a long time so, believe me, I know. He's interviewing today for a new secretary. Barbara got a promotion so she'll be moving to a new office on campus soon. The pay is good but I wouldn't go back to work in his office no matter what they were paying."

Locklear nodded.

"You better get to Professor Rosenberg's office before Barbara gets back. She looks like a pretty little thing but she bites."

Locklear thanked her and left the office quickly.

When he got outside Mendoza was standing at the car, having drunk both their coffees. The cinnamon dust on her shirt told Locklear she had also eaten the donuts, his as well as her own.

"You said five minutes!"

Locklear jumped into the car and, as the engine started, checked the clock. It was twelve forty-five. He had approximately fifteen minutes to get inside Rosenberg's office before his guard dog got back. He looked at Mendoza, reached out and dusted the cinnamon dust from her chest.

"Sarge!" she said, slapping his hand away from her bosom. "I may have invited you to sleep with me last night but I didn't mean ..."

"Relax," Locklear said. "I'm not coming onto you. I need you to look like sugar, not be covered in it."

"Huh?"

Locklear turned out of the parking lot in the direction of Rosenberg's office. He drove slowly past the beautiful Old Main Building and weaved in and out of the small streets of the pretty university campus. He eventually turned onto East Clark and drove by the Native American Center and Faber house. He took the turn off for Willow Street and explained his plan to his less than enthusiastic trooper. He then took an abrupt left onto a small roadway which led to East Hall and to what was probably the most impressive and oldest building on the campus.

"Wow," said Mendoza. "Look at that fairy-tale turret

162

and the pink stone!"

"It's Sioux pink quartzite."

"Sioux?"

"Yeah. That's what they call it."

He pulled in and parked roughly in a space at the back of the lot.

"What a beautiful building!" Mendoza said.

"Yeah, well, now I need you to look beautiful. You got lipstick or something?"

"What? Look, sarge, only hours ago you told me off for getting Torres drunk so she'd give me the information we needed. Now you want me to suck up to Rosenberg so I can get info from him? Don't you think that's a bit rich?"

Locklear looked the cop up and down. He locked his eyes on her shirt which was buttoned almost up to her neck.

"Open a few of those buttons," he said.

"Why don't you show your own chest off to Rosenberg? I didn't join the force to be a pretty plaything for anyone."

Locklear grinned. "And I never for one moment looked on you as one," he said as he pulled Mendoza's purse from the floor of the car and started rummaging in it.

Mendoza pulled it from him. "Hey!"

"Look, Mendoza, we're running out of time to get inside unnoticed. I'd be happy to show Rosenberg what's under my shirt if I thought it would get me inside his office but somehow I don't think I'm his type. Now, I just need you to get me inside the office and *then* you can go back to being Trooper Mendoza."

Mendoza blew out. "Fine, but if he tries anything on –"

"Then feel free to do him some damage."

163

"You think I wouldn't?"

Mendoza pulled a small cream purse from her bag. She took out an eyeliner and deftly drew thick black lines on her lids which accentuated her deep brown eyes. She then took a lipstick from the purse and applied a heavy layer to her lips. She smacked her lips together and turned to her boss.

"Well?"

"You'll do," he replied.

Inside, they found the reception desk still unmanned.

Locklear leant over the desk and lifted a clipboard listing the names and interview times of applicants for Rosenberg's new secretary. He scanned down the list and locked onto the name of the 1.00pm interviewee. *Rita Vasquez*.

"You're in luck, Mendoza. You're Rita Vasquez and you're early for your interview." He used the pen attached to the clipboard to tick the woman off the list as having arrived.

Locklear knocked on the heavy wooden door with Rosenberg's name on it and pushed Mendoza inside when a voice called out for her to come in.

Locklear waited outside to give Mendoza enough time to lure Rosenberg into thinking she was his new plaything. By the sounds of her light-hearted laughter, his trooper was doing a good job. Then he opened a tall filing cabinet placed in an alcove between the reception desk and Rosenberg's door and rummaged through it to see if he could find anything of interest. He stopped when he heard the click-clacking of Rosenberg's secretary's shoes as she returned to her desk. He quietly moved the drawer back into place and as silently as possible turned the handle of Rosenberg's office door and walked inside.

The smile plastered over Rosenberg's face quickly disappeared as he locked on to the presence of the Native American standing in his office. The professor turned to Mendoza who dropped the cheesy smile from her face.

"What's this?" Rosenberg asked as he glanced from Mendoza to Locklear.

Locklear walked over to the huge desk and took a seat beside Mendoza, removing his Stetson and placing it on his knee.

"Who are you?" Rosenberg snarled.

When Locklear made no reply, Rosenberg put his hand on his phone.

"I wouldn't do that if I were you," Locklear began. "Not unless you want my colleague and I leaking a story to the local press that you and your business partners are selling stolen international artefacts and that you've been doing so for years."

Rosenberg straightened up like a cobra ready to strike. He lifted a pen from his desk and tapped its nib off the hard wood.

"Those are pretty serious allegations, Mr ...?"

"Locklear. Detective Sergeant Locklear."

"I believe I know all of the senior cops around here and I don't recall ever hearing your name. Are you a tribal cop?"

Locklear did not answer.

"No, you don't have the look of a reservation cop. Your, em, pretty colleague doesn't either. Shame you barged in when you did. I was just about to give her a typing exam ... see how quickly she can work those long fingers of hers."

Mendoza squirmed but knew Rosenberg's remark was intended to make her uncomfortable and that the Dean possibly hoped the remark would upset Locklear too. It was designed to throw them off guard and deflect them from the information they needed to know. Mendoza looked at her boss and saw that he was mildly irritated by Rosenberg's creepiness but not enough to divert his attention from the business at hand.

"You didn't answer the question," Locklear said.

"Because you didn't ask me one. You made an accusation. One which I have no intention of dignifying with an answer. Perhaps your department would take their enquiry up with my lawyer?" Rosenberg's eyes moved coolly between them. Then he began to laugh. "Oh, *I see.* Now I remember! You can't do that because you have no jurisdiction here. Come on, you think I wasn't expecting you to call? You think Dean Sartre didn't tell me about a troublemaking Native cop who thinks he's figured things out? Your pretty sidekick here did get me though, I'll admit. I didn't know about her. I was actually really taken in by her, em, performance."

"She took lessons," Locklear retorted. "You know, acting classes, like your grandson Tommy took here at USD until he flunked out. The same grandson you brought with you on a dig. A young man I dare say could be identified in a line-up by someone who saw him there."

Rosenberg's smile did not fade. Locklear's threat did not have the impact he had hoped it would.

"Sergeant Locklear, I imagine you're a bright enough man but, believe me, you are looking in the wrong place.

166

I've spent my life protecting and preserving artefacts from around the world. My reputation is quite renowned. May I suggest you try looking for the thief among your own people, eh? Shall we say, among the less, em, *regulated* organisations purporting to protect Native American artefacts?"

Mendoza shot a look at Locklear and swallowed.

"What about Walter Braff?" Locklear said. "I know he worked here and that he was stationed in Iraq with four soldiers who realised what he was up to."

Locklear saw an expression of alarm flicker across Rosenberg's face before he quickly replaced it with an expression of smug superiority.

"Dr. Braff has moved on to another position."

"Oh? And where would that be?" Mendoza asked.

Rosenberg waved his hand. "Oh, he did tell me but ... well, it seems to have slipped my mind."

"You didn't have a permit to undertake the dig with Professor Holton," Locklear said.

"Yes, that's true. It's a pity your young friend didn't have the wisdom to stay away from Holton's lab that morning. Indeed, to stay away from Holton on the unfortunate night someone took his life. Come on, Detective, you think I don't know that Albert Whitefeather had been to Holton's apartment and threatened him? Whitefeather was a thorn in my side for years. The man was crazy and everyone knew it. He finally cracked and killed an innocent man and seems to have rather unfortunately taken your friend down with him. I was at that site to ensure we had left nothing behind that might get into the wrong hands."

"Like the Native American fertility figure that you found but never made its way to the university? You think I'm falling for this bullshit?"

"It went missing. I acknowledge that. It wasn't my fault."

"Then whose fault was it?" Mendoza asked.

"I'm afraid I can't tell you that, officer," Rosenberg smirked. "And not because I don't want to, but because I really don't know."

"Lee Carter described a man who came to the dig site shortly before you arrived," Locklear said. "He said the man was very tall and unnaturally pale. He said Holton appeared nervous of him."

Rosenberg's lips tightened. He blinked twice.

Locklear knew the Dean was about to lie.

"Doesn't ring a bell," he replied.

"I take it you won't mind bringing your grandson in to give a statement to the local police?" Locklear asked, knowing full well there was little chance of him convincing the local force, whom he'd hadn't even had the good manners to inform he was in town, of bringing anyone in for questioning on a case his idiot colleagues Diaz and Hill had most likely closed.

"It seems that my grandson is all you have to go on, that Tommy is essentially your only lead."

Locklear and Mendoza remained silent. Rosenberg laughed.

"I'm afraid that won't be possible," he said quietly. He grinned at Mendoza and then fixed his sneer on Locklear. "You see, my grandson is in Paris with his parents."

"That doesn't stop him from giving a statement. There's

an extradition agreement between France and the U.S. We can force your grandson to provide a statement."

Rosenberg stood and walked to his door. He opened it and stood to one side.

"Oh, I should have added that my son is Josef Rosenberg. A diplomat, high level of course, which of course means ... that he and his family have diplomatic immunity."

Mendoza, unable to look at Rosenberg's face anymore, stood and made her way out the door.

"You couldn't interview my grandson about a parking ticket, missing artefacts or ... even a murder," Rosenberg finished.

Locklear walked to the door and stood, making eye contact with Rosenberg. He tried to think of a clever retort but failed. Rosenberg had boxed him in, and he'd have to find a way to get the information he needed elsewhere.

"This isn't over, Rosenberg. I won't see my friend go to jail for something he didn't do."

He stepped outside.

"Wish I could help," Rosenberg said as he closed the door gently behind him.

In the reception area, Barbara looked perplexed as Mendoza passed the real Rita Vasquez waiting patiently to be interviewed.

When they left the building, Locklear stood on its stone steps beside Mendoza who was unusually silent.

"You OK?" he asked as he donned his Stetson.

Mendoza sighed. "Just pissed off that that creep got the better of us," she said through clenched teeth.

As they walked back to the car, Locklear glanced

around the campus streets and noted how few students were around at this time of year. Across the road, a coffee house was almost empty save for one or two university staff sitting inside, out of the heat. Outside on the pavement, three young women were struggling to lift heavy suitcases onto the roof of an old, beaten-up sedan. Locklear looked at the building beside the coffee house and found it was equally deserted. Three young guys were outside. Two were sitting on the steps, with their noses firmly in books, cramming he assumed for their last exams before heading off to whatever state they called home. The third young guy was standing and looking in the direction of the girls. He called out, offering help to the girls as they struggled to lift the heaviest trunk onto the roof of their car. Locklear watched as the young man made his way towards the girls and smiled to himself to think that chivalry, as outdated as it seemed to some, was not entirely dead.

Locklear watched as the kid approached the girls, his long black hair swaying confidently as he swaggered across the road. It was the Grateful Dead T-shirt that alerted him. Locklear tipped Mendoza's elbow and gave a slight nod in the young man's direction. Mendoza raised a hand up to shield her eyes from the sun, to get a better look at the figure that had caught Locklear's interest. Something about the movement caught the young guy's attention, perhaps the glint of her ring in the strong sunlight. He looked across the wide street and locked not onto Mendoza's ring but onto Locklear's face.

It seemed to Mendoza that the two guys stood for an eternity looking at each other. She recorded every movement as though they occurred in slow motion. The shock as it registered on the student's face, the minute movement of his feet as he rocked back and forth, deciding, she assumed, whether to run or stand his ground. The slow movements of his mouth as he mumbled and then, finally, the overwhelming look of confusion and fear that swept over his face.

He turned and began to run.

"*Hey!*" Locklear yelled as he gave chase.

One of the two guys sitting on the steps decided to help his buddy. He stood and stepped onto the pavement as Mendoza approached at a run.

"*Police! Sit the fuck down!*" she shouted.

She raced after her boss through the maze of buildings and smaller streets in the enormous campus.

Locklear gave chase for three blocks until the kid swung a left past the ID Weeks library. After two more blocks he swung a right and then left towards the Law School but at the last minute kept on straight until he reached Cherry Street where he disappeared into the traffic and narrow buildings on one of the campus's busier streets.

By the time Mendoza caught up with her boss, she found Locklear bent forwards, panting in the heat.

"I take it that was the second kid from the dig?" she gasped.

Locklear nodded. When he caught his breath the pair stood and looked into the distance. Jim Hunter was nowhere to be seen.

"Well, sarge. It looks like your face just scared the life out of yet another Native."

# Chapter 14

"Why didn't you mention this Hunter guy to Rosenberg?" Mendoza asked as she lay down on her bed in their shared hotel room on the other side of Vermillion.

Locklear lay on the bed nearest the window, fully clothed, with his hands beneath his head. The afternoon heat which bore down on the hotel window was intense and they had probably three more hours to wait before the day began to cool.

"Because it was the only card I had left. I didn't want him to know I knew Jim Hunter's identity. We don't know this Rosenberg guy. Maybe it would put the kid in danger."

"Well, at least you got us a good place to stay, sarge. Makes a change from motels."

"I'd have preferred a motel, Mendoza. You can come and go with less people seeing you. No large reception areas to walk through. It's safer. Only reason we're here is this was the last room left in town."

Mendoza nodded. "Who knew that the Historical Preservation Commission meeting would be on today? Or that it was so popular that the town's motels would be booked up? We should go. You never know, we might see people of interest there."

Locklear turned on his side to face Mendoza and nodded. "True."

"What's the plan for talking to Hunter? Should we stake out the dorm after dark, wait for him to get home?"

Locklear blew out and pushed himself into a sitting position. He swung his legs onto the floor to face Mendoza. He glanced briefly at her bare legs in the light cotton dress she had changed into then moved his eyes quickly to the wall on the opposite side of the room.

"Coffee?" he asked.

"Sure," she said.

Locklear moved to the coffee machine as Mendoza got up from her bed.

She turned the air conditioner up to full blast but it coughed and spluttered and then came to a complete halt.

"Well, no wonder this was the last room," she said as she took a seat at the table.

Locklear handed Mendoza a mug of steaming coffee. He took the remaining seat at the tiny table with his mug and faced into the stifling hot room.

"I saw the photo of Hunter on the college's system," he said. "He's a handsome kid but you could see in his face that he's had it tough. I drove through Pine Ridge once looking for a suspect. It was a long time ago. It's like nowhere else on earth you could imagine. There was something about the place that unnerved me. I can't explain it. I just had this ... this feeling ..." His voice trailed off.

"What feeling?"

Locklear shrugged. "I dunno. I felt this kind of ... of anger. I don't know where it came from. And when I drove through the streets looking for this guy my heart was beating so fast it was like I was afraid – but I wasn't. The suspect was pretty harmless, mostly supplied to feed his own habit. We wanted him in connection with selling in Rapid City but we were hoping he could hook us up with people higher up in the drug chain. I couldn't find him though. I said goodbye to the tribal police backing me, two good guys by the name of Grass. They were cousins. I remember that they were a lot older than me and were well respected in the community. Eddie was the younger of the two. Frank was the name of the older one. He was quieter. Never said much. When I got out of the car to say goodbye to them, I was shaking. I think they noticed but they said nothing. They lived together in a small clapboard a few miles out of town on a dirt road off the highway where they looked after their grandmother who raised them. I never met her but she must have been really old. Neither of them were married. I guess they'd be retired now."

"Could it have been just seeing the poverty Native Americans were living in?"

Locklear sighed. "I've driven through plenty of dumps where all kinds of people lived – Native, White, Black, Hispanic. I never reacted that way before and it hasn't happened since. I don't think that was it."

"Hmm. That's interesting. I take it from the expression on your face that we're going there?"

Locklear nodded. "This kid isn't on terra firma here. He sees cops he's going to think he's in trouble. I have to speak to him on home ground. Somewhere he feels safe.

We were going to have to check out that dig site anyway which is about ten miles from the reservation – so while we're there we'll ask around. See if we can find someone who knows him and will encourage him to speak to us."

"Sarge, can I put an idea to you?"

"Shoot," Locklear replied as he stood and poured himself another coffee.

"You told me that Sartre suggested to you that it was Native Americans who stole the artefacts from Richmond University," she said gently.

"And?"

"Well, Rosenberg said something very similar."

She waited for him to absorb what she was saying.

"Your point?"

"Would you give any consideration to the fact that the white guys aren't the bad guys here? That maybe a Native American is stealing the artefacts and maybe Rosenberg is trying to protect the artefacts? It's just one line of thinking ..."

Locklear turned and frowned. He placed his coffee cup roughly onto the table and sat down.

"Look, sarge, we have to at least give some thought to this. If Native Americans have been the ones stealing the artefacts, I understand. They feel that the property is theirs."

"It *is* theirs!" Locklear snapped.

"Sarge, you taught me to be objective. To consider all possibilities. You might be wrong here. Why would someone like Rosenberg risk such a successful career for this? Please, just think about it."

"You think Rosenberg is innocent?" Locklear barked.

Mendoza could see from his expression that her boss was not only surprised but shocked. "We have no evidence on the guy to the contrary, sarge."

"That guy was planning on groping you during a job interview. You think he's a good guy?"

"That makes him a creep, sarge, but not a thief."

"Well, in my eyes, Mendoza, it means the man has no boundaries. It means he's willing to use his position to get what he wants. And what do we know he loves? Artefacts. Digs. Rare finds."

Mendoza sighed. "OK, well, let's go through what we know."

Locklear nodded. "Whitefeather?"

"Innocent. Well, kind of ..." Mendoza replied. "Sartre?"

"Guilty," Locklear replied. "Torres? Lewis? Torres' husband – Hughes?"

"Innocent," she replied.

"Braff?"

"If he's not guilty of the theft of artefacts, then he's guilty of trying to kill Torres and Lewis. He might also have been the one to order Hughes on that drive-out."

"I guess we'll never know," Mendoza said. "Hunter?"

Locklear stood and pulled back the cheap venetian blind on the window and thought for a moment.

"Innocent until I know more," he replied.

Mendoza nodded.

"I guess I already know we differ on Rosenberg but how do you feel about Holton?" he asked.

Mendoza blew out. "Guilty, sarge. He tried to frame Lee."

"Yes, but I have a feeling that Alec Holton is clean. Or

at least he started out that way. One thing that does spark my interest is that Holton's cousin, Amelia Hirsch, and Rosenberg's son are both diplomats. It would give them the ability to fly in and out of countries unchecked. They could be carrying illegally purchased artefacts from anywhere in the world. We need something that connects them though."

"I could call O'Brien? Ask him to check the system and if nothing shows up do a general search."

"Good idea. Do it. And ask him to keep digging into what INTENT might mean. We still have no idea why Holton used that word."

"Why do you think Holton is clean, sarge? After what he did to Lee. Lying to the university about him. Dragging Lee on a search he had no permit for. His actions could cost Lee his career and if he's found guilty, his freedom."

"Something happened to Holton. I think he is, or was, a good man but someone got to him."

"Your White Ghost?" Mendoza suggested.

"Yes. *Our* White Ghost," he replied as he drained his coffee mug. "Rosenberg lied about not knowing him. I'm positive he's the man who arrived at Lee's dig site and I suspect that he's the same man who came to Cindy Geddis's home and scared her. We know he was at Whitefeather's motel and we know he killed Whitefeather in Richmond. We know all that and yet we don't know who he is or where he's from."

"Yeah, well, ghosts are hard to see, sarge."

Mendoza stood and walked to the bathroom at the far end of the room. She filled the sink with cold water and splashed it onto her face and neck. When she finished, she walked back and sat on Locklear's bed.

"OK, sarge. Rosenberg was our big lead and now that's a dead end. At least for now. Most of the rest of our players have one thing in common. Iraq. Hughes, Whitefeather, Lewis and Torres were there. We know Braff was there and this Walsh, the one you know, she obviously knows something or else she wouldn't have put pressure on the army to pay Lewis off. I think this kid Hunter is small potatoes. Could even be he was in the wrong place at the wrong time and that he has nothing to do with this case."

Locklear nodded. "Guess we need to pay Walsh a visit. We'll need to use our cards as there's no way we have enough cash to pay for flights to DC. So if someone is watching, we'll be revealing our whereabouts and our plans."

"We'll have to take the chance. I'd say we blew our low profile as soon as we walked into Rosenberg's office."

"OK, Mendoza, let's go see Walsh in DC. Then, we're going to Pine Ridge and I'm not looking forward to either."

# Chapter 15

The meeting of the South Dakota branch of the Historical Preservation Commission, whose mission was to preserve and restore the area's cultural and historic assets, was not attended by anyone Mendoza or Locklear were interested in. The pair separated and wandered around the room looking for Braff or Rosenberg, or better still, their White Ghost, but the meeting was attended by law-abiding people committed to preserving the area's culture. By nine pm Locklear and Mendoza tired of pretending to be out-of-town culture addicts who wanted to know more about the local area and left for a quick bite in the hotel's restaurant. Then they returned to their room.

Locklear had noticed during their dinner that Mendoza ordered a soda and had refrained from drinking. How long her newfound sobriety would last, he did not know.

"Be careful how much you tell O'Brien," he said before he got in the shower.

Mendoza sat on her bed and dialled O'Brien's number. She spoke quietly to the half-Irish, half-Native American man who, despite the fact that he had only recently joined the station, was already responsible for tracking the many paedophiles and white-collar criminals working out of Richmond – but who always shied away from the station's celebrations each time an offender was finally caught and locked up for child abuse or fraud.

At the end of her call, she asked O'Brien to check the records for anyone referred to as the White Ghost, although she already suspected that this was a nickname used by people the strange man had intimidated and that, if he did have a record, it would be under his real name.

Mendoza noticed how quiet O'Brien became when she gave a description of the man and wondered if her boss was right – if O'Brien was hiding something.

Still on the phone, Mendoza raised her eyebrows at Locklear who had exited from the bathroom fully dressed save for his bare feet. She watched as he put on his shoes and socks in the stifling hot room while she took down O'Brien's private cell number which he insisted she contact him on in future.

"You're going out?" she asked Locklear when she finished her call. "It's late! We have to catch a 6am flight to Washington from Sioux City. That's at least a forty-minute drive from here!"

"I know," Locklear replied quietly as he switched on the TV and lay on his bed with the remote control in his hand.

"Why are you dressed?"

Locklear didn't reply as he channel-surfed.

Mendoza stood and turned her back to Locklear. She raised her arms as she began to pull her cotton shift dress over her head to change for bed. She could sense Locklear tense.

"Get undressed in the bathroom, Mendoza!" he barked.

"Jeez, sarge, you'd think you'd never seen a woman in her underwear before," she joked as she pulled her nightie out of her suitcase.

Locklear did not reply. He found a news channel and raised the volume up as she went into the bathroom. Despite the noise emanating from the TV, he could hear her brush her teeth and turn the shower on. He tried not to imagine her naked under the cold shower but could not erase the image from his mind. He stood and opened the hotel-room door and wandered around the hotel's maze of corridors until he was sure she must be tucked into her bed.

When he finally returned she was turned on her side, facing away from him. He turned off the light and stripped down to his underwear, pulled back the cotton sheet and lowered himself into his bed.

"Night, sarge," she said.

Locklear could hear the mirth in those two words. His trooper was enjoying the impact she had on him and the knowledge of this did not rest easy with him. He made no reply and lay on his back, staring up at the ceiling.

When dawn broke, Locklear was already awake and was going over the case, worrying about the reception he'd get from Susan Walsh and listening to Mendoza's quiet snores. He closed his eyes and pretended to sleep while Mendoza got up and walked to the bathroom and tried to dress in the tiny room.

"Em, you can get dressed while I'm in here – we have a flight to catch," she called out from inside the locked bathroom.

Locklear stood, turned his back to the bathroom door

181

and changed his underwear quickly. As he pulled his jeans on, the bathroom door opened and Mendoza whistled from the doorway.

"Hmm ... not bad for an old guy," she said.

Locklear sighed and pulled a fresh shirt from his travel bag. Mendoza did not move from her position at the bathroom door and was smiling like the Cheshire Cat.

"Do you mind?" he asked.

"Not at all," she replied as she sat down on her bed. "Listen, sarge, we have a bit of time. What say you and I get down to it. Sort out the sexual tension between us here and now." She patted the bed.

"Wha ...what?" Locklear spluttered.

Mendoza laughed, lifted a pillow from her bed and threw it at Locklear.

"Jesus, sarge, I'm just screwing with you. You know you're not my type!"

"Mendoza!" Locklear barked.

"The look on your face, sarge! It was priceless. Really got you going there."

Locklear was still sulking as they packed up the car and headed towards the airport.

He ate a donut and drank his coffee in silence as Mendoza drove south on Route 29, a road she was by now becoming familiar with.

"You still sulking?" she asked.

"No," Locklear replied quietly.

"Did you ever date a colleague, sir?"

"I did. Too many times and it *always* ended badly," he replied. "Never ever eat where you work."

"Or shit where you sleep."

"Whatever. You get my point."

"What's the harm in a few casual dates with a fellow cop?"

"Every harm, Mendoza. Nothing, and I mean *nothing* good comes of being in a relationship with someone you work with. It screws everything up. You should know. You married a cop. A guy from your own precinct, which I might add resulted in you having to move to another station."

The smile faded from Mendoza's face. She nodded twice and gripped the steering wheel tighter. "You're right," she said quietly.

Locklear could hear the sadness in her voice. Since their meeting with Torres, he had sensed that something was bothering his trooper and he did not think that it was simply her ex-husband's shenanigans or her sick grandmother.

"What's going on with you?" he asked, although he really hoped she wouldn't answer. He didn't want to know. He didn't want to deal with anyone else's feelings when he couldn't even deal with his own.

"Nothing," she replied quietly.

"Is it about Manuel? Is that worrying you?"

"A little but it's OK."

"You know, your husband was a fool to do what he did. He was lucky to have you."

"Thank you," she replied meekly.

She could still feel his eyes on her as they drove through Junction City and headed further south towards Jefferson. She blinked to banish the small tears that had suddenly welled up in her eyes.

They reached Sioux City and followed the route further south to the Sioux Gateway Airport. She parked in the long-term car park, returned the keys of their hired car and followed Locklear into the terminal of the small bright airport which was used for both military and public flights. The five-hour American Eagle flight would stop briefly at Chicago O'Hare before taking the final leg of its journey to Washington.

As they sat into their seats, Locklear ordered them coffee and did not look at Mendoza as he took the steaming cup from the flight attendant and handed it to her.

"How are you feeling about seeing Walsh?" she asked.

Locklear inhaled. "Not good."

"You want to tell me about it?"

"Not really."

Mendoza picked up the in-flight magazine and leafed through it as she drank her coffee. Not long after, her boss was snoring loudly in the seat beside her. She smiled and touched his face. This time she knew he was really asleep as he did not move away.

As the plane landed in Ronald Reagan airport, DC, Locklear woke up and stretched.

"You ready for this?" Mendoza asked.

"I'm ready."

# Chapter 16

From the airport terminal, Locklear hailed a cab to take them to their hotel on South Capitol Street. He looked out of the cab window as it followed the George Washington Memorial Parkway, crossed the Potomac River and drove into the District of Columbia until it arrived at their hotel on Capitol Street.

Locklear and Mendoza checked into their rooms, which had an adjoining door, and dropped in their luggage. Fifteen minutes later they left the hotel and hailed a cab on 7th. The cab driver took Maine St SW for two blocks before swinging another right onto 4th street.

"You been to these offices before, Locklear?" Mendoza asked.

Locklear shook his head and stared out of the window as the cabbie swung a sharp left onto Potomac Avenue SW and then a right onto 2nd street on which the main gate to the Fort Lesley J McNair army base was located.

"And we don't have an appointment and you don't think Walsh will want to see you?"

"No, we don't have an appointment and, no, I don't

think Walsh will want to see me."

"Well, this *will* be interesting."

The cab slowed as it climbed up the steep concrete ramp and then came to a halt in front of the boom gate. A tall black army private approached the car and looked into the front passenger seat at Locklear. Mendoza, seated in the back, looked out the opposite window at the second guard, a short, serious-looking Hispanic man who eyed her suspiciously.

"Name?" the first guard asked Locklear.

"Detective Sergeant Locklear. This is my trooper Mendoza," he said as he saluted the young man.

The man looked Locklear over and noted the lack of a uniform. He glanced at Mendoza who was staring at the second guard who had not taken his eyes off her.

"How can I help you today, sir?"

"I'm here to see an old friend of mine. Staff Sergeant Joe Rubin."

"And he's expecting you, sir?" the guard asked as he glanced down at his clipboard.

"No, but I'm in town on official police business and thought I'd stop by and say hi. I'd say he'd be very disappointed if I didn't. He'll be even more disappointed with you if you don't let me in. What's your name, private?"

"Private Valentine, sir."

He stood back from the cab and went to the booth behind the boom gate. Lifting the phone, he spoke urgently into it. He was staring directly at Locklear. After a couple of minutes, he came out of the booth and towards the car.

Mendoza could hear her breathing quicken even though the worst thing that might happen would be that the two serious-looking guards would refuse them entry and direct the cab to reverse back out of the high-security compound.

"You'll have to walk from here, sir. No civilian transport allowed inside the base. You'll also have to surrender any weapons."

Locklear got out of the car and paid the cab driver.

"I'm not armed," Locklear said as he raised his hands upwards to allow the second guard to frisk him. "Trooper Mendoza is also unarmed."

"I thought you said you were on official police business?" the second guard asked.

"We are," Mendoza said as the guard frisked her roughly.

Private Valentine pointed Locklear to a set of double doors on the other side of a large and mostly empty parking lot.

"Go through those and sign in. Staff Sergeant Rubin will meet you just inside the door."

Locklear and Mendoza set off on foot towards the entrance.

"Sir, I hope you really do know this Rubin guy," Mendoza said as they neared the doors where a bald, thin man stood waiting inside a second security area.

"I do."

Locklear opened the door and placed his jacket, keys and wallet onto a table and walked through the metal detector. Mendoza followed and watched as Locklear shook the hand of the waiting man.

"I see the army has stepped up security," Locklear said.

"You can't be too careful these days," Rubin said with a smile.

Locklear nodded as Rubin shook hands with Mendoza.

Rubin gestured for them to follow him down a long narrow hallway lined with the dark closed wooden doors of rooms Mendoza assumed were offices. He opened the sixth door and stepped back to allow Mendoza and Locklear inside before he followed them and gently closed the door. He inhaled and shook his head before taking a seat behind the desk.

"It's been a long time, Locklear," he said.

Locklear nodded.

"I take it this isn't a social call."

"It's not."

Locklear looked at the desk which was overflowing with paperwork. Several more files lay on the ground around the desk and an open filing cabinet looked disorganised and overfull. The phone rang three times and stopped before shrilling again. Rubin ignored it.

"I can see you're busy, Joe, so I'll come right out with it. I want to see Susan Walsh. I know she's based in this building. Can you take me to her office?"

"I see," Rubin said quietly. He rubbed his hands together and pursed his lips. "Locklear, I don't think ..." he began, shaking his head.

"Look, Joe, it's important."

"Can I ask what it's about?"

"It's better you don't know."

"I see."

"Look, I know it's a big ask but you know me well enough to know I wouldn't be asking if I didn't have to."

"No, I expect you wouldn't. Is this something that's likely to get me in trouble?"

Locklear inhaled. "Well, that depends on how much she still hates me," he replied.

Mendoza looked at him, startled.

"Have you seen her since Kate's death?" Rubin asked.

"No."

"Even talked to her?"

"No."

"Well, then, I guess you're about to get me into a hell of a lot of trouble."

"I'll say I cajoled you. Or told you a pack of lies about me and Susan being good buddies."

"She won't buy that, Locklear. Anyone who knows you knows you don't lie."

"Well, I'm getting better at it, Joe. My colleague here, she's real good at it so I'm learning. Talked my way onto the base, didn't I?"

Rubin smiled. "OK. It's good to see you, Locklear," he said quietly.

He stood and opened his office door. He pulled a fob from a long chain around his neck and motioned for them to get into the secure elevator. He pressed the button for the fourth floor and sighed.

When the door opened, two guards standing on either side of the elevator door saluted Rubin. He returned the salute and walked in very quiet shoes to the end of a dark empty corridor until he reached a large desk which sat facing three empty chairs and a windowless wall. At the desk sat a young uniformed man wearing a private second-class insignia on his jacket. He stood and saluted but did not avert his eyes from the bare wall in front of him. To his right was a single door which Mendoza assumed was Walsh's office.

Rubin introduced the visitors and lied that they were on official police business. He motioned for them to sit on two of the empty chairs, wished Locklear good luck and walked away as quickly as he could. Locklear and Mendoza waited in silence while the young man moved his eyes from his paperwork occasionally to glance at them. Mendoza read the name tag on the nervous young man's chest. *Private M. Brodeur.*

"Sir?" he called to Locklear. "Do you have an appointment with Sergeant Major Walsh? She's not in her office at present and I don't seem to be able to locate your name on her itinerary." He had a slight Southern drawl.

Locklear stood and walked sharply to the desk. The man stood. Locklear glanced down at Walsh's appointment list and saw that the woman was due back at her office in ten minutes. He looked at Brodeur and noticed the sweat building on the man's face. He guessed that Susan Walsh was a tough superior and any mistakes on the part of her junior staff would be severely dealt with.

"No. I don't but ..." Locklear began, before his attention was drawn to the sound of high heels clicking along the expensively tiled corridor floor.

Brodeur swallowed. Mendoza heard him whisper 'Oh, Lord' to himself. Locklear looked down the hallway and watched Susan Walsh approach with two female privates, both carrying huge files while Walsh walked unburdened.

He looked the woman up and down. Susan Walsh had not changed that much since he had last seen her. She was, he figured, about five foot ten and her figure had remained slim, her forearms taut. Now in her late fifties he figured her short platinum-blond hair, which showed only a small amount of grey at her temples, was dyed. She wore little make-up and her fitted army skirt moved with her slim hips as she sashayed along the corridor at speed.

He knew the exact moment she recognised him. The serious, business-like expression on her face changed to surprise and then, as he had expected, to rage.

"*Get out!*" she shouted from the twenty-foot distance that remained between her and Locklear.

Mendoza stood while Brodeur placed his hands over his face.

Locklear dug his hands in his pockets but did not move.

"*I said get out!*" Walsh roared. "*You fuck! You complete fuck!*"

"Jeeze, sarge, guess you really pissed this one off," Mendoza whispered as she made her way to her boss's side.

Walsh seemed to suddenly become aware of the eyes of her subordinates on her.

"*Go!*" she screamed at the two young privates who turned and almost ran back to the elevator. "*You too!*" she screamed at the two privates who stood on guard on opposite sides of the elevator.

Brodeur pretended to tidy some loose sheets on his desk.

"*And you!*" she screamed at her secretary. "*You incompetent fool!*" she added as Brodeur lifted his briefcase and ran past her to join the other scurrying rats to the elevator.

When only Mendoza and Locklear remained, Walsh marched up and stopped with her face only inches from the sergeant's face.

"How dare you come here, to my place of work? How fucking dare you? Did you remember that her anniversary is only days away? Oh yes, sure you did. It was both your birthdays. Your shared special day – isn't that what Kate called it?"

Locklear's face remained impassive as he waited for Walsh to finish.

Mendoza felt a small smile rising at the corner of her lips. Locklear, she reasoned, was right. He would make a lousy boyfriend, impossible to argue with, and therefore make up with.

Her boss's silence only seemed to further anger the woman. Walsh drew back her hand and slapped Locklear hard in the face. Mendoza moved in and caught Walsh by the wrist as the woman tried to deliver a second blow.

Locklear did not move.

"*Now just a fucking minute!*" Mendoza yelled.

Walsh turned to face Mendoza. "Take your goddamn hands off of me!" she spat.

She turned back to Locklear and her eyes suddenly filled with tears.

"I see you still like them young," she whispered.

Locklear lowered his head. "Susan, this is my colleague, Trooper Mendoza. I ... I didn't come here about Kate."

"Then what? Why the fuck did you come here if it's not to apologise for what you did to my sister? You know you broke my father's heart? Do you know he spent the entire time at Kate's funeral looking around the crowd for you? He thought you'd be heartbroken. He felt sorry for you. Wondered how you'd cope. But you coped. I can see you got on with your life." She glanced sideways at Mendoza. "You always did like women with dark, smouldering looks," she added through gritted teeth.

192

"Look, lady," said Mendoza, "for the last time I'm his colleague. Nothing more."

"You'll respect my office by addressing me as Sergeant Major!" Walsh spat.

"Well, I'm not in the army so I'll address you any way I please and, also, do you expect respect after that outburst?"

"It's OK, Mendoza, I deserved it," Locklear said.

Walsh inhaled and stepped back. She looked at her right hand as if her appendage had launched its own battle against the man in front of her and had not been directed by her to do so.

"What do you want?" she said, quieter now.

"I want to talk about Private Patrick Lewis. I want to talk about how and why you sorted his army pension out. I want to talk about missing artefacts. I want to talk about Iraq."

"But not about Kate?" she whimpered.

Locklear looked at his shoes. "I'm sorry, I really am," he said quietly.

Walsh looked at Mendoza but could not meet the officer's steely gaze. She opened her door and beckoned for Locklear to come inside.

"You wait outside," she barked at Mendoza.

Mendoza mock-saluted which earned her an angry glare from Locklear. He went inside and closed the door quietly behind him.

At the end of the corridor Mendoza noticed movement. She looked up to see that Rubin had reappeared and was skulking in the corridor with his briefcase in his hand. He smiled weakly at Mendoza.

"Just checking to see if Locklear is still alive! I see he got inside."

"Just about," Mendoza replied with a grin.

"OK, well, think the best thing for me to do is to make myself scarce," he replied weakly.

Mendoza nodded. "Think so."

She walked to where he stood.

"So you knew Sergeant Locklear in the army?"

"Yes. We were both very young – still teenagers when we joined," Rubin said simply.

"What kind of soldier was he?"

"The best," Rubin replied sincerely.

"Why did he leave?"

Rubin shrugged his shoulders and sighed. "He didn't really talk about it but I heard his mother was unwell. There was no-one else to take care of her."

"Can you tell me anything about this Kate woman? About what happened?"

The elevator door opened, Rubin stepped in and pressed the button for the ground floor.

"I think you'll have to ask Locklear himself," he said as the elevator door closed.

Mendoza walked back to the seats and sat heavily on the hard surface. Walsh had obviously calmed because she could hear no voices coming from the room. She lifted her phone and tried to call Santy but there was no signal in the building. She sighed and sat back into the chair and waited for her boss to return.

# Chapter 17

Thirty-five minutes after Locklear entered the office of Sergeant Major Walsh, he exited, looking exhausted. Mendoza stood and followed him down the corridor. Together they got into the elevator where the two privates had once again taken up guard and made their way to the ground floor. Mendoza opened the door for Locklear who had still not spoken one word. She walked with him onto the main road and hailed a cab to their hotel.

"You going to tell me what happened?" she asked.

"I'm starving, Mendoza. Can we just go get something to eat and then we'll talk."

"Sure."

As they settled into a booth in Bert's Diner, Mendoza slurped on a coke while Locklear drank two strong coffees. She thought she noticed a slight tremor in his hands as he lifted the heavy mug to his dry lips.

"I guess seeing Walsh was pretty hard on you," she began.

Locklear nodded.

"Well, at least she didn't think you were my father.

That's a plus, right?" she said as she tried to coax her boss out of the dark mood he appeared to have descended into.

He didn't respond.

"What did you find out about Walsh's involvement in the whole artefacts thing?" she asked.

Locklear lifted the burger from his plate and took a huge bite. Mendoza waited while he chewed on the rubbery meal which she had discarded minutes earlier in favour of the diner's home-made apple pie. He swallowed and took another gulp of his coffee.

"Walsh isn't involved," he said. "I never thought she was. She said the army's legal department asked Torres to sign a disclaimer, saying she'd accept a full pension in exchange for withdrawing her claim that the army was involved in the illegal transportation and sale of artefacts from Iraq."

"But Torres refused the deal."

"Yes. Walsh said she phoned her personally but Torres wasn't backing down."

"I bet the army didn't put any of this in writing?"

"Bet not," Locklear replied.

"Smart."

"And Whitefeather? Did she have any involvement with him?"

Locklear shook his head. "Albert was flown home long before Walsh left Iraq. Susan said she never heard from him again. She never handled any paperwork for him, said she didn't even know he was dead."

"Do you believe her? Lewis said Whitefeather wrote to Walsh."

"I don't have any reason not to. Torres wrote to Walsh

196

asking for her dishonourable discharge to be retracted but the army refused. Walsh brought the case up as far as she could but she came up against a brick wall. She wrote to Torres and said there was nothing she could do. She never heard from Torres again."

"I guess that's when Torres gave up and hit the bottle," Mendoza replied. "Does she know anything about this Rosenberg guy or that Braff had been working in the university with him?"

"She said she never had any contact with Braff after he left the army. Said she'd no idea where he was or what he was doing."

"What about our 'weird ghost' dude?"

Locklear shook his head. "Susan was upset for most of the time I was in there. When I mentioned our 'White Ghost' she smiled a little. Maybe it was even a laugh. Looked like she thought I'd gone mad."

"She's hardly a beacon of sanity herself. Jeeze, sarge, she went from 0 to 90 when she saw you."

"She has good reason."

"You going to tell me about it?" Mendoza asked as Locklear shoved his plate away.

"I'm tired, Mendoza. I think I'll go back to the hotel and lie down," he said as he stood and threw a $20 bill on the table.

She stood to follow him. "Sarge? Are you OK?"

"I'm alright, Mendoza. I just need time to think."


By late evening, Mendoza had tired of wandering the streets of D.C and took a long walk back to the hotel where she hoped she'd find her boss in better mood. She had not enjoyed seeing the White House for the first time as she thought she would nor was she overwhelmed by the Washington Monument or the Lincoln Memorial. Her thoughts were not with her surroundings but with her boss and the dark mood his visit to Susan Walsh seemed to have provoked.

She stopped off in the hotel's bar and drank four beers slowly before taking the elevator to their adjoining rooms on the sixth floor. She went into her room and took her time showering, hoping that by the time she'd finished Locklear would be ready to talk, but when she finished there was no still no sign of life coming from his room.

She walked to the door that separated them and knocked lightly but he did not answer.

"Sarge?" she said as she turned the handle but the door was locked. "Sarge?"

"I'm OK, Mendoza. I'll see you tomorrow," he said.

Mendoza waited on the other side of the door for a moment or two, thinking about what Locklear needed right now as opposed to what he wanted. And what he needed, she reasoned, was someone to tell his sorry tale about Kate Walsh to. Something he had obviously not done in the thirty or more years since the woman had died.

She left her room and tapped lightly on the door leading into Locklear's room on the hotel corridor. She heard rustling and then the sound of feet coming towards the door. She heard the lock unclick and footsteps moving back across the room. She turned the handle, pushed the door in and waited for her eyes to adjust to the darkened room.

"Are you OK?" she asked the still body which lay fully clothed on the large bed in the middle of the room, facing away from her.

Quietly, Mendoza crept to the bed and put her hand on Locklear's shoulder. He flinched and tensed so she backed off and sat on the hard chair in the room.

"Can I do anything for you?"

"No," he replied quietly.

"Did you eat?"

"Not hungry," he replied.

Mendoza remained in her seat and rested her eyes on the loud patterned carpet beneath her chair.

"Do you want me to go?" she asked.

She heard him sniff the air and sigh – a sign, she assumed, of his displeasure that he could smell beer off her.

"Kate was twenty-three the day she died. June 21st," he said.

Mendoza did not move.

"She'd only been with the force two years. She'd joined shortly after her 21st birthday. I was a few years older and there was a world of difference between us. I'd joined the army when I was not much more than eighteen years old. Left three years later and joined the police in Rapid City. My mother died and I travelled around, eventually got a post in New York. I was already a heavy drinker and Kate hardly drank at all. She was innocent until she met me. She'd moved to New York from New Jersey to attend college but had dropped out and joined the force. She'd had a settled, safe, typical childhood whereas I'd had the opposite. Her dad had been a cop in her hometown. Her mom was a full-time homemaker. Susan was her older sister and was already in the army when I met Kate. When Kate graduated police training, she was sent to the same station as me. I spent most of my off-duty time drinking but somehow she was interested in me. We start dating, if you could call it that. She thought there was more to the relationship that there was, and I didn't have the guts to tell her otherwise. I was having too much of a good time. Most of the other cops at the station couldn't believe she chose me. She could have had any of the guys there. She was beautiful. She and Susan looked nothing alike. Kate was short with black hair, brown eyes. She was much softer in temperament than Susan, who took a fairly instant dislike to me when she visited Kate in New York. Anyway, one night I was following up on a case and I was due to meet Kate later on at a restaurant. It was June 21st. We have the same birthday and she had planned a special night. She'd planned it a week or so beforehand and just kept talking about it like it was important to her. I went along with it even though I hate birthdays. My mom always hated my birthday coming up and I guess it rubbed off on me. She always went into a morose state. I never found out why. Anyway, there was this black kid, Tyrone Johnson. His mom was a heroin addict. She took off, left him alone. I think he was only fourteen or fifteen years old at the time. Kept running away from social services, foster homes, juvenile residential services. Every time they picked him up on the streets and took him into care, he ran away and got back to the only life he knew. Eventually he got hooked himself. He was probably born hooked. It was only a matter of time before he started using. He began pushing for this guy Lombardi."

"The guy you met up with again in Harrisonsburg?"

"Yeah," Locklear replied quietly. "My partner and I had got Tyrone on board as an informer. We worked with social services, got him a small place to live in the projects but we knew that some nights he was still sleeping in this squat with a few other kids. It was like he didn't know any other kind of home. But it looked like he was going to make it. He was about seventeen or eighteen by then. I'd been trying to get Lombardi for months. I was supposed to meet the kid that night before I met up with Kate. He had phoned the station earlier to say he had big information on a shipment coming in. The kid never showed up. I checked his apartment but he wasn't there so I walked down to the squat. I found him there with a bullet in his chest, a look of surprise on his face. I sat with him until the ambulance arrived but he was already dead. Probably died instantly alone in a dump with rats crawling all over the place. He never had a chance. From the moment he was born he was fighting to stay alive and his life was cut short that day because Lombardi obviously found out that Tyrone was ratting on him. I felt responsible."

"Did they ever get Lombardi on it?"

"No. He had a watertight alibi. Three other hoodlums said they were playing pool with him from earlier that evening until the early hours of the following morning."

"That's pretty sad," Mendoza offered.

"Anyway, I forgot all about Kate and found myself a bar to drown my sorrows in. Six whiskeys later my partner came in to tell me Kate had been killed by a mugger. Took her purse, shot her in the stomach and left her there to die in an alleyway. When the autopsy results were released to her parents, her dad phoned me to tell me he was sorry for me, for Kate and for the baby."

"Baby?"

"The coroner said that Kate was about two months

pregnant. I didn't know. No-one did. I think she must have been going to tell me that night. I ... I didn't know."

"You couldn't have known that would happen, sarge. You shouldn't blame yourself."

"Maybe Tyrone would have ended up dead from heroin eventually – but Kate, I should have been there. If I had been there no-one would have tried to mug her. She'd still be alive."

"You don't know that. Maybe you'd both have been shot."

Locklear made no reply.

"So Susan Walsh feels you are responsible for her sister's death and for the death of the child?"

"I guess so. But it was what happened after that I think she'll hold against me forever."

Mendoza waited for Locklear to tell her the rest of the story. She stood and turned on a soft lamp on a table by her chair and watched as his body rose and fell and his breathing became heavier. She knew this part of the story was the hardest part for him.

"Her funeral was back in New Jersey. There was a wake in the family home. I couldn't bring myself to go there. I couldn't face seeing her in a coffin. I checked into a local hotel and started drinking. The next morning I was still drunk and wisely decided not to attend the funeral. I had met her father, Brian, a few times when he came to New York. He was a good guy. I think he thought I was going to ask Kate to marry me. I wasn't. Anyway, you heard Susan saying Brian was looking for me at the funeral. He didn't have any sons. I think ... I think he liked me and I let him down. I let Kate down and Tyrone. I let the force down and I let myself down. I hardly remember those first few weeks after the funeral, I was drinking so much. I'd arrive to work, do my shift. Go to a bar afterwards and didn't leave until I was so drunk I couldn't remember getting home. A lot of the guys at the station stopped talking to me. Word had got around that Kate was waiting for me and had left the restaurant to head back to her apartment alone when I didn't show. I didn't blame them. I was drinking so much in the end that I don't know how I didn't lose my job. Eventually I got a transfer to Richmond. I got sober and, well, here I am."

Locklear fell silent, his story now complete.

Mendoza stood and moved to where her boss lay. She leant over and kissed the back of his head.

"Don't, Mendoza. Please don't," he whispered.

Mendoza lightly brushed her lips off his temple.

"What are you doing?" he asked.

"Just being your friend," she replied.

Mendoza ran her hand through his thick black mane and tried to suppress the urge to lie down with him, to hold him, to have him hold her. She took her hand away and looked at him. He had not turned to meet her eyes.

She walked to door and turned the handle.

"Night, sarge. See you tomorrow," she said as she walked out of the room and left her boss to his memories.

# Chapter 18

"You ready for breakfast?" Mendoza asked as she opened her door to Locklear who came in and sat in the only chair in her bedroom.

"Yes," he responded quietly.

Mendoza moved to the bathroom, applied her make-up and tied her long hair into a tight bun on top of her head. He watched through the open door as she deftly applied pins into her thick mane and hung the silver cross, which she wore most days, around her neck. She eyed him through the mirror as she tucked stray wisps of hair into place.

She turned on her phone. It beeped twice but she had something on her mind that she needed to say now before their focus returned to the case and off their troubled personal lives.

She took one final look at herself in the mirror and walked into the room.

"I think we need to talk," she said.

She sat on her bed which faced the chair Locklear sat in. He turned the chair slightly sideways, moving his body away from her.

"Last night, when I kissed you, I felt something," she said. "Something I shouldn't. When I was comforting you, it felt good, it felt right ... I think that I'm beginning to develop feelings for you."

"Mendoza, don't say that," he pleaded as he shifted uncomfortably his chair.

"No, hear me out. Please."

Locklear looked at his shoes and thought about how much they needed to be polished.

Mendoza persisted. "I think I know what's going on."

Locklear looked up and glanced briefly into her eyes. He looked away.

"What's that?" he asked.

Mendoza sighed. "I think it's because of Manuel's marriage. Not that I still have feelings for him. I don't. But I think it's because he's moved on and I haven't. I think it's because I'm alone. I'm lonely, actually. I've seen the way you look at me sometimes and I guess it stirred something in me. Something inappropriate. I never set out to make you uncomfortable last night. You're my boss and I respect you. I don't want to lose that. These feelings are confusing for me and I don't know what to do with them but please don't let me push you away. I need to work through this. I need you in my life. I need your respect."

"Mendoza. I –"

"I know. You've built this wall around yourself because of what happened to Kate and the rest of the women you feel you let down. So I have something else to say to you, sarge. You're wrong. You need friends. We all do. You need affection, physical affection. It's a human need. The need to be touched. Don't shy away from it if it presents itself.

205

Don't be afraid of what it will bring. You're stronger now. You've put your drinking behind you and you have a lot to give. Don't waste the rest of your life because of one mistake. Don't do that to yourself."

She stood and stretched out her arms towards him. Locklear stood and gently accepted her embrace. Three seconds later he had returned to his seat and fixed his eyes on the window.

Mendoza began to throw the last of her clothes in her suitcase.

"I need us to be OK," she said. "I hated seeing you like that yesterday."

"We are OK, Mendoza."

"I think there's something you need to do before we leave DC."

"What's that?" he asked without moving his eyes from the window which he was pretending held something of interest for him.

"You need to go back to see Susan Walsh. You need to at least try to make your peace with her."

"No way, Mendoza. Look, we almost didn't get onto the base yesterday. I can't ask Rubin to get me inside again. He's a much lower rank that Walsh. She'll have him crucified."

"I've thought that out," she said.

A small smile washed over Locklear's tired face. "You have?"

"Yes." Mendoza grinned. "We're going to go to the base together. I'll wait in the cab while you ask to see Walsh directly. If she says no, we'll head to the airport, but at least you'll know you tried. Might be the only chance you get to do this, Locklear. Don't pass on it."

Locklear groaned. "OK, I'll try."

When the cab reached Fort Lesley J McNair army base, Mendoza, good to her word, sat in the cab while Locklear spoke with Private Valentine again. From the rear passenger-seat it looked to Mendoza as if Locklear was telling Valentine the truth about why he wanted to see Walsh. Valentine stood with a deep frown on his face for the entire conversation without moving. When Locklear stopped talking, the army private left him standing on the curb and phoned from his hut.

Locklear glanced towards Mendoza and she smiled reassuringly at him. It was the least confident, most nervous she had ever seen her boss. There was something so lost in the expression on his face that it hurt her to watch. This was clearly unfamiliar territory for Locklear who was not used to apologising for his mistakes, past or present.

A minute later Valentine exited the hut and pointed in the direction of the building, obviously giving Locklear the same directions as he had given them the day before. The second guard frisked Locklear before he was allowed to head in the direction of the double doors.

Mendoza, bored and anxious to know what was happening, tried to chat to the cab driver who was listening to a radio programme. He gave her two or three short polite replies before glancing backwards at her with a look that told her he wasn't looking for conversation.

Mendoza lifted her phone out of her bag and noticed the small envelope on the screen which told her she had

207

messages. She dialled in and listened as O'Brien told her to call him, urgently.

She got out of the car and walked twenty feet in the direction of the roadway. She phoned O'Brien's cell phone.

"What's up?" she said.

"Wait."

She assumed he was moving to a more private location. She listened as O'Brien whispered to her. The information he had for her was upsetting and she was not looking forward to dampening Locklear's mood, especially if the meeting with Walsh didn't go well.

She returned to the cab and thought about her conversation with her boss that morning and wondered what he had made of her revelations. He had not said much but, then, he never did. It was hard to know what was going on inside his troubled and lonely head, but she hoped what she said in some way eased his mind. It had not, she felt, eased hers. The feelings of attraction she now had for him continued and she had played down their impact on her for his sake. She hoped her feelings would fade as these kinds of feelings tended to do with time, or sooner if Locklear managed to piss her off which he was more than capable of doing.

When Locklear finally arrived back at the cab, Mendoza looked at the clock on the dash and noticed that he had been gone for over half an hour. She hoped this was a good sign. He slid back into the front passenger seat and glanced quickly at her. She tried to read his face but all she could see was that her boss looked less anxious coming out of the base than he was going in.

"It went well?" she asked.

"As well as I expected it would," he replied flatly.

Mendoza did not ask any further questions and wondered if her boss would ever tell her what had taken place in Walsh's office. By the look on his face, she didn't really need to know. He had obviously made some sort of peace, however small, with Kate Walsh's sister.

At the airport terminal a few minutes later, Mendoza pulled on Locklear's arm to slow his entrance into the departure lounge.

"Look, I couldn't say anything in the cab in front of the driver but I had two missed calls from O'Brien last night. I spoke to him this morning. It seems Carter was back in jail."

"What?" Locklear snapped.

"It's OK. When O'Brien couldn't reach us, he took the initiative to phone Kowalski. O'Brien told him everything and Kowalski got Lee bailed again."

"When did this happen?"

"Yesterday. Seems Diaz and Hill got a tip-off about the handle of the knife that was used to kill Holton being in Carter's home. An anonymous caller told Diaz exactly where to find it."

"Anonymous, my ass. It's Rosenberg. He's screwing with us. He's just giving us the finger to let us know he's calling the shots."

"Maybe, sarge. But the handle had Carter's prints all over it. It doesn't look good."

"Of course his prints were on it. He was studying it in the lab. It was one of the items that went missing. Someone's been holding onto this to use it because we are getting close to the truth."

"I'm sure you're right, sarge, but that doesn't explain how it was in his house. It makes him look guilty of both stealing the artefact and then using the blade from it to kill Holton. The handle it seems is still worth a lot without the blade. It's carved and in good condition. O'Brien said it would fetch around $30,000."

"How does O'Brien know about this stuff?"

Mendoza shrugged. "Because he's a weird clever guy who uses all his downtime sitting in his apartment scanning the internet?"

"Does O'Brien know where Carter went?" Locklear asked.

"No – he said when Lee was leaving the station he wouldn't tell him where he was going."

"Carter's finally cottoning on."

"You don't suspect O'Brien, sarge? I mean, if he didn't call us with this information, we wouldn't know what was going on."

Locklear thought for a moment. "Did he mention the photo you sent? The one of the protest at the dig site? You'll recall that I noticed someone familiar in the photo."

Mendoza half smiled. "He did."

"And what did he say?"

"He said the photo doesn't show his best side!"

Locklear smirked and shook his head.

"I don't know how you recognised him, sarge. He looks completely different."

"By keeping my eyes open and by expecting the unexpected."

"So, you *do* trust him?"

"Jury is out but I guess he has a right to his political

210

views. And to protest. He should have told Benson though about his connection to the case, however small it was. What else did he say?"

"He still doesn't know anything about INTENT. He said he's tried everything."

Locklear exhaled. "OK. What else?"

"Well, this part will perk you up. It seems Amelia Hirsh and Josef Rosenberg do indeed know each other."

"Oh, yeah?"

"O'Brien did some digging and checked passenger lists for the past few years."

"You can do that without a warrant?"

"Seems O'Brien knows how. They've been in a lot of the same cities at the same time. Occasionally on commercial flights but mostly on private flights for diplomatic use. In the last four years they've travelled together on a total of seventeen flights."

"Where to?"

"Egypt, Greece, China, Iraq and Turkey. All supposedly for diplomatic purposes. If they were there to traffic valuables in and out of these countries, they covered their tracks well."

"All of those countries have vast amounts of valuable antiques," Locklear replied.

"Yes. There's more. It seems young Tommy Rosenberg is getting in on the family business. Before he enrolled in USD last year he travelled back and forth from Paris to Iran six times. Since he left the USA a few weeks ago, he's flown to Paris and twice more between Iran and Paris. Each time for only a couple of days."

"What else?"

"O'Brien had the smarts to check Tommy's future flight plans and it seems he's due to fly into JFK from Cairo just after 1am on the morning of June 19th. His next flight is a five-hour UA flight to South Dakota which leaves two hours later and, allowing for the time difference, should get him into Rapid City a little after 9am. He'll be travelling with a partner. It's Braff. Seems he did move jobs as Rosenberg said but it was to take a low-level position at the American consulate. Seems Tommy's got himself a similar position."

"Interesting. We may just try to meet young Tommy and Braff off the plane. See if we can scare them a little."

"But I kept the best for last!" Mendoza beamed.

'Yeah?'

"Amelia Hirsch is married to ..."

"Come on, Mendoza, we'll miss the flight."

"To one Gerard Sartre."

"What?" Locklear frowned. "Sartre said his wife studied politics in Richmond before getting a post in London. That was years ago. They've had a long-distance marriage ever since."

"Doesn't sound like much of a marriage. Unless it's not really a marriage but more of ... an arrangement?"

"Possibly. It gives her an excuse for flying in and out of the US carrying God knows what. I wonder why Sartre didn't mention that he was related to Holton by marriage? Surely he knew I'd find out sooner or later?"

"I'm sure he did," she said. "But if he told you when you were in his office we'd be a lot further along in the investigation than we are now. By not telling you, he slowed us down."

Locklear thought about what their next move might be.

Mendoza beat him to it. "Henschel said Holton's ex-partner David Horowitz moved to DC. Maybe we should speak with him while we're here? See if he knows anything about Hirsch's relationship with Holton? I think she said he was working with the *Washington Post*."

"Good idea. Listen, I'll take the flight to Sioux City and I'll hire a car and drive to Pine Ridge. See if I can find this Jim Hunter kid. You stay here and talk to this Horowitz guy."

Mendoza nodded. Some time spent apart from each other would, she felt, be good. For both of them.

"Good work, Mendoza. O'Brien too. Least now I know why he's helping us ... and risking his career into the bargain. Guess O'Brien's Native American blood is strong enough for him to want to put a stop to the sale of sacred Native American artefacts."

"And is yours, sarge?"

Locklear looked into the departure hall and squinted at the screen to check that his 1pm flight was still due to take off on time.

"I just want to put the bad guy away, Mendoza, no matter who he is."

Mendoza stood in the departure hall as Locklear waved goodbye to her. She waved back and exited. Hailing a cab, she directed the driver back to the hotel they had been staying at. She was in no humour to sleep somewhere new again tonight. On route, she called the telephone directory for the phone number of the *Washington Post* and then dialled the office and asked to speak with Horowitz. When she was put through to another person, the male employee told her that Horowitz had resigned from his post at the newspaper. She asked for a cell-phone number but the man refused to provide this. She then told the man that she was only looking for Horowitz to ask about an ex-partner of his who had died. Her comment was met with silence until the man agreed to take her number and get Horowitz to phone her. Mendoza thought about the danger of giving the stranger her burner-phone number but she needed to speak with Horowitz so she reluctantly called out the number.

She hung up and looked out at the traffic as the cab weaved its way in and out of the impressive city streets. She sighed and knew that she was already missing her boss and the vulnerability those feelings aroused in her did not sit well with how she saw herself now. She had been dependant on Manuel when she was very young and had put the reliance she'd had on him down to youth and inexperience. Now those feelings were back. It was a long time since she'd cared about a man in that way. Mendoza did a second search and looked for gay bars in the city. She found two close to her hotel and made a decision to have some fun that night. She tried to phone her mother's cell phone but found it was engaged. She left a brief message telling her that she loved her and to get Santy to phone her before he went to bed that night.

When she arrived back at the hotel, Mendoza checked into a more expensive room than her last one and ran herself a bath. She soaked for about an hour and when she got out she dried her hair roughly and ordered room service. When her meal finally arrived, she ate ravenously in her bathrobe. With nothing else she could do, she sat on the bed and turned on the TV but turned it off again when she found the only entertainment on offer was reality TV shows where people were expected to eat bugs and a cringe-inducing amateur dancing competition where people who couldn't dance strutted their stuff in front of a live TV audience.

She checked her phone three times but there was still no word from Horowitz. Then she lay down and fell into a deep, satisfying sleep. She woke briefly and looked at the time on her cell phone. It was 6pm. She had been asleep for about four hours. She checked her phone but there were still no messages. She closed her eyes again and slowly drifted back to sleep.

When she finally woke, it was to the sound of a loud bang against the outer wall of her room. Mendoza looked at her phone again and found that two more hours had passed. She got out of bed and tiptoed to the door. She opened it and saw that the hotel maid's cart had crashed into the corridor wall.

The Hispanic maid blushed and pulled the cart away.

"*Lo siento*," she said.

"*No te preocupes*," Mendoza replied.

The shy smile from the maid reminded Mendoza of her mother who had arrived in America to work in a hotel in Richmond without a word of English and knowing nobody in the large city. She wondered again why her mom had not returned her call.

She closed the door and texted her mother to check that everything was OK. An hour later she received two texts at the same time. She read the first which was from her mother saying Mendoza's grandmother's condition had

215

worsened and she had returned with her to hospital by ambulance. She said she had Santy with her and not to worry but that she was not allowed to have the phone on in the intensive-care section. She finished by saying that Grandma was awake and wanted her to tell her daughter to make sure she got the most out of life and to enjoy it. The second was from Locklear and consisted of four words.

"Arrived OK. Be careful."

She texted "OK" to Locklear and sent her mother a more detailed text saying she would pray for her grandma and to please let her know how things were going. Mendoza thought about her ninety-year-old grandmother's words and decided she would put her advice into action as there was no point in moping around the hotel room, waiting. Mendoza checked the address for the bar she had looked for earlier. She put on the sexiest outfit she could find and applied a heavy layer of make-up. Outside the hotel, she hailed a cab and directed the driver to deliver her to Cobalt on R Street NW and 17th.

When she arrived at the club, the exterior did not look as she had expected it to. The five-storey building on the corner of R Street and 17th had an old colonial feel to it and was similar to many of the surrounding buildings in the old part of the city. Outside, wooden tables were occupied mostly by gay men in leather outfits. Two large motorbikes were parked beside one of the tables. She stopped to take a look at them. The door opened and loud dance music poured onto the street. She got to the door before it closed and stepped inside. Neon lights flashed across the entrance and the music was deafeningly loud. A drag queen passed her followed by another in a similarly outrageous outfit. She watched as they set up their stage for the night in the main bar. Mendoza couldn't have imagined talking Locklear into coming here with her. Not that her boss was homophobic. It was something that she admired about him. Locklear did not see colour or religion or sexual orientation. The man did not judge others about anything except their behaviour and that, she figured, was OK, because applying the law and knowing right from wrong was his job and was something he had devoted his life to. Mendoza shook her head and tried to exorcise Locklear from her mind. She was looking for a good time and was determined to find it.

She climbed the stairs and wandered through three more bars. One looked like any other bar in Richmond. It was full of men all staring at a football match on a large TV screen. Most of the men were holding beers and no-one seemed to be talking to anyone. She wandered down another corridor where loud music boomed. The crowd was smaller and there was a mix of men and women inside, some of whom were dancing on a small neon-lit floor in the centre of the room. She walked to the cocktail bar at the far end of the room and ordered herself a White Russian. The bartender put the cool drink in front of her and she swivelled her chair around to watch the dancers. There were six women on the dance floor. Two of the women were dancing close together and looked like a couple. Two other women looked as though they were hoping to get to know each other better. One of the women who danced alone suddenly drew up her hand and slapped a man beside her for reasons Mendoza had not observed. The woman stormed off and left a dazed and surprised man standing alone on the floor. The sixth woman smiled over at Mendoza and left the floor. She walked to the bar and ordered herself a whiskey. Mendoza swung around and looked at the woman in the mirror behind the bar. She was taller than Mendoza and wore a bright red jumpsuit and high-heeled red shoes. She had thick wavy light-brown hair and wore large dangling earrings. Her lips were painted the same shade of red as her clothes and the smell of her perfume wafted over to Mendoza.

"Hi," she said.

"Hi," Mendoza replied.

"I haven't seen you here before."

Mendoza grinned. "That's some line."

The woman laughed and turned to look at the slapped man on the dance floor who had started to dance by himself.

"I'm Ann. I'm here with my brother. Him."

"Oh," Mendoza replied, now unsure if Ann was accompanying her gay brother to a bar. "Is he OK?" She glanced again at the man who did not seem to mind dancing alone.

"Yeah. He's a bit of an ass but I don't like coming to these places alone. He usually tries to chat a gay woman up and gets nowhere. That's the second time this month he's got a slap."

Mendoza laughed. "I'm Jo," she said.

Ann shook her hand warmly. "Drink?"

Sure."

# Chapter 19

More than twelve hundred miles away, Locklear was four hours into his six-hour drive along Route 20 from the airport at Sioux City to the outskirts of Pine Ridge reservation where he hoped to start by talking with one of the Grass cousins, if, indeed, either of the retired tribal cops were still alive. He relaxed as he drove through the adjoining state of Nebraska, taking in the flat green plains of Breslau, then Orchard, through Inman and O'Neill – towns whose names recorded the plantation of European settlers onto Native lands, a people that were at first welcomed and taught how to live among the Badlands and survive the harsh winters, how to hunt, eat, and thrive in the remote and often barren lands. It was a relationship that was to turn sour with the mass influx of more settlers, with Government-forced evictions and the slaughter of great herds of buffalo to starve out the indigenous people and force them onto tiny parcels of land which became known as reservations. Locklear tried not to think about the sad history of the proud people who once lived with the land, and focused on the beauty around him as his car snaked in a northerly direction through the town of Valentine then westwards through the small Nebraskan towns of Kilgore, Nenzel and then Cody.

Night had fallen and the darkening blue sky lit up with red and pink hues as he turned right at the town of Merriman and onto Route 73 towards Martin. Locklear joined Route 18 which would take him on the last leg of his journey. He slowed as he searched for Big Foot Trail which would take him by Wounded Knee where, if he remembered rightly, the elderly cousins lived in a small house off a dirt road turn-off. He drove through Denby which was little more than two or three houses dotted along the road. With little light to guide him, Locklear slowed to less than ten miles per hour as he squinted into the distance until he saw a lighted window in a single-storey house on the opposite side of the rocky road. He signalled to show his intention to pull over and grinned to himself at his rigid adherence to road safety. He had not seen another vehicle on Route 18 for over an hour and there was even less chance of him meeting another traveller on the tiny dirt road in the middle of the South Dakota plains.

Locklear turned off the engine and stood wearily out of the car. He stretched and yawned. It had been his intention to stop for coffee en route but the light was fading and he was anxious to find the house he had driven to only once during his career as a Rapid City police officer. From where he stood, he could just about make out a lone figure sitting on the porch. He pulled back the creaking gate and stepped onto the property.

"I wouldn't come any further if I were you," a voice said from the porch. "I have a rifle pointed right at your chest."

Locklear put his hands up and approached slowly.

"Is that you, Grass?"

The man stood and put on a porch light.

Locklear climbed the three wooden steps and stepped slowly onto the porch, his arms still raised above his head.

The porch man narrowed his small brown eyes at his unexpected visitor. "I know you," he said.

"Locklear. Detective Sergeant. I used to work out of Rapid City." Locklear lowered his hands.

Grass smiled. "You were a young feller then," he said as he lowered his rifle.

Locklear nodded. If the years had not been good to him, they had been cruel to whichever of the two Grass cousins was standing in front of him. Even in the dull porch light, he could see that Grass's face was heavily lined. He was heavier than Locklear remembered and his black hair that was once worn army-tight, was grey and wispy and blew around his face in the small welcome breeze of the hot summer night.

"Your cousin not around?" Locklear asked, hoping to figure out which of the two Grass men he was speaking to.

"Oh, Frank died a good number of years back, never got to see retirement. I retired a few weeks after his funeral. My heart wasn't in the job without him. We never got to do that fishing we were always planning on doing."

"Sorry to hear that, Grass," he said, still using the man's last name even though he now knew that he was speaking with Eddie, the younger of the two cousins.

"Take a seat," Eddie offered as he shuffled back to his seat on the porch.

"That gun necessary?" Locklear asked, looking out into

the darkness. There wasn't a house around for miles and this didn't look like the kind of place where anyone had anything worth stealing.

"Oh, it's mostly to scare coyotes coming to take my chickens. But, it's also in case any young punks come looking to take something that isn't theirs," he said as he turned his head and looked to the horizon.

Locklear followed Eddie's eyes to the far left of his porch where in the distance he could see the glimmer of streetlights.

"That's Pine Ridge lit up over there. Things ain't like they used to be when we were young and you were even younger. It's much more dangerous now. Was a time the young kids looked up the local police, especially if we were Native. They knew we understood their ways, their struggles. Things were hard for folks. Still are. Worse, I think, now than then."

Eddie leaned to his side and took a cold beer from an ice bucket parked to the side of his seat.

"Beer?"

"No, thanks. I don't drink," Locklear replied.

"Me neither. Never have. It's alcohol free."

Locklear took the bottle from Eddie and checked the label.

"Never knew there was such a thing, thanks," he replied as he unscrewed the cap and gulped down the ice-cold beer.

Eddie opened a bottle, took a small sip and sighed.

"Well, guess you're going to tell me now why you drove to the middle of nowhere to meet someone you haven't seen for – is it thirty years?"

"More," Locklear replied.

Locklear took another gulp and leant forward, staring into the moonlit night.

"It's quiet here," he said.

Eddie raised his bottle and took another sip. "I wasn't born here. Came here, oh, I don't know – when me and Frank were young and got ourselves jobs as tribal police. We were no more than kids. Frank, me and Frank's sister, Rose – we were all born on Rosebud Reservation. Rose is in New York now. Comes back here once a year to keep in touch with her roots. Did real well for herself. She stays here sometimes and, you know, we got little in common except our past, got little to say to each other but it's nice at the same time. She's getting old now. Time will come she's not able to get here. That'll be tough then. She's the only family I have left."

Locklear nodded but did not offer any response. As far as he knew, he didn't have a relative in the world. He wondered if it was possible to miss something you never had. He could not conjure up any feelings of wanting a family. The loneliness that had dogged him throughout his life was, he felt, not due to the absence of relatives but to his nomadic childhood, with the feeling of not having one place where he had a sense of belonging.

Eddie looked at Locklear's empty bottle and took another cold one from his store at his feet. Locklear took it and opened the cap.

"First beers I've had in over thirty years," Locklear said.

Eddie glanced at the Native man on his porch and noticed the fine lines that ran across his face. His visitor had once been a handsome young man, still was to an extent but he could see the damage that alcohol had done to him.

"Almost lost you your job, I expect?"

Locklear nodded but did not look at Eddie Grass.

"Yeah, comes a time when what's inside you fights with what is outside of you. Forces we have little control of. I never drank but Frank and me, we almost lost our jobs for different reasons. It's a long time ago now."

Locklear remained silent and did not look at his drinking companion.

"Frank and Rose's dad and my dad were brothers. We were born in my grandmother's house on the plains outside of Rosebud reservation and she was a proud Lakota Sioux. Knew all of the old tales. When we were little, we went with our parents to live in the centre of the reservation. All four were alcoholics. Drink was a real problem for us growing up. We were just kids when Grandma took us to live with her, all three of us, and she raised us. We didn't see our parents much. One by one the disease took them until the three of us were orphans. Grandma lived until she was ninety-seven years old. Me and Frank took her here to this house when she couldn't live alone anymore and she died right here, on a hot summer night under the stars with me and Frank by her side. She'd had a hard life, endured awful things, but she taught us to be proud Lakotas. She was proud when Frank and I joined the tribal police and Rose went to college. Alcohol has been the scourge of our people. Its sale is banned on the reservation now and that's done some good but ... there's a long way to go."

"How did you almost lose your job?"

"Well, as much as Frank and I were committed to the

law, we were proud of our traditions and lived as close to them as we could. Modern life though doesn't often respect or accept those traditions. A proud Sioux can get caught between two worlds and struggle to know which world is right, the white world or our world. We got word that Rose's husband had been beating her in New York. Frank was her real brother but as we were raised together I looked upon Rose as my sister too. So it was our responsibility as Lakotas to protect her. We went out there and, well, she was in a real bad way. Got teeth missing, face swollen so bad, arm broken. Frank wept. You don't need to know all the details but we made sure he left her apartment for good and that he'd never come back."

"You didn't ...?"

Eddie waved Locklear's suggestion away.

"No. Nothing like that. Men who hit women are cowards I generally find. You stand up to them and give them a worse taste of their own medicine, they generally hide under whatever rock they had the misfortune to climb out from. We did beat him up real bad though. Made sure he felt the same pain he'd inflicted on Rose."

Locklear nodded but did not speak. In his heart he agreed with what the Grass cousins did and felt that, if faced with a similar situation, he might have done the same thing.

"She wouldn't come back here with us to the plains. She had a life in New York. A job, friends. So we helped her move to a new apartment so if he got any ideas he wouldn't know where to find her. We thought it was over but when we got back home we found out he was pressing charges against Frank and me. We were suspended from duty.

Looked like the captain was going to have our badges. Eventually, he dropped the charges in exchange for Rose not filing assault charges against him. Neither Frank nor I wanted her to agree to that, but it seemed the only way we could get on with our lives. We never told Grandma. She would have been confused as to why white law said it was wrong to avenge your sister. She would have thought all men, regardless of their colour, would protect their sisters."

Locklear nodded but could feel the discomfort of the personal nature of Eddie's story rise up in him.

Eddie blew out. "I'm getting maudlin in my old age. Don't mind me. What can I help you with, Locklear?"

Locklear put his beer onto the porch floor and rubbed his hands together. Slowly, he told Eddie Grass the details of the case and the dead ends he was facing.

"So you've come looking for this kid, Jim Hunter?"

"Yes, I need to talk to him. Do you know him or where I can find him?"

Eddie looked towards to the lights of Pine Ridge in the distance.

"Used to be I knew all of the kids and their parents, grandparents, but I've been retired a long time now. There's a whole generation that have grown up over there that I don't know. I don't recognise his name but that's probably his legal name. He probably uses a Native name on the reservation. You might talk to the local elementary school teacher – Lucy Bird. He most likely went to school there."

"OK – Albert Whitefeather, the Native who was killed in Richmond, was a member of the local Native American Rights group here. Who would I speak to if I wanted to know more about the group?"

Eddie thought for a moment. "There's an old guy name of Daccota Looks-Twice who used to be a member – but, well, there was some trouble a while back and I don't think he's associated with the movement anymore. He was a cop on the reservation here for many years. Was very respected. Haven't seen him around for a while but I don't go into town much. I'm a little out of touch with what's happening now but I think it might be best to speak with a guy by the name of Hank Pauls. He's always been involved with the movement."

"Hank Pauls," Locklear repeated, surprised that the man did not have a Native American name.

"That's his legal name. He runs a store downtown selling Native American rugs and jewellery – store's got his name above the door. His Native name is Han."

"Have you ever heard of an organisation, or, well I don't even know if it is an organisation, but, well, does the word INTENT mean anything to you?"

Eddie shook his head. "Other than the actual meaning of the word? No. Why do you ask?"

"The other guy that was killed in Richmond, Holton – that's the last thing he said to the man who found him – or rather, he said "*Not Intent*.""

Grass shook his head and drained what was left of his beer. "Maybe he just meant he didn't intend to do something? Like a confession?"

Locklear sighed. "No. I feel that there's more to it than that. He had files on his computer of the same name which someone had deleted."

"Sorry I can't help," Eddie said genuinely.

"Don't worry. It was a long shot. Here's an even longer

one – you don't happen to know anyone referred to as the 'White Ghost'?" Locklear grinned.

"Ah!" Grass grinned.

"You do?"

Grass pointed. "Not a person, no, but that is the name of that ridge over there."

Locklear looked into the darkness. He shielded his eyes to block out the streetlights of Pine Ridge and focused on the land in front of it. As his eyes adjusted to the darkness, he noticed a long dark ridge in the distance.

He stood and walked to the porch rail.

"It's a small ravine," said Grass. "Runs for about three miles towards the edge of Pine Ridge and it's around ten, maybe fifteen feet deep in the centre."

"Why is it called that?"

"It's just an old Lakota tale. My grandmother told it to me. Used to scare us kids with it when we were young."

Locklear looked at his watch. It was almost eleven.

"I'd like to hear it, unless I'm keeping you up?"

Eddie Grass waved Locklear's suggestion away. He lifted another bottle of beer and saluted Locklear.

"At my age, I'll be up half the night after these anyway!"

Locklear sat and Grass handed him another beer.

"OK," said Grass. "You know about the massacre of Natives that occurred here at Wounded Knee?"

Locklear, slightly embarrassed, shrugged. "Yes, but I've forgotten the details."

"It happened near here in December 1890. Seems like a long time ago but the wounds it inflicted here live on. Lotta people still angry about it. US Army intercepted some Lakota and took them to Wounded Knee where they set

228

up camp. Next day, more cavalry arrived with a Colonel Forsyth. They took the Lakotas' arms and legend has it that one old Sioux man who was deaf refused to give up his gun because he had paid a lot of money for it. The story goes that the old man was performing a Ghost Dance when his gun went off and the army started shooting. The Lakotas were unarmed and tried to fight back but without guns they were sitting ducks. More than two hundred and fifty Lakota were killed that day, including women and children. Army dug a mass grave and threw them into it. Only twenty-five US soldiers died during the massacre and some of those who survived were awarded medals of honour. Medals for killing unarmed men, women and children."

Locklear looked into the darkness at the horror of the story. "Ghost Dance," he said. "That was a ritual dance, wasn't it? Performed to drive away white people from this country?"

"Yes. Sure worked, didn't it?"

"And that's why it's called Ghost Ridge? Because the old man was doing a Ghost Dance?"

"No," Eddie replied. "The so-called 'Battle of Wounded Knee' happened a few miles from here. That ridge over there is named as it is because of what happened a few days after the Wounded Knee massacre."

Locklear nodded and waited.

"My grandma said a wagon train was spotted a few miles beyond that ridge and the tribe at Pine Ridge were angry. They were grieving the loss of family, friends, whole generations of families wiped out. Some braves from the tribe tracked the wagon train to the ridge. It was snowing heavily and there were heavy mounds of snow collecting

229

across the ravine. I guess the wagon-train folk thought the land ahead was just rocky but they couldn't see what they were driving over. Wagons started to sink in the deep snow. The braves rode down and began shooting the people. All of them. Men, women, children, the old, the sick. It was a revenge killing for the loss of their people. Then they just left them there in the snow for buzzards to eat and take their evil spirits away from the land."

Unsure what he could say in response to such a terrible story, Locklear sighed heavily.

"It was wrong, I know, but also understandable. They were different times. My people were fighting for their very survival and any white was a threat to that. More whites meant less land, more reservations. It was a war."

"And the name? How did that come about?"

"The braves drove their horses up out of the ravine and when they reached the top one of them spotted a woman on the opposite side of the ridge. She was wearing a long black dress and she had the whitest hair and whitest skin they had ever seen. She was feeling around the snow until she felt a child. She lifted him but he was motionless. The boy had the same colour hair as her. She began to cry. My grandmother said the sight and sound of the woman terrified these strong, fearless warriors who thought she was the spirit of one of the women they had just killed. The chief's son Wanduta rode over to her and the nearer he got, the louder she wailed. When he reached her, as he told the story for many years, he touched her to see if she was real and she stopped moaning and started screaming. Wanduta told the tribe that the woman had red eyes so he rode off and they left the 'spirit' there where she could be heard moaning into the night. The next day, when they returned with more braves to take any remaining supplies, neither her body, nor the boy she was holding, was there."

Unsure if the story was finished, Locklear waited.

Eddie looked at him and shrugged. "Hence the name. White Ghost Ridge."

"Do you believe that a dead woman's spirit rose up and screamed?" Locklear asked.

Grass grinned. "Oh no, course I don't. But I read an article once in an old magazine. Must have been fifty years ago. I think it explains what happened that day. I told my grandma about it at the time but she wouldn't accept it. The article was about a young man, an antique dealer in Rapid City, who claimed to be the great-grandson of that woman."

"A descendant? So, she survived?"

"Article was old when I came across it," Eddie said. "I think it was written around the late 1950s. This guy said his great-grandmother, a Norwegian settler, survived an attack on a wagon train. He said she climbed out of a ravine with her son in her arms and carried him for days. He said his grandfather, who was four at the time, had been knocked unconscious when their wagon overturned in the snow. Her husband and the rest of the people on the wagon train were shot during the attack by a local Lakota tribe. She and the boy were the only survivors. They walked for three days and were almost dead when a small cavalry unit came across them. She had only managed to walk about eight miles from the site – was probably walking around in circles. She and the kid were badly frostbitten and dehydrated. Guess they were pretty strong to have survived that. They settled in Rapid City but she never remarried. What really got my attention was when the article said that his great-grandmother was an –"

"Albino," Locklear interjected.

"Yes. Which explains why she scared the braves. The article mentioned that albinism in Native peoples is common in the south-west, in tribes like the Hopi – but it's pretty rare among the Sioux. Guess they had just never seen anyone like that before."

"Might also explain why she was feeling around in the snow for the child," Locklear said, "and also why she didn't start screaming until the brave came right up to her. Most people with that condition have poor eyesight. She probably couldn't see him until he was right in front of her."

"Exactly."

"Did the guy in the article also have the condition?" Locklear asked.

"I don't think so, no. It was a black-and-white photo and I could see he was pale and blond but, no, he didn't look like he had albinism. The article didn't say he was either."

"Some story," Locklear said.

If the man Grass was speaking about was alive, he would be an old man now but Locklear knew albinism was hereditary and wondered if his 'White Ghost' was somehow related to this man and was another descendant of the woman who climbed out of a snow-filled ravine almost one hundred and twenty-eight years ago.

"The same day that the braves shot the wagon train, an illness began to spread across the reservation. Our people thought the White Ghost had put a curse on them and felt that the spirits had abandoned them because they believed that illness can only enter the body if it is not protected by the spirits. Soon the old and very young began to die. Offerings were made but more and more of our people died until only the very strong were alive. Wanduta's younger brother Eyota knew it was not because of a curse. He told his father, Red Cloud, that some of the soldiers at Wounded Knee had been ill and their people who survived the attack had returned to Pine Ridge and had spread the disease on the reservation. But Red Cloud did not believe Eyota and sided with Wanduta. He said the spirits had spoken to him and that the illness was a punishment for mixing their sacred blood with the blood of the white man who had no respect for the land or for their beliefs. He ordered that any woman who had been raped by white soldiers should have her male relatives kill the child when it came into the world. Some women with older mixed-blood children could not take their children's lives so they took them into the scrub at night and made them walk into the desert in the hope that they might survive. Indian men who had taken white wives drove them out of the reservation and abandoned them. Wanduta enforced this rule when he became chief until his death and it was carried on by his son. Some of the old folk in Pine Ridge believe in that curse to this day."

Locklear pondered this for a moment. "You said this guy was an antique dealer in Rapid City?"

"Yeah. I remember because the article said he sold a lot of Native crafts in his store. Worked closely with the Native population. Guess he didn't hold a grudge."

"Hmmm," Locklear replied as he got to his feet. He put

out his hand. "It's been good seeing you, Grass."

Eddie stood and took Locklear's hand. "You too. Make sure you check in with the local cops. Let them know you're in town looking into something. Better that way."

"Sure."

Locklear walked to his car and waved before he sat in.

He turned and followed the dark lonely road back to Route 18 where he swung a right towards Oglala and onwards to the Prairie Winds Motel where he would spend the night. Tomorrow he would drive to Pine Ridge and follow up on the leads Grass had given him. He had a lot to tell Mendoza and was looking forward to updating her. He slowed the car as he turned into the motel and checked into his unremarkable room. He wondered if the mounting cost of his and Mendoza's unauthorised investigation would be covered by the station when Kowalski returned. He showered and shaved and lay on his bed, wondering what Mendoza was doing right now.

Tomorrow he would go to Pine Ridge. Tomorrow he would find Jim Hunter and the pieces of the puzzle would begin to fall into place.

Exhaustion overwhelmed him and he fell into a deep sleep.

# Chapter 20

Mendoza reached out from her bed to stop the shrill buzz coming from somewhere in her hotel room. She felt around the top of the bedside locker for an alarm clock. When she found nothing that she could silence, she pulled a pillow over her throbbing head and cringed as memories of what had happened the night before came rushing back. She groaned at flashing images of a hotel reception worker holding her up while a female security guard searched her purse to see what room she was checked into.

She felt her body to check that she was still fully clothed and was relieved to find that the security guard had obviously just placed her face down on the bed and left her to sleep off the copious amounts of alcohol she had consumed.

Mendoza had no idea how she had even got back to the hotel. A fuzzy image of her looking for her shoe on the pavement surfaced and then the face of a man who had tried to help her to stand while she vomited into a street bin. Mendoza lifted the pillow and looked at the carpeted hotel-room floor which revealed only one gold shoe. She moaned out loud at the spectacle she must have made of herself. She swallowed. Her throat was dry and she could smell vomit in her hair. Then she remembered Ann, the beautiful woman she had spoken to, waving her finger angrily at her outside the club and her asshole brother laughing on the pavement. She closed her eyes shut as she tried to remember what had brought the pleasant woman to such a frenzy of anger and sat up.

"Oh God!" she said as she remembered.

Ann had listened intently as an inebriated Mendoza spoke about her complex relationship with her boss: about how much he irritated her yet had taught her so much about being a good cop, but how she had found herself more recently attracted to him which had confused her and unnerved her boss who she respected and who would not welcome the feelings she had for him. Ann had her own stories, a failed marriage to her high-school sweetheart, single parenthood, work pressures, and together they laughed and cried and laughed again.

And then Ann tried to kiss her. Mendoza put her hands to her face and took deep breaths as she remembered pushing Ann away and trying to stand. She remembered suddenly feeling like she shouldn't be there, shouldn't be sitting with Ann. She tried to find her way out of the maze of small bars in the club which seemed more packed than it had been when she arrived and Ann followed her, looking worried. What time had it been? How long had she been there? She rubbed her temples as images flashed of her standing, or rather trying to stand outside the bar with Ann trying to hold her up.

The noise that had been drilling into her head had

stopped but started up suddenly again. She looked around for its source and realised the din was coming from her purse. She stood and stumbled across the room to the purse which was thrown onto a table outside the bathroom. She looked at the unknown number flashing on the screen and another memory surfaced. Mendoza rejected the call and put her hands to her face as she remembered the drunken message she had left on Manuel's cell phone in the early hours of the morning, berating him for asking their son about her drinking.

"*Jesus Christ!*" she screamed as the phone began to ring again.

The caller gave up and Mendoza quickly checked her phone to see if she had made any other calls. She sat on the side of the bed and took deep breaths when she saw that she had made two other calls. One was a two-minute call to her mother which didn't worry her too much. It wasn't the first drunken call her mother had received from her and it probably wouldn't be the last. The second call worried her more. The call to her boss was less than fifty seconds in duration but what she had said to him in that time or if she had spoken with him directly she could not remember. She was a fool, a stupid fool who had given her ex-husband ammunition against her and had probably said things to Locklear that were best left unsaid.

She went to the bathroom where she vomited again and was glad that her boss was not there to witness this and have another opportunity to admonish her. She showered and ordered coffee to her room. It would be hours before she'd be able to put food into her raw stomach. When she was finished trying to wash away the shame of the night before, she replayed the messages on her phone. It was David Horowitz who had phoned twice, apologising for not being available sooner and offering to meet her that night at eight at Toscano restaurant to discuss Alec Holton. She sighed and texted the journalist, saying yes she would meet him, and giving the man a description of herself. She texted Locklear, saying she would be one more night in DC, following which she would take the next plane to meet him and hopefully finish the investigation that right at that moment seemed to be taking forever to solve.

More than fifteen hundred miles away Locklear was already in his car, having played the 4am message from Mendoza that he would probably never speak to her about. His trooper was obviously going through a rough time and was seeing him in a light that he did not deserve or want. It was not in his best interests, or more importantly, in hers.

He was glad that the anxiety he felt driving through the reservation was somewhat distracting him from thinking about her. He remembered how unnerved he had been the last and only time he had driven through it. He passed a pretty white Episcopal church on his right on the corner of Yards Road and SD 407 and the colourful windows of the elementary school to his left which was not yet open. Locklear kept straight on SD 407, passing the Shell service station on his left and an equally pretty Catholic church on his right. The land rose up and he passed several more houses set atop redbrick foundations and small businesses operating out of rundown, dilapidated buildings. The feeling that he'd had when he came to the town as a young man returned. He shivered as he tried to shake off the sensation that he was being watched, as though a force from above was flying overhead, following his path, directing him down unknown streets.

He instinctively turned onto Route 18 which ran through the middle of the town and served as Pine Ridge's main street, hoping that he would find Hank Paul's Antique and Native American craft store. As the stores and businesses thinned and the scenery changed to dry, empty fields, Locklear knew he was lost. He signalled off the highway into a large dusty lot which housed a small gas station and convenience store. The lot was empty save for a broken-down truck parked at the gable end of the store. Locklear parked at the store's one and only gas pump and got out. He looked up at the sign over the store's entrance which read *Maggie's Native American Gift Store,* the red paint of which was chipped and faded from the hot Dakota sun. He filled up his tank as he looked around the desolate place. He noticed a car pass slowly on a steep dirt road behind the store and he wondered briefly where the road led. He shook the gas pump, placed the cap back on his fuel tank and walked slowly to the store.

A bell rang as he opened the door and stepped into the dimly lit store. To his left, two local women pinned a photo of a teenager onto a huge notice board which was crammed with photos of other children and local news notices. One of the women was crying. Locklear wondered if the young Natives in the photos were missing and made a note to go back to the board to see what its contents might tell him about the town and its inhabitants. He looked straight ahead of him at the three rows of shelving which ran the length of the store and held dry goods and convenience foods. There were no fruit or vegetables to be seen and no hot coffee which was what Locklear wanted most. He picked up a bottle of cold water from the refrigerator and a couple of donuts from a tray. He walked to a long counter which ran across the store at the end of the aisles and placed his items on it. The young Native American girl behind the counter did not look up as she scrolled through her cell phone. The girl was wearing long black braids and a traditional buckskin dress. Behind her was a narrow, open door. The remainder of the wall housed hand-made Native American weaves and jewellery.

"Nice dress," Locklear said as he took out his wallet.

The girl looked up from her phone, rolled her eyes and returned to whatever social-media platform she happened to be browsing.

"Are those rugs made here in town?" he asked.

The girl looked behind her as though she had not noticed the items before.

"What the sign says," she replied sarcastically.

Locklear stared at the girl for a moment and decided how best to leave the store with the information he wanted. He moved the items he wanted to buy even nearer to the unhappy server.

"I'm not from around here," he began.

"No shit!" the girl replied.

Locklear ignored the young girl's attitude and persisted. "I'm looking for Hank Paul's craft store. Would you tell me how to get there?"

"Something wrong with the stuff we have here? He just sells the same stuff and some creepy old stuff too," the girl snarled.

Locklear heard a voice coming from the room behind the counter. The door opened into what he assumed were the store owner's living quarters. It was the voice of a woman. An older woman.

"Olowa!" the voice said.

Presumably, Locklear reasoned, a warning for the girl to treat customers better.

"Alright, Grandma! I know." The young woman slammed her phone onto the counter and began scanning Locklear's items.

Locklear grinned as she glowered at him.

"What do you want with Mr Pauls?" she asked as she placed Locklear's items into a paper bag.

"It's business."

"You a cop?"

Locklear laughed. "Is it that obvious?"

"Kinda. What's your name?"

"Detective Sergeant Locklear."

The girl shrugged and took the money Locklear held out to her.

"Go back up three blocks. Take the second left past the pizza place. His store is green. It's kind of a dump. We got much better stuff here." She had raised her voice, no doubt hoping her grandmother would hear her improved customer-service skills.

A motorbike pulled up outside the store. Locklear watched as a young man took his helmet off and waved in to the store assistant.

"*Grandma, that's all I can help you today!*" the girl yelled as she pulled the buckskin dress over her head and threw it underneath the counter. Underneath the dress she wore tight blue jeans and an even tighter white T-shirt. Locklear laughed as she then pulled the wig of long braids off her head revealing a short, modern haircut.

"Have a nice day!" she said as she escaped from the behind the counter.

As Locklear made his way back to the front of the store he was disappointed to find that the two women were still standing in front of the noticeboard. The younger of the two was being comforted by the older who had placed her arm around her companion. He took a quick look at the board which was filled with photographs of Native American teenagers, but found the women soon moved their focus from the photo of the teenage boy to him. He shifted uncomfortably on his feet and decided he'd try to return later to see what information the board might hold.

He walked to his car and placed his purchases on the passenger seat, then went around to the other side. He found himself looking upwards once again at the road which ran behind the store. When he looked back at the store front, he noticed a Native woman staring at him. She was not one of the women who had been blocking his access to the noticeboard and there had been no-one else in the store. He wondered if she was the woman who had admonished her granddaughter from the room behind the store counter. There was something about her that struck him and he stood rooted to the spot, looking back at her. Her lips moved but she was too far away for him to hear what she had said.

He opened his car door, sat into the driver's seat and turned on the engine. As he drove out of the lot and turned back in the direction he had come from, the woman was still standing in the same spot, staring at him.

"Mendoza, I just scared another Native!" he said aloud even though his trooper was a long way away from Pine Ridge.

Five minutes later he pulled up at Hank Paul's Antique and Craft Store. The young Native's directions had been good – and she was right – the store looked like a dump. He opened the door and walked in. It was stifling hot, incredibly small and held only a small amount of goods. He wandered about, picking up the items for sale, none of which cost more than $20. He wondered how the guy made a living selling what looked like junk. Olowa was also right about her grandmother's store having better stuff for sale.

When he had seen pretty much everything, Locklear waited for another five minutes. "Mr Paul?" he then called towards the beaded curtain which hung to the side of the counter. There was no answer.

Locklear dug his hands into his pockets and began to look at the photos on the wall. They were mostly prints of Native Americans in traditional dress which tourists obviously had an interest in buying. He spotted an old photo of a young Native American man standing beside Robert Kennedy on the reservation. Beside it was another photo of the same man, now elderly, with President Obama and a third photograph of the man standing in the front row of a protest group. He scanned that photo to see if Rosenberg, Sartre or Holton were there but the only face he recognised was that of Albert Whitefeather standing right beside the man.

Another five minutes passed so Locklear left the store

and walked down the side entrance to see if Pauls was there. There was no-one in the yard. He walked down to a wood cabin at the back of the property and looked around. He knocked on the door and waited but could hear no sound coming from inside the cabin. He looked through the windows which sat on either side of the wooden door but could see no-one. One of the rooms appeared to be a library. It had a small wood-burner and an old-fashioned TV which sat on a stained black coffee table. An empty wheelchair sat in the corner of the room, its occupant nowhere to be seen. There was only one armchair in the room. Locklear moved to the second window which was a bedroom. He could see a door off to the side of the room which was closed. He wondered if it was a bathroom and if Pauls was inside. He stood back from the window and waited until he heard the sound of footsteps on the pathway behind him. He turned to find an old Native standing there with a pile of firewood in his arms. It was the man from the photos inside the store. The old guy wore two long braids, jeans and a check shirt. His chest was barrel-shaped and his face worn and withered by his advancing years.

"Little hot for a fire," Locklear said but the man did not answer. "Are you Hank Pauls?"

"Han," the man said, giving his Native name as he threw the wood onto a pile outside his front door.

"I want to speak to you about Albert Whitefeather," Locklear said.

"Don't know him." The man dusted off his hands on his jeans.

"Really? There's a photo of you standing right beside him in your store."

244

Han Pauls looked Locklear up and down. He inhaled and looked away as he considered his options.

"What do you want?"

"I'm Detective Sergeant Locklear from Richmond where Whitefeather died. I know he was a member of your movement. I want to know what he did for you."

Han Pauls looked towards his home as if about to take Locklear inside.

"Come back to the store," he said then. "We can talk there."

Locklear walked behind the old man as he shuffled along the side entrance to the store. He reckoned Pauls was over eighty years old but he was still not taking any chances by walking in front of a man who could have a weapon hidden on his person or hidden somewhere along the side entrance to the store. He entered the store in the same way, after Pauls.

Locklear looked in the back to ensure there was no-one else there but the back room, which was a nothing more than a small dusty storeroom, was empty.

Locklear stopped at the photo of Pauls with Barack Obama.

"What was he like?" he asked.

Han took a seat inside the store's front door.

"He was the only president to deliver on a pledge to settle the Native American legal action on our lands and the resources on those lands."

Locklear nodded.

"You got ID?" Han asked.

Locklear took out his driving licence and showed it to him.

"I meant your PD ID."

Locklear shrugged. "Station captain took it off me. It's a long story."

"I see." After a pause he asked, "Where are you from?"

"Everywhere," Locklear replied.

"Do I know you? I think I've seen you before."

"I'm getting that a lot lately."

Han fixed his tiny brown eyes on Locklear from his seat.

Locklear, uncomfortable with the old man's stare, tried to think of something to say.

"I used to be a police officer in Rapid City but that was a long time ago."

Han shook his head. "No, that's not it."

Locklear shrugged.

Han continued to look perturbed by Locklear's presence.

"I know someone whose family is from here," Locklear said. "O'Brien. He's a cop at my station. He'll vouch for me if you want to call him."

"I know O'Brien. He was a young cop here for a short time. Smart guy."

"O'Brien was stationed here?" Locklear asked, surprised by the revelation.

"I'd have thought you would have known that." Another pause. "What does he look like?"

Locklear grinned at the test. "He's a weird-looking guy. Tall, thin. Pale face, jet-black hair. And I know he's a member of your movement."

"Anything else?"

"He has a scar on his cheek where he got a mole or maybe a birthmark removed."

"It was a bullet. A flesh wound. Lucky for him it didn't enter his skull."

"Someone shot him? When?"

Han didn't answer.

"What work does your movement do?" Locklear asked.

"Everything."

"Meaning?"

"We do everything we can to fight for the rights of our people. Economic rights, cultural rights, legal rights, the right to manage our own land and fight for the restoration of our lands and we file legal suits over broken treaties."

"You do all that from here?" Locklear asked as he surveyed the small rundown store which did not appear to even have a computer.

"It's a nationwide movement. We are just a small sister-branch of a much larger organisation."

"And you achieve all this how?"

"Demonstrations. Legal challenges. Marches. We do whatever we can to make our demands known."

"Does that include violence?"

Han looked up from his seat. "No. We advocate achieving our goals through peaceful means."

"Tell me what you can about Whitefeather."

"He's dead," Han replied.

"I know that!" Locklear snapped.

"Then what does it matter? He's with his ancestors now. This life's journey no longer matters for him."

"A friend of mine is being blamed for the murder of a man in Richmond, a man that Whitefeather threatened."

"And you think Whitefeather killed him?" Han laughed.

Locklear did not reply.

"Albert was an angry man – but murder? He wasn't capable of that."

"What *was* he capable of?" Locklear asked.

Han stood and shifted slowly behind his counter. Locklear watched as he lifted a bottle of water from a shelf and drank it down quickly.

"Albert saw a lot in Iraq. He had a propensity for violence that we didn't advocate in the organisation. We started to receive a lot of complaints about him."

"About what exactly?"

"Intimidation. Trying to get access to various Government offices to protest without authorisation. Threatening staff in those organisations. His behaviour became a problem and reflected negatively on the movement."

"How did your organisation afford to fly Albert to the various places he went to support the movement?"

Han lifted a dreamcatcher from the shelf and blew the dust from its web.

"We didn't."

"Albert's landlady said he was frequently away on protests or attending meetings in other states."

"Whitefeather wasn't representing this movement. He was expelled from the organisation more than eighteen months ago."

"Why?"

Han lifted another item from a shelf and stared at it as though he had never seen it before. He shook his head wearily at the tacky six-inch plastic statue of a brave in Native American clothing wielding a spear. Locklear glanced at the item and wondered why a man like Han Pauls would sell such things while simultaneously fighting for respect for indigenous people.

"Sometimes our organisation attracted men and women with more fundamentalist views than those held by the movement," he said. "They were usually younger, less patient folk who became frustrated by the slow progress of the movement."

"And Whitefeather was one of these?"

Han Pauls did not answer.

"What about Daccota Looks-Twice? Was he also expelled?"

Pauls looked alarmed by the question. "Do you know Looks-Twice?" He squinted at Locklear as if to get a better look at him.

"No. Eddie Grass mentioned him to me."

"Eddie spoke out of turn."

"Why?"

"Daccota Looks-Twice was once an important member of our community. A tribal police officer. He made mistakes. He is no longer associated with the movement."

"I asked you if he was expelled."

"There was a disagreement about how to handle some archaeology digs just outside Pine Ridge. Daccota's land adjoined the area the dig was situated on. He said the university people came onto his land and had disturbed his ancestors' graves and took sacred items that they found. He threatened people and he was facing charges from the police who said the university staff insisted they had stayed within the boundaries of government-owned land. There was no evidence that they had come onto his land. I think the townspeople believed him and some may even have agreed with what he did. The case went to court and Looks-Twice was bound to the peace for five years. Two days later, he shot a cop."

"Did the cop live?"

"Yes. It was O'Brien that he shot. Beat him up first and then shot him. Left him for dead on a dirt road. Lucky for him a passer-by stopped and took him to hospital. Looks-Twice wasn't so lucky. He fired the gun with one hand. Recoil made the gun shoot out of his hand and caused a nasty facial wound. Looks like someone etched an arrow across his forehead. O'Brien refused to file charges. Looks-Twice left the movement before he was asked to."

Locklear thought about Jim Hunter and wondered if the young student was related to Looks-Twice.

"Did he have any children?"

"No. He didn't marry. Daccota has had a difficult life. He endured a lot of tragedy. I hear that he is no longer in touch with his extended family. He's more or less cut himself off from the community. My heart is with him. He made mistakes but he has my sympathies."

"Where would I find him?"

"I'd advise against you going near him and I really mean that. Way he is now, he'd shoot anyone coming up onto his land and ask questions later."

"I think I can handle myself," Locklear retorted.

Han smiled wearily. "He lives about ten miles outside of Pine Ridge off Route 18. Turn off after the Shell station and follow the road up about two miles. You'll hear his dogs before you see the house so be careful and don't go there alone."

Locklear inhaled and wondered if he would wait for

Mendoza to return before making a trip to meet Looks-Twice or if it would be better for him to go now in the hope that it would move the investigation forward.

"How much do you know about Pine Ridge or indeed about life on any reservation?" Pauls asked.

"Apart from what's obvious?"

"Used to be we were a proud race, a self-reliant race. We hunted and killed our own food. The land we lived on provided what we needed. Then the whites came and took that land from us. They killed the buffalo and drove us onto reservations. They took our weapons and killed many of our people. To what was left of our people, they gave food we did not know how to cook. They gave us clothes we did not know how to make. They gave us money and said 'this is your new life'. They gave us their alcohol and fed poison into the veins of our children. Now, we live lives without meaning, without honour or pride or hope. There is no work, nothing to hunt. The suicide rate among our young people is 150% higher than the national average. We rely on government commodities and wait in line for our food to be trucked in from faraway places. We cannot grow anything in this wasted dry land. There are not enough homes for people to live in and without jobs we are reliant on the government to put roofs over our heads, to feed us, to treat us like their children. We are like dogs, waiting on scraps from the white people's table. Our people are left with only two choices. To lie panting in the heat waiting for those scraps or to leave this place to go to cities and live where the concrete rises up into the sky, where it runs along the ground and we must live inside this concrete, one person on top of the other, in buildings so tall they block out the Mother Sun until the spirit of our people dies in places they do not belong."

Locklear leant against the wall and folded his arms. Paul's description of the city resonated with him. He had always hated living in the city and ached to feel soil beneath his feet, to touch it, breathe in the air and feel at one with nature.

"But we are fighting back. I am old but there are younger men and women here. They are returning to Pine Ridge with education and with new ideas. They are setting up businesses, giving jobs to our own native children. The children are being taught in our traditions. No more are our children being taken from their families to turn them into white people. We have a long way to go and I will not live to see it, but I will die knowing that there is hope on the horizon."

"I want to know more about Whitefeather. I want to know about his relationship with a Richmond Professor named Alec Holton. And I want to know who paid for him to travel around getting into mischief."

"I am sure I know you," Han said again.

"You don't," Locklear replied. "Now ... Whitefeather?"

Han lifted a plastic bottle of water and threw one in Locklear's direction. He took a seat at the front door and grappled with the tight lid on the bottle. Locklear took it from him and opened it. He handed it back to him.

"Thank you. My bones are old," Han said. "I told you Albert became difficult. He started to show up at places without the approval of our committee. He began to harass the Dean at USD and another lecturer there. He was staking out digs without being asked to. He became a nuisance. The police became involved. Albert was bringing the movement into disrepute. We had a vote and he was expelled from the group."

"Who sits on this committee?" Locklear asked.

"Local people."

"When do you meet?"

Han stared hard at Locklear and moved his lips.

Locklear inhaled. He knew Han was deciding what information he would provide but for now he'd go along with his short answers in the hope of getting information on Whitefeather.

"Tonight."

"Where?"

"At my place, out back. We used to meet in the Community Center but Whitefeather set it alight one night. Needs rebuilding. We don't have the money to do it."

"I'd like to be there."

"Only members can attend."

"Then I'd like to join," Locklear teased.

"Then, let me put it more plainly. Only local Natives or Native Americans whose family come from Pine Ridge can join."

Locklear scoffed. "Seriously?

Han raised his hands upwards in apology. Locklear wasn't sure if the gesture was sincere.

"It's not my rule. I stepped down as chairperson for personal reasons. My health was poor and I ... had other duties. I didn't have enough time to give the movement and Looks-Twice became the chairperson. We were getting a few newcomers who didn't have any Native blood in them at all. Looks-Twice, well, he didn't trust them or their

253

motives so he passed a motion which prevented them from joining."

Locklear exhaled. "Who is the new chairperson?"

"Ohiyes'a. He's a cousin of O'Brien."

Locklear thought about this for a moment. "How well did Whitefeather know Alec Holton? And did you know Holton?"

"I never spoke to him much. It was Albert he became friends with. Albert trusted him. Even let him attend some of the meetings here, back before Looks-Twice prohibited it."

"But he didn't stick to his word?"

"Like many white men, he betrayed us."

"How?"

"Holton said he was going to ensure that the universities returned the sacred items and the bones of our ancestors taken from the earth – that he would return them to us for burial. Instead of this, he stole them."

"Do you have any idea why he did that?"

"We had parted company by then. Whitefeather had disgraced himself so he was no longer attending meetings here. No-one saw Albert or Holton again."

"You said that some of your members were impatient with the movement. It's obvious that Whitefeather was one of those. What other members left and where did they go?"

"I don't know where they went," Han replied sharply.

"I think you do," Locklear replied.

"Some Natives wanted to take things into their own hands. They wanted to take back what was theirs. They started to break the law."

Locklear felt his breathing quicken as Mendoza's words came back to him – her uneasy suggestion that the missing artefacts had been stolen by members of the indigenous population themselves. But, if she was right, that didn't explain Lewis and Torres' account of items being stolen from Iraqi museums or Tommy Rosenberg's frequent travels to and from Iran. Locklear briefly wondered if he had landed in the middle of a tug-of-war game where two groups were stealing the same items back and forth.

"So they set up their own group," Locklear guessed aloud. "A group which is playing a dangerous game in which there are no rules and membership includes the risk of going to prison."

"Yes."

"Where would I find them?"

Han laughed. "They're not exactly in the phone directory. You don't find them. They find you. They have people everywhere. They are an international organisation, sergeant. Highly organised. Good at finding young, intelligent, maladjusted men and women with high ideals and use them to do their dirty work. Their mission is, I accept, noble in that they want to return artefacts stolen around the world to their rightful place. America is a good hunting ground for them. We have people from every religion and ethnicity in this country who will put their lives and their freedom at risk to help the cause."

Locklear remained silent, letting Han talk.

"They've also come up against some very dangerous people who will do anything to protect their crimes. As the group have grown so too has its willingness to do anything to protect artefacts from getting into the hands of these people who have no claim to them."

"People who intend to sell those items on the black market?"

"Yes."

"What is this group called?"

Han swallowed nervously. "I have a son who depends on me. He devoted his life to the military. Served for thirty-five years. He returned from Iraq in a wheelchair. He's in the hospital right now. My wife is dead. My daughters live far away. He depends on me to care for him."

"The police can protect you. You won't be in any danger."

Han let out a short, nervous laugh. Locklear recognised the pitying expression on his face as though the old man felt the Richmond cop had no idea what he had got himself involved in.

"I told you. They are everywhere. Even here, in this small reservation that no-one really cares about."

"Name?"

"INTENT. It's called INTENT."


Before Locklear drove away from the store, Pauls was already dialling a number. It was a phone call to a person he had not had any reason to contact for many years and its purpose was to try to protect the visiting cop from danger and keep him safe until he left the town of Pine Ridge for good.

# Chapter 21

In Washington DC, Mendoza settled in to her table which was situated in the right-hand corner at the back of Toscano restaurant. She chose the seat facing the door which would give her a good view of the other customers as she waited for Horowitz to arrive. There was also a security camera above her head and, while she wasn't expecting trouble from a mild-mannered journalist, she felt the spot she chose would provide her with added safety, if needed. Her head had only stopped throbbing an hour before after she had ordered a large pot of coffee and pastries to her room. She couldn't face seeing the reception staff again and had slithered out through the side door of the hotel on flat, comfortable shoes as she left for her meeting with Holton's ex-partner.

On arrival, Mendoza had looked around the room but could not see any lone male diners who looked around the right age. There were only about fifteen other tables in the dimly lit restaurant and nine of them were surprisingly unoccupied. Three large parties occupied three of the bigger tables in the middle of the long, narrow restaurant and were mostly businessmen in grey suits and ties.

One young woman ate alone at the table by the window and two loved-up couples occupied smaller tables at the back to her left but were too busy staring into each other's eyes to take any notice of the hungover, lone Latina.

Mendoza ordered a bottle of cold mineral water and watched the door. A few of the men at one of the tables began to glance over and throw smiles in her direction. One stared at her, unsmiling, but when she returned his gaze he flushed and looked away nervously. Mendoza cringed at the idea that any of them thought she was looking for a hook-up. She took her phone out of her bag and texted her mom to check on her grandmother and pretended to scroll through social-media platforms that did not exist on the basic burner phone Locklear had sourced. She felt a slight bump at her table and looked up to find a tall, thin, middle-aged man smiling amiably at her.

"I'm waiting for someone," Mendoza said curtly.

"I know. It's me. I'm David Horowitz," the man said, smiling.

Mendoza stared at the man's features and decided he did not look typically Jewish. He had a squat button nose and the distinct mid-western features of fair hair and bright-blue eyes common among people of Scandinavian descent.

"I take it you are Officer Mendoza?" he asked.

Mendoza nodded and gestured for the man to sit.

"You look like you were expecting someone else," he said as he pulled his chair closer to the table.

Mendoza watched the man's body language which gave the impression that he was nervous. She made no reply.

David Horowitz beckoned to the waiter.

"Would you like some wine?" he asked Mendoza. "We could share a bottle?"

Something Meara Henschel had said about David Horowitz came back to Mendoza but she decided to keep her thoughts to herself until she heard the man out.

"I better not."

He ordered red wine from the waiter who also took their dinner orders.

"Pulled one on in a club last night and I'm still feeling shaky," Mendoza said genially as she tried to lessen the man's nervousness.

"Oh, where did you go?"

"A club by the name of Cobalt."

"Oh, I've been there. Not since my college days though. It's a real pick-up place."

Mendoza put her head in her hands and blushed as the memories came rushing back.

"You OK?" he asked.

"Yeah," Mendoza replied. "I'm afraid I drank a little too much and made an ass of myself. Don't think I'll ever be showing my face there again."

"Been there." He grinned and waved his hand towards her.

"Do you mind if I ask you how you met Alec?"

The waiter arrived with the wine and David immediately took a large gulp and patted his mouth dry.

"We met in a cocktail bar."

Mendoza sighed. The man in front of her had said the second thing that did not fit with the way Henschel had described Horowitz. She folded her napkin on the table and leaned forward.

259

"Who are you? Because I know you are not David Horowitz."

Mendoza could see the alarm in the man's face.

"What do you mean? I am David Horowitz."

"The real David Horowitz doesn't drink and he met Alec Holton at an art exhibition." She lifted her phone off the table. "Now – I could phone Holton's neighbour and ask her for a description of David Horowitz. So do you want to keep this charade up or are you going to tell me who you are and where I can find the real David Horowitz?"

The man caved and looked towards one of the large tables behind him. Mendoza followed his eyes and realised he was looking at the serious man who had been staring at her earlier. The real David Horowitz stood and walked over to her table. His impersonator stood, walked quickly to the packed table and took a seat facing away from Mendoza.

"I knew the moment you sat down that you wouldn't be fooled," the real Horowitz began.

Mendoza kept her eyes on the large table which was occupied by around eleven people.

"That's a lot of back-up," she said.

Horowitz sighed. "They're all colleagues from the newspaper. Ex-colleagues. They don't know why I'm here. They think this is my goodbye party. I thought it would be safer to come in a group, in case you weren't who you said you were."

"Who else would I be?"

Horowitz did not answer.

Mendoza looked him over and decided the man looked

like he hadn't slept in days. David Horowitz had dark loose skin under his brown eyes and his curly greying hair and beard looked like they badly needed a trim.

"Who's your stand-in?" Mendoza asked.

"He's just a friend of mine. He insisted on meeting you in my place to protect me."

"He works at *The Post*, doesn't he?" Mendoza asked, as she recalled the voice she had spoken to when she contacted the newspaper looking for Horowitz.

"Yes."

"So were you in contact with Alec after you left?"

"Not much. A few phone calls to check on him and sort out my mail and bills, that sort of thing."

"How did you find out that Alec had died?"

"Sartre's girlfriend, Mai Nguyen, phoned me at work the day after Alec died. She'd found me on the internet. Saw articles I had written recently for the *Post* and phoned the newspaper."

"Did you say Nguyen is Sartre's girlfriend? I thought he was married to Alec's cousin Amelia Hirsch?"

The food arrived. The waiter put Mendoza's plate down in front of her while the real Horowitz directed the waiter to where his friend was now seated.

"He is. Nguyen is also his secretary. She's a nice lady. We had a good talk. She asked for my address. I saw no reason not to give it to her at the time."

"She's the woman who witnessed Albert Whitefeather being thrown off the bridge," Mendoza said, more to herself than her companion.

"Who?"

"Doesn't matter," she replied as the reason for Nguyen

withdrawing her statement about the pale man she saw throwing Albert off the bridge became clear. Sartre's girlfriend had probably coincidentally driven over the bridge at the same time that the murder took place, a killing Mendoza felt Sartre had something to do with, and he had obviously exerted pressure over his unwitting girlfriend to change her statement.

"Did you give her your home number or cell number?"

"Neither. Both are unlisted anyway. She just asked for my address."

"And you didn't think that was strange?"

"I just thought she wanted to send me a condolence card. The day after Mai phoned, someone came to my apartment block looking for me. He mistook a neighbour for me and tried to force his way into the house. He asked my neighbour what he knew about the 'missing goods'. There was a struggle. Another neighbour came out of her apartment and the guy ran off."

"Was your neighbour able to give a good description of the man?"

"Yes. He wanted me to go with him to the police and give a statement but, after what happened to Alec, I knew it was better to keep quiet. I begged him to let it go. He said the guy was huge and looked like he needed a blood transfusion."

"Meaning he was very pale?" she asked.

Horowitz nodded.

Mendoza smiled. The pieces were beginning to come together.

"What did he mean when he referred to 'the missing goods'?"

262

"It's complicated."

"I got time," Mendoza replied.

"A few months before Alec and I split up, he had been on a dig at a Native American settlement. He found a lot of important artefacts. It was a real coup for Richmond University. All of the items were photographed and a record taken of their descriptions. A few days after Alec got back to the university, his mother became ill so he flew to London to be with her. While he was on his way to London, Amelia Hirsch was flying in the opposite direction to visit Sartre. When Alec got back to Richmond, three of the items he found on the dig site were missing."

"And you think Sartre and Hirsch had something to do with it?"

Horowitz exhaled. "I don't know. Like I said, I can't prove anything but when Alec got back he wanted to phone the police. Sartre tried to talk him out of it but Alec was enraged. He asked Alec to wait until the board met the following morning and Alec agreed to do that. That same day, campus security searched Alec's briefcase on his way off campus and inside was a priceless Native American necklace."

"Which Sartre had had planted on him?"

Horowitz rested his eyes on his lap. "Sartre said the board was considering Alec's position at the university and that he was facing police charges and might lose his job. Alec was distraught. He couldn't eat or sleep. He began to drink heavily. Two days later, he was shocked when he found that $100,000 had been deposited into an account the university used to pay his salary into. It had come from an unknown account. Alec never used that account for anything other than his salary so the only people who knew the account number was the university. The money had been paid in a couple of days after the artefacts had gone missing."

"Making it look like Alec had sold them," Mendoza surmised.

Horowitz nodded. "Alec phoned his bank and they said the money had been wired through an account on the Cayman Islands. They tried to search back and it had been routed from Paris, through Switzerland first. He wrote to the bank and said the money was not his but they couldn't give it back. It had legitimately been paid from an account that was subsequently closed."

"So what happened with Sartre?"

"Sartre told Alec he knew about the money that had been paid into his account and that the university would drop all charges ..."

"In exchange for his silence about the missing artefacts," Mendoza replied.

"Yes."

Mendoza sighed. Alec Holton was being blackmailed by his employer, his cousin, his shady lover Simon Caird and had an angry Native American threatening to expose him. She wondered how the man had coped under such pressure.

"What happened between you two?"

Horowitz slumped back in his chair. "You mean apart from the pressure caused by Sartre? After the necklace incident, Alec was different. There was sadness to him, a desperation. He stopped talking to me about it. He became distant. I got lonely. We started to argue a lot. Eventually, the relationship just fizzled out."

"There's no way my friend who is being blamed for the murder did it," Mendoza said. "I know him. He couldn't. But the night Alec was killed, no-one was seen coming in or out of his apartment except him. I can't explain that. Can you?"

Horowitz exhaled and thought about this. "Only other way in or out is through the garbage chute. But who on earth would climb up a garbage chute? Plus, they'd need to have had keys to get into the basement."

"The janitor never mentioned a garbage chute."

"Probably because Alec didn't use it. He had these fears and annoying quirks. Like smells. He was convinced he could smell garbage wafting up through the shaft. It was nonsense of course. He was also scared stiff of rats. He thought if someone didn't lock the hatch, they'd get in. He once told me that Amelia left it open for a whole weekend while he was away so he locked it and had the janitor change the key so Amelia could never open it again. He put the kitchen table in front of it. The police probably didn't even notice it when ... when they found him."

"Hirsch lived with him?"

"A long time ago. She's a lot younger than Alec and came to USD to do her PhD when Alec was already working there – so she slept on his couch until she found her own place."

"Who would have had keys to the apartment?"

"I didn't have one for the garbage hatch. Alec didn't trust me not to take the easy way out of disposing of garbage. I gave him my keys to the lobby door and the apartment door when I was leaving. Meara Henschel had a full set of keys but we can surely discount her. I don't

265

know if Amelia still has keys. I mean, why would she keep them for all this time?"

"Did you ever have any more visits from the pale guy?"

"The day after he came to my apartment, someone phoned the main switch at work three times and asked if I was there, but they wouldn't leave a message or a number. That evening, I was leaving the office around ten thirty. It was dark but I saw a man matching his description standing across the road. I went back inside and asked the security guard to call a cab for me. When the cab arrived, the security guard walked me to it and when we reached my apartment block I asked the cab driver to wait at the curb until I got inside. About two hours before the guy turned up at my office, the same pale guy had been trying to buzz up into the apartment. My partner could see him on the camera. He went to a neighbour's apartment and stayed there until I got home."

"What did you do?"

"I resigned from my post with immediate effect and we've been staying somewhere else until we find another apartment to rent."

Mendoza thought about what Horowitz had just told her. Sartre had no way of knowing if Holton had told his partner about the missing artefacts. Perhaps, she thought, Sartre was just sorting out loose ends but her gut feeling was that there was another reason why Sartre wanted to silence him.

"So, I take it the Hirsch and Sartre marriage is a sham?"

"Everything about Hirsch is fake. She's been using her marriage to Sartre for years to hide her affair with a well-known married politician in London. She claims to be a humanitarian and a political activist and I admit I only met her twice but she came across as very materialistic. She was dripping in expensive jewellery and I'd say the outfits she was wearing cost a half year of my salary."

"*Hmmm*, how did she get along with Alec?"

"She didn't. Alec liked her better I think, least he did when they were younger. He tried hard to keep up a relationship with her but she was – may I be blunt?"

Mendoza nodded.

"A complete fucking bitch."

Mendoza laughed.

"Hirsch was jealous that Alec was going to come in for the majority of the inheritance from his mother who had been a bigger shareholder than Amelia's parents. The family had been in banking. A trust was overseeing the company until Mrs Holton died. Neither Alec nor Amelia had any interest in banking. Amelia doesn't like to work hard. She makes it look like she does, flying all around the world supposedly doing diplomatic work but it's the jet-set lifestyle she's after. The old lady made sure Amelia had to do something. She was offered a chair on the board of directors but she refused that, so Alec's mother gave her a paltry yearly payment which was low enough to ensure Amelia had to earn a living. Alec and Amelia had agreed that as soon as the old lady died they were going to sell their shares."

"And if Alec was dead before that happened?" Mendoza asked.

The smile slowly slipped from Horowitz's face. "You don't think?"

Mendoza shrugged.

"But she was going to be rich enough to do nothing for the rest of her life even without Alec's share of the inheritance," Horowitz said.

Mendoza could see the genuine upset on his face. "It's just a thought. I'm probably wrong. But can I ask you – do you know the terms of Alec's will? Do you think he might have left his inheritance to you in the event of his death?"

"No. We never discussed it. I doubt it. I mean, I left him."

Mendoza tapped the table and ruminated over the new information.

"He may not have had time to change the will or he may have wanted you to have the money regardless."

"Oh, I hope not. I mean, not that I couldn't do with it – but I'd feel, I don't know, guilty. You know, I'm happy with my new partner who is completely different from Alec and it took a while to see that I've found the right person for me. I hadn't been happy for a long time. But ... I feel so guilty that I left Alec. I keep thinking that if I'd been there that night, I might have been able to save him."

"You couldn't have known. And I'm glad you've found someone."

Horowitz smiled as he thought about the person he had fallen in love with, a love that took him by complete surprise at a time of his life that he thought he knew what he was looking for.

"Sometimes love comes when we're not looking for it and maybe not in the shape we expected it to. We don't get to choose who we love. It's fate."

Mendoza nodded. "I agree," she said.

Her phone buzzed. She lifted it and read the text from

Locklear updating her on what he knew.

She stood and lifted her wallet from her purse.

Horowitz raised his hands in protest. "Please! Let me get the check."

Mendoza smiled and thanked him.

As she left the restaurant, she checked the street to ensure there was no-one watching her and phoned Meara Henschel. Henschel answered the phone after eight rings and appeared to have been sleeping.

"I *know* who you are," she barked as Mendoza reminded the woman of their meeting. "Just because I'm old doesn't mean I'm stupid."

"Miss Henschel, do you happen to know the name of the lawyer Alec would have used for his will?"

"Why?" the old woman barked.

"It's a line of enquiry we're following. It's important."

"He uses the same one as me. Ethan Blank on Ellwood."

"Thank you," Mendoza said.

She ended the call and got a cab to her hotel, checking all the way that she was not being followed.

As she entered her room, she dialled Locklear's number. When he answered, she felt her face flush.

She stuttered as she tried to speak, unsure what, if anything, to say about her early-morning call to him. "S–sarge?"

"Hi, Mendoza."

"Em ... just calling in with an update."

"I'm driving around Pine Ridge. I've pulled in, so shoot."

Mendoza updated Locklear on what she had found out and stated that she would not be joining him in South

Dakota the following day but would fly to Richmond and check out the hidden garbage hatch in Holton's apartment and would also try to meet with Holton's lawyer. Her boss remained quiet throughout the call.

"So, that's everything," Mendoza said nervously.

"OK. Good work," Locklear said and updated his trooper on his own plans.

She waited nervously until he finished.

"Is there anything else we need to discuss, sarge?" she asked, anxious now to get everything said so they could get back to their semi-fractious yet mutually respectful relationship.

"Nothing that I can think of right now," he replied.

"OK. Well, then, see you soon."


Locklear ended his call with Mendoza, signalled back onto the road and drove his car around the block, hoping to see the faces of people leaving Han Paul's house having attended the Native American movement meeting and hoping that Jim Hunter's face would be among them. He had deliberately not asked the craft-store owner about Hunter in case the old man warned the USD student and the kid skipped town before Locklear had a chance to ask him about the day he went to the dig site with Tommy Rosenberg and Carter.

Locklear's visit to the elementary school had not resulted in any leads. He was disappointed to find that the contact Eddie Grass had given him was out of town and would not be back to work until the new school term. He did manage to talk the new teacher into checking the register for a past pupil named Jim Hunter but the search

270

had come up with nothing. No-one by that name had ever attended the school.

His short, cursory meeting with local cops was also unremarkable. The station's head, Adam Clark, was white and an Alaskan who had come to the town the previous winter. His deputy was a young Native named Biyan Goulden, who remained silent throughout the short meeting. Neither seemed perturbed by his presence or his unauthorised investigation and vaguely offered to assist him if needed.

As Locklear passed Maggie's craft store and gas station, he saw the woman pumping gas into a rundown truck. She looked up as he drove by the lot. For reasons unknown to him Locklear slowed the car and stared at the woman who returned his gaze with intensity. He wondered if the woman was the proprietor whose name appeared over the door and if her long braids and old-fashioned clothing was, like her granddaughter, a gimmick to draw in tourists searching for the Native American experience. He smiled at her but her expression, which Locklear could not read, did not alter.

Locklear turned left off Route 18 onto Eastridge. As he neared the corner of Old Poolside Road, he noticed a gang of youths standing on the corner, kicking a football and roughhousing. Two of them were drinking from paper bags. Locklear cringed and wondered about the town's alcohol ban. Bootlegging, he assumed, was a thriving business wherever prohibition was in place. A motorbike was parked in the middle of the group. He recognised Olowa, the short-haired girl from the craft store and a tall gangly youth wearing a Grateful Dead T-shirt who stood awkwardly in the group. Locklear jammed on the brakes and pulled in to the curb. He got out, locked the car and began to walk over to the group. As he neared, the short-haired girl said something which made Jim Hunter run across the road in between moving traffic. Locklear gave chase through the intersection of East Ridge Loop Road, turning right at its junction where Hunter continued to run at a pace Locklear could not match. The road looped back onto Route 18. He stopped as he reached the crossroad and tried to catch his breath and then ran on. He could still see the figure of Jim Hunter running in the distance. The kid took a left onto Old Sundance Road and crossed Wolf Creek where he disappeared into the dense scrub. Locklear waited for a moment to see if he would emerge from the wilderness but there was no sign of him.

He turned and walked back to his car. The short-haired girl from the gift store stared angrily at him on the corner. Most of the other youths had gone, no doubt had run away because Olowa had told them that Locklear was a cop.

Locklear sighed and turned his car to face the twenty-mile journey to his motel. Darkness was falling and he had learnt little today that would further the investigation. He could only hope that tomorrow would be a better day.

# Chapter 22

As dawn broke, Locklear was already in Pine Ridge, driving around the streets, looking for Jim Hunter in the hope that the youth had a part-time job and might be seen making his way through the town on foot. The previous evening's call from Mendoza had proved interesting as she had learnt of the blackmailing of Holton which Mendoza was at pains to remind him, could not, as yet, be proven. He was surprised by his mild disappointment that she would not be joining him that day and tried to shake off the feeling that he was missing her.

He parked off the main street and walked along to a coffee house with a good view of the main street. He took his Stetson off and looked out of the window as he drank two strong coffees and ate more donuts than was good for him. He tapped his empty paper coffee cup on the table and reasoned that the time might have been better spent lying on his bed, thinking out what he knew so far and what direction the information Mendoza had gleaned from Holton's ex-partner would take them.

The only other lead he had was the old guy Han Pauls

warned him against visiting alone. He exhaled as he tried to decide if it would be smart to take Han's advice and wait for his trooper to return or if a visit to the guy alone was worth it to move the investigation forward.

He decided that it was worth the risk. He stood, threw his paper coffee cup into the bin, put his hat on his head and left.

He turned the car towards Route 18 where Han had said Daccota Looks-Twice lived alone in a rundown clapboard on an isolated prairie ten miles outside of Pine Ridge. He passed Maggie's gas station and craft store again but the woman was not standing outside.

He took the turn-off at the Shell station and followed the steep incline up the dirt road. He already knew that he was at a disadvantage. He was unarmed and if Looks-Twice was home, he would most likely already be able to see him as his car wound up the hilly road. He stopped the car a short distance before the house and got out slowly. Locklear listened for the dogs Han said he would be able to hear but there was no sound except the breeze whistling through the long grass on the prairie. He walked closer and looked at the wooden house from the distance but there was no sign of anyone. He glanced to the side and noticed a huge barn to the left of the dilapidated home. He wondered why anyone would bother building such a large, modern-looking barn when they lived in a house that obviously needed rebuilding. Locklear moved forward slowly.

When he reached the house he tilted his hat back and crept towards the front door. He listened at the door for signs of movement but again he heard nothing. He placed his hand on the handle of the fly screen and pulled it towards him. But the hinges of the door were unscrewed and, as he pulled it forward, it fell. As he grappled with the metal mesh, the solid inner door opened and before Locklear could react, a big Native man lunged towards him with a rifle in his hand.

Locklear threw the screen door off him and leapt to his feet, putting his hands up in the hope that he would at least get to explain his presence to the man he could see was Daccota Looks-Twice because of the long arrow-shaped scar across his forehead.

Before he got a chance to utter one word, Looks-Twice brought the butt of the rifle up into his jaw. He fell back and tried to regain his balance as the sound of ringing shrilled in his ears.

Looks-Twice laughed.

"I'm a cop." Locklear said when he could manage to speak. "My name is Detective Sergeant Locklear. I'm from Richmond PD."

"Half-breed!" the man spat as he slammed his rifle into Locklear's face again. The sky spun above him and Locklear fell to his knees.

"Wait!" he pleaded but Looks-Twice landed one final blow to Locklear's head. He fell back onto the dry earth and as his eyes slowly closed he could see an eagle above him, soaring in the clear blue sky.

# Chapter 23

Mendoza's 6.10 am flight from DC to Richmond took three hours and seven minutes and got her into her home town at 9.17am. She hailed a cab and directed the driver to take her to the office of Ethan Blank on Elwood Street.

The cab continued on through the downtown boulevard and then took a left onto the upmarket, pretty tree-lined street which was not a part of the city she was familiar with. She got out of the cab and demanded a receipt from the driver. She had, as requested by Locklear, made a rough record of their outlay during the investigation but knew that emailing this to Benson now was not wise. Her sergeant's view that they should delay their claim until Kowalski, who might be less irate with them, returned, or until the case had been solved, was a far better idea. Unless their money ran out first, or rather Locklear's money as she had begun using his credit card knowing her own would most likely burst into flames if she tried to swipe it at any more airports or hotels.

As she sat in the waiting area, she entertained herself reading glossy magazines until the door opened and Ethan

Blank stepped into the reception area to greet her. Mendoza stood and stretched out her hand which Blank shook warmly. He motioned for her to come inside and sit on one of the huge comfortable armchairs. Mendoza suddenly felt like she was not entering an office of business but a shrink's den. It was an experience she'd had on only one occasion when forced to speak to the force's psychiatrist after the shooting of two colleagues while she was on a call-out with them. Both survived but neither of the two men recovered enough to return to work. Her thoughts moved to their wives and children and she wondered how they were doing now.

"You seem distracted," Blank began.

Mendoza smiled. Blank was an ordinary-looking man. He had thinning brown hair and light grey eyes beneath his clear framed glasses. His skin was the washy white colour of an indoor worker. His suit was a dark navy and he wore shiny brown shoes which looked comfortable. His face was smooth save for long laughter lines at the side of his eyes and a few worry lines on his forehead.

"It's just that this room reminded me of a shrink's office I had to go to once."

Blank looked surprised by the revelation and the easy smile slipped from his face.

Mendoza raised her hands up and laughed.

"Don't worry, I'm not crazy! Two of my colleagues got shot in the line of duty and, you know, it's procedure – you have to go talk with the force's shrink to make sure you're fit for duty."

"Did you pass?" Blank grinned.

"Guess so. I'm sitting here!" Mendoza laughed.

On Blank's large and unbelievably tidy desk sat a photo

of the lawyer with a woman, two teenage girls and a large dog.

"You've got children?" Mendoza asked as she glanced at the photo.

Blank looked over at his desk as if he had forgotten about the family that was waiting for him at home. He smiled warmly.

"Yes. They're fifteen and seventeen now. Each time they threaten to run away because they can't have tickets to see whichever singer they're obsessed with at the moment, my wife and I suggest that she and I will leave instead and they can stay and pay all the bills!"

Mendoza laughed.

"What about you?" he asked.

"A son. He's with my mom in Mexico at the moment."

"What can I do for you, officer?"

"You prepared Alec Holton's will, yes?"

"Yes, about a month ago. It was a revised will. I heard about what happened. Terrible. Just terrible. He seemed such a nice man. Gentle. He came across as, well, naive for someone born into such wealth. Meara Henschel called me this morning and gave me strict instructions to tell you everything I know."

Mendoza smiled. "She's a tough cookie."

"Miss Henschel seems to have woken up this morning with a sudden dislike of Mr Holton's cousin Amelia Hirsch. She thinks she's up to no good."

"And is she?"

"Meara referred Mr Holton to this firm about eighteen months ago. She thought the firm could help him with some legal queries he had."

"What kind of queries?"

"Holton's mother's will stated that if either Alec or his cousin predeceased each other, then the entire inheritance went to the surviving cousin. He wanted to know if that was watertight."

"And was it?"

"Well, no. I think it was probably wishful thinking on behalf of Mrs Holton. It took us a while to familiarise ourselves with the UK's Common Law and to get original manuscripts from London, but it seemed that Mr Holton's mother was not in fact the owner of the assets. The inheritance had already been left to Alec and his cousin by their respective fathers and Alec's mother was, well, a gatekeeper I suppose until she died and then the assets were to be divided between Alec and Ms Hirsch. Seventy per cent for Mr Holton and thirty per cent for Ms Hirsch."

"So, am I right in assuming that Alec could have left his share of the inheritance to whoever he pleased? That it didn't automatically have to go to his cousin?"

"Yes. Exactly."

"I wonder if Amelia Hirsch knew this?"

"She does now. She arrived here unannounced a couple of days ago demanding to see Mr Holton's will. She said Mr Holton's mother died on June 12th, just a few days after her son. She showed me the death certificate."

"Mrs Holton is dead?"

"Yes, she was quite old. The death cert said she died of pneumonia. Ms Hirsch was with her when she passed away."

"How convenient," Mendoza said sarcastically.

"Anyway, Ms Hirsch said she had to delay the funeral

as she had business in the States and thought she'd fly to Richmond and make some enquiries. She was flying back to London the following day. Mr Holton was hardly cold when she arrived. We thought it to be in very bad taste."

"How did she know Alec had changed his legal firm?"

"Well, when Mr Holton first asked this firm to represent him, we wrote to his mother's lawyer requesting various documents so they would have had all of our contact details. I imagine the company must have told Ms Hirsch that Alec had changed law firms."

"Do you know what the terms of Mr Holton's previous will was?"

"No. I'm sorry."

"And did he give any reason why he wanted to write a new will?"

"No. I had only met him once before but he did seem different during our second meeting. He was definitely on edge and wanted the will written as soon as possible."

Mendoza thought about this. It was clear that Alec Holton feared that his life was in danger.

"So, what happened when Hirsch arrived?"

"Well, I simply answered her questions and told her that she was not named as a major beneficiary in Alec's will. In fact, all he left her was a painting from an unknown Native American painter named Albert Whitefeather. Alec left it here, with me. He insisted on my placing it in the safe which amused me at the time. I don't know a lot about art, but it really isn't very good. The scenery is pretty, I suppose. Would you like to see it?"

"Hirsch didn't take it?"

"She wouldn't even open it. She actually lifted it and

threatened to smash it over my head! She's tiny but seems to be unexpectedly strong for someone so small."

Blank stood, pressed a button on his phone and asked for the painting to be brought to his office. When his secretary brought it in, he gently peeled back the brown paper and held it up for Mendoza to see. The scenery was of beautiful prairie land in springtime. Long golden grass swayed in varying shades of yellow and gold. In the background, a small forest dotted the landscape and buffalo roamed freely. Teepees could be seen in a deep valley in the centre of the frame. It was a peaceful scene. Mendoza glanced at the corner of the painting which was entitled 'Before Betrayal' and was signed by Albert Whitefeather Mills.

She stood back and inhaled.

"Can you make any sense of it?" Blank asked.

Mendoza grinned and nodded.

"Apart from threatening to knock you out with a painting, did Hirsch say anything else?"

"She threatened to sue my firm but she's wasting her time. The will is completely legal and Mr Holton was in a fit state to make his wishes known. She insisted on knowing who the beneficiaries were."

"And you told her?"

"I had no reason not to. The will would have been formally read at some point anyway."

"Can I ask who the beneficiaries were?"

"Well, $50,000 is to go to the janitor at Mr Holton's building. The rest of the estate is to go to a former partner by the name of David Horowitz. He left a letter for Mr Horowitz, asking him to use some of the money to establish a trust to provide educational opportunities for Native Americans."

"What would happen if Horowitz was deceased when the will was read?"

Blank stared at Mendoza as he tried to digest what she was saying.

"*Is* he dead? I've found it impossible to get in contact with him."

"No. But what if he was?"

"Em, well, Mr Moretti the janitor would receive his payment and then the estate would go to probate. I imagine Ms Hirsch would file a motion that the remainder of the estate should go to her as Mr Holton's next of kin."

Mendoza thought about the danger Horowitz was in.

"I may know where he is, but I think it's safer if I get him to contact you."

Blank nodded. "I see."

"Thanks for talking to me, Mr Blank."

Mendoza made her way back onto Ellwood. She hailed a passing cab and asked the driver to take her to Holton's apartment where she hoped to get the janitor to let her in to see the hatch Horowitz had told her about.

Outside the apartment, Mendoza buzzed the janitor's storeroom and waited while Matteo Moretti made his way to the door. He didn't look too pleased to see her on the doorstep but after a brief conversation he agreed to let her back into Holton's home.

They took the elevator to the second-floor apartment and Moretti opened the door.

"This place will be sold at some stage of course," he

said. "Soon as the lawyers are finished up doing whatever it is they do."

"Is everything OK?" Moretti had been more than helpful to her when they last spoke but now he appeared somewhat unfriendly.

"Not really. The building's board has moved to retire me. That's a nice word for 'fired'. Five votes. Used to be Mr Holton voted against and it was an all or nothing deal."

"I'm sorry."

"It's probably for the best. There have been too many changes here. I'm tired and I'm old."

"I heard about the money Mr Holton left you," Mendoza said.

Moretti smiled for the first time. "I guess he knew they'd fire me as soon as he was gone."

Mendoza wandered down the hallway to the kitchen. The kitchen table, which was still covered with a long, old-fashioned tablecloth, was pushed up against the wall as Horowitz had said.

Mendoza pulled back the table, revealing a squat chute door.

"Can you give me the key, please?"

"Sure," Moretti said as he singled out a long silver key and handed it to her.

Mendoza felt around her pockets but found no gloves. She took a paper towel from beside the sink and covered her fingers with it. She slid the key in but the hinged door opened before she had a chance to turn the key.

"It wasn't locked," Mendoza said as she pointed at the open chute.

Moretti came forward and stared at the lock. "But ... how?"

Mendoza borrowed the janitor's torch. She pointed it down into the metal shaft which was probably less than two feet wide and would allow only the slightest-framed person to climb up. About fifteen feet down she saw a suction cup, obviously left behind by the killer in his rush to get away.

She phoned O'Brien and told him to get forensics down to the building ASAP. O'Brien tried to argue with her about what he'd tell Benson but she ended the call and stared at Moretti.

"No-one uses the chute until after the cops are done with it, OK?"

"OK," Moretti replied weakly as he anticipated the wrath of the well-heeled residents who wouldn't take too kindly to having to travel to the basement with their garbage.

"Can you show me where the chute ends?"

She followed the janitor down the stairs into the basement. A large black dumpster sat underneath the end of the metal opening. Mendoza shone her torch into the dumpster but it was less than a quarter full.

"When was it collected?"

"Three days ago. It's collected once a week. Time before that was the day before Mr Holton died."

Mendoza scanned the distance between the metal chute, the opening to which was finished with a sharp, serrated metal edge and the bottom of the dumpster. Even if the dumpster had been a quarter way full, a person of average height standing inside the bin would have found it impossible to reach the opening and, if they did manage it somehow, would have cut their hands to shreds trying to hold on to its razor-sharp edge. She looked around the basement to see if there was anything a murderer could have used to give them height but there was nothing.

"So, if it was almost empty there's no way someone would have reached up to grab onto the chute. There was nothing to stand on."

Moretti looked up at the metal opening and shook his head. "Not unless he was ten feet tall and had hands made of leather."

"What's outside there?" Mendoza asked as she pointed towards a shard of light coming through a door at the back of the basement.

"It's small yard that leads onto a side street. Directly across the yard is the building's parking lot. The owners got together and bought a derelict house behind here, knocked it down and put in some parking spaces. Before that there was only on-street parking and there were always rows about it."

Moretti opened the exit door which led onto the paved yard. Strong sunlight flooded into the musty basement. Mendoza walked across the yard to the parking area which was accessed through a locked metal gate. There were no vehicles in the small lot which looked as though it would hold no more than eight cars.

"Everybody's at work. Just Miss Henschel here by day and she needs a janitor all to herself," he quipped.

"Yeah. She's a real piece of work alright."

"But she's had a difficult life with a lot of sadness. Must be hard to carry around all that anger. I think about my blessings every day. Life in a new country. I thank God for my wife, children, grandchildren. I've even got a great-grandchild on the way. I'm grateful. Each time I feel angry about the way she treats me, I think, 'Matteo, God blessed you more than he did this old lady so be kind' and I am. I do my best for her."

"Even though she voted to fire you?"

"Maybe she did me a favour?" he said with a laugh.

Mendoza looked up at the back wall of the building and was disappointed to see no cameras. She turned to the parking area and could see no cameras there either. She walked onto the side street and glanced up at the fire escape which gave access to the side window of the apartment's bedroom. But Locklear had discounted entry by the fire escape from the start. A camera was placed on the gable end looking towards the main road and away from Mendoza's area of interest.

"There are no cameras at the back of the building?" she asked.

Moretti shook his head.

"Sometimes rich people are too mean to protect their riches. It makes no sense to me."

Mendoza turned and looked across the road to where a pizza shop blared Italian music from two huge speakers which hung on each side of its store front. The music stopped abruptly, made a booming noise and began to play again. The noise had sounded a little like a gun firing and Mendoza had jumped.

"That noise makes Miss Henschel mad. She makes all her carers go to the store and complain but it's a problem with the music system. It makes a loud noise when it rewinds to the beginning again. I don't know how she can even hear it. She says she's a little deaf and her apartment is on the other side of the building, but I guess she looks for any reason to complain. The owner doesn't care if she is mad because Miss Henschel doesn't buy any pizzas."

Mendoza nodded. "All her carers? Rosa isn't the only one?"

"She is now but they come and go so quickly. An agency sends them and they all get sick of Miss Henschel ordering them about and they leave. Last one stayed three days and never came back. Never said she was going neither. Just left Miss Henschel high and dry. I was surprised. She seemed nice. She got the job after the previous carer was in an accident. She didn't make it. It was a hit and run. Cops haven't got anyone for it yet."

"So how long has Rosa been working for Miss Henschel?" Mendoza asked as an idea popped into her head.

"Eh … I think she started on June 1st. I remember because the day before was my grandson's birthday. The carer didn't show and I was late getting home because I had to run an errand for Miss Henschel. She can't get to the store on her own anymore."

"So, she started working here just over a week before Mr Holton died?"

"Yeah, that'd be about right."

"And you say the previous carer just never showed up on, what, May 31st?"

"Yes. She only stayed three days. I figured she'd last longer because she was quiet and very timid. Just the type Miss Henschel likes to boss around."

"What was her name?"

"Her first name was unusual – Nubia. She had a name

tag on her with the agency logo. Her last name was Ardavan."

"American?"

Moretti shrugged. "No, she was foreign-born but she never said where she was from. She hardly spoke to me. Like I said, she seemed shy."

"Do you still have security tapes from then?" Mendoza asked hopefully.

Moretti smiled. "I keep the footage for a month before I delete it and not for the reason you'd think. I get paid once a month – second week of every month. Miss Henschel made three complaints about me going home early or coming in late which were not true. She got me brought in front of the committee. I got a warning so I began to save the tape for four weeks at a time. When I get paid, I delete them. That way, if she ever accuses me again, I can be clearly seen on the front-door tape coming in and going home."

"What about the hallway surveillance?"

"It all runs on the same system so anything you want, I got."

"So, you'd need a key to get into the basement but you can only open the chute from inside the apartment?"

"Yes. The doors came with locks so kids in the apartments couldn't open the chute and fall down."

Mendoza nodded as she thought about how someone had managed to jump up to the chute. There was no way a killer would arrive carrying a ladder. Mendoza figured she knew the answer.

The music from the Italian pizzeria changed to a slow melodic tune. She turned to look at the store again and noticed a camera placed high to the left of the door. She crossed the road, followed by Moretti, and stood under it to see what direction it was pointing. Mendoza grinned. The killers, because she knew now there was not one, but two, had come into the basement on the night Holton was killed and would have been caught on the pizzeria's camera.

She looked into the store and saw one man standing at the counter staring into space. She could see the arms of a woman through the service hatch, beating dough into a flat round shape.

"Matteo, would you please bring the tapes from the hallway outside Mr Holton's apartment from May 30th and 31st over to the pizzeria? I can view them at the same time that I view their footage."

"Sure," he said and left.

After a two-minute conversation with the proprietor, Mendoza was directed to a small room at the back of the store to view their security tapes.

The owner's wife, Sofia, brought the tape of the night Holton was killed to her.

"I knew the man who died – he came in here a lot. It's sad," she said.

Mendoza insisted on viewing the tape alone and Sofia left her. She waited while the grainy tape moved slowly, recounting each minute of the rainy evening. Several people passed the store with umbrellas, blocking her view. She exhaled and moved the tape on a little, aware that the killer might have been in the building for hours before the murder actually took place. Ten painstakingly slow minutes passed with no movement other than the normal customers coming and going.

Matteo arrived with the two tapes from Holton's building. Mendoza popped the tape from May 30th into the pizzeria's second monitor and watched as Miss Henschel and the carer she now knew to be Nubia Ardavan came and went on their landing. She watched Holton leave for work and arrive home looking exhausted. She fast-forwarded her way through the tape and, with nothing to see, ejected it and placed the tape from May 31st into the machine. She let the tape roll slowly while she watched the second screen of the roadside outside the pizzeria. Then she took a chance and fast-forwarded the pizzeria tape to 10.10pm on the night Holton died. She slowed the tape again and watched. Business at the store slowed and between ten-fifteen and ten-twenty only three customers collected pizzas from the store. She moved back to the apartment-landing screen and watched it in fast motion until her attention was drawn to the pretty young carer walking across the hall from Meara Henschel's door to Holton's at 11.30am, with a small rucksack on her back, three and a half hours after the man had left for work and possibly the time the old woman took a nap. The woman let herself into Holton's apartment, presumably having relieved the sleeping Henschel of her set of keys, and closed the door behind her. Mendoza noted the time. Fifteen minutes later the cool young woman exited the apartment. Mendoza locked in on her company ID: *Nightingale Home Care Services*. Then the carer re-entered Henschel's home to complete her work at the job she was never to show up at again.

Mendoza phoned the company while she watched the tapes from the pizzeria move slowly. By the time she finished the call, she had learnt that the carer had only joined the agency a few days before she got a post with Henschel and had insisted on a post on Creek Avenue, stating that her child attended the school at the top of the small avenue and as she was a lone parent, who did not own a car, she needed work close to her child's school. The woman, or whoever had put her up to posing as a carer in order to unlock the chute leading up to Holton's apartment, had done her homework and must have known that Henschel was the only customer the company had on the avenue. The company rep she spoke to also said that Ardavan never showed up for work again and their attempts to contact her had failed. Ardavan had completed her mission and had provided access to the apartment to someone who could not afford to be seen on the premises. Someone who would be easily recognisable on camera. Someone Holton knew.

Mendoza moved her focus back to the pizzeria footage and at exactly 10.22 pm a dark sedan pulled up and parked at the curb across the street. Two people dressed in dark hooded clothing got out and walked into the yard at the back of the building and towards the locked basement.

Mendoza froze the screen and scanned the back of the figures. One was very tall and broad and most probably male and the other short and thin. Mendoza felt that the shape of the figure of the smaller person was that of a woman but she couldn't be sure. She moved the tape on a little and watched as the smaller of the two handed the other a set of keys. The door to the basement opened and the pair disappeared inside the building. Mendoza waited. She could feel her breathing quicken, knowing that these were to be the last few minutes of Alec Holton's life. She waited for ten minutes and did not take her eyes from the screen. The small moths that flew across the screen were the only movements on the isolated street. Her finger itched to fast-forward the camera but she knew she couldn't. She knew that each moment unfolding before her could unlock the mystery of Alec Holton's murder.

Sofia knocked and offered her a coffee. Mendoza refused as she kept her eyes fixed on the footage. Suddenly, the basement door opened and the two figures emerged. Mendoza checked the clock. 10.55pm. An unwitting Carter was probably parking his car at this very moment outside the front of the building, thinking that he was visiting to make peace with his colleague who was gasping for breath in his office on the second floor.

"*Come on!*" Mendoza said to the two figures as they skulked towards the car.

"*Look up!*" she shouted but the figures kept moving towards their parked car with their heads down.

Then abruptly they halted and their heads shot up.

They were looking across at the pizzeria and Mendoza knew why.

The pizzeria's music system must have come to a halt with its usual loud bang.

Mendoza froze the screen and smiled at the faces that she had never seen in person but whose identities she knew.

"*Gotcha.*"

# Chapter 24

By the time she'd made the seventh unanswered call to Locklear's phone, Mendoza knew something was wrong. As she made her way to the airport, she called O'Brien from her cab but he had not heard from the detective sergeant. O'Brien had managed to get forensics to Holton's apartment and had avoided telling Diaz and Hill who he knew would somehow mess up the crime scene.

"You don't trust Diaz or Hill, do you?" Mendoza asked.

"No," O'Brien replied simply.

"I want to know more about that, O'Brien, but right now I need to find Sergeant Locklear."

O'Brien made no reply.

"O'Brien?"

"Yes?"

"First, I need you to talk Benson into contacting the DC police and arrange for a man by the name of David Horowitz to be taken into protective custody."

"Are you crazy, Mendoza? I'm a desk officer. A computer nerd. How do you suppose I'll talk Benson into that?"

"Use your head, O'Brien. If you can't talk Benson into taking Horowitz to safety then make something up about him and have him taken in for questioning. He'll be safer in a jail cell than on the streets."

"I'll try."

"Second, find out everything you can about a young woman named Nubia Ardavan."

O'Brien went quiet again.

"*O'Brien!*" Mendoza yelled.

"She's the daughter of an Iranian diplomat based in Paris. Until two years ago he was the curator of the National Museum of Iran. She has no convictions, holds full diplomatic immunity and last flew out of Richmond on the evening of June 1st. She married an American in Paris a few days later. I guess she's waiting for her new passport to arrive before we see her again. If we ever do."

"O'Brien, how do you know all this? And, more importantly, why? Why are you watching Ardavan?"

"It's a hobby," he replied quietly.

Mendoza thought for a moment. "O'Brien ... what are you not telling me?"

"Mendoza, this post was supposed to be my fresh start – my last move. I ... I've had to move around a lot and it's been hell. All I ever wanted was to be a police officer, a good one, but the past keeps coming back to bite me and old habits die hard. That's all you need to know."

Mendoza remained silent, surprised by the sudden emotion O'Brien was displaying. She suddenly felt like Locklear, uncomfortable and unskilled in the face of human emotion. Perhaps she was learning a little too much from her boss.

"Alright, O'Brien, but I'll be telling the sergeant about this. If he finds out you've been hiding things from him, for whatever reason, you'll be sorry you ever heard his name."

As Mendoza moved the phone from her ear she thought she heard O'Brien mutter something. She put the phone back to her ear but he was gone. Mendoza thought about phoning Kowalski but the captain was still on vacation and if something had happened, Locklear would have called her and not Kowalski who was most likely spending some of his time off thinking of ways he would punish them for ruining his much-awaited vacation. She took out her notes and decided to call Eddie Grass whose number Locklear had given her and who appeared to be the only person her sergeant knew in Pine Ridge.

"Is this Eddie Grass?" she asked when the stranger answered.

Grass was silent for a while.

"Who wants to know?" the retired cop cautiously replied.

Mendoza sighed.

"I'm Trooper Mendoza. I work with Detective Sergeant Locklear. I've been trying to get in touch with him but he isn't answering his phone. I know something is wrong. You are the only contact I know in Pine Ridge. So, do you have any idea where he'd be?"

Grass took a moment to reply.

"Maybe. But I know someone who might know for sure, someone I told him to contact. I'll phone and find out."

Mendoza paced the departures waiting area. Sweat trickled down her brow as she waited for her plane to take off. She dialled her boss three more times and left urgent messages. In the last call, she was close to tears as she pleaded with him to call her. With only the worst imaginings going through her mind, she shed some silent tears in the window seat and was thankful that there was no-one else seated beside her on the small regional plane. She had cancelled her planned flight to Rapid City from where she would have travelled to Pine Ridge by car as this was no longer an option. She didn't have time to take that route, needing the quickest route that would get her to her boss. After a ten-minute discussion with a less than enthusiastic desk clerk, she had booked a seven-and-a-half-hour flight with a one-and-a-half-hour layover in Denver to Chadron municipal airport. But the Nebraskan airport would still leave her around 40 miles from Pine Ridge.

She had sent a text to Grass giving him her arrival time and asking if he would pick her up as she could not waste time trying to rent a car when she felt in her bones that Locklear was in deep trouble. The sooner she got there and found him, the better.

# Chapter 25

Locklear woke to find that the face looking down at him was not that of Daccota Looks-Twice but of a young Native. He tried to open his eyes fully and moaned aloud.

"Quiet! Don't wake him!" the young guy said.

Locklear tried to push himself up from his supine position. He sat on the hard floor, touched his temple and smoothed out the hard-dried blood between his fingers.

"Looks like you might need sutures," the young man said.

Locklear looked around the room he found himself in. There were track marks on the ground where he had been pulled through the straw and left to lie on the cold hard ground beneath him. The walls were lined with square hay bales and he could smell chicken shit.

"I'm in the barn?" Locklear asked as he tried to stand. The room spun and he fell forward into the young man's arms.

Locklear noticed a small handle on the floor behind the young guy. He disentangled himself and crawled on his knees towards it.

"Wait now!" the kid said. "Please, don't make noise. I'm going to get you out of here before he wakes up."

"Before who wakes up?" Locklear rubbed his temples to try to reduce the sharp pain in his head.

"Looks-Twice."

Locklear remembered the man coming at him at the front door of the house and hitting him. What he couldn't understand was why he was still alive, why Looks-Twice had not finished him off.

"Where's my hat?" he asked suddenly as though his Stetson mattered at this very moment in time.

The kid lifted it from the dusty ground behind Locklear, blew it clean and handed it to him.

"You're Jim Hunter," Locklear said. "I've been looking for you. I know you're a friend of Tommy Rosenberg. I want to know what the two of you were doing on that dig."

"Look, we can talk about that some other time. I begged Looks-Twice to get you out of here but he became really angry. I took him into the house to get him some medication but he has these blackouts and fell down on the kitchen floor. You have about ten or fifteen minutes before he comes to."

Locklear lifted the handle of the trapdoor which led down to a squat basement.

"Where's my phone?" he asked.

"Looks-Twice took it. He smashed it up."

"Give me your phone. I need to use its torch to look down here."

"Please don't look down there. It's better that you walk away now while you still can. I'll make sure he doesn't hurt you."

"Give me that goddamn phone!" Locklear barked.

Hunter handed over his phone and hung his head. Locklear shone its light down into the space which was nothing more than a dirt-floored shallow crawl space about three feet beneath the foundation of the barn. In it he saw several Native American artefacts and, if he was right, among the artefacts was the Native American Fertility figure Carter said was stolen during the dig.

"You stole that fertility figure from the dig here?"

"I did not steal them. These are our sacred things. I took back what belonged to my people. We would prefer to bury them back in the earth where our ancestors placed them but, when we did that before, the professor returned with his team and dug them up again. Please, I am asking you to just go and forget what you saw. They should not be put in a museum or sold to the highest bidder but placed where our ancestors intended them to be."

"*Intended!* Is this what *INTENT* means? That there was an agreed *intent* for people provided with consent for digs to return those items to their owners but they never did and, in fact, sold them?"

"Yes. And it means our *INTENT* is to get those items back whatever the personal cost to us."

Locklear looked at the handsome youth and the passion in his dark-brown eyes.

"Jim, you're a law student. If you're charged with the theft of these items, you know that you'll probably go to prison. That will finish any hope you have of using your education to help your people. Think about this."

"Please, you need to get you out of here before Looks-Twice wakes."

"The hell I will. I'm taking him in for questioning and I'm taking these artefacts with us."

Hunter stood to his full height. Locklear stood and faced him. The two men were about the same height but Hunter was younger, and stronger.

"I don't want to fight you," Locklear began as he inched toward the young Native.

He was interrupted by the sound of police sirens wailing onto the lot. He moved to the barn door, followed closely by Hunter.

Two policemen got out of the car and Locklear walked towards them.

"Looks-Twice is passed out on the floor inside the house. He assaulted me," Locklear told local cops Goulden and Clark. He left out the part about the missing artefacts, for now.

The cops entered Looks-Twice's house and pulled the man out in handcuffs.

Locklear walked across the dusty site.

"Mind if I speak with him alone?"

Clark nodded and he and Goulden walked casually back to their car.

Looks-Twice gave Locklear a look of disdain and spat in his face.

Locklear wiped his face and stared the man down.

"This kid, you've got him involved in something that's way over his head," he said. "He's got a good future. Don't take him down with you."

Looks-Twice stared at Jim Hunter.

Locklear waved the kid over and the three of them stood in a circle.

300

"What do you want?" Looks-Twice asked.

"You go with the police. You say the kid had nothing to do with anything. I know that you thought you were doing right. All you've done is take back things that were taken from your own land so hopefully you'll get off with probation."

"And for that?"

Locklear indicated Hunter. "For that I convince the police to let you keep the artefacts that rightfully belong to you, and I don't press charges for the assault. You agree to that and the kid tells me all he knows about who is buying the pieces. It's not INTENT I'm after, Looks-Twice. I know your organisation is only trying to protect artefacts from being wrenched from their proper heritage. I'm trying to help you stop the people who are taking those items in the first place. Hunter – I need you to come with me to meet Tommy Rosenberg off a flight that lands into Rapid City tomorrow morning at 9.00am. That's the next step in this investigation. That's how I think we can put an end to this."

Looks-Twice gave Locklear a cold hard stare while he considered the offer.

"Let's hope your white blood does not betray us."

Goulden and Clark strode over and took Looks-Twice to the police car.

Before the old man got in, he turned to Locklear.

"Half-breed?"

Locklear reluctantly looked in Looks-Twice's direction.

"You don't remember me, do you?"

Locklear shook his head.

"Probably better that way," Looks-Twice said.

301

Goulden placed his hand on the old man's head and pushed him into the car.

The police car drove off and another car pulled into the site, followed by an ambulance.

Eddie Grass climbed slowly out of his beaten-down vehicle as two paramedics made for Locklear and sat him on the steps of the ambulance to see to his wounds.

Grass blew out and dug his hands into his pockets.

"I spoke to Han. Seems that he phoned Looks-Twice and warned him that you'd be coming. He pleaded with him not to do you any harm or get himself into further serious trouble with the law. Guess Looks-Twice had other ideas."

Locklear sighed.

Grass looked over at Hunter who now stood alone at the edge of the site.

"That the kid you were looking for?" he asked.

Locklear nodded.

"His name is Paytah Little-Eagle, Locklear. Parents are dead – road accident when he was no more than three or four years old. Drunk driver killed them outright. Nobody here would know him as Jim Hunter. No wonder you couldn't find him. I think he's a distant relative of Looks-Twice."

Locklear beckoned for the young Native to come closer.

"OK, Jim, or Paytah, you better get out of here but tomorrow at first light I'll pick you up and we're meeting that flight. If you don't show up, I will find you and you will be charged with the theft of that fertility figure. Do you understand me?"

"You've made yourself clear," Hunter spat.

"Where do you live?"

Hunter hesitated. "I'll be at the corner of Village and 18."

Locklear nodded as the ambulance crew continued to check him over.

"You might have concussion. We're taking you to hospital," the ambulance man said.

"No, you're not," Locklear replied.

Grass touched Locklear's arm.

"Your trooper's pretty worried about you. I'm picking her up this evening when she lands. Just go and get checked out. Then you can finish the investigation."

Locklear rubbed his throbbing head. "OK."

# Chapter 26

Locklear woke for the second time that day with someone standing over him. Mendoza was staring down at him with a worried expression on her face. Through the window beside his hospital bed he could see that night had fallen and he had slept for hours since his arrival in the small regional hospital.

"Thank God you're OK."

"It's you who should be thanked. If you hadn't phoned Grass who in turn phoned Han, no-one would have known I was on Looks-Twice's isolated property. Right about now I expect I'd be in a shallow grave on his land."

"Seems like I saved your life twice?"

"Huh?"

"Remember, Beth Stoll, our weird case in Harrisonburg? She tried to shoot you? Mennonites? No?"

Locklear stared blankly at Mendoza.

"Jeez, sarge, if you're pretending, stop it. You're scaring me."

Locklear grinned and coughed. His left eye was black and swollen and a large purple bruise covered his cheek.

"Seems like the old guy gave you a going-over. Can't believe he did so much damage."

"He wasn't that old, Mendoza, and he was strong. I didn't see him coming. Simple as that."

Mendoza waited as Locklear told her about Han Pauls, about Looks-Twice and the coincidence that he had shot a young O'Brien when he served as a native cop in the area some years before, about Rosenberg and about Paytah Hunter's reluctant agreement to go with him to the airport with Locklear to meet the young frequent flyer who Locklear hoped to make sing like a canary..

Mendoza, in turn, told Locklear about the unused garbage chute in Holton's apartment, about the will which essentially meant Amelia Hirsch would be no richer from Holton's death and about Henschel's carer Ardavan who had used her position to gain access to Holton's apartment and ensure easy access for the person who planned to murder the mild-mannered professor.

She left the part about the security camera at the pizzeria to last.

"Hirsch and the albino?"

"Your White Ghost," Mendoza said.

"Seems he's been getting around. He came to Holton's ex-partner's apartment in DC armed. Had a tussle with a neighbour and fled. Horowitz has been living in fear ever since."

"And it was definitely them? You saw them clearly?"

"Well, the albino guy is easy to identify even though his face isn't really clear on the footage. The guy is huge with thick snow-white hair. I didn't know exactly what Hirsch looked like so I googled her. She's a five-foot, one-hundred-

and-twelve-pound powerhouse who won medals for gymnastics in high school and college."

"Why two of them? Why not use one of them to take Holton out?"

"I'll tell you why. You see, Hirsch knew the front and sides of the building had security cameras so she couldn't enter the building using either and a guy like our White Ghost, I mean, how hard would he be to find?"

"Very hard, as it turns out, Mendoza. This guy has been giving us the run-around ever since Carter first mentioned him. But go on."

"Anyway, Hirsch knew that the back entrance had no cameras. She had keys to the basement and, once inside, she just needed the ghost guy to lift her up to the chute. She wore thick leather gloves to climb in over the serrated edge. Then she used suction cups to climb up the chute. Thankfully she left one of them behind. It's with forensics now. Cops must have arrived on the scene sooner than she expected them to and she got sloppy."

"But the call to emergency services from Holton's home. It was a man who made that call."

"Could have been a tape played by Hirsch while she was inside," Mendoza offered.

Locklear nodded as he digested the information.

"You understand why I didn't issue a warrant for their arrests?" she asked.

Locklear inhaled. "Yes. Hirsch can't be arrested because she has diplomatic immunity. There's no way Benson would have touched that one. And the White Ghost, we don't even know who he is."

"And, if we alerted Hirsch that we were on to her, our

ghost friend would have disappeared, Tommy Rosenberg and Braff wouldn't board their flights and we'd never solve this case."

"Sartre and his gang of thieves went to a lot of trouble to point the finger at INTENT. What I don't understand is why Holton involved Carter and why Sartre worked hard to point the finger at him by planting evidence at his house."

Mendoza nodded. "I've been thinking about that. At first I thought Sartre had deliberately implicated Carter in the theft at the lab to blackmail him and get Carter to do his dirty work like he did with Holton. But he could have got anyone to steal artefacts on digs. He didn't need Carter for that. I think that Holton may have brought Carter to the site for his own safety in case Rosenberg tried anything. I think he feared for his life. Carter was simply in the wrong place at the wrong time. Sartre seized the opportunity then and had us running in two directions at once, or at least he thought he did. I doubt he knew of our relationship to Carter and that we'd know he wasn't guilty. He had to know we'd find out who INTENT were eventually but he was free to transport and sell artefacts during the time it would take for us to figure it out. Who knows, perhaps whatever Braff and Rosenberg are bringing in tomorrow is the jewel in the crown. Their retirement pot."

"Yes, seems plausible," Locklear replied.

"There's something else. O'Brien seemed to know all about Ardavan and her family. Seems he was tracking her movements. I couldn't get any more out of him than that but, I don't know, it's been bothering me. Why would he have been doing that? Why her? What else does he know that he's not saying?"

"You think Benson had him track her?"

"No. He said it's a hobby for him. I told him I'd tell you what he was up to. He'll be expecting you to question him."

Locklear thought about O'Brien's moonlighting for a moment. Slowly, he swung his legs over the side of the bed and tried to untie the hospital gown which was secured at the back.

"OK, I'll get to him later. Help me," he asked.

"Where do you think you're going?"

"Back to the motel," Locklear replied.

"No, you're not, sarge. You're staying here overnight and tomorrow we'll see how you are before we go chasing any more angry natives."

"I think I'm done pissing off the natives, Mendoza. I've moved my focus to Tommy Rosenberg and to whoever he is selling the artefacts to. You know Looks-Twice asked me today if I recognised him. I didn't but it got me thinking ..."

"About?"

Locklear squirmed as he tried to loosen the gown from about him. "Mendoza, will you help get me out of this thing?" he snarled.

Mendoza walked to the other side of the bed and began to untie the hospital gown's cords. Locklear reached back and pulled the gown off to the front and reached out for his clothes.

"Em, sarge," Mendoza said as she stood behind him.

"What?"

"You kinda don't have any underwear on."

"Damn it! Sorry!" he said as he used the gown to cover himself. "Guess they took off all my clothes when I passed out. I woke up in some scanning machine. Thought I was dead! Anyway, nothing you haven't seen before, Mendoza."

"Yes, but not *that* much!"

"Look away."

Locklear stood shakily and pulled on his clothes. Then he sat again on the bed and, as he bent down to put his socks on, the ground shot up towards him. He took a deep breath and waited for the dizziness to settle.

"Are you OK, sarge?"

"Yeah."

Mendoza came closer and pulled his socks and boots on.

"I'm helping you get dressed but I'm not taking you out of here. I'll pick you up first thing in the morning when the doctor is satisfied that you're OK."

Locklear frowned and lay back on the bed.

"I was telling you about Looks-Twice ..."

"Yes, you were, right before you flashed me."

Locklear grinned. "My head hurts so much I can't think straight but he ..."

"He what?"

"He called me a half-breed."

"And that hurt you?"

"No, it didn't *hurt* me, Mendoza. It's just ... he said it as soon as I walked up his steps. He didn't have time to get that good a look at me. It made me wonder if he knew who I was and knew who my family were."

"Sarge, when I first learnt that you were Native American, I hadn't noticed it before that. I mean, I could see you weren't white but I didn't guess what your exact background was. But now that I know, yes, it's obvious and I'm sure people around here can see it a lot quicker than people over east."

"I don't think it's that, Mendoza. There's more to this. Something is unsettling me. I feel ... strange."

"Yes, it's called concussion."

"Oh, Mendoza will you *listen* to me?"

"Sorry. OK, what's troubling you?"

"I realise that maybe I'm looking at it the wrong way around. I've been scaring people since I got here and if I'm not scaring them they're insisting they know me. First Cindy Geddis, then a native woman at the craft store, Han Pauls and now Looks-Twice. He actually spat at me."

"So, what are you saying?"

"Maybe Looks-Twice doesn't know who my native family are. Maybe it's my white family he knows. Grass told me a story about how the ridge near his house came to be known as White Ghost Ridge. It's a pretty awful tale. A lot of Native Americans were killed at Wounded Knee and in retaliation the tribe in Pine Ridge killed a whole wagon train of white settlers. There were only two survivors. An albino woman and her little boy."

"And what? You think that our White Ghost is related to this woman and that ... what? That you're both descendants of her? That you're related to the White Ghost?" Mendoza laughed. "Sarge, your concussion is worse than I thought!"

"I'm serious, Mendoza!" Locklear snapped.

The smile slipped from the young cop's face. "OK, sarge. Sorry! Well, look, let's just get this Tommy Rosenberg thing out of the way and then go back and talk to Looks-Twice. See what he can tell you. Unless, of course, sarge ..."

Mendoza stood, walked to the window and turned to face him.

"Unless you don't want to know? Maybe that's what's really troubling you. Finding out you have family somewhere would change your life completely. You'd have people to care for. People who might want to care for you. Or maybe you'd find out they're not good people. People who are different from you and your principles. I guess that's something you need to think about. Do you want to open that can of worms? Is it something you can handle?"

Locklear stood and walked to the window. He looked out into the dark night. A flash of lightning lit up the sky beyond White Ghost Ridge.

Mendoza turned to him and studied his side profile. She raised her hand up and smoothed down his thick black hair which had become matted on the pillow.

"It would still be better to know, though? Wouldn't it?" she said. "If he knows something about you, you can decide what to do with that information. You can walk away or you can face it. Whatever you decide, I'm here for you."

Locklear exhaled. "OK. I'll see you first thing in the morning, Mendoza, and don't be late. It's time to wrap up this case."

# Chapter 27

Paytah Hunter was exactly where he said he would be when Locklear drove by the intersection of Village and 18. The casually dressed youth was standing on the corner with a colourful backpack strung on his shoulder. He slithered into the car and shook Mendoza's hand – but he didn't look at her.

She noticed that the young man's hand was sweaty and his face was tightly set. Locklear pulled out and joined 18 due west.

"Why are you going this way? Take the loop around Bia road. It's shorter," Paytah ordered, without looking up.

"I don't know that way," Locklear replied as he eyed the nervous youth in the back seat.

He noticed Paytah slide lower down in the back seat as they passed Maggie's craft store. The woman was outside, looking into the distance as though she was searching for something. For the third time in days she locked onto Locklear's car with such intensity that he too wanted to sink in the seat to avoid her stare. After they passed the store, Paytah sat up again and began to play with his cell phone. Locklear wondered if the woman was a relative of Paytah's and if it was him she was looking for.

"Do you live on this street?" he asked.

Paytah made no reply.

"OK, good to know," Locklear said sarcastically as he glanced sideways at Mendoza for help.

"*Hey, kid!*" she barked.

Paytah put his phone down and shyly looked the trooper in the eye.

"I think we should use this time for you to educate us on your activities," she said.

Paytah thrust his phone into his pocket and stared out of the window. "OK."

For the rest of the one-hour-and-forty-minute drive, Paytah Little-Eagle told Locklear and Mendoza about how, at Looks-Twice and Albert Whitefeather's suggestion, he singled Tommy Rosenberg out on campus and built up a friendship with the socially awkward, lonely young man. He told them how Tommy trusted him and believed his story about being a city Native and how he had no interest in the culture or the history of his people. Paytah passed on information given to him by the trusting student about his parents and their colleagues' travel plans which resulted in INTENT having valuable information about their next targets. Paytah explained how INTENT knew that they could not bring the diplomats to justice but instead waged a war on them by intercepting their missions and retrieving many artefacts being transported for sale.

"So that's what Professor Rosenberg meant when he said Whitefeather had been a thorn in his side for a long time," Locklear said.

Paytah told how they were funded to stop the traffickers by thousands of philanthropists but that they had failed to prevent a huge percentage of the thefts as items appeared on a secret website for sale, about how the group cared not only about the artefacts of their own community but of others and how a global movement was soon established to try stop the illegal sales. Paytah recalled how many of the items were never noticed as being stolen due to the cunning of museum curators, skilled forgers and money-hungry diplomats whose immunity made them excellent transporters of the goods.

"How did Tommy get his grandfather to allow him to bring a Native American to an illegal dig?"

Paytah laughed. "The professor didn't want any of his students on site. They'd have to record what they found and he didn't want any paper trail or to answer any awkward questions from smart grad students. These goods were going directly for sale. I was hoping I'd find out where but I couldn't get that out of Tommy. He probably didn't know. He told his grandfather he'd bring a friend named Jim Hunter to help dig. I guess he was expecting a white kid. Tommy picked me up on campus and we drove to the site. Met Professor Rosenberg there. You should have seen his face when he saw me!" Paytah grinned.

Even Locklear laughed at this.

"I had Tommy prepared for how his grandfather might not like Native Americans so he told him this big story about how I was a city kid who didn't have any involvement with the culture. Rosenberg had no option but to buy it. I was already there. It's funny, right?"

"It's funny, Paytah, but it could have been dangerous," Locklear said.

Paytah said nothing for a while, then added, "On the way there Tommy told me that the other professor meeting us there was bringing one guy to dig but that he was pretty gullible."

"Poor Carter," whispered Mendoza.

Locklear tapped at the steering wheel as a question came to him. It was about the failures, the artefacts INTENT didn't manage to save from being sold.

"How did you know about the failures? Say the museum puts a copy of an artefact in place and sells the original, how would INTENT know it was ever stolen, especially if the website selling the goods is secret?"

"That's the biggest problem we face now. We don't know as much as we used to. There was a guy working for INTENT a while back. He was able to find out what was stolen and who was selling it, but in the end it became too risky for him. It was long before I met up with Tommy Rosenberg and the group were trying to focus in on the professor. The guy was a cop but he left the organisation and joined the Native movement instead. Looks-twice said he was a coward in the end and couldn't take the heat."

"A cop?"

"Yeah, he was a mastermind at computers. That's how he knew what was for sale. There was nothing he couldn't find on the internet. He could literally infiltrate any site."

Mendoza looked at Locklear and watched as his hands tightened around the steering wheel.

"What was his name?" she asked as nonchalantly as she could muster.

Paytah shrugged. "I've only been working with Looks-Twice a couple of years so it was before my time but I know the guy was only part Native. Part-Irish, I think."

Mendoza turned and raised her eyebrows at Locklear.

Locklear kept his eyes on the road and gave a very slight shake of his head, so Mendoza knew not to reveal that they knew O'Brien and now knew that O'Brien was a double agent or had been. She also knew that the fact that he had been giving information to a side that was fighting for a good cause was immaterial to Locklear.

"How are we going to do this? Mendoza asked.

Locklear took a sharp intake of breath. "I didn't sleep a wink after you left. Some patient was roaring all night. So, I've had a long night in the hospital to think about this. I drove the nurses crazy until they let me out of bed to use the phone and I put in a call to Rubin in the early hours of the morning. He knows a little about diplomatic relations and he said that we can't arrest Tommy Rosenberg no matter what we find on his actual person."

"What? Jesus, sarge! What's the point in going to the airport then?"

"Calm down! I have a plan. We couldn't have arrested him anyway, Mendoza. Don't forget we have no jurisdiction here and we'll be relying on the local cops to help us. Rubin said that the cops can't arrest or detain a close family member of a high-ranking diplomat like Tommy's father but Walter Braff is also on that plane and, as a low-ranking diplomat, the cops can detain him if they have good cause to search him."

"But I don't know what he looks like," Paytah said.

"I do," Locklear said as he unfolded a piece of paper from his pocket and handed it to Mendoza.

"Where did you get this?"

"When Patrick Lewis organised to meet a seller on the pretence of wanting to buy artefacts, he took photos of Braff for evidence. I phoned him and asked if he would scan the photo in and email it to the nurse's desk."

"And the nurses agreed to that? Jesus, Locklear, you have concussion. You shouldn't even be driving."

"I used my charm," he said with a grin.

"You keep talking about your charm but I haven't seen a shred of evidence that it exists," she retorted.

"And you keep saying what a great driver you are, but *I* haven't seen any evidence of *that*! You drive too fast and you're reckless. And I think better when I'm driving."

"You're delusional," Mendoza said, rolling her eyes.

Locklear shrugged. "I described the man in the photo to Rubin. He checked their system and it looks like the man Lewis photographed in the car is definitely Braff. They're coming in on a commercial flight so we'll wait at arrivals. Paytah, I need you to get Tommy's attention and walk outside with him. I'll be with you. I'm your uncle and we've come to collect your aunt but her flight was cancelled. Mendoza, you stay in the car directly behind the cab line-up area and be ready to take off as soon as Paytah and I get out of the terminal. OK? Hopefully we'll mange to convince Tommy to take a ride with us and find out where exactly Braff is going."

Paytah nodded but the look on his face said he'd rather be anywhere else than sitting in the car right now.

Locklear turned and looked into the back seat to give Paytah a look that said 'don't mess with me'.

The UA flight from JFK landed in Rapid City on schedule at exactly 9.02am. Locklear and Paytah stood in the background watching out for a redheaded, freckle-faced kid carrying a heavy carry-on case. Crowds surrounded the area waiting for their loved ones to return from vacation and the noise emanating from the arrivals hall was unbearable.

"How can you hang around with a kid like Rosenberg when you know what he does?" Locklear asked while keeping his eyes firmly trained on the glass arrivals door.

Paytah sighed. "I just kept focused on what the organisation was trying to achieve. I joined the drama group to get close to him though I didn't like lying to him. After a while, Tommy started confiding in me. He told me how lonely he was, how he didn't want to go back to Paris, that he had no friends there and what he really wanted was to finish his degree in drama studies and become an actor."

"A degree? There's such a thing?"

Paytah laughed. "Yeah, old-timer. Tommy's kind of lonely. Parents don't really want him. They fly around here and there, stuff him in one school after another and take off, come back, uproot him again. It's been like that his whole life. He's got no community. Tommy thinks he's important in the family now but, if he got busted, I know they'd walk away from him and hope he wouldn't sing. I didn't like using him but it was for a better cause."

"You're a good kid, Paytah."

Slowly, the arrivals hall began to fill with people from regional and international flights. Locklear watched as they hugged their waiting family members and made their way to the exit. He watched reunion after reunion but there was still no sign of Braff or Tommy Rosenberg.

After twenty further minutes of waiting, Tommy

Rosenberg's shock of wiry, untamed red hair appeared through the arrivals door. Locklear watched the young man closely as he executed his 'easy-going hipster dude without a care in the world' look. He swung his hips to music plugged into his ears but held tightly onto a holdall that looked like it weighed a ton. His clothes were also a good disguise: filthy blue jeans, worn sneakers and a creased black T-shirt depicting a skull and bones. Tommy did not look like a boy whose parents were rich. The diplomatic pass which allowed him to move unchecked through customs would gain envious glances from airport security staff standing in starched uniforms for twelve-hours shifts while the hippy-looking kid breezed through the crowds, and through life. His friendly demeanour would, to Locklear's mind, only add to airport staff's desire to move him on quickly. Nobody doing their crappy jobs wanted to look at a condescending rich kid asking how their day has been for any longer than they had to. Rosenberg, he reasoned, was not as stupid as he looked.

"Well, let's hope your acting classes in USD pay off here."

Paytah followed Locklear's eyes and sprang into his routine. He waved from the distance and called out. Tommy looked around and smiled warmly when he saw his college friend.

"Hey, it's The Chief! Jimmy, what's up, man?" he asked as he swaggered over to where Locklear and Paytah stood.

Locklear got a strong smell of dope off the kid's clothes and wondered how security could bear to let him pass through. He guessed that stopping a high-ranking diplomat's son on suspicion of carrying drugs was more than their job was worth.

Paytah introduced Locklear as his uncle, Two-Sides, and explained that they had come to meet his aunt but her flight had been cancelled so she wouldn't be arriving until the following day and they were just about to leave the airport and head to Rapid City.

"Wanna ride with us?" he asked.

"Sure. But first I gotta drop off something, if that's cool?"

"Cool."

"Hey, dude, what happened to your face?" Tommy asked Locklear.

"You should see the other guy!" Locklear joked.

Locklear stared into Tommy Rosenberg's freckled face and, in particular, his dilated pupils. The kid was stoned. It was probably how he got through each of his deliveries. His nerves were probably shattered and the only way he could pull off his laissez-faire attitude was to get cooked before he got onto a plane and maybe even top himself up throughout the journey.

Tommy's eyes moved quickly around the room.

"You looking for someone?" Locklear asked.

"Yeah, my buddy – well, he isn't my buddy. I'm just travelling with him – well, not with him – I'm on the same plane. I was supposed to take a cab ride behind him."

"*Behind* him?" Locklear asked.

"Yeah, we don't ride together … you know, cos … em … who did you say you were?"

Tommy stopped talking and his face became serious. Locklear could see that the kid was starting to wonder if he was safe.

"I already told you," Paytah laughed. "This is my Uncle Two-Sides."

"Jimmy, dude, your uncle looks kinda white," Tommy sniggered.

"Yeah, he doesn't get out much," Paytah joked. "Sits at his desk all day managing an insurance company. He's kind of a pasty-faced embarrassment to me."

"OK, guys, very funny," said Locklear, "but I gotta get back to town. Tommy, I can give you a ride and then you and Jimmy could go have a few beers."

Paytah looked at Locklear. "Uncle, I keep telling you I don't drink," he warned.

"Yes, and I keep telling you you're a pussy. A real man has a few beers, damn it. Am I right, Tommy?"

"Fucking A straight, Mr Indian," Tommy said, laughing. "The Chief's a pussy. He don't drink, smoke, do drugs, don't run around with a lotta girls despite being a goddamn handsome dude. Girls are throwing themselves at him at college but he just says nah, he's looking for a special woman. Like there's just one! Ha! He's like a fucking priest."

"Is that right?" Locklear replied as he smiled at Paytah.

Paytah looked away, embarrassed.

"Well, let's go," Locklear said. "My assistant is waiting and, Tommy, a word of warning – she's hot but she bites."

"Well, Jesus, that's exactly the way I like 'em."

They passed through arrivals and made their way to Mendoza sitting in the car. Locklear opened the car door for Tommy. He slid into the back seat and Locklear climbed in beside him. Paytah sat in upfront with Mendoza.

"Hi, babe," Tommy said as he pulled on Mendoza's seat to get a better look at her. "Oh, you weren't wrong, Mr Two-Sides – she *is* hot!"

Mendoza glanced back at him and scowled.

"Look, there's my – travel companion," Tommy said as he pointed to a man loading his case into the trunk of a cab. "I bet he's wondering where I am. Quick, we need to follow him."

Mendoza pulled out to follow the cab and drove behind it as it exited the airport and drove north-east on Route 44.

"You need another smoke?" Locklear asked. "Go ahead if you want to."

"I'm all out. You got one?"

Locklear shook his head.

"No point in asking Mister Pussy for one!" Tommy laughed as he elbowed Locklear, reminding him about their joke at Paytah's expense.

"I do," offered Mendoza. She felt down to her purse on the floor of the car and pulled out a small silver tin.

"Watch the goddamn road!" Locklear barked.

Mendoza straightened up the car and handed the silver container back to Locklear.

Locklear opened it and sighed at the two half-smoked joints inside. He'd had no idea she was into marijuana.

Mendoza looked at her boss through the rear-view mirror.

"Relax. I took them by accident from a woman in a club."

"What club? When?"

"In DC. I'll tell you about it another time. OK?"

When the idea had come to Locklear to keep Rosenberg as stoned as possible, it had seemed like a good idea but his conscience told him this was wrong. This kid was someone's child, a neglected young man by the way Paytah told it. He couldn't abuse him any more than the people in his life already had.

Too late. Tommy's light fingers lifted the larger of the two joints before he could shut the box.

Tommy put the joint in his mouth and rummaged through his travel bag looking for a lighter.

"Hey, cute babe, you got a light?" he asked, tapping Mendoza on the shoulder.

Mendoza stared angrily at him through her rear-view mirror.

"No. Sorry."

"Fuck, you offer me a joint and then I can't fucking light it?"

He rummaged through his travel bag which lay on the seat between him and Locklear.

"Do you want me to try help you find it?" Locklear asked.

"I'm not allowed to show anyone what's inside."

Locklear pretended to let out a short laugh. "Why? You got a bomb in there?"

"Fuck bombs. Who wants to mess with that shit? There's way more money in this."

"What is it?" Locklear asked as Tommy finally found a lighter at the bottom of his packed bag.

Tommy lit up, inhaled deeply and lay back in the seat.

"This is good shit, babe. You wanna share it?"

"Sorry, I can't. Working!"

Tommy pulled himself forward and pushed his long thin body suggestively into the back of Mendoza's seat. Locklear watched as he smelt Mendoza's hair. She flinched and pulled herself forward towards the steering wheel. Tommy inhaled again and blew smoke all over the crown of her head and then raised his hand to touch her thick black hair.

"Hey, Tommy, do you mind – that's my girlfriend," Locklear said.

Tommy raised his hands up in the air. "Jesus, sorry, man. You said she's your assistant and, like, weren't you going to the airport to, like, pick up your wife? I checked to see if the babe had a wedding ring and she doesn't so I thought why not give her a go?"

"Give her a go?" Locklear snapped but then tried to regain his composure. "You know how it is, Tommy. You try working with someone who looks like she does every day and not feel the need to, well, you know ..."

"I dig you, man. You're a little old for her but I dig. Legend!" And he raised his hand to high-five Locklear.

Locklear did not raise his hand.

Paytah let out a big sigh to show his disapproval of the tone of the conversation.

"Hey, Jimmy, this guy is cool – you sure he's your uncle?"

"I'm sure."

"For real? Like, not just one of those Indian uncles – you know, where every Indian you know is an 'uncle'?" Tommy placed his hand over his mouth, made Indian war-whooping sounds and snorted.

Paytah turned in his seat and looked at Locklear. A moment passed between the two men.

"No. He's really my uncle but he's a bad example to me," Paytah said.

When the 44 merged with Omaha street, Mendoza

drove two further blocks and swung a right onto Haines Avenue. The cab in front of her slowed and pulled to the curb as it searched for its final destination.

Mendoza pulled in and pretended to check her phone.

"I don't know which building I'm going to," Tommy said as he began to lower the window. "I'll just shout out to Mr Braff. He knows where."

Then he gasped as Locklear clamped his huge hand over his mouth. The redhead's alarmed eyes swam as he tried to digest what was happening.

Mendoza put the car in reverse and, as quietly as she could, moved the car about 100 feet back and parked behind an empty yellow sedan, out of the view of Braff's cab. She turned off the engine, twisted around and reached back to roll up the car window lest Rosenberg manage to warn Braff of their presence.

Mendoza got out and opened the rear passenger door. She leaned in and assisted Locklear to secure Tommy by sticking a long strip of tape over his mouth. As she reached across Tommy's thin body, she thought about punching him for coming on to her so crudely but she didn't want to knock the guy out before Locklear had a chance to interrogate him. They taped his legs together and his hands behind his back. Locklear began to empty the contents of the bag which was full of dirty socks and underwear as well as other grubby clothes, which Locklear reckoned was another trick Rosenberg deployed to deter airport staff from going through his bag. When he managed to empty the bag of its disgusting contents, he lifted out a heavy object. It was covered in dark-green silk and inside the silk was a heavily taped cardboard box. Locklear looked at

Braff's car. He ducked as the tall black-haired man he knew to be Braff got out, carrying a travel bag, and made his way to a side door of a massive steel warehouse. Outside the building a sign read *Olsen International Distributors*.

"Paytah, this is what I need you to do," Locklear said as he handed the young Native the box which no doubt contained precious artefacts. "You're going to drive the car far out of town to an isolated spot and set Tommy loose."

Both Paytah and Mendoza registered surprise.

Locklear reached into his own bag and took a bottle of water and a sandwich from it. "Take his phone and money but leave him with these."

Paytah nodded.

Locklear held Tommy's face as the frightened young man stared at him in horror.

"Guess you're starting to come down from your high now, Tommy, and you're real paranoid. Don't worry. I've been there. It's a bad feeling. But here's what's going to happen to you now. Paytah's going to drive to an isolated spot and keep you there for, oh, at least four hours or so until you can't do us any harm. He'll set you free when I tell him it's safe to do so."

Locklear looked the dishevelled young man up and down and then looked out of the car at the bright-blue sun-filled sky.

"When you're eventually set free, best thing for you to do is to keep your mouth shut. Your friend Braff will go down and I guess he'll sing like a canary about your parents' involvement and maybe even yours – but you're a dumb kid – you tell the police your parents asked you to carry some boxes and that you never knew what was in any of them. Best thing that could happen to you, kid, is your grandfather and parents get locked up for a long time and you get free of them and start thinking for yourself."

Tommy remained still as Locklear's words sank in.

"You see, Tommy, I'm not really after a little fish like you. You seem like a good enough kid apart from the fact that you're a misogynistic pig with no morals and a penchant for drugs which will almost certainly ruin whatever little life you could have carved out for yourself. Now – and here's the only lesson I have time to give you today – never ever disrespect any woman the way you did here."

Drawing back his hand, he slapped Tommy Rosenberg hard on the face.

"That's for disrespecting my friend. I'd say from the look on her face, she was hoping to do that herself but I wanted the satisfaction."

Mendoza grinned.

"And *this*," he said as he landed another slap across the groaning boy's face, "is for disrespecting Jimmy's culture. And mine."

# Chapter 28

Locklear stood out of the car and tied the seatbelt around Rosenberg's body, pinning him to the back seat so he couldn't cause Paytah any trouble on the long drive into the wilderness. He tried to kick out as Locklear secured another belt around his legs

"Would you prefer to finish your ride in the trunk? It's about 30 degrees in the car. Hotter in the trunk. No? Didn't think so," he said as Tommy became motionless.

"Two-Sides? Look here," Paytah said as he climbed over to the driver's seat.

Locklear leaned into the car as Paytah opened his backpack and took out two handguns.

"Don't worry. They aren't mine. They belong to Looks-Twice but whoever is in there isn't going down without a fight. Two-Sides, please take them."

Locklear was taken aback by the offer but then was struck by something else. "Why did you call me Two-Sides?" he asked.

"I made it up. Natives receive many names during their lifetime."

"Yes, but why that name? Why *Two-Sides*?"

"Because I can see the dark side to you, and the light side. Both fight each other until one side wins."

"I can only be on the side that's right," Locklear replied.

"Then, you must decide which side that is."

Locklear stepped away from the car as Paytah pulled away from the curb. He handed Mendoza one of the guns and scanned the building on the other side of the scorched street.

"Are you ready for whatever is inside there?" she asked.

"Yes, but first we're calling for back-up," he said as he borrowed her phone and phoned the Rapid City police force. He wouldn't know anyone there now. Too many years had passed since he had served as a rookie cop but he knew the mention of his popular captain's name from that time would encourage those stationed there now to come to his aid.

He finished the call, relieved that back-up would be provided by the captain who remembered Locklear's old boss.

He walked with Mendoza to the white metal building. There were no windows on the side that faced the roadway. They walked to the right of the building and made their way along the gable end which also had no doors and no windows. Parked along the back wall were about a dozen new Ford trucks.

Mendoza pointed to them. "You reckon Diaz and Hill are involved and that they got their shiny new trucks as some kind of payoff? O'Brien doesn't trust them."

"O'Brien's got some answering of his own to do but, yeah, I suspect the trucks were payment from Sartre and his gang. Who knows how long they've been keeping their mouths shut about things."

Together, they crept along the back of the building until they came to a large roller door which was closed. A fork truck was parked outside a small door which had been left ajar. There were three cigarette butts on the ground outside the door and the keys were still in the fork truck's ignition. One of the butts was still smouldering. Someone would be back very soon and Locklear reckoned they had only seconds to slip inside before being seen.

They looked inside as they held their guns out, ready to fire. Inside the dimly lit building were multiple rows of racking on which goods were boxed for distribution.

"Surely these can't all be artefacts? There must be thousands of items here," Mendoza whispered.

"They must be running a legitimate distribution business here to cover up what's really going on. Otherwise, the cops would have been all over this place."

Mendoza listened but the only sound coming from within the building was music humming softly in some distant corner of the huge unit.

"Why can't we hear anything?" she said. "We saw Braff coming in. There must be other people here."

Locklear signalled for Mendoza to follow him deeper into the warehouse. They crept at a snail's pace as they moved through the long aisles, the racking of which was backed with wire caging, making it easy to see movement further into the warehouse.

"I don't like this. If someone comes upon us, we're sitting ducks," Mendoza whispered.

Locklear nodded. "It's too open. We need cover."

When she thought her boss was not looking, Mendoza blessed herself, thought of her mother, her son and her sick grandmother and prayed that she would get out of this place alive.

"I saw that," Locklear said.

Mendoza snorted. "You've got eyes in the back of your head."

Locklear signalled for Mendoza to take another aisle in the hope that one of them would find Braff quickly. As they searched the sixth aisle they had still not seen or heard any movement in the building.

Then Mendoza heard footsteps outside. She turned and stared at Locklear, who was three aisles down, through the wire cages. Her eyes turned towards the door which was still open.

Standing just inside the door, with the brilliant light behind him, was a huge man with a revolver pointed at her.

Locklear watched as his trooper put her hands up.

"*Drop the gun*," a male voice ordered.

Mendoza did not look at her boss for fear of giving his position away.

"*I said, drop your gun*."

Mendoza thought about the order for a moment.

Locklear tensed. He knew she wouldn't relinquish her weapon easily.

"I'm a cop," she said.

"No shit," the man replied. "What are you doing here?"

"I have back-up on the way. I'd advise you to put your weapon down."

"Where's your partner?"

"I'm here alone."

Locklear heard a loud raspy laugh. "I saw the two of you sneak in here. You think I wasn't watching you on my cameras. I let you creep far enough into this rabbit-hole that you can't get out."

The huge man raised his gun higher and moved closer to Mendoza until she could see his face clearly. Mendoza took in his shock of white hair and deathly pale skin but it was his eyes that held her attention. The man's pupils were so pale they were almost without colour. She had come face to face with the White Ghost.

"Now I asked you, where is your friend?"

"He's gone upstairs to see Braff."

"Upstairs?" he asked as he moved even closer to her.

"Yes."

The man lifted a radio from his belt and spoke urgently into it. Locklear heard loud footsteps running above him – one, possibly two, people. He hunkered down and crept in the direction of the man.

"Do you know anything about albinism?" the man asked.

Mendoza nodded towards the man who now stood no more than thirty feet from her.

"Yes," she said. "It's caused by a lack of melanin so people with the condition are pale and have white hair."

"Anything else?"

"It's usually genetic."

"Good girl. What a shame you wasted your intelligence and became a police officer. *Tut-tut*. But not all family members are born with this condition. Some show no signs of it at all."

Mendoza nodded. "So you have siblings who don't have

the condition? That must have been hard on you. It must have seemed unfair."

The albino laughed. "Oh, don't try to mind-fuck me, officer. The condition can come with its advantages. Can you think of one?"

While Mendoza tried to think of an answer, Locklear continued to creep towards the man.

"Oh! You can't think of an answer. What a shame! Well, then, let's move to the disadvantages, will we?"

Mendoza swallowed. "You can't see very well."

"Very good but it's really only strong light that affects me. Confuses me a little. It takes me a while to get my bearings. Otherwise I get around just like anybody else. But do you know what happens to people with poor eyesight? What special skill people like me sometimes have? What compensation?"

Mendoza could hear movement behind her. She could feel her heart quicken and wondered what was taking their back-up so long.

"I guess ... I guess you can hear very well?"

"*Bingo!*"

"I ... also think ..." Mendoza began, stalling for time.

"No, that's enough chat for now, honey, because I'm just going to shoot your friend in the head."

Locklear leapt up and charged at the man from the side, ramming him into the wall. They fell to the ground and began to tussle. Mendoza raised her gun and looked behind to see an old man hobbling in her direction with a firearm in his hand.

"*Gun,*" he demanded.

"Gun?" Mendoza said.

"*Gun.*"

"OK," she said as she pretended to be about to throw the gun in his direction – but she twisted and, as she threw herself on the ground, fired two shots into the old man's leg. He fell down and was still. Blood oozed from his leg and he groaned quietly.

Mendoza ran to where Locklear continued to wrestle with the white-haired man on the ground.

"*Shoot him!*" Locklear shouted as he tried to gain control.

Mendoza lifted her gun but the man kept pulling Locklear on top of him, blocking Mendoza's aim.

"*Shoot him!*"

"*I'm trying! I'll hit you!*" she shouted.

Locklear saw his gun lying on the ground beside him. The albino reached forward to grab it but Locklear got there first and hammered two blows into the man's temple, knocking him unconscious.

Locklear stood up, gasping, as Mendoza ran to his side.

The sounds of police sirens screamed outside.

Locklear and Mendoza stood over the unconscious man and took in his unusual features. The man's snow-white hair and milky-pale skin were expected given his condition but it was his features that led Locklear and Mendoza to stare down at him in shock. His thick hair was the same length as Locklear's and he shared the same high cheekbones and strong jawline as the detective sergeant. His broad face and high furrowed brow also mirrored Locklear's face. He also shared the same full, albeit paler, lips and his thick white eyebrows were the same shape as Locklear's jet-black brows.

"Jeez, sarge! He's you!" she gasped as police rushed into the warehouse, two paramedics following more cautiously behind them.

She reached into the man's trouser pocket and lifted his wallet.

"Samuel Olsen," she said aloud as she read the man's ID. "He turned 58 years old in March."

"That means he was born three months before me," Locklear said.

In the middle of the aisle, a cop stood over the old man Mendoza shot while paramedics saw to his wounds.

Mendoza walked to where the old man lay in a pool of blood.

The cop was holding a wallet.

"Did you take some ID?" Mendoza asked urgently.

"Henry Olsen," the cop replied.

"He took two to the knee," one of the paramedics said.

She squatted next to the old man. "Sir?" she said.

The man's eyes blinked but he did not open them.

"Sir?" she repeated.

The old man opened his eyes and looked at Mendoza as she focused on the strong features he shared with the huge man who still lay unconscious at Locklear feet's, and with Locklear himself.

"Is Samuel Olsen your son?" she asked.

"Yes. Is he OK?" the old man whispered.

"Sir, do you have any other children?" she asked as the paramedics lifted him onto a stretcher.

An oxygen mask was placed over his face.

"Wait!" Mendoza said to the paramedics who glared at her.

"We've got to get him to a hospital. You can ask your questions later,"

Mendoza turned to look at her boss. She walked slowly back to him where another paramedic attended to Olsen Junior.

"Well, sarge. Seems like your suspicions were right. I think you just knocked out your brother and I think I just shot your father."

# Chapter 29

In the waiting area of Rapid City's regional hospital, Locklear and Mendoza waited for two hours to hear how the two Olsen men were faring. Wilson, the senior cop who had led the back-up at the warehouse, came to the doorway.

"The old man is out of surgery. It'll be a while before we can speak to him. His son is fine. Concussion. He'll be kept here overnight and then transferred into police custody. The warehouse contained artefacts from all over the world. They've been taken to a secure location. We won't know if they are replicas until specialists can study them but the captain has contacted the FBI. They'll be taking over the case."

"Has the son said anything?" Mendoza asked.

"Won't talk. Wants to speak to his lawyer."

"Braff?"

"We found him hiding in a vault upstairs. He had six wooden carvings with him, possibly Egyptian. Captain contacted the consulate who contacted the museums there and sent through a photo. The curator said there are twelve carvings in all and they are priceless, thought to be around four thousand years old and they're definitely where they are supposed to be – in a locked case with security cameras trained on them. Guess the ones Braff had must be fakes."

Locklear, who had hardly spoken since they arrived at the hospital, raised his weary bones from his seat.

"The ones in the museum are fake. Tell them to check again. Tell them to check their security footage again. They were most likely swapped by a senior staff member at night when the museum was closed. It will be someone in a position of trust who had access to all areas."

"Will do," Wilson said as he left the room.

"I phoned Paytah and told him to set Tommy loose," Mendoza said. "He said he'd drop him in the middle of Badlands National Park. Said it'll take the city boy at least five hours to get to the main roadway – if he ever finds his way back to civilisation, that is." She grinned.

"I guess young Rosenberg was carrying the other six carvings?" Locklear asked.

"Yeah. Paytah dropped them into the station, marked for Wilson's attention like I told him to. He gave the desk clerk your car keys and walked away."

"Good. Let's hope Paytah has the sense to lie low now for a few days until this blows over."

"You want to talk about your half-brother and your father?"

"I don't know they are for sure!" Locklear barked.

Mendoza flinched. "Sarge –"

"OK, I'm sorry. I guess it seems that way but I really wish it wasn't. What I was hoping to find, if anything, would have been ..."

"Would have been what?"

Locklear looked at his shoes and inhaled. He did not raise his eyes to his trooper.

He swallowed. "Would have been my Native family."

"Do you want me to talk to Olsen? See what I can find out?"

Locklear shook his head. "No," he said quietly.

"What about Looks-Twice? He must know something. Couldn't you just ask him?"

"I remembered something, Mendoza ... something that happened a long time ago."

"What?"

Locklear inhaled. "I'll tell you another time."

Mendoza put her arms around her boss and hugged him.

"I'm sorry it didn't turn out better for you, but we solved the case. Braff will rat Hirsch, Sartre, the Olsens and the Rosenbergs out. INTENT's work will be finished. And more important than anything, Carter will be cleared." She loosened her embrace.

"There are still loose ends, Mendoza. This won't stop INTENT because whoever is masterminding the theft of artefacts around the world will find willing replacements for Hirsch and the Rosenbergs. But you're right, it will clear Carter and that's what we set out to do. The rest will be down to the FBI and how it handles the case from here."

Mendoza's phone rang. She moved into the corridor and put her finger in her ear as she tried to hear the voice of a long-distance caller. Locklear watched from the glass wall of the waiting room as tears welled in his trooper's eyes. He followed and stood behind her.

"OK, tell Mom I'll be there as soon as I can," she said as she ended the call.

Locklear turned Mendoza around to face him.

"That was my brother, Diego. Grandma died a couple of hours ago. Mom was trying to call me but she couldn't get through. The funeral won't be for a few days. Diego is teaching at an art college all summer in Europe so he's not going to be able to get there. My mom really needs me."

"Go. You need to be with your family now."

"But ... what about you?"

"I'll be fine. I'll see you back in Richmond."

As Mendoza slipped from view Locklear sank back in his seat. He brought all of the case's loose ends to the forefront of his mind. He made a mental note of the what he needed to do to knit those loose ends together.

He knew where his first stop would be and he was not looking forward to it.

When his mind was clearer, Locklear stood on the periphery of the dwindling number of cops at Rapid City's hospital and, knowing there was little else he could do there for the rest of the day, he exited the facility and walked the short distance to the police station to collect his car keys from the desk.

From there he went to the precinct's parking lot and got into his car. Then he drove south on Highway 41 for the one-and-a-half-hour journey to Pine Ridge Reservation. By the time he arrived on the outskirts of the town, the day was almost at an end and the cloudless sky had transformed into a deep midnight-blue canvas with long silvery lines on the horizon.

When he reached the jail, he found that Daccota Looks-Twice had been moved to hospital following another blackout and according to Goulden he was not doing well. Locklear drove his car to the parking lot of the local hospital and made his way to the ward where Looks-Twice was handcuffed to the side of his hospital bed. The old Native was awake and was sitting up, staring into space. Locklear pulled a chair over to the bed and sat down.

Looks-Twice stared at him with dark pools full of hatred.

"I remember you," Locklear began.

Looks-Twice snorted.

"You came to the trailer where I lived with my mother. I was about nine years old. I remember you both argued in your language. You were driving a yellow mustang. Who are you?"

"I am Wachiwi's brother."

"You're my uncle?"

"I'm not *your* uncle. Knowing that my blood runs through your veins makes me sick. I hate you. I've always hated you."

"I remember how you looked at me and what you called me. *Paleface*. Why did you hate me? I was just a child. What could I have possibly done to make you hate me?"

"It's not what you did to me but what you did to my sister."

"What did I do?"

Looks-Twice did not answer. He looked out the window into the night sky and began to hum a tune to himself.

"You wanted her to do something. Something she wouldn't agree to," Locklear said.

Looks-Twice sneered.

"What was it?" Locklear asked.

"They say I've got a brain tumour. Soon my memories will be all gone and then I will die. You might never find out what we talked about."

"I want to know."

"*You* want? You got everything *you* wanted. You, Half-breed, got Wachiwi while her full-blood children were left with only me to fend for them."

"Her children? I don't understand. My mother had other children? Where are they?"

"Your brother is dead. Chaska died in my arms crying out for his mother and still she did not come. No-one wants to see you. You are hated among our people. The ancestors of your white father brought a curse on our village. Wachiwi brought his evil into our lives and it ruined her."

"Then Henry Olsen really is my father?"

Looks-Twice spat on the ground of the hospital floor and turned his face away from Locklear.

"Do not speak his name to me."

Locklear inhaled. "And the so-called White Ghost who killed Albert Whitefeather? He's my brother?"

"Yes."

"How? How did this happen?"

"She was beautiful and what Olsen did to her ..." he whimpered.

Locklear looked away as the realisation of how he may have been conceived dawned on him.

"I didn't ask to be born," he said quietly.

Looks-Twice did not answer.

"I know that Paytah is a relation of yours. Is he also related to me? How does the kid fit into the picture?"

Looks-Twice turned his face back to Locklear. His nostrils flared and his mouth set in a hard, angry line.

"You stay away from Paytah. You keep your evil away from him. I will protect him for as long as there is breath left in my body."

"You got him involved in crime. He could have gone to jail. Is that what you want? You aren't teaching him the ways of your people. Anger is not the Sioux way."

"How would you know what the Sioux way is? Did your mother teach you? I don't think she did. She knew you were a curse for her, a punishment. That's why the chief gave you your name on the day you were born."

"Where was that?"

"In Pine Ridge."

"I was born here? When did my mother and I leave?"

"The day after you were born. I took her away in my car. There was no other way."

Looks-Twice turned his eyes once more to the window of his stifling hospital room.

"What happened? I deserve to know. I need to know. If you tell me, you won't ever see me again. For your sister's sake, tell me. Tell me what happened to my mother."

"Be careful what you wish for, Half-breed. Some things are best left unspoken."

Five minutes passed and still the old man did not speak. He pulled his wrinkled arm twice against the handcuffs that imprisoned him and began to hum. Locklear went to the door and gestured to the young cop to come inside.

"Untie him, please," he said. "I'll take responsibility. You can tell Clark I ordered you to."

The young cop shrugged, unlocked the cuffs and walked quickly out of the room.

"OK," said Looks-Twice. "You want to know, so you will know and you will be sorry you ever asked me how you came to be."

# Chapter 30

Locklear listened as Looks-twice told him the story of his mother's arranged marriage to the chief's son when she was just sixteen years old and how she had agreed to the marriage to keep her father happy. The following year she gave birth to a daughter followed two years later by a son. The marriage had not been good for Wachiwi and she endured many years of suffering at the hands of her alcoholic husband who was more than three times her age and whose first wife had taken her own life to free herself from his cruelty. Looks-Twice told how his sister had begged their father to agree to her divorcing her husband but, despite this being possible in their tribe, he refused as he had given the chief his word and it could not be broken. Wachiwi was unhappy and used every opportunity she could to get away from the reservation by travelling to nearby towns to sell Native American rugs to craft-store owners. It was in Rapid City that she met Henry Olsen and the young beauty was taken in by his kindness and generosity to her. Olsen gave her good prices for her weaving which he displayed prominently in his craft store.

He began to buy her clothes and gave her money to help look after her children. He treated her with what she understood then to be nothing more than brotherly kindness. Soon, though, she had fallen in love with him and she thought her father would release her from her marriage. Olsen began to give Wachiwi whiskey which he made her drink every time she crept off the reservation to see him. Slowly, she became dependant on him and the alcohol he brought which soothed her troubled thoughts and enveloped her in a false sense of happiness. She spent more and more time seeking him out, often walking long distances to find him. She began to neglect her children, leaving them in the care of her mother who had divorced her own abusive husband to live in a hut alone at the top of the valley. It was here that Wachiwi was to run for protection when she found herself pregnant by Olsen who she insisted had forced himself on her.

Locklear held up his hand to Looks-Twice when he uttered those words. He inhaled and wondered if he could bear to hear any more of his mother's sorrowful past.

"I told you. Sometimes it is better not to know," Looks-Twice said.

"No. Go on."

"Wachiwi stayed in our mother's hut trying to hide her pregnancy but word had spread among the tribe that she had lain down with a descendant of the White Ghost. Wachiwi tried to hide her shame and swore to the chief that the child inside her was her husband's child. She prayed to her ancestors to make this true and she was not without hope because her husband had continued to inflict his cruelty on her in the same way he had done since the first night of their marriage."

"And then I was born?"

"Three months before you were born Wachiwi had a dream that you came into the world with colourless eyes and white hair which stood high on your head. She screamed in the night and my mother said the dream would come true. Each night for a week my sister had the same dream. On the eight day she walked to the main road and hitched a ride to Rapid City in the hope that Henry Olsen would find it in his heart to help her. When she got there, he was not at his store. She went inside and saw a woman standing in the store with a new baby covered in one of Wachiwi's weaves. Wachiwi asked the woman if she could see the baby and when she pulled back the shawl the baby had the same white hair as she had seen in the dream and skin whiter than milk. Wachiwi fainted and, when she came to, the woman was standing over her with some warm tea. She told my sister that she was Henry Olsen's wife and that this was his son born only days before. Wachiwi had not known that he was married. He had deceived her. When Wachiwi told my mother that story she said the baby had pink eyes and every night until you were born she cried and worried about what it was that was growing inside her."

Locklear looked away and swallowed.

"Do you want to hear the rest of the story, Half-breed?"

"No," Locklear whispered.

Looks-Twice closed his eyes and waited.

"Yes. Please, just finish it," Locklear said.

"The day you came into the world the tribe were celebrating the Sun Dance. It was the day of the summer solstice, June 21st."

"The Sun Dance?"

Looks-Twice sneered. "It is a celebration of the renewal of our tribe and of our land. It is a day we make sacrifices for the good of our people, when we ask the spirits for guidance and well-being for our people."

"I see," Locklear said.

"Back then, the reservation was a few miles from where the town is today, set in a deep valley with views of the mountains on all sides. The sun was high in the sky and the valley was lit up with its energy. Our ancestors were smiling down on us. Our men were dressed in traditional clothing preparing to celebrate the dance. People were eating, laughing, dancing and the sound of our drums echoed around the valley. We were to have a naming ceremony for babies and for our young people as they prepared to become men and women. While our people were celebrating, my sister was screaming in our mother's hut at the top of the valley as she tried to bring you into the world. None of the old women came to help as they would have done. They were afraid of what they might see. I waited outside until I could no longer bear to listen to her. I feared she would die. Seven hours passed and still she screamed out until at last she screamed so loud that the very eagles in the sky took flight from their nests and hid among the mountains. Soon after, my sister came out of the hut with you covered in a shawl. Her white dress was covered in her blood. I could hear my mother weeping in the cabin. I took you from Wachiwi and looked at you and my heart broke for her. She began to climb down into the valley where our chief was finishing the naming ceremony. I followed behind her with you and tried to steady her and as she reached level ground the singing stopped and the drums did not beat. The world suddenly seemed silent. Not even a bird could be heard. The sun disappeared behind dark clouds that had risen up out of nowhere and the sky fell into darkness. Wachiwi kept walking while blood flowed down her legs and the people moved out of the way. Most turned away from her but I remained by her side. She took you from my arms and handed you to Chief Akecheta. He was a very old man and he was very wise. He took you and pulled the shawl from your head and held you up close to his old eyes. Old women cried out at the sight of your white hair. The White Ghost is among us, they said, but the chief did not show any fear. He held you out and stared into your eyes as though he was communicating with you."

Locklear swallowed. "My hair was white?"

"You had the eyes and skin of our people but just like my sister saw in her dream, your hair was the same as the White Ghost. Akecheta decided that you were sent to curse us and that Wachiwi had allowed evil to use her womb to destroy us from within. He prayed over you and asked our spirits for guidance. As he prayed the sky darkened further and a dark shadow spread over the valley."

Locklear looked to the ground. "And so he named me."

"Yes. *Ohanzee*. Shadow."

"The chief then told my sister the decision of the spirits. He told Wachiwi she must take the child and leave him in the city where white people would care for him."

"But she refused."

"Yes."

Locklear inhaled and waited although he knew. He

knew the rest of the story because he had lived it.

"As Wachiwi's brother, I promised I would see that it was done. I took Wachiwi back to the hut and my mother washed her. As my sister fed you for the first time, she was not joyful as a mother should have been. She cried. She was weak from blood loss. I waited until she slept and I tried to take you from her arms so that I could drive you to Rapid City and leave you there."

Locklear could feel anger rising up inside him. Anger for himself, at what had happened to him during the first hours of his life and anger for his mother and the suffering she had endured.

"Each time I tried to take you she awoke and I could not free you from her arms. I agreed with my mother that I would wait until morning came and would allow my sister to come with me to deliver you to where you belonged. When morning came, I took Wachiwi to my car and drove with you to Rapid City but when we got there she would not part with you. I told her to come inside the hospital so that she could say goodbye to you but she pleaded with me to take her back to her children. She could not have both. She had to choose."

"So, you left her there, on the street with a new baby?"

"No. I took her inside the hospital and the doctor was worried about how much blood she was still losing. It was as if your birth was taking her life from her. They asked me to let my sister stay. They told me to come back in a few days for her. They said they would take care of you and see that a good home was found for you."

"So you left?"

"Yes. And when I returned a few days later, Wachiwi

was gone and she had taken you with her. She had chosen you. She left a note for me saying ..."

Looks-Twice's chin trembled and his small brown eyes filled with tears.

"Saying, '*Ohanzee has nobody but me. I accept my punishment but I cannot leave him alone in the world. Look after my children.*'"

Locklear's eyes filled with hot tears. His mother had chosen him. All those years he was angry with her for giving him the rootless life he endured but she had sacrificed everything for him. He remembered how his birthday always coincided with his mother's black mood and worsening drinking. It was the day her world changed forever. Something Mendoza had once said to him when he complained about how his mother was always running from something flooded back to him. His trooper had said that a mother will always put her child first and that, if she was running, it was to protect him.

"Why did you come to our trailer that day?"

Looks-Twice sighed. "It was not the first time I found your mother. I used my job as a police officer to find out where she was. Each time I found her I pleaded that she give you up and come home but she refused."

Locklear sighed.

"I came to your trailer that day to make my sister see sense. Your brother was twelve years old and he was sick. My mother died three years after Wachiwi disappeared. She died not knowing what became of her daughter. Chaska had leukaemia. He was calling out for her. I had every school looking out for a Native woman with a boy your age. I figured she wouldn't change your name. She knew it was a sentence for her and she would accept it. What I didn't figure was that she would use my grandmother's last name. It was pronounced Loc-a-leer. It took some detective work to find you but I did."

"And you asked her again to leave me behind?"

"Yes. Nothing had changed on the reservation except Wachiwi's husband was now chief. He would not let me take the children even to see her. I stayed with her for three days pleading with her to come back and look after her dying child – but she would not abandon you. You, who were conceived through violence and hatred. She chose you with your white face and Olsen's blood running through your veins. When I saw how my sister was living, sleeping with men who were not her husband, drinking, letting you run wild, I knew that she was no longer who she had been. The children had stability. They were better off without her. I drove away from that trailer knowing I would never see her again. I would tell the children that Wachiwi and her half-breed child were dead. Three days after I returned to Pine Ridge, Chaska died in my arms, calling out for his mother."

"And she died calling out for him," Locklear said quietly.

Looks-Twice looked at him. "She made her choice."

"You gave her no choice. You were her brother. Under Sioux tradition you were supposed to protect her but you didn't. All because she made a mistake and she was facing up to her mistake by caring for a child that didn't ask to come into the world in the way that he did. You abandoned her, Looks-Twice. You dishonoured her."

"You know nothing of what I did. After that last time I

saw her, I was filled with anger because I knew then that I would spend my life caring for Wachiwi's children and that I would not have my own family. No woman wanted to care for the children of my cursed sister. From time to time I would find out where she was and I would write to her. Sometimes I would threaten to tell the authorities that she was neglecting her son. I never did it, but I wanted to hurt her. I wanted her to lose the only child she had left, the one she had chosen above her full-blood children."

"Which explains our many sudden moves. You were tormenting her."

Looks-Twice looked down but his expression did not alter.

"How did she die?" he asked.

"In a haze of dementia and torment. Looks like you are going to face the same awful death. In the end, my mother no longer knew who I was, but she died calling my brother's name. She called for Chaska and Magaskawee. She called out over and over and I didn't understand what she wanted. I didn't know what those words meant."

Locklear exhaled at the thought that he'd had a brother, a brother he would now never get to know. He did not look on the white-haired man in Rapid City as his brother. Not now that he knew the kind of man he, and their father, was.

"When Chaska died, I lost my soul. He was like my own son. I began to drink. I was full of anger and I channelled that anger into protecting all I had left: my land, the soil my father left me. When I realised that our sacred artefacts were being stolen by white people, I joined INTENT and I devoted my time to putting things right."

"You shot a cop."

Looks-Twice nodded. "It was my darkest moment. I asked the spirits to take away my anger and to put peace in my heart. But then they came."

"Who?"

"Scientists with digging machines, upsetting the graves of my ancestors, scraping at their bones and pulling up the sacred things my people had placed in the earth as offerings. They came onto my land, three, four, five times. Han Pauls and his activists stood in unison with me. Peaceful demonstrations which achieved nothing. Photographs in white newspapers."

"What happened to my mother's other child, my sister?"

Looks-Twice snorted. "Forget her. No-one is looking for you, Locklear. No-one. Now, you made a promise to leave if I told you the story. Now you know it all. There's nothing more I can do for you. *E wang oh ma nee yo.*"

"What does that mean?"

"It means 'Be careful how you travel'. It is a warning."

Locklear stood and stared at the old man.

"You never did anything for me, Uncle. You are as much to blame for what happened to my mother as Olsen, maybe even more because you were supposed to love her, to protect her. You failed her and you failed me."

He walked to the door and left the room.

Outside, he asked the young cop if he could use his phone. He spoke with Goulden, said he was not pressing assault charges on Looks-Twice and pleaded for his release whenever the hospital felt he was well enough to be discharged. Goulden argued that Looks-Twice's case also involved the discovery of stolen goods on his property.

"You can't steal what you already own, Goulden. All he did was take back what was stolen from him."

When Goulden finally conceded, Locklear returned to the room and stood in the doorway but the old man had already fallen asleep.

"Goodbye, Uncle," he said quietly as he closed the door and thought about what his next step would be.

# Chapter 31

When morning came Locklear found himself back in Rapid City police station by sunrise, assisting Wilson with local aspects of the case which was now being largely handled by the FBI. At seven thirty Mendoza called from Richmond Airport to say that the first flight she could get to Mexico City was due to leave Richmond at nine fifty and that she was not looking forward to making the six-hour flight alone.

"I enjoyed working on this case, sarge, just you and me with no Kowalski or Benson harassing us. Felt like we were a couple of private investigators with no-one to answer to but ourselves."

"Sounds like something I could live with," Locklear replied.

He did not tell Mendoza about his visit to Looks-Twice or the depressing story of his conception and birth. That tale could wait until another time, if indeed he ever uttered it to another living soul, which he doubted he would.

Mendoza listened intently as he told her how the investigation had so far uncovered the involvement of museum curators, forgers, diplomats and university archaeology departments.

Olsen Junior had changed his tune the previous evening and was now willing to testify that he had been with British diplomat Amelia Hirsh on the night that her cousin Alec Holton had been murdered and that, while he had no hand in the killing, he assisted the diplomat to enter the building through a garbage chute. Olsen had confessed that he and Hirsch tried to make the Native American branch of INTENT look guilty of the murder by leaving the stick key in the professor's computer. He also claimed that cutting into Holton's scalp in an effort to further point the finger at the Native American branch of the movement had been a childish, cringeworthy attempt by Hirsch to cover her tracks. Olsen admitted to hacking into Holton's computer to send an email to Holton's colleague Lee Carter inviting him to the apartment shortly after they expected to have left, which would provide the police with not only one but two suspects and would hopefully slow the investigation down until their prized shipment of twelve ancient Egyptian carvings were safely in the US and readied for sale. Olsen was going to jail for a long time and his father, who had obviously been a part of the business, would spend what days remained to him behind bars.

Hirsch's public denial of Olsen's claims were broadcast overnight around the world before the footage of her leaving the scene with Olsen was provided to the British Government who immediately revoked Hirsch's diplomatic immunity and agreed for her extradition to the US for trial. It seemed the inheritance that Hirsch seemed so desperate to get her hands on would be tied up until she was very old. On Locklear's information, the FBI advised Scotland Yard to arrange for the exhumation of Holton's mother for an autopsy which meant Hirsh could be facing two life sentences in two countries.

Sartre, for his part, was clever enough to know the game was up and handed himself in, hoping that he might get a reduced sentence for adding to the information the cops already had on his estranged wife and, with it, information on the bribes taken by Richmond cops Diaz and Hill for planting evidence in the home of Lee Carter, who was innocent.

Braff was also in confessional mode and had implicated the US army in the transport of artefacts during the war in Iraq and was claiming that involvement went up to the highest ranks at that time. He had also hung the Rosenbergs out to dry. The professor was arrested in Vermillion but his son and daughter-in-law were in hiding in the US consulate in Paris. Word had it that the US would follow Britain and strip the Rosenbergs of their diplomatic immunity and send them to the US for trial. Tommy Rosenberg was spotted in the early hours of the morning boarding a plane for South America. The sun-burnt, crack-lipped photo of the ginger-haired young man had made Locklear smile. He hoped he had learnt his lesson and would go straight from here but somehow he knew he'd be hearing about young Tommy Rosenberg in the future. His life of privilege and free licence meant he would find it difficult to live on a meagre wage and live like ordinary people do.

The police's only lead into the organisation known as INTENT was an old Native American with dementia who would soon die from a brain tumour which was clouding his memories. Looks-Twice claimed to have no memory of the organisation and, with Whitefeather dead, the wealthy philanthropists who reportedly funded the organisation's illegal activities would remain unknown.

Paytah Hunter was nowhere to be seen.

"Wow," Mendoza said when Locklear finished giving her the update.

Locklear waited for her to expand on that.

Then she said, "I was thinking, sarge, I didn't get to say goodbye to my grandmother. I mean, I knew she was ill but you always think there will be time to say the things you want to say but sometimes things happen and you don't get that chance."

Locklear swallowed. "What are you saying, Mendoza? Is this your way of telling me you're looking for another position? Thought you just said you enjoyed working with me?"

Mendoza laughed but he could hear the sadness in her voice.

"No. That's not what I mean. What I want to say is, if something happened and this was the last time I spoke to you, I want you to know how much you mean to me."

Locklear did not reply.

Mendoza could hear his quick breath on the phone.

"Sarge?"

"Jo," he began. It was the first time he had ever used her first name. "My relationship with you is the best I've ever had with any woman. I want to keep it that way. If anything were to change," his voice dropped to a whisper, "if we were to become more than friends ... well ... it would change everything."

He listened and thought he could hear her sobbing quietly.

"Mendoza, you are grieving. So much has been going on for you between your ex-husband coming back into your life, your worries for your child and your grandmother dying. I think we need to talk about this some other time, when things are better for you and you can see things clearly. Please, please, don't cry, Mendoza."

Locklear's words were met with silence. He noticed Wilson standing to the side, obviously waiting to talk to him about the case that was still unfolding. He waited until the cop realised the detective sergeant's phone conversation was of a private nature and walked away.

"*Ohanzee,*" Locklear whispered.

"What?" Mendoza asked.

"*Ohanzee*. That's my name. I've always hated it which I'll explain another time. The only other person at the station who knows it is Kowalski and I've known him for over thirty years. What I'm trying to say is ... that's how much you mean to me."

"Well, that's a start, sarge," she said as gently she hung up.

Locklear felt a tap on his shoulder. It was Wilson again.

"Want to go see old man Olsen? Few things I have to ask him now that he's doing better."

"No. I can't. I'm sure you've heard ..."

"It's all around the station. His son told the guard stationed outside his room last night and, well, you know how these things go. But, there's still the case ..."

Locklear flushed and set his eyes on his footwear. "OK, I'll come but I'll wait outside the room."

"Suit yourself."

While Wilson gathered up his paperwork, Locklear sent a quick email to Kowalski totting up the expenses he and Mendoza had incurred during the unauthorised investigation. He held his finger over the button for a minute and inhaled, knowing how Kowalski would react when he saw the total. Locklear reasoned he might only see a small amount of the money repaid to him or maybe none, depending on how mad Kowalski was with him. He pressed *send* and followed Wilson out to the car.

In Rapid City hospital, Henry Wilson was not handcuffed to his bed as Looks-Twice had been. The old man's leg was in a large cast with a wire cage over it. He wasn't going to be running anywhere anytime soon. Locklear stood outside on the quiet corridor and peered in through the glass panel while Wilson sat down and began taking Olsen's statement. Twice the old man's eyes flickered towards the glass that separated them and Locklear instinctively looked away. He did not want to meet his father's eyes and as he stood there he began to question why he had come with Wilson at all. His conversation with Looks-Twice resurfaced and thoughts about how he came to be rose up in him. He felt sick and the dizziness that had subsided following Looks-Twice's beating returned. He looked down and tried to steady his breathing as he gripped onto the handrails that ran along the corridor wall. Vivid images of Olsen's attack on his mother flashed before his eyes. He saw his birth, her screams with no-one but her mother to help her bring him into the world. He watched her walk through the valley in her blood-soaked clothes and present her son to the chief who would decide her fate and that of her half-breed son. He heard the drums, witnessed the Sun Dance and the silence settle in the valley Looks-Twice had described to him.

Locklear moved away from the room and stood alone at the end of the long corridor, out of sight.

Then he heard her voice, singing what he assumed was a Lakota lullaby.

*Cante waste hoksila ake istima*
*Hanhepi ki waste ...*

Over and over he listened to the two lines being sung by his mother. He had no memory of her having ever sung to him except in the dreams and visions he sometimes had of her but this must be a real memory of her singing to him when he was little, when they had begun their life of running and hiding, the reasons for which had only now become clear to him. Wachiwi had not subjected him to their nomadic life because she could not settle. She was running from Looks-Twice who wanted to separate her from her youngest child, who wanted her to return to her responsibilities so he could have a life of his own. Locklear closed his eyes and found himself rocking back and forth on his heels to the sound of her voice. He began to hum along to the haunting tune and felt himself to be a long way from the hospital corridor he was standing in, as though he had fallen asleep and was floating in a dream with his mother and another boy beside him.

When he opened his eyes, he found himself standing in Olsen's room. Wilson had gone and the old man was staring at him from his bed. Locklear stared at the old man and knew that, if he wanted to, he could kill Henry Olsen right now. He could take the soft white pillow from under his head and smother the life out of him as Olsen had taken his mother's life slowly. He swallowed as the overriding temptation to end the man's life coursed through his veins. He closed his eyes and asked his mother what he should do but all he could hear was the sound of her peaceful voice humming the lullaby in his head. He had never remembered her sounding so serene when she was alive. He knew what Wachiwi was telling him. She was at peace. She did not need her son to avenge her. She did not need another one of her children suffering because of the course she'd had to take in life.

"Do you know who I am?" Locklear asked the old man.

"Yes," Olsen said.

Locklear noticed how strong the old man's voice sounded, how calm and measured he was, as if he knew this day would somehow come, that someday he would face the child he had abandoned.

"You are my son."

"Wrong," Locklear replied. "I am Ohanzee Localeer, son of Wachiwi. A proud Lakota Sioux."

Locklear heard the words flowing from his mouth but it was as if those words were being spoken not by him but through him – but by whom he did not know.

Olsen did not show any sign of fear.

"I don't blame you if you want to kill me. I would do the same myself."

Locklear stared down the cold hard stare of the old man and wrapped his long fingers around the end of the metal bed with a force and intensity he did not know he possessed.

"Your death will come soon enough and when you die you will answer for what you did to Wachiwi and to her children," his voice said.

Locklear unfurled his fingers and stepped back to find Wilson standing in the doorway.

"Where were you? I was looking all over for you."

"I was standing right out there," Locklear gestured. "I didn't see you come out."

Wilson shook his head. "No, you weren't. This corridor was empty when I came out. All I could hear was humming. Creeped me out so I waited in the lobby for you but you didn't show."

Locklear looked into the corridor and then back to the spot his feet stood in. He could not remember coming into Olsen's room.

"How did I get in here?" Locklear asked.

Wilson looked from Locklear to the old man.

"You don't remember coming in here?" he asked.

Locklear shook his head.

"*E wang oh ma nee yo*," he said as he walked away from Olsen.

"What does that mean?" Wilson asked.

"It means 'Be careful how you travel'. An uncle of mine said it to me yesterday. I have a feeling he just died."

# Chapter 32

When Locklear awoke in Prairie Winds Motel the following morning, he felt refreshed and ready to close the remaining business of the case. He had known as he lay down in his bed the previous night that it would be his last night in South Dakota and that by nightfall he would be back in Richmond. He would miss the State, would miss the wide-open prairies and the dry, sun-scorched ground which all felt like home to him. He ate one of Mendoza's unhealthy breakfasts of coffee and pastries in his room. He showered and shaved and dressed in the last clean shirt he had packed into his light travel bag and sat on his bed to make the first of three calls he needed to make before he left the area for good.

After he had left the hospital in Rapid City the previous afternoon, he had checked in on Norma Macken to ensure her lazy son was sticking to his word and was respectful to his mother. When he arrived at the motel, Raymond was cleaning out the swimming pool which was now transformed from the filthy scum-covered mess it had been to a shining blue-tiled body of water.

"I did what you said, now stop sending those guys around to check on me," Raymond had begged.

Locklear had smiled at the young man's paranoia. He had sent no-one but he didn't tell Raymond this, nor did he suggest he cut down on the weed which was obviously making every straight-looking customer seem like a plainclothes cop keeping an eye on him. When he had entered the reception area, he had checked in on Norma who was still reading trashy magazines. The hardworking woman looked more rested than she had before and was wearing new clothes. She had her hair died a light red and was wearing lipstick. She willingly handed over the three boxes of Whitefeather's belongings and smiled sadly at Locklear.

"I'll be glad for his sister to have them. They make me sad every time I look at them," she had said.

Locklear had waved as he drove out of the parking lot towards Cindy Geddis's place of work and had hoped the presence of other people in her workplace would make her less afraid of him than she had been the last time she set eyes on him from across the car park of the school she worked in. He had waited in reception until she crept up behind him. The Native American woman was even smaller than he remembered and there was a sad, worn expression on her pretty face.

"Last time I was here, you mistook me for someone else. You don't need to be afraid of me," he had told her.

Geddis had nodded nervously as Locklear handed over the three cardboard boxes containing her brother's meagre belongings. He told the younger sister of Albert Whitefeather that he was going to see to it that she received the compensation that Albert had been due.

"How?" Geddis had asked.

"I just will. I promise," he had said as he headed back to his motel to get what he hoped would be a good night's sleep.

Locklear sat on his bed and waited until it was the right time to make the first of his three calls. He checked the date on the local newspaper which had been left outside his motel room door. June 21$^{st}$. His fifty-eight birthday.

O'Brien answered after the first ring.

"It's Locklear," Locklear snapped when he heard the officer's voice on the other end of the line.

"I expected you'd call."

"You played me for a fool, O'Brien, and when I get back I'm going to see to it that Kowalski fires you."

"You can't prove my involvement with INTENT – the only person who could identify me as having ever been a member died yesterday," he said quietly.

"Well, if I can't prove it, at the very least I'll make sure Kowalski gets you packed off to the furthest shitty little station in Alaska."

"I understand," O'Brien said quietly.

"You deleted stuff from Holton's computer, I know."

"I only deleted anything that would have led you to INTENT before I needed you to get there."

"You knew about INTENT the whole time – you goddamn-well moonlighted for them. You knew artefacts were being stolen and instead of informing the police, who I might add you work for, you used your skills to incite maladjusted young men and women across this country to put their lives in danger retrieving those artefacts."

O'Brien remained silent.

"You knew about Ardavan and how she'd been planted in Holton's apartment block. Did you know they were going to kill him?"

"No. I didn't. I was watching her but it was only when he died that I figured out the connection."

"And you didn't inform the police? You're a cop – did you forget that you promised to uphold the law?"

"What would I have said? That I was hacking into computers watching people? I wouldn't have been a cop for long if I did that."

"That's your defence? You self-protecting little shit!"

"Will you hear me out if I explain?"

Locklear took a few seconds to decide if he'd allow the dishonest cop time to concoct an elaborate story. He decided he had time before he took on Susan Walsh on the anniversary of her sister's death and decided that prolonging the call might be a good idea.

"I'm listening."

"And this is off the record?"

"No, it's goddamn not," Locklear retorted.

"Right. I worked for INTENT for years while I was stationed in Pine Ridge. I could see what was going on around me. Big shots coming in, taking our resources – oil, gas, our sacred artefacts – while our people waited in line for commodities and handouts. I became one of your so-called maladjusted young people except there was something different about me. I was smart. Very smart as it turns out and I knew there was a way to win the war and keep our heads out of the firing line at the same time."

"I know the story, O'Brien, and it stinks. I know it and you know it. It didn't give you the right to take the law into your own hands."

"Looks-Twice didn't think so."

"Did you know who I was the whole time? Did you know Looks-Twice was my uncle? Is that why you don't like me? I know he shot you."

"No, I didn't know. I didn't like you because I didn't like the way you spoke to me."

"I don't believe you. I wouldn't take you for the sensitive type, O'Brien."

O'Brien said nothing.

"Well, go on, tell me the rest of your tale," Locklear snapped.

"That's the kind of thing I'm talking about."

"O'Brien!"

"OK! I left INTENT shortly before Looks-Twice shot me. I had already decided to leave the organisation. Too many things were happening, things were getting rough. I was just the IT guy. I didn't pay anyone any visits, nothing like that. The people who were beginning to join the organisation were tough and were capable of anything."

"Like Whitefeather?"

"Whitefeather was like a kitten compared to some of these guys. I was worried about my job. I decided to leave and join the Native Movement again. It was more my speed."

"And Looks-Twice took offence?"

"Looks-Twice was itching for a reason to get me. He put up with me for as long as I was useful to the organisation but, once I said I was leaving, he was out to get me. He hadn't liked me anyway because I'm a –"

"Half-breed," Locklear said.

"Not a word I'd choose, sir, but yes, in a nutshell, that's why he shot me. He phoned in a phony car accident when he knew I was on duty and waited for me down an isolated turn-off. He beat me first. Nearly broke my jaw."

"Well, that's something we have in common, O'Brien," Locklear quipped as he rubbed his jaw which remained sore.

"I think we also have being half-breeds in common, sir."

"I thought you didn't know anything about me, O'Brien."

"I have eyes."

"Why did you play me? The information you had could have cut this investigation short and, who knows, it might have even stopped Holton from being killed."

"I already told you that I knew nothing about that but, if I led you to INTENT straight away, you wouldn't have known about Hirsch, Sartre or the Rosenbergs. All that would have happened is innocent people would get locked up for reclaiming what was rightfully theirs and the case would be closed."

Locklear thought about this for a moment. "OK, that's true. Go on."

"I'd been watching Sartre for almost a year. The Rosenbergs I knew much longer but they weren't anywhere near as smart as Sartre. When Holton ended up dead I joined the dots between him and Hirsch."

"And Diaz and Hill?"

"For a while it was just a hunch. I suspected that they

were dirty so I watched them. Took a look into their bank accounts. Saw amounts that didn't add up to what they would be getting paid so –"

"You know that's illegal, right?"

O'Brien didn't answer.

"Did you look into my bank account? Did you check me out? Did you check Mendoza out?"

"I didn't need to. I know good people when I see them. Kinda got a sixth sense for that sort of thing."

"What about Benson?"

"He's an ass but he's an honest ass. Sooner Kowalski's back the better."

"Kowalski will be back today and with the trouble you're in I wouldn't wish for his return so soon if I were you. I've yet to tell him what you were up to."

O'Brien fell silent. Locklear could almost hear the guy adding up his next move like he was playing chess.

"I'm much more use to you here than in Alaska."

Locklear exhaled loudly into the receiver. "Take my advice, O'Brien, and this is coming from someone with experience – tell Kowalski everything. Better that no-one has anything to hold over you in years to come. I don't reckon you'll keep your job but come clean and hope to God he's in a good mood."

"But you're friends with him, right? You could put in a word in my defence?"

"I'll think about it but, if I defend you, you'll do everything by the book from now on?"

"You have my word."

"Good, I've already got Mendoza breaking rules. I don't think I could handle two loose cannons at once."

Locklear hung up and poured himself another coffee. He needed the caffeine before he spoke to Susan Walsh. He had dreamt of Kate the previous night. He had almost forgotten what she looked like and the way she laughed. He swallowed and tried not to think about the night she had been killed and how her death and the death of his unborn child had driven him further into his spiralling alcoholism which in turn had changed the course of his life. Susan Walsh's line rang three times before her assistant answered. Locklear had to shout at the man to put him through or to at least tell Walsh that he needed to speak with her urgently.

When Walsh finally took the call, he found her tone muted.

"What do you want, Locklear? A happy-birthday wish?"

"No," he said quietly. "I dreamt of Kate last night."

Walsh sighed. "I did too."

"She was happy," Locklear said.

"Uh-huh," Walsh replied weakly.

Locklear knew the stern army leader was upset but that she would do everything in her power not to reveal this to him.

"I meant what I said in DC. I'm sorry for what happened."

Twenty seconds passed and Walsh did not speak.

"I spoke to my dad," she said. "He said he'd like you to come see him next time you're in town."

"I'd like that," Locklear replied.

There was a pause.

"There's something I have to tell you, Susan," he began.

"Something you need to act on today before it hits the newspapers."

"Hold on, Locklear. Brodeur, get off the line!"

Locklear heard a loud click.

"Go on," Walsh said.

Locklear updated Walsh on Braff's statements and how his testimony in court would shine a light on the army's involvement in the transportation and sale of Iraqi artefacts. He told her that he fully expected Braff to say in court that, as his commanding officer, Walsh had known about and had possibly masterminded the murder of Private Hughes and the attempted murder of Lewis, Torres and Albert Whitefeather.

"Locklear, you believe me when I say I had nothing to do with that, don't you? You have my word."

"I believe you but Braff is going to want to point the finger at someone else. He knows it won't get him off the hook but I suspect he'll try to at least shorten his sentence. Your superiors are going to find it hard to believe that this happened under your watch without you knowing. You know the army are going to throw you under the bus."

Susan Walsh did not speak. Locklear knew the smart woman was considering her options. She came up with nothing. There were none.

"What would you do?" she asked.

"Start by sorting out some of the human mess. It'll look better if you bring the situation to your superiors before Washington does. Give Whitefeather's sister the compensation Albert was due and, if you can, get the army to retract their statement that he was insane."

"Then?"

"Have the army declare Private Hughes dead. Then Torres can finally put her husband to rest. Then give Torres what she is due and have her reinstated to the army, if she still wants it."

"And?"

"Then go and warn your superiors. You better hope you have time to warn them about what's coming their way before Braff gives his testimony in court."

"That's a tall order, Locklear. Sounds like a job for the Tooth Fairy or Santa Claus."

"It's the only chance you have of saving your career and, more importantly, doing the right thing. If the army feels its reputation is in question nationally, it might force them to do what's right by the people who served them with honour."

"I'll see what I can do," Walsh said quietly.

"Good luck, Susan," he whispered as he hung up.

Locklear lifted the phone to the last person he needed to speak with today.

Lee Carter answered on the second ring.

"Sarge!" he said merrily.

Locklear could almost see the genial smile of his pleasant friend.

"You back home?" Locklear asked.

"Yes. Benson said it was OK. Is it safe to talk?"

"Yes. Are you OK?"

Carter stalled a little. "Yes, sir. Yes, I am."

"That's good."

"You did it, sir, you proved me innocent."

"You don't have to call me 'sir', Carter. You don't work for me anymore, remember? Right – Hirsch hasn't been tried yet but there's enough evidence now to prove she killed Holton and that she had the help of two cops to plant evidence on you. They've entered a plea and admitted to planting the knife handle in your house."

"You believed me, sarge, when I said I didn't do it, didn't you?"

Locklear blew out. "Of course I did – but next time someone you've fallen out with invites you to their home in the dead of night, say no, Carter!"

Carter laughed. "I owe you, sarge. Oh, by the way, I'm not sure if I have a job now. I expect to be reinstated but I don't know if I want it anymore, not with what was going on under my nose so ... if you're looking for an assistant?"

"To do *what*, Carter? You're afraid of your own shadow!"

Carter guffawed. "Well, if you ever need anyone who knows about anthropology, geology or theology, keep me in mind."

Locklear laughed. "Will do. Goodbye, Carter, and stay out of trouble."

Locklear put down the phone and noticed a missed call from Paytah Hunter. He decided he would call the young man after he got to the airport for his flight back to Richmond. He zipped up his bag and threw it into the trunk of his hire car. There was something he wanted to see before he left Pine Ridge for good. One more thing to see before he honoured his promise to Looks-Twice never to return.

# Chapter 33

The view from the top of Pine Ridge was as stunning as Looks-Twice had described it. Locklear had driven his hired car through the deserted town and had searched for signs of the valley where Looks-Twice said the reservation once stood off Route 18 and had been the place where he had been born. There was hardly anybody on the streets and, as he slowed at the lights, he noticed the cafés and takeout joints were all deserted. As he passed Maggie's gift store he looked into the lot but found that the woman was not there and the store appeared to be closed which Locklear found himself somewhat disappointed about. He would have liked to have got to say goodbye to the woman he had never spoken to but who had looked at him in a way that had wrenched at him. He took a sharp left onto the steep dirt road that ran directly behind her store and made a mental note to check in again on his way back onto the highway.

The road was dry and the grit spun beneath his tyres as he tried to climb the steep hill. Twice more his wheels spun on the gritty surface. He dropped a gear and slowed but managed to make it only another half mile before he pulled into a small widening in the road. He locked the car and decided to make the rest of his journey on foot.

The sun beat down on him as he climbed further and he panted in the morning heat. He stopped to draw his breath and wiped the sweat from his forehead. The sky was clear blue and in the distance he could hear the faint sound of beating drums. He climbed further and pushed his way through dense scrub until he felt he could climb no more. He searched for somewhere to sit but the trees were parched and wilting and the rocks at his feet were small and sharp. He listened and focused on the distant sound of cars revving and shook his head.

"Guess there's another way up here, you idiot," he said although there was no-one there to hear him.

He remained still as he thought about the fact that on this day, fifty-eight years ago, he was born somewhere close to where he now stood. He walked on further and noticed movement below in the valley, a gathering of people. And remembered it was the day of the Sun Dance. He squinted at the tiny figures dressed in Native clothing dancing in the burning sun. Small fires were lit upon which food was being cooked. Six men beat drums rhythmically and whooping war cries could be heard from young men standing on the perimeter. Locklear became so lost in the sight before him that he did not hear the sound of footsteps coming from behind him.

"Brother, is it you?" a woman's voice said.

Locklear turned to find a woman standing on the dry path, smiling. It was the woman from the craft store, the woman who had stared so intently at him. His mouth opened but no words came out.

"Brother?" she asked again.

"I'm ... I'm Locklear," was all he could think of to say.

The woman stepped forward and stretched out her arms.

"I always hoped I would see you again, that you would find your way back home."

She placed her arms about his body and pulled him to her.

Locklear tensed but she did not seem to notice.

"I'm Magaskawee. Maggie. I am the daughter of Wachiwi, your mother."

The woman smiled and Locklear could see his mother's face in hers. He could see Wachiwi's deep brown eyes, her soft brown skin and her thick, slightly greying hair in long braids on either side of her small face.

"Looks-Twice ... he said there was no-one looking for me."

"Uncle told me you were dead. That you and my mother had both passed a long time ago."

"She asked for you, when she was ill. She cried out for Magaskawee. I thought you were a place."

"In a way, I was. I am. She was looking for home."

Maggie pointed behind him, into the dense scrub.

"Come with me."

Locklear followed the woman along an old path until she came to a clearing where a modern wood cabin stood alone in the wilderness. She opened the door and he followed her inside.

"This is where the cabin you were born in once stood. I was here standing outside with Looks-Twice, waiting to hear your cry."

378

Locklear looked around the modern cabin which had one large living area to the front. Three doors stood at the back. A large wood stove sat in the centre of the simply furnished, wood-panelled room.

"The old cabin didn't have two bedrooms and a bathroom. It was just one room where my grandmother lived alone – but I always loved it here. My late husband rebuilt it when it fell into ruin. I couldn't bear to see nothing in its place. It was the last place I saw my mother and you. I rent it to tourists from time to time but I always hoped that if you ever found your way home, there would be a place for you. I come up here often and sit here alone, especially during the Sun Dance ceremony. It should be a sad day but for me it always made me feel closer to you because I knew it was the day you were born and I tried to send out to you a message that I remembered you, that you and my mother were in my heart, wherever you were."

"So you didn't know that Looks-Twice actually found us?"

"When our brother was dying he drove to find you. When he returned he told us that you were both dead but I did not believe him. I knew he was protecting Chaska and me from something but, even after I felt my mother had died, I knew you were out there. I didn't know your name so I couldn't find you. I see now she gave you our grandmother's name but I didn't know the first name she gave to you."

"She didn't change my name – the name the chief gave me. It is still my name."

Maggie's eyes filled with tears and she shook her head. "Shadow," she said sadly. "We will need to change that."

Locklear looked at his feet.

"Come," she said.

She took his hand and led him along a steep path towards the centre of the valley.

Locklear's head swam in the heat. His throat was like sandpaper. The ground seemed to rise up towards him as he tried to move his large feet along the narrow pathway. He stopped and moved his free hand to his head.

"I got concussed a few days ago. I'm still a little off balance."

"Let me help you. This is the same path our mother carried you on the day you were born."

"Please. I don't want to hear it," he said as images of his blood-soaked mother flashed again before his eyes. "Looks-Twice told me. I can't hear it again."

"Did he tell you how proudly she held you up to the chief? How she stared down the eyes of the men and the women who turned their backs on her? Wachiwi walked bravely to the centre of that valley and held you up for the world to see. She was not afraid although she should have been."

Locklear shook his head.

"Did he tell you that she stood her ground? Did he tell you about her strength and that she was burdened with an impossible choice?"

"To choose between her children," Locklear said.

"She made the right choice. She made the only choice a mother could," Maggie said. "We had our grandmother. We had Looks-Twice. Chaska died and I grew up. I married and had my daughter and she had two children. When my daughter and her husband died, I thought I would never be able to breathe again but I found a reason to live by caring for her children."

Locklear could not speak, moved by her words.

"Come," she said and they made their way down to where the land flattened and the valley stood before them.

Locklear looked around at the unfamiliar faces at the gathering and found himself inching closer to his sister's side.

"It is alright, brother. You are among your family here."

Maggie led Locklear by the hand and brought him closer to the centre of the large gathering.

Paytah, dressed in a ceremonial headdress, stood in a line of young natives, preparing for the ceremony.

"Paytah, this is your Uncle Ohanzee," she said to the shocked young Native.

The young man looked different without his Grateful Dead T-shirt and jeans. His long hair was loose under the headdress and his face was painted with long red streaks across his high cheekbones. The expression on Paytah's face told Locklear that his grandnephew did not want him to reveal their previous meeting or the trouble he had almost landed himself in through his dealings with his estranged granduncle, Looks-Twice.

Locklear put out his hand but Paytah pulled him into a strong embrace.

"Don't worry, Paytah," Locklear murmured. "I'm not here to rat you out but I do need to know this. Are your days with INTENT over?"

Paytah smiled and nodded.

Maggie was drawing a young woman in traditional dress towards Locklear.

"This is Olowa. My granddaughter."

The girl from the shop rolled her eyes but then gave Locklear a warm hug.

"And now my brother needs a new name," Maggie said as she led him to the elderly chief who sat in the centre of the large gathering.

Paytah followed and stepped close to the chief.

"May I rename my uncle, please?" he begged the chief.

The old man nodded and smiled patiently.

Paytah pretended to look Locklear over as if he was trying to decide what name would suit the 'stranger' in front of him.

"At first glance I would choose 'Two-Sides'," he teased.

Then he looked into the clear blue sky and smiled.

"But I think I will name you 'Misae'."

"Mis-saa-eh?" Locklear repeated as the crowd laughed.

"It means 'white sun' because your return has brought bright light back to my grandmother's face but I'm also giving it to you to mean 'white son'."

Locklear laughed. "I don't think I'll be putting that on my driving licence!"

Maggie led Locklear to the chief and beckoned for him to kneel in front of the old man who began to hum quietly. Men began to join in the chant. Drums began to beat in rhythm from behind him. Locklear's heart began to race as the sounds seemed somehow familiar to him. He felt tears sting in his eyes and looked up at the kindly face of the old man.

"You are home. My white son. Your wait in the wilderness is over. Here, you will have water," he said as a woman handed Locklear a drink. "Here, you will have food," he said as another offered him a bowl of steaming soup. "The shadow has lifted from your heart and your mind. Peace is now yours. Peace from your ancestors. Peace from your tribe. Rise now, Misae, and join your brothers and sisters."

Locklear stood and turned to watch the tribesmen chant and drum faster and faster.

Paytah grinned and began to dance as Locklear retreated from the centre of the crowd to sit and watch the proceedings with his sister by his side.

Much later he walked with Maggie halfway to the top of the ridge.

"I have to go back to Richmond," he said.

"But you'll come back?" She pressed a key in his hand. "This is for the cabin. Whenever you want to come home, it is here waiting for you and so are we."

Locklear thought about the pledge he made to his dying uncle.

"I promised Looks-Twice that I would never come back."

"Uncle was a damaged man. He blamed you for everything that happened to our mother but none of it was your fault. Wachiwi's children shouldn't have to suffer anymore for what happened so long ago. Will you come visit again? For me?"

"I will."

Maggie hugged her brother one more time and watched as he climbed the rest of the hill to the top of the valley. He turned and waved to her and watched the gathering for a moment. His chest swelled as he felt a wave of emotion wash over him. An eagle soared above him. Wachiwi, guiding him, as he knew she always did.

As he reached his car, Locklear's phone beeped four times. He took it from his pocket to see he had two missed calls, one hour apart, followed by two text messages. The calls and texts were all from Kowalski.

The first text said, **"Are you shitting me?"** – an obvious response to Locklear's 'expenses claim' and the second **'Urgent! Get back here now'**.

Locklear pressed the button and waited until a familiar voice answered.

"Kowalski?"

# The End

# Author's Note

The massacre at Wounded Knee is documented fact, but the episodes of the retaliatory attack on the wagon train and that of the expelling of mixed-blood children from the community are drawn from the author's imagination and are not to be construed as fact.

Also published by Poolbeg Crimson

# THE PACT

## Carol Coffey

When Richmond homicide detective Locklear is called in to investigate the attempted murder of a young Mennonite in a Virginian farming town, he is instantly drawn into a web of secrecy and lies spanning back to the American Civil War.

Frustrated by the refusal of locals to co-operate with the investigation, Locklear realises that to find the perpetrator he must first solve a 150-year-old mystery. With his leads restricted to historical records, the Native American is running out of time to save the orphaned boy's siblings from a similar fate. As the body count in a seeming local feud rises, Locklear is no nearer to solving the most complex case of his career.

Flanked by his trusted colleague Jo Mendoza and local cop Carter, Locklear finds himself embroiled in a silent religious community where nothing is as it seems and everyone has something to hide.

*Fiction with an edge*

'A strong plot and clever storytelling ...
giving the novel that unputdownable quality'
*Irish Independent*

ISBN 978-178199-8199

Also published by Poolbeg Crimson

# THE BUTTERFLY STATE

## Carol Coffey

*Wrong time, wrong place, or could
a ten-year-old be guilty of murder?*

Tess Byrne has a secret. Alone and forgotten in an institution for
troubled children for the past ten years, Tess has kept the secret
with her. But now, at the age of twenty-one, she is coming home.

Waiting for her at home on the farm in Árd Glen,
County Wicklow, are sister Kate and brothers
Seán and Ben. But why are Kate and Seán dreading Tess's return?
What lies behind Seán's hostility towards his young sister? And
just what is the secret that threatens to destroy the Byrne family?

Can Tess finally live the normal life she craves with
the people she loves, or will their tragic family
history tear them all apart forever?

*Fiction with an edge*

ISBN 978-184-223-3979

Also published by Poolbeg

# WINTER FLOWERS

## Carol Coffey

'A must-read for fans of Jodi Picoult'
*Sunday Independent*

When her dishevelled, eight-year-old nephew Luke comes knocking on her door in the middle of the night, Iris Fay knows her sister Hazel is in trouble again. This time, it is a house fire started by her drunken boyfriend Pete Doyle.

As Iris is drawn back into Hazel's dysfunctional lifestyle, she is haunted by her own past and also by the childhood memories she has kept secret from her sister.

When Pete becomes an even greater threat to the family and her sons are placed in danger, Hazel realises she must turn her life around or else lose them. But then she stumbles on a pile of letters in her mother's attic and their contents spiral her into an even darker place.

Meanwhile Iris, too, is confronted by her past when her former husband Mark suddenly comes back into her life, looking for answers. Can the sisters face up to their memories and find the future they long for? Or will the secrets of their childhood continue to destroy them and those they hold dear?

ISBN 978-184223-502-7

Also published by Poolbeg

# The Penance Room

## Carol Coffey

Broken Hill Nursing Home is a house laden down with secrets, its
residents now settled in Australia but living out their troubled lives
trapped in the past.

Thirteen-year-old Christopher, whose parents run the home,
is its self-appointed guardian. Deaf since childhood, his foot severed
in a horrific accident, he notices what others miss. Isolated and
ignored, he is obsessed with helping these damaged souls find the
peace they crave.

He befriends the beautiful young Maria whose strange sadness
puzzles him, then gains an ally when a mysterious young man
arrives to record the extraordinary lives of the aging immigrants.
Christopher eagerly awaits the transformations he expects will
result from these 'confessions'.

But will delving into the past disturb the residents' fragile mental
state and open up a Pandora's box that was best left closed?

*And can Christopher himself survive their terrible disclosures?*

ISBN 978-184223-452-5

Also published by Poolbeg

# The Incredible Life of Jonathan Doe

## Carol Coffey

Brendan Martin is an American-born loner raised in Ireland by his silent, embittered mother before escaping back to New York, where he lives and works each day in blissful isolation in the crowded city. Brendan spends his days happily labouring on building sites and his evenings drinking alone in bars and hooking up with a constant stream of one-night stands.

Following a second DUI, Brendan's peaceful and predictable life ends abruptly and he is forced to go to live in the town of Dover, New Jersey, with his overbearing uncle. There he forms an unlikely friendship with his meek,downtrodden cousin Eileen.

Forced into completing his community service, he meets Jonathan Doe, an intriguing man living in a local homeless shelter whose amazing stories of a happy childhood in the Appalachian Mountains captivate him. Within weeks of his arrival in Dover, Brendan loses himself in the strange man's incredible stories.

Fascinated by the fact that Jonathan Doe can no longer remember exactly where he is from, Brendan becomes obsessed with helping his new friend find his way back to the kind of home he himself has always dreamed of.

But is Jonathan's past real or are his memories the product of a deeply troubled mind? The closer Brendan gets to the truth, the more he realises that all is not what it seems with Jonathan Doe.

ISBN 978-184223-607-9